Ready to Fly

BATYA RUDDELL

Published by: Hamodia Treasures
207 Foster Avenue, Brooklyn, NY 11230

Jacket design: Shoshana Radunsky
Typesetting: Brocha Mirel Strizower

Distributed by: Israel Book Shop
501 Prospect Street #97, Lakewood, New Jersey 08701
Telephone 732-901-3009 Fax 732-901-4012
www.israelbookshoppublications.com

Printed in Canada

I dedicate this book

to all of you, because there's a story inside each and every one of us. The greatest, most authentic narration of all is the Torah, written by the Master storyteller. Often, all we need is a little extra help from Him to look inside ourselves — and bring it out!

Thank you...

to *Hakadosh Baruch Hu* for having
given me my gift to write,

to my husband for all his
patience and support,

and to my editors at *Hamodia
Publications* for believing that
my words are worth sharing.

Table of Contents

Introduction

I HEAR IT everywhere I go. "*What made you write that story? Where did you get the idea for that one?*"

They are interesting questions; ones I often have, too, when reading other authors' work. *How on earth did she think that up?* I marvel.

After encountering these questions repeatedly, I found myself asking, "Where *did* that story come from? How did it get from my head onto the paper (or more accurately, my computer screen)? I started thinking (I do that sometimes) and an idea began to sprout. What if I gathered my stories together in one volume and gave the readers a peek behind the scenes, a first-hand glimpse into how a story came about?

The idea germinated in my head for a while until I finally decided to pitch it to my editor. When I got the green light with it I was excited to get started. I began reading my old stories and trying to remember why I had written them. Some of the reasons came back to me very quickly but for some stories I had to dig out the subconscious motives for writing them. Surprisingly, the process turned out to be a fascinating learning experience. I discovered things about myself as I understood why and how I'd come up with various ideas.

Fiction is often more real than non-fiction. Certainly, the facts in fiction stories have to be believable in order to have credibility unless they are fantasy or science fiction. Most of my fiction stories are based on truth — ideas that have sprung from real-life situations. Some of the stories came from deep places inside me that I myself wasn't aware of at the time until I revisited them for this anthology.

So… while striving to provide you with a deeper understanding about the things I write, this has been an eye-opening experience for me too.

I haven't been disappointed with what I found — and I hope you won't be either!

Batya Ruddell

Secrets

"SO WHAT DID he say then?" Asher asked.

"Who?" Kayla said absently, staring out of the spattered car window as they drove slowly down the tree-lined road. She made a mental note to clean the windows later at home.

"The doctor, of course. That's where you went, isn't it?" A flicker of exasperation passed over Asher's face.

"Oh, that." Splashes of sunlight winked through the leaves of the trees.

"Well?"

Kayla took a deep, tremulous breath. "He said I need a biopsy."

Asher turned to look at his wife, who was staring straight ahead, unmoving. "A biopsy? Does he think it's… that?"

"Yes, he thinks it's that."

They drove on in silence, deafened by unspoken thoughts.

"So," Asher said at last, "when is it?"

"This Thursday," Kayla replied.

"I'll be there with you, don't worry."

"No," Kayla said firmly. "I need to do this alone."

IT WAS SUPPOSED to have been a routine visit. The lump on her neck had been growing steadily for some months, and her family doctor insisted she check it out. Actually, he'd suggested it a while back, when she'd first noticed the hard, round nodule about the size of a marble, but she'd ignored his urging. She was just too busy for stuff like that. Kayla was a high school teacher and she had a nice handful of children at home, *baruch Hashem*. Anyway, the lump didn't hurt, so what was the urgency?

Eventually, Asher had convinced her to go to the specialist. He didn't like the look of the lump; it made him nervous. So, to keep him happy, she'd made the appointment and soon found herself sitting in a spacious office in the city hospital. Dr. Benjamin had examined her carefully, turning her neck this way and that, gently palpating the lymph nodes on her neck.

"How long have you had this?" he asked.

"I think about six months," Kayla said, trying to recall just when she'd first noticed it.

"Any coughing, low-grade fevers?" the doctor continued.

"On and off, yes."

"What about night sweats?"

"Actually, I do have," Kayla exclaimed in astonishment. "Do you think that's connected?"

"Could be," Dr. Benjamin answered gravely. "You have all the symptoms of Hodgkin's lymphoma."

IN THE DAYS leading up to the biopsy, life went on as usual in the Marks household. Kayla behaved as if nothing out of the ordinary was happening, seemingly oblivious to the ominous cloud looming on the horizon. She efficiently made arrangements for the children, who were very excited to sleep out at various cousins' homes. All, except her daughter, Miriam.

"Ima," fourteen-year-old Miriam asked worriedly, "where are you going?"

Kayla looked at her firstborn child, who had always been wise for her age.

"I just have to undergo a small procedure in the hospital," she answered. "One night and then I'll be home."

"Are you sure it's nothing serious?" Miriam wrinkled her forehead in concern. *This was really strange. Her mother never went away anywhere by herself, even after birth or on vacation.*

"Don't worry," Kayla said, stroking her daughter's hair. "It's nothing. You see, even Abba doesn't need to come with me. Everything's fine."

ASHER RUBBED HIS hands together nervously as he sat next to his wife in Dr. Benjamin's office. He looked around the room, noting all the framed certificates on the walls and trying to suppress a feeling of dread. At least Kayla had let him come with her this time. Actually, he'd insisted — enough of this stiff-upper-lip business! A husband belonged at his wife's side. He was coming, and that was that.

Even though the room was air-conditioned, Asher felt so stifled that he started hyperventilating. Dr. Benjamin finished reading the reports laid out in front of him, paused for a significant few moments, then lowered his glasses and cleared his throat.

"It's like I suspected," he said. "Hodgkins lymphoma, stage two." Asher felt his heart plummet downward. "You'll need six rounds of chemotherapy and then a month of radiation. Here are the forms for all the preliminary tests you need to do before you start. Luckily," he continued, smiling encouragingly, "of all the types of lymphoma, you have the best one."

Kayla and Asher looked at each other in astonishment. If this was the best, then what was the worst?

"HOW," ASHER ASKED tensely, "are we going to get through this?" They were sitting in a quiet coffee shop in downtown Jerusalem. They looked like any normal couple enjoying time out together, not like a pair whose world had utterly collapsed.

"With Hashem's help, we'll get through," Kayla declared firmly. "But we must keep it to ourselves. I don't want anyone to know."

Asher looked incredulously at his wife. "How on earth do you think we will manage that?"

THE TESTS BEGAN, followed almost immediately by the treatments. A thin tube was threaded into a main vein in Kayla's neck, its point of exit sitting in a small plastic connector under the chest wall. Instead of poking and prodding her veins every time she needed a treatment or a blood test, this porthole was used instead. Once every two weeks she disappeared for a day into the shadowy domain of the hospital where various chemical poisons, meant to cure her, were pumped into her body.

The vomiting and chills came quickly. Nausea hit her like a tsunami; the retching, like waves. She was washed out, spun and hung to dry. When the first clumps of hair greeted her from her pillow, she shook her head and cried. *How would she recognize herself?* But she gritted her teeth and battled on. Her wigs covered the hair loss, and she told the kids she had a virus- mononucleosis- and that it would take time to get over it but she would recover. And they believed her.

Well, maybe Miriam didn't. Her daughter's probing questions suggested her suspicions, which rippled, like a subtle undercurrent, between them.

"I FEEL SO useless! She refuses to let me help her." Asher was at his early-morning learning *seder* in the *beis medrash*, speaking with his *chavrusa* and good friend Naftali. The open *Gemara* lay on the *shtender* in front of them, its holy words swimming before Asher's unfocused eyes.

"She'd hate it if she knew I'd told you. She insists that no one must know, but I can't do it anymore." Asher sank his head into his hands, heavy with the weight of his worry.

"Why do you think she's determined to keep it quiet?" Naftali asked gently.

"Mostly because of Miriam," Asher answered. "She's worried about *shidduchim*... you know how it is."

"Yes," said Naftali thoughtfully, "I do know. But there might be another reason as well. Maybe if she allows herself to be weak, to be seen as a person to be pitied, she's afraid she'll collapse completely."

Asher nodded slowly. "But there is something you can do for her," his *chavrusa* said solemnly. "You can learn in her *zechus* and *daven* for her."

"I THINK MY mother's very sick," Miriam said to Tova. Schoolbooks were scattered all over the floor of her friend's bedroom. She and Tova had been best friends from kindergarten and were practically inseparable.

Tova barely looked up from her history book. "Well, she has mono, doesn't she? Isn't that what you told me?" She was trying hard to concentrate on the difficult material for an upcoming test.

"No, I mean *really* sick," Miriam repeated, "like, something serious."

"Like what?"

"Like, you know... the *machalah*."

Tova's head jerked up. She was paying attention now. They sat in silence, fear strangling their words. After a moment Tova spoke.

"What makes you think that?" she ventured tentatively.

"I know," Miriam replied. "I just know."

MONTHS PASSED. KAYLA fought valiantly. Except for a few close family members and, of course, the principal of the high school where she taught, no one knew about the battle she was fighting. It was her own private war.

Gradually she adjusted to the rigorous treatments, recognizing when she'd be knocked down by them and when she'd get up again. And she hardly missed a day of work.

Asher wasn't too happy about it. He wanted her to rest more, to push herself less. Secretly though, she was proud of herself. If she could get through this, she could get through anything. And Miriam… well, she'd thank her in the end when it was time to start on *shidduchim*. There wasn't much money to marry her off with, and to have a sick mother on top of that… Yes, her daughter would be grateful that she'd done it this way.

THE PHONE RANG just as Kayla was leaving for the hospital. With one foot out the door, she was undecided whether to answer.

"Good morning, Mrs. Marks. This is Leah Dunner, Miriam's teacher."

"Oh, hello. I'm so sorry, but it's not a good time now. I'm on the way out."

"Well, I won't keep you if you're rushed, but maybe we could make a time to talk about Miriam," the teacher suggested.

"What's wrong with Miriam?" Kayla sat down on a chair in the hallway.

"Well, she hasn't been herself lately. She looks sad and worried most of the time, and she isn't concentrating like usual in class."

"Oh," Kayla said, an uneasy sensation pooling in her stomach.

"So I was wondering if everything's all right at home," Mrs. Dunner plowed on. "She mentioned something about you being sick…"

"No, I'm not sick. I'm fine." Kayla's defensive answer snapped sharply across the line. "I've just had a touch of mono, and it's taking me time to get back to myself."

"I see. Well, maybe Miriam's carrying the burden at home? Might that be possible?"

"Yes, that could be it," Kayla murmured.

If only the teacher knew that she was desperately trying to carry that load for her.

THIS TIME DR. Benjamin had a wide smile stretching across his face.

"Everything looks good," he announced, having checked through the results one more time. "I can say with certainty that you're in remission. Another five years like this, and you're considered cured."

Kayla slipped Asher a shy smile. He held her gaze, not daring to breathe lest the doctor change his prognosis.

"I must say, Mrs. Marks, you've been a remarkable patient. I've never seen such strength and determination to survive."

They were all smiling now, great big beams of sunlight shining from their eyes.

"Come back in three months for a check-up. And keep up the good work!"

MAZEL TOV, MAZEL tov! The brachos rained down, invoking blessings from Above. Kayla was in a daze. This was the moment she'd been waiting for… to see her eldest daughter glow with the true light of a kallah. Miriam had just turned nineteen… perfect! And what a chassan she had gotten. Reuven was everything she could have wished for in a son-in-law: a ben Torah, kind, clever, well-mannered, a fine reflection of the home he'd been raised in. Of course, they'd checked the family out properly and had heard nothing but favorable reports. Everything on their side seemed fine, too; she had stayed healthy all this time, thank G-d. Her ordeal was almost behind her.

The Markovitzes were similar to them in so many ways — lifestyle, hashkafah. She was thrilled to have such mechutanim. Her thoughts floated dreamily through her head like light, cottony clouds. Her mind flicked back to the present as the *chassan* approached for the *badeken*. Gently, Reuven lowered the veil over his *kallah's* face. Kayla grasped the lighted lamp tightly in her right hand, linked her left arm through Miriam's, and they made the slow, measured walk to the *chuppah*.

"ARE YOU COMING for Shabbos this week?" Kayla asked her daughter. She was folding laundry, the phone propped in the crook of her neck. *Sheva brachos* were long over, but she had still not fully climbed down from the dizzying heights she'd reached.

"We'd love to come, Ima, of course we would. It's just that…"

"What?"

"Well, Reuven's pretty picky with his food and I don't want that to be a burden on you. There are a lot of things he won't eat."

"Like what, for example?" Kayla wasn't concerned in the slightest. She was warmed by her daughter's concern for her new husband.

"Oh, I don't know myself yet. The main thing seems to be carbohydrates. He's very careful."

SHABBOS IN THE Marks home with the new couple was simply wonderful. Kayla and Asher were euphoric. Had they ever dared to imagine during the difficult years that this day would come? Reuven and Miriam seemed so happy together. Kayla's heart was singing, filled with thanks and praise to Hashem, the Bestower of good. How lucky they all were!

One thing Miriam was right about, though — her new husband was certainly particular about his food. Kayla had done her best to tone down the carbs and restrict sugar from her menu, but with her perennial sweet tooth, it wasn't easy. Still, as she watched her son-in-law scrutinize every item of food, she had a feeling of unease that she couldn't quite put her finger on. It hovered over her head like a fly she couldn't catch.

"IMA!" MIRIAM'S VOICE was hardly recognizable over the phone lines; sobs drowned her words. "I need to talk to you."

"I'm just going out to teach." Kayla fumbled in her bag, trying to find her car keys. "What happened? You sound terrible."

The sobs were stronger. "Ima, I need to talk to you *now*. Please... could you cancel work?"

"HOW LONG HAVE you known?" Kayla gently asked her daughter, who had dropped, distraught, onto the living-room couch.

"He told me last night," Miriam stammered. "But I'd kind of guessed, really. It's not something you can hide."

No, Kayla said silently to herself. *You definitely can't hide diabetes.* Miriam buried her face in her hands as she sobbed. Kayla sat quietly with her arm around her daughter's shoulders and let her cry herself dry.

"You know what the worst thing is?" Miriam said at last. "It's that he hid it from me. He lied."

Kayla reeled from the punch even though she'd known it was coming. It felt as if a second tsunami was hitting her, this one harder than the first, knocking her right off her feet. The unspoken accusation slashed at her, opening a Titanic-sized gash into which freezing water flowed. She moved away from her daughter, clutching tightly to the arm of the couch for fear of drowning.

"How could he do that? How can I ever trust him?" Miriam continued, the anger in her voice rising.

Kayla struggled bravely to surface and face her child. Inhaling a deep breath, she chose her words carefully.

"I don't think it was him, sweetheart. It was probably his parents, maybe his mother."

Her broken daughter, dreams shattered into a million shards of glass, appraised her mother carefully.

"You did that too, right… hid your illness from us. But I knew the whole time that you were very sick."

Pain struck Kayla's face like lightning, and tears cascaded down her cheeks, like rain from a storm cloud.

"I… I thought it was the best thing to do at the time, to protect you, to give you the best chance you could have."

"But I suffered too. At school I was a mess — I couldn't concentrate on anything. You never let me talk about your big secret. Do you have any idea how frightened I was?" Miriam was crying harder now, releasing all the anguish of the past.

Kayla's heart ached. *Oh, what had she done?* She had never imagined Miriam had felt that way. She reached across the chasm dividing them and pulled her daughter close.

"You know," she began softly, "sometimes it's the fight that keeps you going. I fought for you — in the wrong way, I realize now. And I believe that Reuven's mother fought for him too, to lead a normal life. Each of us fights the battle with his or her own arsenal. But I made a mistake that hurt you and for that, I'm really, really sorry."

They stayed — for hours, it seemed — curled on the living-room couch with their arms wrapped around each other. The hall clock ticked loudly on, yet time stood still for them, making up for all the lost moments. Mother and daughter sat, each immersed in her own thoughts, cleansing her grief.

Finally, Kayla spoke. She tilted Miriam's chin toward her and looked deeply into her eyes.

"Go home and talk to your husband," she said. "He's got his work cut out for him to earn your trust back. But, if anyone can understand him, it's you. The main thing" — and a warm smile glowed in her eyes like the soft flame of a Shabbos candle — "is not to have secrets."

This was my very first fiction story to be published in Hamodia Magazine *(known as* Inyan *today). Although I'd already had numerous personal essays published, this was my first attempt at fiction writing since my high school days, when I'd earned top marks for creative essays. Somehow, over the years, I had simply stopped writing in this genre for reasons I don't understand. Yet somehow, I felt the need to be accomplished in this area too if I were to consider myself a "real" writer. So I simply decided to start… and I loved it. Writing dialogue is a special favorite of mine. Today I can say that even though fiction is the hardest to write, it is by far the most creative and rewarding. I absolutely love it!*

Yael Mermelstein was my role model for frum fiction at that time. I used to say, "When I can write stories like hers, then I can call myself a writer!" "Secrets" was my first such attempt.

The story was inspired by a tragic situation that occurred in my community. A young mother of six children was diagnosed with the machalah. *Throughout her arduous treatment she told very few people about her illness, including her own children, because she did not want to cause them pain. All they knew was she had mono (mononucleosis), which was why she was so weak, but that she'd slowly get better. Unfortunately, the woman passed away. At her* levayah, *six brokenhearted children wailed for their mother. As I stood there watching the tragic scene, I found myself pondering the pros and cons of keeping such a thing hidden, and the idea for "Secrets" began to form in my head. I then gave the story an added twist by developing the* shidduch *angle and what hiding things can do to a relationship.*

Even though this story is not my best from a literary point (I even cringed when reading it again now after four years), there will always be a special place in my heart for it. It marked the beginning of my fiction-writing career and a beautiful relationship with my editor.

Looking for Mother

I USED TO think my mother was a ghost.

Not that I'd ever seen a ghost, of course, only read about them in children's books, but she had to be the closest thing there was to one. To my childish eyes, she was something formless that I could never touch; huddled inside a white room where the only splash of color was on visiting days. We'd crowd in, all seven of us, including Mommy, and make enough noise for everyone else.

My eldest sister, Shaindy, would set out the hot food she always prepared that Mommy never ate, and her children would present pictures they'd made at school, which Mommy never looked at. Tatty would chatter about nothing in particular while Avrumi's wife would check the closets and place freshly laundered nightgowns on the shelves. With all the whoops and laughter that pealed from Mommy's room, anyone would think we were having a party, and some of the other patients would watch the show enviously.

Sometimes, I'd slip out of the room and go sit by the bed of one of those lonely souls until my father would find me and with an irritated sigh, haul me back to our production. "Without you, it's missing," he would say, as if no one else could take my part.

But as I looked at Mommy staring at me with her empty eyes, I knew he was wrong. The character with the missing role was my mother!

"COME ON, CHAYALEH, you have to make a decision already!" Shaindy says in exasperation. "How many boys can you meet? There can't be something wrong with all of them!"

"I've only met three," I mumble. "Hashem created many more boys than that."

"Yes, but you only need to marry *one*," Shaindy exclaims in frustration.

I have a lot I could say to that but I don't, keeping it all squished inside me like I've done since I was a small child. Sometimes I think I'll run out of room to stuff in the thoughts, especially now that I'm supposed to be finding a husband and I have so many stifled opinions.

"So," Shaindy continues. "What about Leiby?"

"No," I say through gritted teeth.

"Why not? He seems like a nice boy and his family is our type… he'd fit in perfectly."

"Oh, so he also doesn't have a mother?" I blurt out.

"No, that's not what I meant. I was talking about *Yiddishkeit*."

"And his autistic brother," I shoot back.

Shaindy's face falls. "Oy, Chayaleh," she says, coming over to sit beside me on the couch and putting her arm around my shoulder. "I know this isn't easy for you." She pauses as if she's searching for some words that will soothe me. "You *do* have a mother," she attempts. "She's just not able to take care of you right now."

"Same thing," I mutter. "It doesn't matter… no point talking about it." There, I've managed to push it back down, keep my emotions neatly stacked away like the good girl that I am.

"Will you try Leiby again?" Shaindy sounds relieved that I've changed the subject.

I know I can't tell her that I don't like the silly way he giggles or how he smells of musty clothes. Or try to explain that the habit he has of sniffing like a tracker dog irritates me. She'll nod wisely and just say, "I know, I know, but these aren't major issues, Chayaleh. The main thing is that he's a good boy."

I sigh heavily like I have a lead blanket hanging over my head. It's not worth arguing about all these things. In quiet resignation, I nod. "Fine, I'll see him again... but just one more time."

IN THE END, Tatty makes the decision, together with the *shadchan*. After three meetings, Leiby and I are officially engaged. Here I am, strong, capable, responsible Chayaleh, who's been taking care of my father since I'm old enough to boil an egg, yet I cannot decide who I want to marry. But maybe that's because it's not a husband I'm looking for?

I decide to take Mommy away for a few days before the wedding. Shaindy and my other sisters encourage it because they still have lots to do and this way, maybe I can get her in the right mood. We go to a quaint bed-and-breakfast off the coast of Devon.

It's windy but we walk along the beach anyway because there's nothing much else to do. Mommy seems "here" in a distant sort of way. At least she's not in her manic phase and she realizes I'm getting married. I ask her if she likes the gown I've picked out for her and she nods and smiles and tells me that she loves the color before going back to gazing at the ocean. She sits on the promenade while I run after the outgoing tide, scooping up the frigid cold sea water in my hands, trying to catch it before it slips through my fingers forever.

SHAINDY PATS THE ruffles on my dress and adjusts my veil for about the tenth time.

"It's fine," I tell her, pushing her hand away irritably. "Don't fuss."

She steps back. "Sorry," she says. "I just want you to look perfect."

I look at her hurt expression and feel a twinge of guilt. "You've done an amazing job... really," I say reassuringly.

"I tried my best," Shaindy says. "I know it's not the same as having a mother, but..." Her voice trails off as if it's surprised by the unusual display of emotion but I lunge for it quickly before the opening closes.

"Shaindy, tell me about Mommy. What was she like before she got sick?"

A shadow crosses Shaindy's face. "Not now, Chayaleh, not on the day of your wedding."

I grasp my sister's hand tightly. "Especially *now*," I reply fiercely, "especially today when I miss her the most. Share a few of your memories. Help me understand what I'm missing."

Shaindy leans against the dressing table in my room and wraps her arms around herself as if she's cold. "She was wonderful. I remember her tucking us into bed at night and saying *Shema*, and then she'd sing lovely lullabies until each one of us was sound asleep. She'd have done it for you, too, if..."

"Tell me more," I beg, even though I can see tears creeping into the corners of Shaindy's eyes. I am thirsty for the memories, images that I can gather together in my imaginary album and take with me into my marriage.

"She used to make a delicious tomato soup in the winter and we'd all run into the house and empty the pot as soon as we got home from school," Shaindy smiles. "Once, we begged her to take us ice skating. She took us to the other side of town, two buses there and back, and sat frozen for an hour, watching us fall down over and over again on the ice."

Now it's me with the tears and I catch them quickly before they run in salty streaks down my face and ruin my make-up. "When did things change?" I ask quietly, even though I know the answer.

"Mommy always had her ups and downs... we thought she was moody... you know, sometimes very happy and overly energetic or she wouldn't get out of bed for days, weeks even. But after your birth..." Shaindy's lip quivers, "she wasn't the same... she never really recovered."

It's enough for now, not just for Shaindy but for me too. I reach out to give her a hug. "Thank you," I whisper, "for my wedding gift."

SHAINDY WAS RIGHT about Leiby. He's a fine boy... kind and very good to me. And now that I am the one laundering his clothes, he no longer smells like moth balls, I hardly notice his giggle anymore and the sniffing has disappeared along with his nervousness. Sometimes I cannot understand why he cares for me so much and when I ask him, he seems baffled by my question.

"Because you're my wife, Chayaleh… why wouldn't I care?" he replies.

I'm left with a lingering discomfort over his answer. I cannot quite grasp why, except that maybe I'm more comfortable taking care of others than this way around.

When I'm expecting our first child, Leiby's father invites him to move to London and join the family business.

"Well, I guess the weather's better there," I shrug and he flinches, hurt from my lack of enthusiasm.

"We'll be closer to my parents," he says. "My mother will be able to help you after the birth."

I stop to consider that. I've not really had much to do with Leiby's mother but she seems like a nice woman, although a drop intimidating. Much more put together than mine. That last thought almost makes me laugh.

"Maybe my mother will be able to come too?" I say foolishly, feeling my heart stretch out towards invisible hands.

Leiby smiles patiently. "Perhaps," he nods. "Anything is possible."

"She's been doing a lot better, you know. The doctor is hoping that with this new medication, she'll be able to go home for good soon."

"G-d willing," Leiby says seriously. "Let's pray that he's right."

THE WEATHER IN London *is* better; the sky is only gray for half a day instead of a whole, and the sun stays out long enough for me to get warm and feel like there's hope in the world. I like Leiby's family, especially his father, a rotund man with a hearty sense of humor, and his sister, Bayla, who's a little older than me and has two-year-old twin girls. My mother-in-law is very pleasant in her efficient, polished sort of way.

My beautiful little boy is the most miraculous thing I've ever seen.

I cannot stop looking at him; I am transfixed by his every movement, the puckering of his lips and scrunching of his eyes. But what I like most of all, what sends a tingle running all the way down to my toes, is when he wraps his little fist around my finger, holding on for dear life, as if he intuitively knows… I'm his mother.

"WHY DON'T YOU let my mother help you more?" Leiby asks, looking at me with a worried expression on his face.

I rock Shimmy back and forth, watching his face become redder, listening to his screams grow louder, and I cry. Sometimes I'm not sure who cries more. I haven't stopped crying since the *bris*. Leiby's family catered a lovely affair and I really appreciated my father and siblings traveling down for it. Mommy wasn't up to the journey but sent a cute little stretchy along with a note that I could barely decipher. When Shaindy handed it to me, as if giving me a gift from a friend, I cried.

"Maybe I should send you to the mother-and-baby convalescent home?" Leiby suggests. "You'll be able to rest there… unless you want to move in with my parents?"

I shake my head, "No."

I don't know what I want. I know what I *don't* want, though. I don't want someone else's mother replacing mine. I don't want someone else's arms around me, trying to give the love and reassurance that should be coming from my own flesh and blood.

Leiby sends me anyway. He orders a taxi and carries my suitcase down the shiny corridors to my private room and helps me settle in.

"It looks nice," he says, looking around. "Cheerful colors."

"Probably supposed to help with the postpartum depression," I respond.

For a moment, Leiby looks alarmed.

"Is your mother very offended?" I ask quickly.

"Not really… I think she understands."

"That's good," I say.

"You're sure you'll be okay?" Leiby asks, his eyes soft with concern.

"Yes, I'll be fine. Come, let me walk you out."

I wave at Leiby as he enters the elevator. The doors slide closed and the elevator moves off with a sudden lurch, leaving me alone, rudderless in a sea of emotions. I wander listlessly to the nursery. At the bassinet next to Shimmy's, a young girl is passing her baby to an older woman.

"Who do you think he looks like, Mommy?" she says excitedly. " I think he's our side of the family."

I watch the two of them walk out into the corridor, chattering animatedly together, and touch my cheeks to find they're wet again. I thought I'd escape this here, mothers and daughters right in my face. I push Shimmy in his clear plastic, wheeled box back to my room, sit down on the bed and punch the numbers on my phone.

"Leiby," I say when he answers. "Please come and take me home."

I AM SETTLING down in London like a puppy dog delighted with its new surroundings. I never imagined that my life here would become as familiar as the fog. Through Bayla, I've made some friends and we often get together at the park or each other's houses. Leiby's family is very welcoming, yet I find myself holding back, always leaving a space inside that one day will be filled with… something.

Tired from my second pregnancy, I'm just about to take a nap when I get the call.

"Chayaleh," Shaindy calls breathlessly down the phone. "Mommy's back!"

I'm slightly bewildered. "Back… from where… where did she go?"

"No," my sister says excitedly, her voice tinkling like bells. "I mean *back with us*… the new medication is working!"

The shock has knocked the wind out of me. "Are you… are you saying that she's *normal?*"

"Mostly. She's been through a lot, of course, and it shows, but she's functioning again, pretty well, actually. It's a miracle!"

I inhale elated air, letting that unfilled space inside me expand as I breathe.

"You must come to see her, Chayaleh. We'll make a *seudas hoda'ah* for the family and everyone will travel in. I still can't believe it. I'm shmoozing with Mommy just like old times… it's incredible." Shaindy is babbling, strings of beaded sentences that sway in rows, sometimes banging into each other.

"Yes, yes… of course I'll come. When is it?"

"Soon," Shaindy says. "I'll be in touch as soon as I've finalized the arrangements. Must run… got lots to do…"

And then she's gone, leaving me with a silent telephone and my gigantic gap whose outer walls are trembling with anticipation.

"Mommy's back," I say to Leiby when he comes home later. He looks at me strangely.

"You don't understand," I exclaim, lifting up Shimmy with a sudden burst of energy and spinning him around in the air. I pull Shimmy's head down towards me so his face is touching mine and nuzzle his neck. "Bubby's back," I whisper. "Mommy is with us again!"

AS WE LEAVE the south behind, we watch the sky turn grainy and say good-bye to the last remnants of the sun. I shiver, even though we're nowhere near my hometown yet, but just thinking of it makes me feel cold. Twisted up with the excitement, I'm aware of a knot of guilt for not having been back to visit in months and I hope I can untangle it.

The taxi pulls up outside my house and I quickly gather my belongings, take Shimmy's hand, and spill out onto the pavement. Leiby stands beside me, and still holding Shimmy's hand, I stare at the house that was once my home. I can feel the cobwebbed memories before I even enter; the pervasive hush that hung like heavy drapes over every window, the silence that slid along the windowsills. I look at Leiby and he nods.

"Come, let's go in."

Suddenly the door flies open and I'm engulfed in jumbled embraces that carry me inside. I feel myself pulled down the hallway to the living room and then I see her. The petite woman sitting in my favorite armchair, neatly dressed in a navy blue knit suit, her *sheitel* tastefully styled in a short, wavy cut, must be my mother! I walk tentatively towards her and she looks up at me and smiles.

"Chayaleh," she says softly, her eyes crinkling at the corners.

"Mommy?"

She rises slowly from her chair and comes to hug me. I close my eyes and wait for that first true motherly hug, but when it comes I feel… nothing… just an empty space inside that's still aching to be filled.

"I DON'T EVEN recognize her!" I wail when Leiby and I are alone. "She's a total stranger."

Leiby shrugs helplessly. "I suppose you have to get to know her."

"Get to know her! She's my mother! Since when is one supposed to get to know one's own mother?"

Leiby sits down on the sofa and waits patiently for me to calm down. "Even when we have a mother, we don't always know her," he says quietly.

I blow my nose and sniff into the handkerchief.

"At least your mother wasn't malicious. She just wasn't well enough to look after you," Leiby continues, trying to make me feel better.

"That's exactly the point!" I retort, frustrated by his over-understanding. "It's still neglect, isn't it? Mothering is a mother's job. That's what she's supposed to do!"

"But she couldn't," Leiby states simply.

I start to cry again… angry, agonized tears that mingle in confusion down my cheeks. I lean forward in the chair, clutching my stomach to soothe the pain even though it's my heart that's shattered.

"I… I thought I'd find Mommy, the *real* one, the one I want… but I didn't." Another round of sobs racks my body. "All I ever wanted was a mother. Is… is that so terrible?"

Leiby looks at me compassionately, his eyes mirroring my pain. "Of course it's not."

"But I'm never going to have one, am I?"

We both let the question hover like a wide-winged eagle over our heads, waiting for it to swoop down and take me in its clutches. But instead of carrying me off to some deserted destination, it merely circles the sky.

I turn to Leiby, surprised. "I... I've never said that before. Those words were supposed to destroy me."

"And they haven't," he murmurs.

I am so startled by that realization that the tears pause in the corner of my eyes as if they're also uncertain.

"You need to grieve," Leiby says with a wisdom I'd have never imagined. I don't know why I'm surprised, though, because growing up with an autistic brother has to have made him different... more understanding and mature.

I start to cry again. "It's going to take a while."

Leiby nods. "However long it takes. But meanwhile..." he hesitates, "there's always *my* mother. I know it's not the same, and she's also not what you wanted, but..."

"Thank you," I give an uncertain smile. "Maybe... we'll see."

THERE ARE PIECES, I've discovered, of mothers; little bits of love and nurturing from those who are not my own. I'm learning to recognize them, to put them in my pocket when I find them.

Leiby's mother is one of those parts, a large slice of a multi-layered cake. After Pessy was born, we moved in with Leiby's parents and this time, I let his mother look after me.

Shaindy is another one of those pieces. She always was and always will be. And even Bayla has a portion to give when I feel like taking it.

Mommy is many slices, sometimes coated in frosting, sometimes in sweet, whipped cream. We've been tasting our relationship slowly, taking tentative bites. I know she'd like to be included in my life more but I'm not comfortable with that yet. Like Leiby said, it will take time.

And then, of course, there's my mothering of myself and learning that it's not something selfish or indulgent like I once thought.

I'm chopping vegetables for lunch one morning when the phone rings.

"Chayaleh," I can hardly hear Shaindy's raspy voice. "Mommy's gone back."

I take in a sharp breath and feel the pain in my ribs.

"When?" I ask.

"Last night. Tatty took her into the hospital. She went into a depressive state again."

"So sad," I whisper, "poor, poor Mommy."

Leiby, who is home sick, appears at my side with two steaming mugs of cocoa and a big slice of himself. He sees my eyes glistening and nods knowingly.

I ache for both her and me, but this time, the gaping hole inside is smaller, filling itself up gradually like water in a man-made lake. As I sadly hang up the phone, I stare out of the kitchen window and see that the sun is still there, behind the clouds.

This story is based on true events in the life of Sorahle, a close friend of mine. Just like in the story, Sorahle grew up with a mother who was mentally ill. She was raised by her father who had no idea how to marry her off. Her shidduchim went as described in the story, and my friend did in fact have to prepare her mother to attend her own wedding. A few years later, Sorahle's mother passed away. After hearing my friend's sad story, I thought a lot about what mothers mean to us. I tried to imagine what it would have been like to grow up without a mother, the nurturing that would be absent and the effect that would have on a child's life.

This is one of those stories that just flowed from my fingertips. I wrote it in first person, which I find much more powerful because I can be so much more expressive. I enjoyed reading this story to myself afterwards — which means it was a winner, because usually I can't stand the sight of my pieces anymore by the time they've gone to print!

Choices

"SHE'S GETTING WEAKER, you know, and her numbers aren't good," the familiar voice says softly. "Did you get an answer from her uncle yet?"

"No," says another voice that's very dear to me. "We're trying; it's difficult to locate him."

Silence… and darkness… but love, lots of love… and tenderness… all bound together in the cluster of people huddled around the stained, wooden table in the hospital waiting room.

"Let's hope this shunt lasts a while," the first voice says. "I don't think she has place for another one."

Sighs and heaviness and worry weighing on their slumped shoulders, almost forcing them to their knees on the shiny, linoleum floor.

And all… because of me!

I SLIP BACK into bed without them seeing me and snuggle under my blanket… the fluffy eiderdown with the horse cover and matching pillowcase that I've been allowed to bring from home. Ah, the privileges of being a long-term patient.

My bed-table is laden with lots of thirteen-year-old girl things… photo albums, letters, an MP3 player, candy wrappers, and low-salt potato chips that Matti sneaked in yesterday. Devoiry has recently added the newest stuffed animal to my soft toy collection, an odd-looking bear I've named Tigger after the character in Winnie the Pooh. Now he is firmly holed up with the rest of the menagerie, including Sausage, a long, skinny dog from Miri; and Daffy, a beautiful blue and white dolphin. I scrunch up my forehead in thought: Who had brought the dolphin?

Things… there are so many things! On the shelves, on the wall… I am dwarfed by things — posters, pictures, photographs, notes stuck to my bed for the nurses. Anyone would think this was my bedroom.

"Becky," whispers one of the voices I'd heard earlier. "Are you awake?" Dr. Weiss sits down carefully on my bed; she is light and airy, like an angel floating in. "Becky," she says again, using the shortened version of my English name, as usual. "You need to go for dialysis, I'm afraid. Your creatinine and urea levels are high."

"Now?" I raise myself up and rest on my elbows. "At this time of night? What about sleeping?"

Dr. Weiss smiles her sweet, crooked smile, with the one dimple dipping into her left cheek. "You can sleep once you're hooked up. Unless, that is, you'd rather play cards?"

"Yay!" I whoop, suddenly no longer tired. "Just you and me in the dialysis unit… you're on!"

She helps me into a wheelchair because I am too tired to walk and pushes me through long, sleepy corridors to the elevator and down to the fourth floor. When she unlocks the door, the dialysis room is dark, deep in slumber, gathering its energy for the next day's patients. It certainly wasn't expecting me.

Dr. Weiss flips on the lights and I shuffle over to my usual place — the chair I've been occupying for the last two years.

"Maybe we can make it shorter this time," Dr. Weiss suggests, while connecting me to the machine. "You've already had one session today so I'll see if you can do three hours instead of four."

"Whatever," I say breezily. "What's the difference? It just gives me more time to beat you at cards."

Dr. Weiss chuckles and pulls up a chair next to the leather recliner that I, the patient, have the honor of lying on. She dips her hand into the pocket of her white coat and pulls out a pack of shiny, plastic playing cards and begins to deal, passing cards back and forth between us, and in the stillness of the night, with the only sound coming from soft songs on the radio… we play.

"Becky, I'd like to talk about things," Dr. Weiss says at last as I scoop up another winning pile.

"I know."

Dr. Weiss narrows her eyes and looks at me curiously.

"I heard you talking with my parents this evening when you thought I was asleep."

"Ah… I see." Dr. Weiss raises her eyebrows in mock disapproval. Gathering her breath like she's about to inflate a rubber tube, she takes my hand and says, "We can't continue like this much longer. You need a kidney as soon as possible."

I nod.

"You're requiring much more extra dialysis now…" her voice trails off, clearly reaching its own threshold.

I blink back tears and stare at the ceiling, hoping to find some solace in the bright lights above, or even a kidney floating around somewhere with the name Rivka Glass emblazoned on it in bold, black letters.

Dr. Weiss squeezes my hand again. "You're at the top of the transplant list, and I understand your mother is still trying to track down her brother to see if he's a match. None of the other family members are suitable donors because of the genetic component."

I swallow whatever it is in my throat, lay my head back, and close my eyes.

"I think you're too old and mature for me to hide the situation from you," Dr. Weiss continues, "and anyway, you probably know what's going on even without eavesdropping on our conversation."

"Yes," I say, with a grin.

"So in the meantime we carry on as usual," Dr. Weiss pats my arm firmly. "It's going to be okay… really… I feel it. See, all of your faith has rubbed off on me after all!"

SOMETIMES I FEEL as if I've known Dr. Weiss my entire life, or certainly since I'm old enough to understand things. But then again, it feels like I've had polycystic kidney disease my whole life when really I've only had it since I'm nine. Still, four years is a long time when your friends are running races along the beach, playing color war and having pajama parties. I shouldn't complain really, because it's only affected my life in any major way these last two years, since I started the hemodialysis. Until then I was more or less managing, doing the dialysis through my stomach at home and not needing to go to the hospital. Lately, though, I feel like I live here.

Dr. Weiss is almost like part of our family. Sometimes I look at her as an aunt, or maybe even a replacement for Uncle Seth, Mom's brother who disappeared off the face of the earth twenty years ago. Actually, he was thrown out of the house by my grandfather when he wanted to marry out after he stopped keeping Torah and *mitzvos* and we've never heard from him since. I wonder about him sometimes.

Mom especially likes to invite Dr. Weiss to our home during the Yamim Tovim, which she rarely experiences, and I have the best time explaining our customs to her. At those moments I feel as if I am the doctor and she, the patient.

"I'M NOT GOING back," I declare angrily, stamping my foot. "I've only been home for three days!"

"I'm sorry," my mother says, and the sadness on her face squeezes my heart real tight. "It's only overnight," she pleads. "Dr. Weiss wants to have you on the ward in case you need extra dialysis."

"No!" I stomp upstairs to my bedroom and kick the door closed behind me. I'm not going — I'm not! They can't make me!

I beat my fists on my purple poof that's on the floor over in the corner and fight back angry tears until I lay back, exhausted. Of course I am going. Who am I kidding? Do I have a choice? Come to think about it, do I really have a choice about anything? If only it were so simple that I could just saunter over to the supermarket and choose myself a kidney from the shelf, or stand in the aisles and shout, "Hey, anyone have a kidney to give me?" But no, those are only fantasies… my unfulfilled dreams.

Over the last few months, since my late night rendezvous with Dr. Weiss, I've been more in the hospital than at home, and there's still no kidney in sight. Of course, Uncle Seth came up empty; his wife said he wouldn't even do the testing. That made me feel horrible and I don't know why, but I cried so hard when I heard that, even though it's what I'd expected; it was a miracle that Mom even found him in the first place, although I think we Jews can always find one another, wherever we are. Still, I wept for days on end, copious amounts of tears, until my pillowcase was thoroughly soaked and needed changing, and I wished my kidneys worked half as well as my tear ducts.

Anyway, I'm not going so easily this time, I decide, flopping down onto my bed. It's time to stand my ground, to choose rebellion for as long as I can. Downstairs, I hear the sound of the phone ringing in the kitchen and my mother's flustered answer. It's probably Dr. Weiss, nagging again; too bad, she'll just have to wait until I'm ready. Suddenly, I hear my mother shouting, and her voice is not the same as it was a few minutes ago.

"Rivka, Rivka!" She's charging upstairs, and in a second she's bursting through my door, a crazed look on her face. "They've got a kidney for you! Oh my goodness, do you hear me? You have a kidney!"

I bolt upright in bed. "W… what… who… how?"

"It doesn't matter; no time to talk now. I need to call Tatty — just get your things and let's go!"

"LET'S PRAY THAT this will be the last time," Dr. Weiss says when she visits me in the dialysis unit later. "You may need a session or two straight after the transplant, though, so be prepared for that."

I nod, although I don't really register what she's saying, because ripples of excitement or maybe nerves are fluttering inside me like butterfly wings. My brain feels jellified, as if it's all dissolved into one big blob, and I can't think straight.

"Scared?" Dr. Weiss asks softly.

"Uh-huh."

"That's normal," she reassures me. "I would be too."

I look at her in surprise. "You would?"

"Sure. It's a big thing you're about to go through, and that's without the actual operation."

"Yeah, but just think — I'll be able to drink as much Coca Cola as I want, and I won't have to measure my food portions anymore," I say jokingly.

Dr. Weiss smiles and leans casually on my armrest.

"Who's giving me the kidney?" I ask suddenly, struck by the urge to know whose body part I'll be receiving.

"The donor would rather not say at this stage," Dr. Weiss answers, "and that's their right."

"Do you know who it is?"

"Of course," she nods, and that only makes me more curious. I want to know who has chosen to give their kidney to me! It feels so strange that some stranger out there has willingly decided to give up one of their kidneys. It's not coming from anyone who has just died, *chas v'shalom*, but from someone very much alive and healthy and with a heart bigger than all the kidneys in the world, and I want to know what kind of person would do that.

"Don't worry about it now. Let's just concentrate on getting you through the surgery," Dr. Weiss says. "I want you to rest as much as you can over the next few days and gather some strength."

I wonder about that, because I'm already so tired, and energy doesn't seem to me like something you can unpeg from a clothesline. But right this minute I don't feel the weariness, only the trembling of fear and anticipation — and impatience with this stupid lump of metal next to my chair that's taking forever to clean all the junk from my blood.

"Becky," Dr. Weiss takes my hand between hers, as if she's guarding a precious diamond. "I have something to tell you."

I wait expectantly, wondering if she's going to tell me that she's getting married and that I'll be guest of honor at her wedding.

"I'm afraid I won't be here after you have the surgery; I'll be away for a couple of weeks."

"What?" I gape at her in disbelief, feeling like she's just punched me in the stomach. "You mean you're not going to be with me? Who's going to take care of me? W… where are you going?" I bite my bottom lip hard to stop the tears from falling, but they are in my eyes, not my mouth.

"I'm sorry, Becky. Something urgent has come up that I need to attend to… Dr. Kagen will be taking over, and he already knows your case."

"But it's not the same!" I begin to shout, my voice rising with each level of hurt. "He's not you. He hardly knows me. How could you just… isn't there something you can do to get out of it?"

Dr. Weiss shakes her head slowly and clasps my hands so tightly that my fingers are almost squished together and don't have room to move.

"So I'll be alone then," I pout.

"No, of course not; you'll have your parents and your amazing family and all your friends to love and support you, and Dr. Kagen will be here for the medical things. You don't need me, Becky — you can do this without me. You're very strong."

"I'm not so sure about that," I snivel, and I cannot see anything beyond the rain that falls in sheets across my eyes.

IT'S SO DARK when I wake up that I think I'm back in the nighttime dialysis room, but then I realize that my eyes are still closed. Somewhere, around my head, I can hear my parents' voices poured into a long, loving monologue and dripping over me like fresh cream. I drift in and out of somewhere that isn't here, a place in between the vomiting and headaches and temperature taking. And then one day I hear cries and Mommy is shaking me, unable to wait any longer, and she's shrieking, "Rivka, Rivka, wake up… it's working… the kidney is working!" I lean drowsily over the side of the bed, gaze at the tubing snaking down to the silicone bag tied to the side, give a tired, contented smile and go back to sleep.

"DR. KAGEN IS thrilled with your progress," Mommy is saying. "He says that so far the kidney's working beautifully."

Dr. Kagen, Dr. Kagen… that's what I hear all day long. Well, I'm tired of Dr. Kagen.

"Where's Dr. Weiss?" I ask again, for the umpteenth time. "How come she hasn't even called?"

"I told you already that she phoned a few times while you were sleeping. She sends her love and is happy you're doing so well," Mommy answers, pouring me a cup of raspberry tea.

I take the tea and scowl. "I still don't understand why she had to have an emergency right when I had my surgery."

Mommy pours herself a cup too and flops down tiredly on the recliner beside my bed. I can see the lines on her face, the puckered skin. Suddenly she looks so old, and a nip of guilt pinches me like a pair of tweezers. All of this is taking its toll on her, and here I am whining like a spoiled child.

"It's not that I don't appreciate you, Mommy… it's just that Dr. Weiss has been with us right from the beginning," I try to explain.

"Oh, I didn't think that at all," says Mommy, patting my knee. "Of course I understand how you feel… it's only normal."

I look at my mother curiously. "How come you seem so okay with it? Don't you wish she was here too?"

"She is here," Mommy answers, in a voice coated with chocolate bits and sugar candy. "She might not be here physically, but believe me, she's with you."

I scowl. What does my mother's sickly sweet understanding do for me? The fact is that my doctor has gone. She's not with me at the most important time of my life. After everything we've been through together as doctor and patient, she is missing. My mother's calm, accepting demeanor is annoying, and all it does is make me feel thoroughly frustrated, because inside a lonely chamber of my heart, I feel that Dr. Weiss has let me down.

I'M GOING HOME tomorrow. Yes, home… I'm really going home, and I won't have to come back three times a week for dialysis. Whew! I cannot imagine my life without being in the hospital all the time and I admit that I'm more than a little nervous. I'll be coming back for follow-up visits, of course, with Doctor — well, actually, I'm not sure whom, but I suppose for now it's Dr. Kagen.

We packed my things this evening… wow, so much stuff… We'll need several trips to get it home. Mommy left me the cherry-apple drink that I love and the peanuts that Bubby gave her for me, in case I get hungry in the night. The fact that I can eat them is wild! I still have some dietary restrictions, but far less than before, and it's so much fun being able to have choices. You cannot imagine how that feels, almost like a prisoner being allowed his first visit home. All of the "no's" are slowly receding. The "no salt or potassium"; the "no, you can't drink anymore today, because you're over the limit"; the "no, you can't go on the school trip because you'll miss two days of dialysis…"

I'm too excited to sleep, so I lay in bed in the semi-darkened room with my eyes closed, just floating inside my thoughts. It's when I'm drifting off to a place without dialysis machines that I sense a presence by my bed, but for some inexplicable reason

I don't open my eyes. Despite the dark the presence is familiar and comforting, like the return of a long lost friend, and immediately I know it's her… she's come back. I lay still as if I'm paralyzed and make no effort to acknowledge she's here, for I understand, even without words, that she wants things this way.

She leans over me and moves some loose strands of hair off my forehead and my heart pounds as I feel her warm breath on my face. It feels like she's standing here forever, just watching me, until suddenly she moves to the end of my bed and I hear her lifting up the metal chart that's hanging there. As she turns the pages, I cannot resist taking a tiny little peek and through my squinty eyes, I see that yes, it is her, just as I thought. Even in the semi-darkness she looks pale and tired, and for a brief moment I wonder if she's sick… maybe that's why she hasn't come to see me? And then it happens… this absolutely astonishing revelation that could have come from heaven itself, and I'm filled with the deep, unquestionable knowledge that it is Dr. Weiss who has given me her own kidney.

"WHY DIDN'T SHE tell me, Mommy?" I'm barely able to get the words out in my shell-shocked state. It's 3 a.m., but my mother is here — she just jumped into the car and raced to the hospital after receiving my hysterical phone call.

"Because she didn't want you to feel uncomfortable, or perhaps try to talk her out of it," Mommy explains gently.

"But why did she do it?" I don't really want to hear my mother's words, even though I'm asking for them. I screw my face up and look like I've just eaten something sour. "I don't get it… I'm her patient!"

"Right," Mommy pauses. "But she obviously feels that you're more than that."

"This is beyond weird. I cannot believe that I just received a kidney from my own doctor!"

Mommy nods. "Yes, you're right. It's hard to understand…

Tatty and I struggled with the idea too at first. And Dr. Weiss has been getting quite a lot of criticism as well."

I raise my eyebrows.

"From the medical ethics board and her fellow doctors," Mommy explains. "It's been quite a roller coaster for her, but she was determined."

I lean back wearily against my pillows. This is too much to wrap my brain around. I feel as if all my neurons are slamming into one another and they're making my head bang.

"When did you and Tatty find out?" I ask tiredly.

"The day after the surgery, but Dr. Weiss asked us not to say anything... she wanted to tell you herself."

My head is pounding even more from those dizzy neurons, punching different parts of my brain, and I just wish they would keep still so I could think about something other than, "My doctor gave me her kidney," but I can't.

"It's an incredible thing that she did," Mommy says, and I notice that she's fighting to stay awake, her eyelids drooping. "I know it's confusing for you, but she's just given you the most precious gift she could."

A warm rush of emotion burns my veins and it feels almost like the times I was on the kidney machine. Gratitude and confusion and a deep, searing love are tangled up in those tubes of dialysis and the many months of yearning for the right match, and I'm unable to separate them. Where, inside of all of that, do I put Dr. Weiss?

My voice is shaking as I ask the question. "Mommy, what do we do now? Is she still my doctor?"

Mommy shakes her head. "No, she can't be; it wouldn't be ethical. The relationship has gone beyond that."

My eyes begin to close and I sink into clouds that are full of disappearing dialysis tubing and the strangest of choices.

WE'RE ALMOST READY to leave when Tatty gets the phone call from Uncle Seth's wife that he passed away last night.

It wasn't that he didn't want to help us out, she explained, but he was already very sick by then. I am so sad to hear this — so very sorry that he couldn't spend his final months with his family.

"It was his choice," Mommy says sadly. "Sometimes it's hard for us to understand the decisions people make."

We say good-bye to the entire staff. Some of them have made me Going Home signs and hung helium balloons from the bedposts, and we hug one another until we're all squeezed out like fresh oranges. And then we're gone, sweeping through the door like a royal entourage, waving behind us until we get to the elevator and press the button to go down. When we reach the lobby, Mommy and Tatty tell me to sit and wait while they take care of some paperwork, so I park myself in a chair and start rereading some of the get-well cards I've received.

"Hello, Becky."

I look up to see Dr. Weiss standing before me.

"May I sit down?" she asks, inclining her head towards the seat next to me.

"Y-yes, of course."

"You look good," she says. "I hope you feel as well as you look."

"I… I'm doing fine." I look down at the pile of cards in my lap and for a moment we sit in silence.

"You realized I was there last night," Dr. Weiss begins.

I'm not sure if this is a question or a statement, so I just nod.

Dr. Weiss touches my arm gently. "Please don't feel uncomfortable, Becky. I wanted to do this… it was my choice."

I wish I could say something, anything, that would express all that I feel, but I'm not sure what that is, so all I can do is childishly stutter, "B-but you won't be my doctor anymore."

Dr. Weiss smiles, her familiar, lopsided, one-dimpled smile, and my confusion explodes into a galaxy of stars filled with gratitude and love.

"You're right — I won't be your physician," Dr. Weiss is saying, "but giving you this chance was more important to me than being your doctor. It's the choice I made."

"A choice that gives me choices," I whisper softly, "and a chance to live."

Dr. Weiss, who is no longer my doctor, lets out a sigh that's so contented it could almost smile all by itself.

"I've never done anything as meaningful as this in my life," she says. "Somehow, being a doctor wasn't enough... I had to do more."

"You already are more," I blurt out. I'm not really sure how to explain this, only that I suddenly see her as someone so much bigger than everyone else — all those people who have stayed within the limits. It's like she glided out of a skating rink and found far more ice on the other side — and the partner she picked to skate with was... me!

I love writing medical stories! And of course, my years of experience working as a pediatric and NICU nurse gives me the edge here. When I write something in a medical setting I can envision the scenes as if I'm there.

"Choices" was inspired after reading a newspaper article about a Chinese doctor who donated a kidney to one of her patients. She was taken to task by the medical ethics board of the hospital where she worked. That got me thinking. Was there anything wrong with what she did or not? From the medical committee's point of view there clearly was, but from a moral and spiritual perspective it seemed to me that this doctor performed a noble act of chessed. I expanded this topic into the choices that we make and why we make them, until voila, there was my story!

I have to also mention that I very much enjoy writing from a teenager's perspective like I did in "Choices." Perhaps that's because, as my children like to tell me, I still am one!

Ready to Fly

"LOOK, MOMMY, IT'S got a broken wing!"

I crouched down beside Ayelet, my eight-year-old daughter, and examined the plump black creature that was huddled on our doorstep.

"You're right, honey, it has," I confirmed.

"Can we take it in?" Ayelet pleaded irresistibly. "I'll find a box for it and feed it my hamster's food."

I smiled at my sweet, caring, angelic-looking daughter and ruffled her hair affectionately. "Okay," I nodded, "bring her in. We'll take care of her until she's ready to fly."

"Get that thing out of here," ten-year-old Yanki ordered angrily. "It smells."

Ayelet gently elbowed the front door closed behind her and proudly carried her new companion into the living room.

"It's a pigeon, Yanki, it's supposed to smell."

That's pretty wise for an eight-year-old, I thought. Especially a girl who still plays with dolls and never dirties her delicate hands.

Ayelet cradled the injured bird in her hands as though it were made of china, supporting the damaged wing so it didn't droop. I looked the creature over; the beak and beady eyes, the neck that could stretch itself out and retract like a telescope. It wasn't the cleanest houseguest I would have liked, or the prettiest, but

I couldn't in good conscience leave it outside alone — the cats would gobble it up for supper.

"I said get rid of it," Yanki complained. "I hate birds."

I glanced at my son, puzzled. "You usually like animals, Yanki. What's the matter?"

"Yeah, I like real animals like dogs and things, not birds… they don't do anything."

"Except fly," I answered. "That's pretty amazing, isn't it?" I studied the grounded bird again and sensed her vulnerability. "Well, I'm sorry," I replied firmly. "She's injured, and she stays."

"YANKI," I CALLED for the tenth time that morning, "get down from that tree." I sighed. What was the point of his being suspended from *cheder* if all he did was perform dangerous acrobatic feats in our backyard?

"Yanki, I'm warning you, you're going to break something, *chas v'shalom*. Come down now."

He was high up in the great oak that graced our garden, half hidden in a thick blanket of leafy branches. I peered upward, searching for a flash of his dirty-blonde hair and freckled face among the foliage.

"Nope," Yanki's voice rang out merrily. "It's fun up here."

"WILL YOU STOP moving your leg so I can clean it!"

"Ow, ow, ow!" Yanki shrieked, yowling like a cat. "It hurts!"

"Of course it does, but if you let me clean it and put a bandage on, it will feel much better."

"But the plaster is going to stick to the sore I got last week," Yanki moaned.

I looked at Yanki's leg and swallowed the words, "I told you so." The lines, bruises and suture scars running along his limb had turned it into a road map. The previous week's fall had been from the top of the *cheder* fence, which he'd been scaling because he was late. A couple of days later he'd gouged a piece of flesh out of his thigh while building his latest wooden fortress in yet another tree, and just yesterday he'd knocked out two teeth in a fight with a sixth-grader, landing him back home in my tender loving care… again. I scanned my baby-faced son's limbs. He looked like little Moshe's chewed-up teddy bear, which was running out of places to bite.

"It doesn't matter," Yanki said. He stood up grumpily, unable to sit still any longer. "I'll do it myself."

As he stomped off in a huff, I wondered for the millionth time what would become of him.

WITH AN INNATE mothering tendency, Ayelet was fussing over her pigeon. She fed it tiny crusts of bread, fashioned a drinking basin from the cap of a soda bottle, and had even "borrowed" some of my white printing paper to layer the bottom of a small plastic crate she'd found outside, sprinkling it liberally with twigs and leaves from the garden. Once the bird was installed underneath our *netilas yadayim* sink, it officially became Yonah and began to recover in its temporary quarters in the Resnick residence.

"Maybe we could get her a cage or something?" Ayelet suggested. "That box doesn't look very comfortable. Look how squashed she is."

I raised my eyebrows in mock severity. "May I remind you that dear Yonah is getting all of these superb living conditions for free, so she'd better be grateful."

Laughing, Ayelet skipped off happily to retrieve some more stale bread, and I smiled after her, delighting in her enthusiasm.

On the third day, Yonah showed signs of being something more than just a lump in a box.

"Look, Mommy," Ayelet called down the hallway, "Yonah's trying to get out."

She clapped her hands gleefully. "See how clever she is — she's jumped up on the top of the box. Maybe she's getting better?"

"She's just a stupid pigeon, Ayelet," growled Yanki as he passed by. "And she still smells!"

"So what?" Ayelet was undeterred. "She deserves to be taken care of, and that's exactly what I'm going to do until she's well again."

For a second, Yanki paused to stare at his sister. He looked back and forth between her and the bird, abruptly kicked the box, and stormed out.

He was angry. I understood that he was angry. Why shouldn't he be? After all, my hyperactive, delightfully creative son had endured repeated insults, humiliation in class and more suspensions from school than I could count. These days it seemed as if they were sending him home simply for breathing. We were desperate to find another school that would meet the needs of our energetic, imaginative child.

It wasn't easy at home, either. Ayelet would get irritated when her brother bothered her, which was far too frequently, and we were always running out of new, interesting ways to keep him occupied and prevent him from leaving the house lest he end up in more trouble.

Yes, I understood his anger, even felt his frustration. He believed he could conquer the world but no one would let him do it. Of course, if he took his medication, things could be a lot easier, and that was yet another battle. We'd tried just about everything short of force-feeding to get him to swallow that one tiny white pill, and to be honest, I was getting tired of it. My patience was almost exhausted. Medication prescribed instead of Ritalin hadn't helped at all, so there was no question that Yanki really needed to follow his doctor's orders.

"UGH, CAN'T YOU try harder to keep her in her box?" I wrinkled my nose and pressed down harder on the mop.

"I can't stop her, Mommy, she jumps out by herself," Ayelet explained patiently, like a teacher to a small child.

"Well, she'd better jump right back in," I said firmly, "because I'm not planning on cleaning up her messes for the next few weeks."

"But she's getting better, isn't she? She can walk now." My daughter pointed at Yonah, who was waddling across my once-sparkling living-room floor and dropping messy splatters on the tiles.

"Sure she is, sweetheart, but walking isn't flying. She still has a long way to go."

"IT'S NOT FAIR," Yanki cried, hot, angry tears running down his cheeks. "Why can't I go?"

My heart flooded with my son's misery and pain.

"I'm sorry, honey," I said, but my empathy bounced off his hurt, empty and hollow.

"Everyone else is going except me. It's not fair!" He stamped his foot and reached for the cushions on the couch. I readied myself to duck.

"They don't feel they can take the responsibility," I said as a beige cushion whizzed over my head. "And Naomi doesn't think you're quite ready for sleepaway camp yet." The next cushion landed dangerously close to my glass display cabinets, so I quickly gathered up all the other potential missiles.

"What does Naomi know?" he yelled back. "She's just a shrink!" He reached for the flowerpot on the windowsill, so I quickly handed back a couple of cushions.

"Well, she has been your therapist for the last year," I gasped breathlessly. "I think she knows you by now."

"No, she doesn't. She's supposed to be on my side, isn't she? I'm not going back to her anymore!"

I don't know whose heart ached more, mine or his. I felt the hurt, humiliation and rejection that rained down on him repeatedly from all sides. The blows just never stopped coming.

"I'm sorry, Yanki, really I am. I'm sure you'll be ready by next year. Meanwhile we'll find other things to do, honest — we'll try to make the vacation nice for you." I was already dreading his boredom and imagining the likely explosions that would result during the summer. Just thinking about it tired me. He collapsed heavily onto the couch, the fight draining out of him like air from a punctured balloon.

"But you know, honey…" I paused. He wasn't going to like this. "If you'd take the medicine like you're supposed to, maybe you wouldn't need to suffer so much."

Yanki clenched his teeth tightly. "I told you, I'm not going to take it. It will make me short and skinny like Shlomo, and everyone will laugh at me."

I sighed again. I was doing a lot of that these days. The kids laughed at him anyway, for other reasons, but he didn't seem to realize that. He was ten years old; how could we force him to take his medicine?

"DON'T CRY, HONEY, she'll be okay."

"But she's supposed to be better, isn't she? Why can't she fly yet?"

I looked at the bird that was still strutting around the house a week later, leaving droppings all over, and I really wished that she'd take off already so I could regain control of my kingdom. Unfortunately for me — and for her too, if I were only selfless enough to admit it — she was showing no signs of being ready to fly.

"Her wing hasn't healed yet; look how it's still drooping lower than the other one." I knelt down beside my daughter. "We have to be patient, you know. These things take time. Come," I said, standing up.

She looked at me questioningly.

"Go catch her and we'll take her to the vet."

Ayelet whooped and ran excitedly to collect her bird while I grabbed the car keys from the microwave shelf. Suddenly, from the corner of my eye, I spied Yanki, who'd been quietly watching the scene from the kitchen.

"Yanki, you want to come?" I tossed the keys to him — he liked to open the car doors.

"WOW," SAID YANKI in amazement. "It's like a real doctor's office here."

We looked around the clinic, taking everything in — the medical equipment interspersed with birdcages and animal pens. Avi, the friendly young veterinarian, dressed in green hospital scrubs, stood behind a stainless-steel table that could have come straight from an operating theater.

Moshe, Ayelet and Yanki edged closer. We'd decided to make a family outing of our first visit to a veterinary clinic, and I must admit that I, too, was impressed. The X-rays hanging from the illuminated screen on the wall made it seem as if we were visiting our pediatrician.

"Bring her over here," Avi beckoned. Ayelet placed the small crate on the steel table, and the vet lifted the bird out confidently to examine its wings. It was strange, but the pigeon no longer seemed so unattractive in this man's caring hands; in fact, she suddenly looked quite sweet.

"What's this, Mom?" asked Yanki, fingering some plastic medicine containers.

"I don't know, but please don't touch," I quickly replied.

"If you'd like," Avi said to Yanki pleasantly, "I'll show you around after we've finished."

Yonah's wing was neatly splinted and thick animal tape was wrapped around and under her belly, making her look like a war veteran. Yanki's eyes were shining. I hadn't seen them glow like that in the longest time. He'd helped Avi administer medicine to a sick cat, clean a Labrador's ear wound, vaccinate a puppy, and when Avi took him on a tour of the clinic, he looked like he was ready to move in. The other two kids, however, were more than ready to move out by then.

"Come on," said Ayelet impatiently. "Let's go home already."

"Can I stay a bit longer?" Yanki turned to me earnestly.

Ayelet was heading for the door. "Come on," she said again. She wrinkled her nose and sniffed. "It smells in here." Aha! She was still a dainty little girl after all.

"Don't worry," Avi said, winking at Yanki. "You can come back tomorrow."

YANKI FOUND A second home at the veterinary clinic, which was just fine with me because the school wouldn't take him back unless he took his medicine. There wasn't long to go before summer vacation anyway, and he wasn't allowed to attend summer camp, so I was deeply grateful to Avi for his unending patience with my son. Yanki was radiant, the shine in his eyes brighter than ever, and he was much calmer. He still wouldn't hear about taking the Ritalin, though.

"It's nothing to be ashamed of," my husband and I repeatedly reassured him. "Everyone has something they need help with; even those animals you love take medicine."

Yanki was adamant. "I told you already, I don't want to be scrawny like Shlomo. When he takes Ritalin, he doesn't eat anything. And anyway, I don't need help… there's nothing wrong with me."

I WAS DROPPING Yanki off at Avi's animal hospital every day while I tried to find another school for him. Meanwhile, our pigeon was sitting under our sink waiting for its splinted wing to mend. Surprisingly, Ayelet, our young Florence Nightingale, had lost interest in her smelly bird and happily handed her over to the tender loving care of Yanki, our amateur vet, who no longer seemed bothered by the odor. He was, however, impatient.

"Mom, when can we take the bandage off? She's had it on for ages."

"Not yet, sweetheart," I warned him. "It's too soon. Avi said three to four weeks, and it's only been two. We need to wait a little longer."

"Oof," Yanki said, scooping up the bird and holding her tenderly in his hands. We'd become quite attached to this little creature, especially since Yanki had taken over cleaning up its messes. "Maybe I could just take off the bandage and let her walk around the house?"

"I don't recommend it," I said, shaking my head in disagreement. "That could cause more damage. Yonah needs her splint now. It's not the right time to take it off."

I DIDN'T NOTICE right away. I was weighed down by my heavy shopping bags, which I dropped with a thump onto the kitchen floor, and sat down at the table to catch my breath. There was a welcome pitcher of orange juice on the table and I gulped down a cup of it gratefully. The house was quiet... too quiet. Where was everybody? "Yanki, Ayelet, Moshe... kids, where are you?" I called out.

Silence answered me.

It was strange. I'd only run down to the local supermarket and I'd left them all busy with various activities. Ayelet had been doing homework with a friend, Moshe was building an army base with his new toy soldiers, and Yanki was cleaning Yonah's crate. I'd asked a neighbor to be on call in case of crisis. Uh-oh... where was Yonah? Her box was empty and she was nowhere in sight. Where had the bird gone? She couldn't have climbed out of the crate by herself with her taped wing. Oh, no... Yanki couldn't have... could he?

I flew out the door, rushed down the steps and out onto the street calling Yanki's name. Then I saw them: Yanki in the middle, Ayelet and Moshe like soldiers on guard at his side. They walked down the street toward me, and as they approached, I felt his tears before I saw them, streaming down his cheeks. Yanki cradled something in his arms, and I wasn't sure which one was more broken, Yanki or Yonah.

They buried her in the back garden. It was a grand funeral for a pigeon and fitting for a heartbroken ten-year-old boy and his siblings. I watched them work in silence while they dug a far-too-big hole, gently placed her inside and covered her with soil. Yanki had a tin full of small stones that he'd painstakingly painted in beautiful, bright colors.

"I'm going to put them in a circle around her," he announced, "so we'll always know where she is."

What was there to say? His pain, his guilt, was deeper than the hole he'd dug. Ayelet and Moshe went back indoors while Yanki sat cross-legged on the ground and began placing the stones.

"They blame me, don't they?" he stated matter-of-factly, without looking up.

I paused a moment. "What about you? Do you blame yourself?"

"I just wanted to see, that's all," Yanki murmured, so quietly I could barely hear him. "I so much wanted her to fly."

"Like you do, right?" I sat down on the floor beside him and reached for a handful of pebbles. "You want to fly too, don't you?"

He didn't answer, not with words, anyway. The tears ran down his cheeks like rain down a windowpane.

"You know," I said, leaning forward to place some pebbles, "we can't always do things on our own, especially if we're not ready. Sometimes we need restraints before we can fly. For Yonah, that was her splint; for people, it can be other things that set them free."

"I couldn't wait," he said, crying harder. "I let her go too soon." Suddenly he looked up, a new awareness flitting across his face. "Do I have a broken wing too, Mommy?"

I thought my heart would snap from the weight of that question. I took a long, deep, prayer-filled breath.

"We all do, honey. Some wings need more repair than others. But everyone needs some kind of splint; if we didn't, we wouldn't need Hashem's help, and He's the strongest splint we have."

It was growing dark. Our little back garden was so quiet that for a moment I forgot where we were. We worked silently together placing the stones, Yanki on one side of the mound, me on the other… soon we would meet in the middle.

"What's my splint, Mommy? Is it the medicine?"

I shivered both from the cool breeze and from the ripples of courage that radiated outward from my proud, spunky little boy. We laid down our last pebbles to complete the circle.

"Could be, Yanki. What do you think?"

Our hands touched on the last stones and he played with my fingers, entwining them with his while he searched inside himself for wisdom. Reluctantly, he nodded. It wasn't easy for him to say it, but I didn't rush him. We had all the time in the world, time to be, time to enjoy the connection, to touch the togetherness. I could hardly hear the words when they came.

"Yeah, Mommy," he whispered softly. "I suppose it is."

Fiction is so often truth. I always remember my editor saying that fiction has to be even more believable than non-fiction. I was reminded of this when I reread "Ready to Fly" recently. The story read to me like a personal essay, as if I was describing an event in my life. I don't think I realized when I wrote it just how much truth I'd infused there, how much of my real life circumstances were woven into this "fiction" story. I don't think I understood that I was writing about my own son!

Those of you who read Binah *will be familiar with my* Viewpoints *column about my son "Ari" who suffers from ADHD. In "Ready to Fly," Yanki is clearly my "Ari," replete with all his idiosyncrasies. We actually did come home one day to find a wounded pigeon on our doorstep, and with his usual enthusiasm, Ari rushed to take care of it. Most of the events in the story have actually happened at some time or other, except for the ending where Yanki took off the bird's splint and tried to get it to fly. However, even though he didn't do this, it is something that Ari could easily have done in a moment of impulsivity. In real life, the pigeon did not die; we gave it to a neighbor who had an animal corner in her yard. Also, Ari did take his Ritalin; baruch Hashem for that a thousand times over.*

As with many of my stories, I began with true-to-life events and let them take me to places I hadn't necessarily planned to go to. This happens to me a lot when I write fiction. I love that journey. It's at those times that I wait to see where I'll end up and marvel over the creative process along the way. There's a certain "letting go," just flowing with it. For example, when I first put in the part about the splint on the pigeon's wing I had no idea at that moment that I would develop it into a concept of "splints" for life like Ritalin and even Hashem. That wasn't part of the plan.

For this reason, it is not easy for me to write up story summaries beforehand because truthfully, many times I have no idea where the story will go!

Forever Her Child

TALI HUMMED QUIETLY to herself as she crossed the busy street. Life was good… no, it was wonderful; the unusually sunny winter day matched her mood perfectly. Business was going well, the new house was taking shape, the kids were settled, and she… well, *she* was blooming, bathed in the expectant glow of pregnancy. She entered a well-kept, red-brick building and pressed the elevator for the fifth floor. Moments later, she stood before the squeaky-clean glass doors of the doctors' offices and pushed them open with her shoulder while searching for the ringing cell phone inside her bag.

"Oh, hi, Shimon," she answered breathlessly. "Yes, I'm fine, don't worry. Yes, I know you have a meeting. This is just a regular ultrasound; it's no big deal."

She snapped the phone closed, checked in with the receptionist, and settled back in her seat to wait for her appointment. While leafing through the magazines on the table, she was so content that she felt like singing; soaring melodies to *Hakadosh Baruch Hu*, thanking Him for her blessed life. After a few minutes, the technician beckoned her into a darkened room.

"Thanks," said Tali gratefully as she stepped up to the examining table. "This won't take long, will it? I have so much to do."

She lay back on the hard surface and started punching numbers into her cell phone.

"Could you shut that off, please?" said the technician. "It damages the equipment and there's very little reception in here anyway."

"Oh yes, sure." Tali shut the phone off and closed her eyes; she may as well rest a little. The technician was in another world over in her dark corner, her eyes glued to the screen, squinting as she brought the picture into focus. Tali felt lighter and lighter as she drifted off to sleep. Goodness, I really must be tired, she thought… unless the test was taking longer than usual.

"I'm just going to call the doctor," Tali heard a voice through her haziness.

"Fine," she muttered sleepily. "*What?*" Something jarred her awake. "Wait… hold on, why do you need the doctor?"

But the words stuck inside her throat as two strangers in white coats peered at the screen, muttering to each other in low tones, and fear rippled through her from head to toe. Finally, as if she was inside the other end of a long tunnel, they looked at her.

"Mrs. Slater," the doctor said gently, his eyes clouded with concern, "I think we have a problem."

"WHAT KIND OF a problem?" Shimon exclaimed. "We don't *have* problems!"

Tali laughed sardonically. "Well, we do now."

She understood what her husband meant. They had indeed been blessed with uncomplicated lives; the predictable strolls down straight paths of school, seminary/yeshivah and *shidduchim*. Shimon had been the only boy she'd met at the tender age of eighteen and their first child had arrived a year later. Shimon had joined his father's successful business and they were presently renovating a new house. Of course there'd been the normal hiccups, but nothing they couldn't control. Yes, life had mostly gone according to plan... until now.

"So tell me what the doctor said," Shimon prodded gently.

Tali kept her eyes down, unable to face him, and began to speak in a low voice. "They..." she paused to take a deep breath. "They think... that the baby has Down Syndrome."

Shimon's mouth flopped open.

"He has all the signs," Tali continued, her voice wobbly, "but I still need to take some more tests."

"So maybe it's not?" Shimon recovered quickly.

"Right, maybe it's not, but most likely it is. It looks as if there are some other serious medical conditions too... his heart and... and other deformities."

At that moment, had Shimon been thrown a lifeboat, he would have jumped in and paddled frantically for safe ground.

"Shimon," Tali's voice sounded like the waves that threatened to engulf him, "however will we manage with a child... like that? What will we do?

THEY WENT TO their Rav who told them which of the tests they should take and blessed them with *hatzlachah* and good health.

"We haven't spent this much time together in ages," Shimon joked feebly while they waited for the fetal echocardiogram. Tali glanced at him sideways, then returned to staring at the white-washed wall across the corridor.

"How long is this supposed to take?" Shimon attempted again. "Do you think we'll be finished in time for me to hear the six o'clock news?" He laughed lamely at his own joke.

"I don't think I can handle this." Tali's face was as blank as the wall in front of her.

"Sorry?"

"Having a child like... *this*; I can't do it."

Shimon stared at his wife. "Well, of course it won't be easy and we'll have to adjust to a new situation, but we'll cope. Hashem will help us. He wouldn't have sent us this test otherwise. And anyway, I heard that children who have Down Syndrome are very warm and loving."

"It's not only Down Syndrome."

"We don't know that yet."

"I do."

Shimon looked at the ground, hoping to find answers to the questions rolling around in his head.

"I said that I can't do it," Tali said again.

Shimon fumbled for words but the ones he found didn't fit into his wife's last sentence. "Like I said, I know it's hard but you *can* do it… what's the alternative?"

For the first time since they'd been sitting there, Tali turned to look at him, but her eyes and words were as cold as the sterile walls. "The alternative is… that we give the baby up for adoption."

EVERYWHERE TALI WENT, she saw them. Suddenly there were so many of "those" children; jumping rope on street corners, folding napkins at a shul *kiddush*, stocking shelves in the local supermarket. There were other children too, with different handicaps; the ones with cerebral palsy, the neighbor across the road whose child was autistic. Funny that she'd never noticed before how many people had less than perfect children. But she didn't want to see them, only to slip back into her previously blissful, ignorant state and pretend that everything was normal.

Everywhere Shimon went, he saw them. Suddenly there were so many of "those" children. One of his business associates had a "special" child… how come he hadn't known about it until now? And Cousin Yaakov's little Chaim, who had been born prematurely and couldn't do much of anything unaided, but was content and well taken care of. How come he hadn't noticed the difficulties that people were struggling with? But he wanted to see; to know how it would be, because he could no longer go back to a blissful state of ignorance and pretend that everything was normal.

"COME IN AND sit down," said Dr. Sanders, holding the door open. Shimon and Tali nervously took seats in front of the shiny, mahogany desk.

"I feel as if I'm back at school," Tali whispered to her husband. "I wonder what I've done wrong."

"Nothing," Shimon whispered back firmly. "This has absolutely nothing to do with you."

Tali shot him a grateful glance. Not that his words really helped. His strong sense of *emunah* and *bitachon* only made her feel more guilty; guilty for being confused, even guilty for feeling. Dr. Sanders had laid out the file of their baby's pictures on his desk and for a moment, Tali stifled a laugh. *The most photographed unborn baby around,* she thought ironically. If only the baby knew what a celebrity he or she was. Dr. Sanders was speaking… not to her, of course, because she wasn't listening, but to her dear, devoted husband who was leaning forward, elbows on the table, peering at the pictures in an effort to understand them. Shimon turned towards Tali, pain and confusion drawing lines across his face.

"Tali," he began gently, "do you understand what Dr. Sanders is saying?"

"I guess," his wife shrugged. "But it doesn't matter anyway."

Shimon gaped at her. "Meaning what?"

"None of this is going to happen."

While Shimon continued staring, speechless, Dr. Sanders gently interrupted.

"Mrs. Slater, your baby has all the signs of Down Syndrome, and in addition, we found a serious heart defect on the echocardiogram, as well as a cleft lip on the other ultrasound. The baby will need surgery to correct both things."

"When do you think that would be?" Shimon was alert again.

"Well," Dr. Sanders paused, "it's not so simple because of the heart defect. Correcting that will be the first priority and until we know how serious it is, it's not possible to plan anything else."

"What if I decide not to keep it?" a toneless voice interrupted.

Dr. Sanders and Shimon turned together to look at Tali. "Sorry?"

"What if I want to give it up for adoption?"

Dr. Sanders glanced at Shimon and cleared his throat. "It's always an option, of course, although the baby might not be a good candidate because of all the other medical conditions."

"So what happens in that case?"

Dr. Sanders spoke slowly and carefully. "There's a special room in the nursery for the babies with no parents, and when they're well enough to be discharged they're either fostered or sent to an institution."

"SO YOU REALLY *are* serious about this?" Shimon gripped the steering wheel until his knuckles went white.

Tali watched the rain lashing at the car window and shuddered. She wrapped her arms around herself as if *she* was the baby who needed protecting.

"Tali," Shimon glanced sharply at his wife. "I'm talking to you."

"I… I can't."

"Can't what?"

"Talk."

"Well, you have to."

Tali felt steam mounting from the heat inside the car as the rain continued beating against the glass.

"You can't make a decision like that without including me."

"It's my child," she said flatly.

"And it's also mine," Shimon countered. He leaned forward, trying to see through the windshield wipers, his fury flying fast, back and forth with them.

"What are you doing?" Tali noticed his sudden turn.

"Pulling off to the side; it's insane to drive in this weather. I think we should wait for the storm to pass."

"It's not going to," Tali muttered.

"What?"

"Our storm — not that one," she nodded at the blustery gale outside. "Our hurricane is going to last a lot longer."

Shimon pulled up the handbrake sharply, switched off the engine, and rested his head on the steering wheel. "But the question, of course," he said to no one in particular, "is will we survive it?"

THERE WAS A space inside her that was frozen, like the giant stainless steel freezers in the belly of a hospital basement. On the outside, like smooth, shiny refrigerator doors, she hung up her children's pictures, reminder notes and wedding invitations with brightly colored magnets, but the inside was empty, storing only the basic items. She tried not to open the doors too often and venture out, preferring to stay inside the bitter chill of frosty mazes and corridors of ice.

"IT'S PERFECTLY NORMAL that she's reacting this way," said Rabbi Mendlebaum, an understanding expression on his aging face. Shimon raised his eyebrows.

"It's your wife's way of coping," Rabbi Mendlebaum continued, swiveling slightly in his leather office chair. ""She's disconnecting herself from the pain because it's too hard to feel it."

"So what am I supposed to do?" Shimon asked miserably from

the other side of the polished table, its surface lacquered and shiny while his own life was lusterless and splintered.

"Give her time," said Rabbi Mendlebaum kindly. "Don't fight with her. Try to understand and empathize. I'm sure that once she sees her baby and holds it in her arms, she'll come around."

"I hope you're right," Shimon said with a sigh. "Right now I can't imagine her ever thawing out."

"TALI!" A FAMILIAR, cheerful voice bubbled down the line. "Where did you disappear to? I've been trying to reach you for weeks."

"Oh, hi, Leba." Tali's heart plummeted at the sound of her sister's voice. "I'm really sorry; just been very busy, as usual."

Leba sighed. "How I wish that we lived closer; we never seem to see each other anymore. But you will come out for my birth, right?"

Tali's stomach tightened. She'd been dreading this conversation. Normally, she'd have leapt into the car and rushed upstate at the first sound of the phone ringing. She would have charged into her sister's hospital room, arms laden with flowers and packages of baby clothes, fresh orange juice and granola bars. How could she possibly miss the birth of Leba's first baby after so many years without children? But of course she couldn't go; not in her condition, the doctors would never allow her to be far away from the hospital and anyway, she wasn't in the mood.

"Um, you know that I'd love to be there with you…"

"Don't tell me you're not coming?" Her sister's disappointed voice sounded like one of her children's.

"I… I really want to… honestly, I do. I'm just not sure I can manage it."

For a moment there was silence. "Tali, is everything okay?" Leba asked at last. "You've been awfully distant lately; everyone has noticed it."

Tali swallowed back tears. Her sister's selfless concern had made a chip in the ice. "Well… you see… I'm sort of expecting myself…"

"Oh, that's wonderful," Leba squealed. "Why didn't you tell me?"

"I've not been feeling too well so I didn't want to bother anyone."

"Sorry to hear that, but it is great news. Does Mom know?"

"Actually, I haven't told her either." Tali squirmed in her chair.

"Ah, I understand. It must still be early then, but thank you so much for sharing it with *me*."

"Well, that's just it," said Tali hesitantly. "It's not so early. Iy"H, I'll be having a baby shortly after you have yours!"

SHE WAS PACKING a suitcase for the hospital when the call came. Better to be prepared, her doctors had advised; in her situation anything was possible. At Shimon's insistence, she was getting ready, gathering her belongings with slow, mechanical movements. She stared at the closed drawers, half expecting them to open by themselves and all the necessary items to jump into the bag. Where were the baby clothes? What would she bring him home in? She shook her head quickly as if rousing herself from a bad dream; no, she wouldn't need those. Really, there was nothing much to take, she thought to herself while zipping up the case, when Shimon suddenly appeared at the doorway, clutching the phone and looking as white as a freshly laundered tablecloth.

"It's your mother," he said, his eyes wide and dilated in distress. "Leba lost the baby!"

SHE WAS SUPPOSED to cry, of course. But then again, there were lots of things she was supposed to do these days, but didn't. She was supposed to weep and wail for her beloved sister who, after ten hope-filled years, was yet to have a child. But her eyes remained dry and dusty, not even a tease of a tear trickling out. She felt like a dried up well, deep and dark in the ground, dead leaves, tree branches and discarded wrappers covering the opening. Sometimes, in curiosity, people peered down the shaft, blocking any possible sunlight, intrigued by the never ending blackness, searching for something, anything, even a sliver of light, but finding nothing.

When her time came, she carried her cumbersome self to the hospital and listened in silence when the nurse told her that she'd had a boy… a tiny, sick, baby boy who'd arrived early and was whisked away in an incubator to the neonatal intensive care unit. In a single moment, he had disappeared. Actually, he had never been there.

"I WENT TO visit the baby today," Shimon said, scrutinizing Tali's face carefully.

"Oh, that's nice."

"Still no talk of a *bris* yet," Shimon continued, "not while he's on the respirator; it looks like it will be quite a while."

"I see." Tali plunged her arms into the warm, soapy water she'd prepared for three-year-old Motti's bath.

"The doctors say that he's not strong enough for the heart surgery yet." Shimon watched as Tali tracked bubbles with her fingers. "He's really cute though, despite…" He stopped as a rush of resentment hit him. He stared at his wife. What was *wrong* with her? How could her heart remain frozen when her precious baby was fighting for his life inside his sterile home? He watched as she ran the bath water and couldn't understand how she could fill up the tub for one child, yet almost pull the plug on another. He wanted to shake her back to life, force her to feel, to cry out in pain, but he didn't, because the words of his Rav echoed in his head… be patient, don't fight with her.

Suddenly, the image of his baby struggling to breathe all alone inside his incubator swam before his eyes, and he could almost see the cold edges of the same box, surrounding his wife. Mother and baby were not so far apart after all.

TALI STRETCHED HERSELF awake like a sleepy cat. It was so unlike her to take a nap in the afternoon and she found it irritating. She slipped her feet into her slippers and was surprised to see they were still swollen. Yes, well, she had just had a baby, hadn't she? Sometimes she wasn't sure about that. All she knew was there was an emptiness inside her and in the crib where her sweet smelling newborn should have been lying. Occasionally, she wondered how her son looked; Shimon had said he was similar to Motti. At those moments she felt like jumping in a taxi and racing off to the hospital to visit him, to sit beside his bed and gently stroke his face or cradle him in her arms. But she never went. Each time she had the urge, she stopped herself, holding back from doing anything that would allow him to wriggle into her heart. No, she couldn't let that happen.

As Tali shuffled down the corridor, she heard the sound of her husband's voice through the glass partitioned door to the living room. There was something in his tone that made her pause.

"Dovid, I'm very grateful to you for offering this. I'll have to talk to Tali, of course, and see what she says."

Tali's radar went off. Who was Shimon talking to?

"It might be just the solution for now," he was saying. "Of course, I'm hoping that Tali will come around eventually, but in the meantime, if you and Leba are willing to take him…"

Tali didn't hear the rest of the conversation because she doubled up from the blow she'd just been dealt, and as she sank to the floor, she screamed.

The door flew open and Shimon came dashing out. "What happened? I'll call you back," he rasped into the phone as soon as he saw his wife.

"Nooo!" Tali cried. "I won't let you." She clutched her stomach as if she was feeling the kicking inside of her.

Shimon stared in shock, looking as if he, too, had been punched.

He lifted his arms in a helpless gesture. "Come... get up. W...why don't we go into the living room and talk about it?" he suggested.

Tali managed to drag herself to the couch and sat, clutching a cushion tightly.

"I... I'm sorry that you heard about it like this... I was going to talk to you..." Shimon began.

"He's *my* child, not Leba's! What makes you all think you can take him from me so easily?" Tali attacked angrily.

Shimon didn't know what to do. His brother-in-law's offer to take the baby had seemed like a good temporary solution after the hospital called to say he was being discharged.

."I... I'm sorry, but I don't understand," Shimon said finally, in a defeated tone. "Leba doesn't have any children yet and she'd love to look after the baby for us. It's very generous on her part. Why is it so hard? It's not as if you..."

"Love him, right!" Tali shouted the words so loudly that if the children had been home from school, they'd have come running straight away to see what was shaking their house. "That's what you think, isn't it... you, everyone... that I don't love my baby?" She started to shake, trembling violently like a small child with febrile convulsions.

Shimon watched the pain slash Tali's stone face, its brute force causing it to crack, and he felt it too, inside every living cell of himself. "It didn't seem as if you cared. You didn't talk to me... I had to guess." He trailed off miserably, his words suddenly swept away by the sound of racking sobs that caught him by surprise because it had been so long.

"Of *course* I care," Tali gulped between spasms. "Can you possibly ever know what it means to love your child so desperately that it turns you to stone? Can you understand how it feels to shatter into a million shards of glass every time you think of him, and spend every day stepping on the sharp splinters with bare feet?"

"No," Shimon bowed his head. "I can't."

Tali curled her legs underneath her on the couch and rested her head in her hands as her sobs slowly subsided. "Maybe," she murmured tearfully, "I didn't rise to the test like you did; maybe I wasn't strong enough, didn't have enough *emunah* and *bitachon*; I always had things easy, remember?"

Shimon nodded.

"I envy you," Tali said simply, and Shimon shook his head in an unspoken question. "Your acceptance and faith; I'm just trying to hold on, to do what I can to survive." She looked up at him with soft, sad eyes. "Maybe I haven't handled this in the best way, but don't ever think that I don't love our child!"

TALI WATCHED FROM the upstairs bedroom window. From the inside, looking out, it was as if everything happening on the street below was in slow motion. Dovid was helping Leba and the delicate bundle in her arms carefully into the car, and her father was lifting their luggage into the trunk.

The *bris* had been an emotional affair for all of them. Dovid and Leba had been *kvatter*, of course, and when the name, Natanel, was given, there was hardly a dry eye in the shul. Tali had held him afterwards, rocked him gently back and forth in soothing motions and let him suck on her wine-soaked finger. It had almost felt... normal. Normal... that was funny... whatever was that? Their "normal" was no longer the same, so what was it now? she wondered. Natanel had squirmed in her arms, opened his squinty eyes and looked at her as if challenging her with this question, and when she'd handed him over to Leba, her heart had hurt so much that she'd wished she could take it out and hold it too.

Down below, they were almost ready to leave. Tali pressed her face closer to the glass and her tears ran down the pane like streaks of rain.

"Not easy, is it?" Shimon appeared beside her at the window and Tali nodded. "But we can go to see him whenever we want, until… until you're ready."

Tali nodded again. "I'd like that."

"I guess this is part of the process and you've taken the first steps," said Shimon reflectively.

"Yes," Tali whispered, "and G-d willing, I'll get there, wherever that is."

Downstairs, the car was moving off, trickling down the street. Tali raised her hand slowly… and waved.

In one of the neonatal units I worked in, there was a special room off to the side for babies with various medical conditions such as Down Syndrome, Trisomy 13 or hydrocephalus. They were in this room because they no longer needed intensive care but still required more care than babies in the regular nursery, and they had nowhere to go. Their parents, for whatever reason, had left them in the hospital. I wish I could say that this doesn't happen within frum circles, but unfortunately it does and it saddens me to no end.

Now, please don't misunderstand… I'm not judging people in any way. One can never know people's circumstances and we should never be tested like this. But several times a week, when I passed that room on my way to the intensive care unit where I worked, I thought about those babies, often wondering where they'd end up if they survived. Throughout the many years in my profession I met families whose lives had been turned upside down through the birth of a severely premature baby or a child with multiple handicaps. Some were more equipped to deal with it than others. Yet whenever I visited that baby room and held a baby in my arms, I couldn't help thinking about the many child- less couples and how they would have probably run to take one of those babies home. Slowly but surely, a story formed in my head.

"Forever Her Child" was a painful story to write, but, I feel, an important one. I particularly wanted to normalize those feelings of rejection that a mother can have for her child, feelings that we often don't understand and feel guilty about. And I especially wanted to show that a mother's (sometimes it's the father's) rejection is frequently coming from a place of pain, a fear of bonding with a child who may not survive. If this story can in any way help readers gain a better understanding of this, then it was successful.

Borders

THE FLASHING BRIGHT lights exploded in her face like firecrackers. She squeezed her eyes tightly shut, letting the sea of frantic voices wash over her while she struggled to breathe. They were carrying her now — no, running, pulling her like the sled rides she'd had with her brother when he'd raced her down the snow-covered hill behind their house. Why so fast? What was the hurry? She felt as if she were going to fall off the sides. Slow down. Please, she prayed, don't let me fall. Lowering her hands sluggishly to the sides of the gurney, she tried to grasp the metal rails but her fingers slid off them like melting butter.

Danny, where was Danny? She couldn't pick out his voice from among all the others. *I want my husband*, she tried to mouth, but the words wouldn't come. They were moving her, hoisting her off the stretcher like a slab of meat, onto another, softer mattress. She allowed herself to sink into it, to let the frenzied activity around her wear itself out. Tired… she was so tired. Her eyelids were closing.

They left her then, and stuck a big, bold notice on her door: "Isolation." And like the flick of a light switch, everything went black.

WHEN SHE AWOKE, it was still dark. Her head hurt; oh, how it hurt, like hammers pounding relentlessly on her skull.

Where was she? She lay alone in the blackness. Hugging her knees to her chest, she curled herself tightly into a ball. Voices… she could hear voices… somewhere…

Straining to see through swollen eyes, she tried to find the owners of the words, but there was nothing, just darkness. Was she dreaming? No, there were people there, rumbling into her room through a long, yawning tunnel.

"How long was she abroad?"

"Two weeks."

Danny! That was Danny speaking… she was sure!

"And where did she stay?"

"With her sister and brother-in-law. There was a family event."

"I see. Anyone else in the family sick?"

"No, not that we know of." Danny sounded strained, weary, as if he'd been stretched across an ocean.

"Did she eat at any restaurants?"

"No, we're religious Jews, we keep kosher."

"Oh? Which means what?"

"Well, we usually don't eat any food outside the house that we haven't prepared ourselves, and if we do, then only at places that observe our dietary laws."

"Okay. So when did your wife become ill?"

"On Sunday. It was about three days after she returned."

"Fever?"

"Yes, very high."

"Coughing, chills, shortness of breath?"

She could hear Danny's voice shaking now, each word wobbling unsteadily.

"Yes, she's been hallucinating — not really with us, if you know what I mean."

"Yes," the doctor replied gravely, "I certainly do."

She was drifting off again, the sounds swirling around her like soft, woolly clouds. Sinking lower and lower, she let them cushion her in their safe embrace. It was simply too hard to stay awake.

THE NEXT TIME she awoke it was raining, steady streams of water cascading down outside the window of her room. Tracing her face with her fingers, she was surprised to find that the wetness was her own tears; they were deep enough to drown in.

"DASSI, IT'S ME, are you awake? Can you hear me?"

His voice floated over her like a soft sprinkling of confetti and she searched for his face.

"Yes, I'm awake. Where are you?"

"Look to the right, Dassi, toward the window in the door. I'm over here, talking to you through the intercom."

Dassi turned her head with difficulty toward the glass, stretching the tubes that led from her nose to the oxygen supply. "Why don't you come in?" she asked, puzzled.

A look of sadness, frustration even, passed over Danny's face. "I can't. You're in isolation. You've been very sick."

She lifted her head slightly to see the IV tubes snaking from a vein in her arm, the quiet bubbling of the oxygen humidifier by her bed, the steady rhythm of the heart monitor bleeping above her.

"You caught that virus, the one everyone's talking about. You went to your sister's wedding, and when you got back you came down with it."

"How long," she wanted to know, still battling for air with each breath, "have I been here?"

"You've been here ten days already," Danny replied, "unconscious mostly. As I said, you've been very sick."

"Danny," she whispered, her voice straining with the effort, "I want to rinse my hands… wash *negel vasser*. Can you do that for me?"

"I'm sorry, Dassi." Danny shook his head sadly, small tears

gathering in the corners of his eyes. He looked at her through the great divide that separated them. "I'm not allowed to."

THE NEXT TIME he came, Dassi was sitting up in bed, the oxygen gone, the tubes tossed inside a special sealed plastic bag for incineration. Still nobody touched her, not directly anyway. Medical personnel, when they came, wore paper masks over their faces, their beady eyes peering out alertly above them. The powder from their latex gloves made her itch whenever they performed a procedure, like changing her IV line or giving her an injection of some thick, foul-smelling medicine.

They worked quickly and quietly… too quietly, as if merely talking with her would infect them. When they left, tasks completed, she'd watch them through the window in the door, feeling like a lone fish swimming inside an aquarium. Just how, she pondered, does a fish leave its watery existence in the tank and stay alive? It wouldn't survive outside and right now, neither would she.

"SURPRISE!"

Danny appeared in the doorway, posing in hospital greens as though it were Purim. The long hospital gown reached down to his ankles and a blue paper mask covered the lower half of his face. His hands were encased in beige rubber gloves. She looked up at him and laughed.

"Very becoming," she murmured. "What's the occasion?"

Danny sat down on the white plastic chair beside her and played absently with the IV tubes dangling from the pole.

"I see you've got your sense of humor back," he grinned.

Dassi nodded at her husband, encased almost from head to toe like an astronaut. "You've changed." She smiled, and started to cry.

A few days later he was allowed to bring the children. All four of them crept cautiously into the room, their small faces painted in bewilderment. They approached her awkwardly, the long gowns seeming to pull them down like quicksand, and the masks over their noses obviously making them uncomfortable. She wanted to leap up, gather them close to her and hold on to them forever. But she couldn't.

"How much longer?" she begged her husband, tears running down her cheeks.

"Soon, very soon," he said soothingly. "They just want to be sure you're not still contagious. Just be patient a little longer."

That night Danny returned to comfort her and they sat together in the dimly lit room, listening to the sounds of the bustling ward outside.

"You know," said Danny, "they're closing the international borders now. The virus is spreading so fast, they can't contain it."

"What does that mean?" Dassi asked. "No more traveling, everyone staying at home?"

"Well," said Danny pensively, "that's how it seems. People can't leave their countries meanwhile. Airports are empty. Just think about the ramifications, the disruptions — everyone trapped behind borders. Can you imagine?"

"Yes," Dassi muttered, "I can, because my borders closed a few weeks ago."

After Danny left, Dassi lay awake long into the night, reflecting on his words, thinking about borders and where exactly they opened or closed. She'd had hers too, of course, before she had been abruptly cut off from the outside world, but had they been too all-inclusive? Had she, a successful businesswoman, cut too many holes in her fences, allowing unnecessary things to sneak in and distract her? Now, after serious illness and enforced confinement, she found herself examining those perimeters. Perhaps, with her fresh, uncluttered perspective, it was time to redefine them.

AT LAST! SHE was out of danger and no longer posed a threat to others. Initially visitors poured in, unimpeded, unlimited,

but she quickly realized that not everyone needed to pass her reno-
vated gates and she closed them when necessary. For her family
they were always open, and when her children came to visit, she
hugged them hard, ran her fingers through their hair and stroked
their faces, familiarizing herself again with each one's features, like
a sculptress with her clay. Human touch was welcome after all this
time in isolation; she was thirsty for it, desperate to rehydrate. She
reveled in the heat of their breath on her face, the faint scraping
of their nails on her skin, a small knee or elbow poking her side.
They snuggled up close to her on the hospital bed, like newborn
puppies. This, she smiled to herself, felt like home.

"So that's it!" announced Danny, tossing aside the local Jewish
newspaper he'd been reading. "Total border shutdown! They say
it's the only way to control this virus."

Dassi gazed at him and their children, and a warm, contented
feeling flowed through her like a life-giving infusion. Let them
seal up their borders because hers had reopened, but within newly
adjusted boundaries. She would take control of her border cross-
ings from now on, let in what truly mattered and keep the rest out.

A quiet, peaceful sigh escaped from deep within her and
wrapped itself around her precious family in a comforting embrace.
They could close the whole world down for all she cared, because
right now, at this moment, she had all she'd ever wanted, inside her
gates.

This story seems like it is just another medical story, but it really isn't. It was actually inspired by the shiurim I attended every Shabbos afternoon about the geulah and the End of Days. The lecturer, Rabbi Pinchas Winston, taught a small group of ladies on this subject, based on teachings from the Arizal and the Zohar. During one of his inspirational classes, Rabbi Winston spoke about the importance of coming to live in Eretz Yisrael as soon as possible, before it became too difficult. He gave the example of Yaakov hurrying to leave Lavan's house after he heard Lavan's sons talking about him. Yaakov recognized the beginnings of anti- Semitism in Lavan's sons and therefore knew he had to leave immediately and return to Eretz Yisrael.

In class, the Rav made the comparison to the resurgence of anti-Semitism in chutz laAretz today, warning that these are signs for the Yidden to come home and not wait too long because it might not be possible to leave. While he spoke, I had an image of all the international borders closing and not letting people in or out, thus leaving each country isolated. And then I began thinking how it would feel if every person was forced into a form of isolation or definitive space. In addition, the first emergence of the SARS virus was making news headlines around this time. Combine that with my imaginary closure of borders and I had my story! And what started out as an adventure tale then morphed into something more thought-provoking about the definitions of our own borders and what we consider important enough to allow in or keep out.

Growing Up Together

IT WAS LIKE a dream. She'd imagined this day, although never really believed it would arrive. As the summer sun set behind the Jerusalem hills, casting a warm glow over the *chuppah*, Tova felt her heart swell with happiness. Her Yitzi was getting married! Twenty years ago, when she and Yehuda were a young couple, new immigrants, Hebrew illiterates, struggling to acclimatize to life in Eretz Yisrael without family, she could not have dreamed it was happening. Because they'd struggled with something else as well, something that had shaken her to the core, and had slowly and stealthily stolen all her self-confidence. As she watched Yitzi and his radiant *kallah* leave the *chuppah*, basking in the joyous *mazel tov* blessings, her mind traveled backward…

TWENTY YEARS EARLIER:
   "Well," said Miri, the nurse at the local mother-and-baby clinic, "it looks like he's gone down again!"
   Tova tried not to look at the numbers on the scale as the nurse handed her wriggling six-week-old baby back to her. Could it be her imagination, or was there a hint of disapproval in the professional woman's eyes?
   "Six weeks old," Miri muttered as she strode down the corridor, "and he hasn't gained a gram."

A lady in the waiting room, the one with the gurgling, rosy-cheeked infant bouncing on her lap, gave Tova a sympathetic glance.

"Hard when they don't gain weight, isn't it?" she empathized. "But don't worry, he'll be big and fat before you know it."

"Do you really think so?" Tova pounced on the optimistic hook she'd been thrown. "It's my first baby, so I don't know what's normal."

"Sure," said the woman, whom Tova was ready to appoint as her expert adviser on the spot, "it happens all the time."

Suddenly the nurse reappeared, deflating whatever optimism Tova had developed.

"Okay," the nurse announced authoritatively, handing Tova the little blue card with all the heights and weights recorded neatly on it. "Come back in a week, but see your doctor first and do these tests."

HE WAS CRYING again. Screaming. Tova felt his screams shooting into her head like sharp arrows. She opened her eyes groggily. What time was it? She groaned. Did it really matter? Time for her had become a continual jumble of crying, screaming and feeding — all the hours of the day seemed rolled into one. She was so terribly tired. Leaning over the bassinet, she picked up her baby and staggered sleepily down the hallway to the living room where she could feed him quietly without waking her husband. She gazed down at her son squirming in her arms. He seemed hungry now, rooting for food with a normal, healthy desire. The thought of feeding him, of pouring nourishment and vitamins into his tiny body, brought a rush of satisfaction that only a mother can truly feel. He was soon lustily gulping down the life force as if he would never stop. Tova leaned back contentedly on the couch, watching the dark night through the window as it rose slowly upward, giving way to the dawn. She allowed herself a sliver of hope. Maybe this time it would go well?

And then he stopped! Just like that! Throwing back his head, he let out a shrill scream that pierced the silent house. How long had he been at it this time… five minutes? How much could he have ingested? As usual, he was inconsolable. He'd stay that way, screaming his high-pitched scream that shattered any illusion of serenity. He'd scream and scream, on and on, while Tova rocked him, soothed him, walked with him, rubbed his tiny tummy until, exhausted, he'd fall asleep.

Her pain was so raw that her tears hurt as they poured down her cheeks. She had so many questions. Was all this screaming normal? Why wasn't he hungrier? What, she asked herself for the hundredth time, was she doing wrong?

"WE NEED TO know how much he's eating."

Tova looked blankly at the young pediatrician sitting opposite her. "Uh, how do we do that?"

"Bottles," he announced, "that's the best way… much more accurate. Let's see if he's actually getting enough to eat or if he's just burning up too many calories. Maybe he's tiring from the effort. I'll need to check his heart."

"It might be his heart," she told her husband worriedly when she got home. This was all a foreign language to her, but at least, she thought quietly to herself, it might not be her fault after all.

"HEART'S FINE," PRONOUNCED Dr. Kaplan, carefully examining the echocardiogram report in front of him. "Come, let's put him on the scale."

A wave of nausea rose up inside her, catching in her throat. Little Yitzi floundered uncomfortably on the cold metal weighing tray. She'd have thought he'd be used to it by now. Tova averted her eyes from the flashing numbers. They reminded her of the red signal flashing on her dashboard, alerting her that the tank was almost out of gas. Actually, that's exactly how she felt, like an empty tank, unable to supply what was needed.

"His weight's gone down," the good doctor announced, tight-lipped and obviously displeased. "I'll give you another week," he said, as if he was doing her a favor. "If there's no change, I'll have to hospitalize him."

EVERYONE, IT SEEMED, had something to say. She was surrounded by concerned experts who all, unlike her, had raised healthy, happy, thriving infants. Suggestions swept in uninvited, well meant, of course, but nonetheless suffocating, pulling her deeper into confusion and self-doubt. Her head was reeling, spinning with images of baby bottles and formulas. Every formula boasted more calories than the others; each feeding bottle was more "state-of-the-art" than the next. Both sets of grandparents worried frantically from afar, their twice-daily phone calls often making her wish that modern methods of communication had never been invented. Why didn't she and Yehuda just come home, their parents pleaded; all this religious business was bad enough without them moving to Eretz Yisrael by themselves! Poor Yehuda was just as frazzled as she. This was new, uncharted territory and they had no idea how to navigate it.

"TOVA," HER BEST friend Mali began. Mali was sitting beside her on the living room couch, holding her own newborn in the crook of her arm. "Tova, are you bonding with your baby?"

Bonding with… of course she was! Well… she supposed so. She kissed him, didn't she? Held him, hugged him, worried about him — wasn't that bonding? But did she love him? Oh, she wasn't sure of anything anymore. She just knew that there was a huge, empty hole inside her that she desperately wanted to be filled with a contented, well-nourished child. Maybe *he* didn't love *her* yet? Was there such a thing? He still hadn't given even a suggestion of a smile. Tova let out a deep weary sigh.

"Yes," she murmured to Mali, "we're getting there."

IN THE HOSPITAL they were installed in a small, one-windowed cubicle where she could sleep on a fold-out bed next to Yitzi's crib. Nurses bustled busily around her. They were quite nice really, some of them even motherly, but she was certain she knew their unspoken thoughts. *Poor thing… a young mother… overwhelmed… not coping.* All she was now, it seemed, was an inexperienced first-time mother who couldn't feed her baby. But she was also other things… a good wife and daughter, a loyal friend and neighbor. She'd illustrated children's books in her past life… and was actually quite good at it. And not too long ago, though now it seemed like a decade, she'd never left the house without a well-styled *sheitel*, light make-up and well-coordinated clothes. Was anyone interested in that?

When had she begun to lose a sense of herself? She'd always been competent… or had she? This plunge into motherhood had pulled the rug of self-confidence from under her feet and she was floundering in the insecurity she had found beneath it.

But now, almost immediately upon their arrival, a super-efficient nurse slipped a feeding tube into Yitzi's little mouth at the speed of lightning.

"We need to bring his weight up quickly," she explained. "He's very weak."

Tova could hardly find Yitzi's face underneath the white, sticky plaster taped on his cheek to keep the thin pipe in place. Then an IV was inserted into his skinny arm, "to keep his electrolytes balanced," she learned. If she was struggling to stay connected to him before, now she really felt as if he didn't belong to her. Just what was this strange new world she found herself in?

They ran test after test after test. Blood went into his tiny veins; blood was taken out. They snapped pictures of almost every part of his body. He was fed with the tube; he was fed without it. More calories were added to the formula; the IV was removed and then put back. And they, the experts, observed her while she fed him.

Over and over again they sat beside her, guiding and instructing her. She felt like a laboratory rat beneath a microscope.

During the day, visitors came. Many offered to take over so she could go home for a few hours of rest, but she always refused. She was NOT leaving her child with anyone else! Of course, Yehuda stayed with her whenever he could take a break from *kollel*, but he too was confused. He heard words like *postpartum depression, over-exhaustion* and *anxiety*. What connection did that have with his wife? What did it all mean?

Life slipped into a series of dark nights. Everything beyond the four clinical walls had ceased to exist. It was during those long, lonesome nights that she cried herself to sleep, pleading and begging Hashem for strength and to clear her bewildered mind.

But there *was* a bright side to this insulated existence, a flicker of light flashing in the darkness. For there in the hospital, she met other mothers who also couldn't feed their babies. Some even had a houseful of healthy children at home and could not be relegated to the realm of the inexperienced like her. She discovered there were many reasons why a child didn't thrive. Some infants possessed their own unique physical blueprints that didn't allow them to grow. For some there was no medical explanation for failing to thrive, and the parents of those children required patience and prayer, and the hope that over time they'd outgrow it. Funny, but the other mothers didn't seem to blame themselves like she did, but then, that was her area of expertise: bowing her head humbly while soaking up guilt as it rained down on her. It was her childhood legacy. Maybe... and the thought flitted through her mind with more frequency now... it was not her fault after all. But if not, then what was wrong with her child?

ONE COOL, COLORLESS morning, the resident doctor breezed into Tova's room.

"Mrs. Berger, you can go home tomorrow," he announced cheerfully. Tova was momentarily stunned into silence.

"There's nothing more we can do for your baby now. We haven't found out why he's failing to thrive and all the tests results were normal." Tova stared at this messenger of so-called good tidings and forced a few words from her lips.

"So how," she asked timidly, "am I supposed to feed him?"

"Oh, you can keep the tube in at home. Try to give him a bottle first and then top up with the tube afterwards."

"But he's not…" In a flash, he was gone.

"… gaining weight," her voice reached out, like an extended arm, to the empty doorway.

So that was that! Dismissed, like a naughty schoolgirl… after three weeks. She had never felt so abandoned.

Once the door stopped swinging and the air settled, Tova gently lifted her sleeping baby out of his crib and laid him on the mattress beside her. With one finger she tracked the translucent blue veins snaking across his pale, bald head, like rivers on a road map. She felt his fragile body, his fleshless fingers weakly clasping hers, watched the feeble kicking of his feet. He couldn't even raise his head, and she was still waiting for that first smile. Suddenly she saw him… really saw *him*, instead of herself, the inadequate mother, failing at her job.

"You," she said to him softly, "are a sick baby. Even *I* can see that."

In a moment of clarity, a newfound confidence surged through her like a huge tidal wave. She picked up her child, strode over to the doctor's room and rapped loudly on the door. The man in white who opened the door loomed over her, but this time Tova stood her ground like a soldier in the front line of battle.

"Something," she declared, nodding towards the sleeping bundle in her arms, "is wrong with my baby. I am not leaving this hospital until you find out what it is!"

And this time, the one who swept away, leaving an aura of determination behind… was she!

TWELVE MONTHS LATER:

Hopefully Yitzi wouldn't need the feeding tube much longer. The rare enzyme he was missing had been flown in from Italy where it was manufactured in its pure form. It still amazed her, each time she crushed it up before his feeds and syringed it down the tube, how one small gray pill could change a life, how some messed up molecules could send a system haywire.

The paralyzing, self-criticizing voice inside had been replaced by an all-encompassing worry and fear for her child that fueled her to search for a diagnosis. Her husband had called, consulted and conferred with as many experienced Rabbis and medical experts as he could. Tova and Yehuda had become relentless in their search for an answer.

When the results finally came, Tova collapsed; every bone in her body felt like it had finally crumbled from the weight it had been bearing. The release, the lifting of that huge boulder from her shoulders, was liberating. She felt it shift, relished the feel of it sliding off her, envisioned it rolling off and away until it was gone. At last, she could let go! She and Yehuda had done whatever they could for their little boy; now it was up to Hashem.

Of course they still had to adjust to Yitzi's unusual condition, deal with the enzymes he'd need forever, cope with the constant follow-ups and occasional hospitalizations. Then there were the sympathetic whispers and people's curious stares at the thin pipe threaded through Yitzi's nose, but that was nothing, a small price to pay for his blossoming health. Actually, they considered themselves lucky because at least now they had a diagnosis. Everything was easier once they knew what they were dealing with. Not everybody was that fortunate.

Whenever she looked at her healthy baby these days, she couldn't take her eyes off him. She filled herself with his very existence; drawing his sweet laughter inside her, infusing it into all her spaces. There were fewer of those spaces now, since Yitzi's perilous predicament had forced her to turn inwards and pull out strengths and confidence she didn't know she had. She'd learned to believe in herself, to not give up but grow up instead. Just this morning in the park, while enjoying the warm, soothing sunshine, she had turned his chubby face toward hers so she could soak up his huge, wide, wonderful smile. Yes, she marveled, he was growing nicely now… and so was she!

This story came about after I was asked to help out a young mother who was struggling following the birth of her first baby. Her son was extremely pale and not thriving on his feeding schedule. This poor girl was riddled with guilt and self-doubt, in addition to being postpartum and exhausted with no family living nearby who could help her out. She was subjected to weekly weighings of her baby, which she dreaded, as well as endless rounds of tests and doctors' visits to check his health. Understandably, this mother was frazzled.

While I was helping her, I was reminded of a friend of mine who had been in a similar situation several years before, and her baby was, in fact, suffering from a serious metabolic disease. The initial guilt and self-doubt had been there as well, followed by a palpable sense of relief at receiving a diagnosis for her child. I combined the two real-life scenarios and got my story.

Interestingly enough, there was a lot of feedback on this piece. I received e-mails and phone calls from women in similar situations with their babies who wanted advice and guidance. I hope that I was able to help them in some way.

EVEN THOUGH I was new and inexperienced, I immediately saw that something was wrong. It was her ever-changing chameleon eyes, which were at times haunted, lifeless or cold, yet on other occasions frenzied and agitated, darting back and forth in preparation for flight. No, it wasn't hard to see it at all; in fact, the non-verbal cry for help shrieked out at me. And if I noticed it, so did everyone else. At least that's what I assumed.

I WAS ENTHUSIASTIC, idealistic and young. That was the part I was mostly reminded of when I began teaching at Proctors, a girls' elementary school in the city. It hadn't been easy to get the job and the school wasn't exactly "my type," but beggars can't be choosers when looking for work these days. Anyway, I was excited, because as a homeroom teacher, I would have my very own class.

"Naomi, do you really have to move out in order to take this job?" my parents pleaded, rather than asked. They weren't thrilled about their twenty-four-year-old single daughter sharing an apartment with friends.

"Well, even if I stay, you won't see me, because it's two hours traveling time each way."

"We know, but..."

"Don't worry," I reassured them. "I'll be home for Shabbosos, and we'll speak every day on the phone."

It wasn't the same, though; I knew that. And of course they were somewhat embarrassed — better I should be moving out to get married than to become a roommate!

"How do you think you'll manage?" my father inquired, practical as usual. "Are you okay with working in a less religious school?"

I raised my eyebrows and grimaced. "They're still *frum* girls, Tatty, just more open and modern than Bais Yaakov, that's all. I won't be the only Bais Yaakov teacher there."

"Well," said my father, stroking his beard thoughtfully, "I've never had a daughter do this before, but seeing as how you are… it should be with *brachah* and *mazel*."

"Thanks, Tatty." I smiled and lowered my head to get his blessing. Fortified with my father's precious *brachah*, I was ready — and off I went.

SHE WAS SO pale and fragile that she reminded me of one of those fine, blown-glass sculptures that could snap in a second. If not for those huge haunted eyes, it would have been easy to miss her. Maybe that's what she wanted — to shrink more and more until she was invisible, the way the other girls treated her. But I did see her. Those eyes never left me. They followed me around the classroom and out the door, along the corridors, through the school exit and to the bus stop. Even at home they accompanied me. What was it about them? Why did they disturb me so much?

"SO, HOW'S IT going?" Shaindy plopped herself down on the couch next to me in the teachers' staff room.

"Great," I replied, munching on my tuna-lettuce sandwich. "I like my class, the girls are listening to me; what more could I want?"

"Oh, just you wait," Shaindy grinned. "You've only been here a month. Once they get to know you, they become much more feisty."

"Yes," I nodded, "I know that, but meanwhile I'm just enjoying having my own class and being able to make a difference in my students' lives."

Shaindy looked at me thoughtfully. "Yes, that's always fulfilling," she said seriously, "although in some situations, there's a limit to what we can do."

I examined her face. She wasn't much older than I was, already married and a mother of two. Maybe she was tired, I thought; after all, juggling a full-time job, a husband and children was probably pretty exhausting.

"Well." I stood up and brushed the crumbs off my skirt. "I'm going to try anyway. You never know what can help — a kind word, a smile, an encouraging note."

"Go for it," said Shaindy, "and good luck." She gathered her books together for the next lesson.

"Oh, Naomi." I had one foot out the door when she called after me. "Is Sara Cohen in your class?"

I stopped abruptly. "Yes, she is," I replied cautiously. "Why do you ask?"

"Oh, nothing really," Shaindy answered, shaking her head. "I taught her last year. Send her my regards and keep a special eye on her for me."

MY FIFTH GRADERS were awfully cute. I adored that age; a perfect in-between — not yet enmeshed in teenage turmoil, yet old enough to engage in proper conversation. As the weeks passed by, I delighted in them more and more, as if I was the gardener, watering my young seedlings and helping them grow. Each child was a different plant, with her own unique kind of flowers and leaves. Some were root-bound, some not; some required more watering than others. Some were strong enough to survive the lashing of heavy rains, while others were blown over by a mere whiff of wind. It was fascinating to see who needed what in order to grow up strong and healthy.

As I watered them daily, I observed them closely to see who was or wasn't flourishing, while trying to identify the areas where my green fingers could make a difference.

One of my treasured plants was clearly not blooming properly. Sara Cohen didn't seem to change, no matter how much I tried to nurture her, straightening out her leaves, picking off dead flowers so new ones could grow, and moving her in and out of the sun. Nothing seemed to make a difference and each day, as I sprinkled water on her, I prayed that she'd still be there the next morning. Why did I have the queasy feeling that something was terribly wrong?

"SIT DOWN, MISS Lerner, I'll be with you in a minute." Mrs. Rosen waved her hand towards a chair and I sat obediently. Even though Mrs. Rosen was a fair and compassionate woman, I still felt as if I were a student again, a little girl back in the principal's office. She closed the file she'd been reading, rested her chin on her hands, and leaned slightly forward.

"How are you getting on, Miss Lerner? Any difficulties so far?"

"No, it's going really well. I mean, I think it is; that is, if you think it is…" My tongue was getting knottier by the second.

Mrs. Rosen smiled warmly. "Relax, I've been getting very good reports. Both the girls and staff like you, and I hear you are original and creative."

I beamed a big, bright smile that stretched from one side of the room to the other.

"That's the advantage of having fresh, young teachers," the principal continued. "Of course, there's a lot for them to learn, too…"

I coughed nervously. "There's just one thing," I began. "Sara Cohen… I was wondering if everything's all right there? Maybe she's sick or something?"

Mrs. Rosen's face tightened ever so slightly and her jaw tensed. "Why are you asking?" she questioned politely.

"I just can't seem to get through to her. She seems so remote, so distant, yet at other times she's like a frightened animal, terrified of her own shadow."

"Have you met Sara's parents yet?" Mrs. Rosen inquired.

"Actually, no. They didn't come to the PTA meeting last week. I was about to follow that up."

"Sara's father, as you will soon discover, is a very powerful, influential man... and rich. He donates money to many institutions, including our school. Sara's mother is not an emotionally well woman, I believe. Nobody sees her out much." Mrs. Rosen leaned forward and looked at me earnestly. "It's not clear what goes on in that home, Miss Lerner, but whenever we've tried to find out, the results have not been pleasant. I suggest you leave things alone for now. Do you understand?"

Understand? I understood nothing except that I'd just received a warning. Well, I was the wrong person for that, because my idealistic nature and natural pull toward justice would only make me dig deeper to find whatever was buried.

I TOOK TO calling her the shadow girl. In my mind she was just that, nothing more than an empty shape. I could see through her, but not into her. The other girls pretty much left her alone so all she had was herself... and me, who persisted in trying to catch her shadow before it slipped through my fingers. She was a pretty good student, considering. She never opened her mouth in class or raised her hand to answer a question, and if it weren't for my snippets of conversation with her, I wouldn't have even known she could talk. But she was bright, I could see that; wise, even, based on answers she wrote in her notebooks. There was something inside her, I was certain. If only I could bring it out.

"Sara," I called her as the girls were leaving the classroom for recess. She rarely went outside to play, preferring to sit and read instead. She looked up at me with her big, green, haunted eyes.

"Sara," I began, once we were alone, "I'd like to talk to your parents. They didn't come to the PTA meeting. Could you give them this note and ask them to call me to set up a time?"

Sara shrank back from the note as if it would burn her. "Oh, no... I can't do that. They're very busy, so they won't come." Her empty eyes were now filled with fear, and she bit the fingernails of one hand while nervously twisting her long, wavy hair with the other.

"Well, maybe I can come to your house if it's hard for them. I don't mind."

"No!" Sara looked like a runaway child about to be caught. "They're not usually home, and they don't like visitors."

"I see." I gently laid my hand on the young girl's shoulder and she flinched. "Don't worry, I won't do anything you're not comfortable with. Perhaps we can speak on the phone instead."

A palpable release of tension seeped out of her and she gently removed my hand and reached for her schoolbag. Hurriedly, she gathered her things and headed for the door.

"Oh, Sara, one last thing," I called after her. "Is everything all right? At home, I mean."

The fear was back; tight fingers of it closing around her face and neck and squeezing it into her eyes. "Yes," she answered, too quickly, "everything's fine."

"WHAT CAN YOU tell me about Sara Cohen's family?" I asked Shaindy in the staff room a few days later.

"Oh ho, Detective Lerner is on the loose. Be careful, my dear, be careful."

"I don't get it. Why all the cloak-and-dagger stuff? Who are we dealing with, the Mafia?"

"Almost," Shaindy grinned. Then her expression changed. "Seriously, though, Mr. Cohen is not someone to mess around with. He can get very angry."

"So I gather," I mumbled, more to myself than her. "But I think there's a problem with his daughter, so what can I do about that?"

"Nothing much," my friend admitted reluctantly. "Just give Sara some extra attention and TLC, that's all."

"No way," I said to myself. I would not be intimidated. I was determined to find a way to help my shadow girl.

I CALLED SARA'S house several times to arrange an appointment. Nobody ever answered the phone, which was strange, because I understood Mrs. Cohen was usually at home. Meanwhile, I gave Sara as much attention as I could. For a start, I noticed she was missing basic school supplies, and after frequent reminders yielded no results, I bought them myself. At first she was shy and hesitant to take them, but I insisted. Next, I got into the habit of bringing fruits and vegetables to school to add to her meager lunchbox, hoping they would bring some color to her paper-white complexion. She especially enjoyed the oranges and carrot sticks and devoured them hungrily. Every so often I would catch a glint of a smile on that sad face, a flicker of life in her haunted eyes. But it was only fleeting. She'd quickly slip back inside herself — the shadow girl.

One evening, I'd finally had enough. That's it, I decided. I'm going over to the Cohens' house. The lack of communication could continue no longer; I needed to have someone to work with. It was almost as if Sara was "dumped" at school every morning, dropped off like used clothing at the local *gemach*.

I found the house easily; couldn't miss it as it rose majestically, dwarfing the lesser structures around it. As I clambered up the white marble steps and faced the thick, formidable door with its intercom and impressive array of buttons, I felt my courage waver and almost turned around. *How foolish*, I thought to myself. It was only a door, a piece of wood, just one small part of the intimidating edifice of stone and concrete, but I guess it represented what was behind it.

Tentatively, I pressed the main buzzer and waited for a welcoming voice. Silence stretched all the way down the stone steps. I pressed again, allowing my finger to linger a little longer. After a few seconds, Sara's hello crackled through the static, and then I heard a sharp gasp when she recognized my voice.

The huge wooden door creaked open slightly and Sara's frightened face appeared around it. "Go away," she hissed. "Please." Suddenly, she was pulled back roughly as the door swung wildly open. A giant, imposing man, almost as big as the doorway, towered over me, and when I caught the look of sheer terror on Sara's face as she cowered behind her father, I knew immediately that I'd made a grave mistake.

"I'M SORRY," MRS. Rosen shook her head apologetically. "He says he'll have you fired if you ever go near his house again."

There was no chance of that, I thought gloomily. Once was more than enough.

"What I don't understand," I began carefully, "is how he controls everything, even you."

"Money," Mrs. Rosen replied. "It buys power and intimidation. Believe me, we've tried everything, but nothing has worked. Everyone's afraid of him and his threats, and he has powerful contacts just about everywhere. Sara, of course, doesn't speak up, so even social workers haven't been able to get near his house, because there's no 'proof' of anything untoward happening there. The truth is that nobody really knows what's going on."

"And what about Sara?" I asked sadly. "How does she get help?"

"Just keep up with what you're doing," the older woman replied tiredly, weariness hanging like a cobweb around her shoulders. "Give her whatever you can."

SARA DIDN'T SHOW up for the next few days. On the third day she crept quietly into the classroom and placed the school supplies I'd bought her on my desk.

"My father says I must return these," she whispered, her head slightly bent.

"It's okay, Sara." I lifted her chin up slightly. "How are you, anyway?" And that's when I saw it: the purplish-blue mark staining the side of her face! "What happened to you, Sara? How did you get that?"

She pulled her hair forward and wrapped it around her face like a winter scarf. "I fell down the steps," she answered, with well-rehearsed words. I watched my shadow girl disappear into herself and my heart raged.

WE WERE NEARING the end of the school year and it would be hard to say good-bye to all my flowers, who'd nearly all blossomed in some way over the last ten months. We had grown nicely together, and I loved them all, but my heart continually wept for Sara. She had bloomed briefly before my disastrous visit, but now she looked withered and dry. I'd done my best, though, hadn't I?

I wasn't so sure. Every time I overlooked a suspicious mark or slight limp, I ate myself up with guilt, and there were moments when I was too ashamed to look in the mirror. And yet, if I were to get involved, I'd only make things worse for her; I'd seen that. Still, there wasn't a day that went by when I didn't wish I could take her hand, bring her home with me, and close the door forever on her sad, miserable life.

One evening, while I was marking history tests, the phone rang. "Naomi!"

"Oh, hi, Mommy, how are you and Tatty? Sorry I've not called over the last few days."

"It's fine," my mother shrugged it off. "But listen, we have a wonderful *shidduch* for you. Naftali thought of it… a boy from his yeshivah."

I sighed. Mommy had a way of getting straight to the point. *What would it be this time*, I wondered. In general, nice normal suggestions didn't come too frequently anymore, but if my brother was involved, then it was worth hearing it out. Surprisingly, by the end of the phone conversation, Daniel Kohn did indeed sound very promising, and for the first time in months I felt a flutter of anticipation. "Just one last thing, Mommy," I remembered before hanging up. "If he's all the wonderful things you say he is, then how come he's twenty-six and still not married?"

"Ah, yes," my father was in on our three-way conversation. "Naftali says that he comes from a much more modern background than ours, but he's spent the last few years strengthening himself in Torah and *mitzvos*."

"Have you checked him out yourself, Tatty?"

"Well, actually, no." His voice sounded weary. "We've checked out so many boys in the past, and Naftali is so impressed by his excellent *middos* and refined personality that we decided to trust his opinion on this one."

"Oh," I said, surprised. "Okay."

"I guess you could describe him as more of a *baal teshuvah*; does that bother you?"

"Of course not," I smiled through the telephone. "It doesn't bother me at all."

THE FIRST MEETING lasted five hours, and could have lasted another five as far as we were concerned. I practically floated home. He was so… nice… and interesting, sensitive and compassionate, as well as obviously serious about his deepening connection to *Yiddishkeit*. Even though we hadn't discussed more personal topics, these traits of his shone through like sun rays, and I couldn't remember the last time I'd felt so completely comfortable with somebody.

"Nu," said my mother the next morning. "Naftali says he's interested. How about you?"

I was still up in the air, floating from the night before.

"Speak up now," she said impatiently. "I can't hear you."

The second meeting he took me for a drive to the beach, where we sat on the sand dunes, ate sandwiches that he'd packed in newspaper, and watched the sun sink down into the sea. As the evening wrapped itself up like a pretty gift package, we eagerly awaited the next one.

WHEN WE MET again, I was determined to find out more about his family, about whom he seemed particularly reticent.

"Tell me about your parents," I encouraged him. "What do they do?"

"My father's a businessman; my mother's a housewife. We're not so close," he added quickly. "I don't have much contact with them anymore."

"How sad," I empathized. "Is that because you became more *frum?*"

"Kind of, I'll tell you about it another time." Daniel changed the subject quickly. "Which school did you say you teach in?"

"Oh, I'm at Proctors," I replied breezily, "and I love it."

"What a small world," Daniel remarked. "I have a younger sister there. She's in fifth grade. What do you teach?"

I stared at him, scrutinized him carefully, a light suddenly blinking in my head. Yes, there was a resemblance. But Naftali had said his name was Kohn, hadn't he?

"Maybe you know her…?" Daniel's voice trailed off when he saw the look on my face.

"What… did you say your family name was?" I could barely get the question out.

"Cohen," Daniel answered, far too quietly.

"Oh, my gosh." I was going to be sick. Cohen… Kohn… how could I have been so blind as to miss the connection? But there were lots of Cohens out there, weren't there? Just our street alone had three of them. Maybe it wasn't the same one?

"Sara," I whispered. "She's your sister, right?"

Daniel looked at me, and it was clear that he knew what I knew, or wasn't supposed to know.

"That man," — I tried to hide my revulsion — "he's your father?"

He lowered his head in shame. "Yes."

MY PARENTS WERE devastated beyond words, especially because this time, they hadn't checked the *shidduch* out themselves. Naftali apologized profusely for not finding out more information first, although, as he said, it didn't change his opinion of Daniel. There would be no marriage; my parents were adamant about that.

After a while I stopped talking to all of them about it. I wanted to curl up into a tiny ball like a new puppy dog, lie near the crackling flames of the fireplace and go to sleep. I wanted to cry, to shout, to scream and yell and experience every emotion possible until I was empty, hollow inside, an illusion — like my shadow girl.

A self-made prisoner in my home, I became just like her: solitary, sad, and struggling to stay connected. And I mourned. I grieved for a little girl called Sara and her wonderful brother, whom I'd liked more than I'd liked anyone before, but who descended from a cruel, tyrannical man and an emotionally ill mother. I grieved for myself, for my loss, for my lack of courage. Was it fair to judge him by his genetics? But there had to be something of his father in him, didn't there? Some DNA that would pass character traits down? Or had he bypassed all of that with his will, his determination, and his special *neshamah*? Could I take that chance?

Of all my questions, there was one that I couldn't shake off. Just like Sara's haunted eyes, it attached itself to me wherever I went, never leaving me alone. So one evening, I had to do it; I had to ask.

"Daniel, it's Naomi."

"I know," Daniel answered warmly. "I haven't forgotten your voice."

"I… I have a question; I need to know. Why didn't you protect

Sara? How could you have left her in that house to suffer by herself?"

His sigh slithered down the line and his voice, when it came, was choked, as if an incredibly large stone was stuck in his throat.

"My father threw me out of the house when I was nineteen years old and Sara was only four." The retelling was obviously hard for him. "At first I was broken, emotionally and physically, from my father's abuse. I had nowhere to go, no self-worth, and was afraid of my own shadow."

"Like Sara," I whispered.

"Yes," said Daniel sadly, "like her. It's a long story, but it took me a few years to pull myself together, and during that time I had no contact with Sara. I couldn't, even if I'd wanted to, because I was forbidden to go near the house."

"And now?" I gently prodded.

"I do see her now," his voice trembled. "It's complicated, because she's not allowed out alone, so I wait after school sometimes, just to say hello or give her a small present. It's hard, though, because she doesn't really talk."

"I know." He didn't need to explain. "But Daniel," the words came out in a rush, "couldn't you have taken her out of there; gone to your Rav, even the police?"

"I tried, believe me, I tried. But if Sara doesn't talk there's no proof of anything. I was afraid to make things worse for her, so I just did whatever I could in any small way to make her life a little better."

"So did I," I sobbed, "but it wasn't enough!"

DURING THE SUMMER Sara was taken into foster care. Her broken arm was the evidence Daniel needed in order to finally act, and she eventually opened up and told him everything. I heard all of this from Naftali, who continued to rave about Daniel and sing his praises. I went to visit Sara at her foster parents' home to tell her I was sorry, to purge myself of the guilt, to rid myself of the searing, red-hot pain I felt every time I thought of my weakness in succumbing to pressure to overlook the signs. She seemed lighter, brighter, even laughed a little, and her eyes were not as haunted; she was less of a shadow girl.

During summer vacation I handed in my resignation, packed up my things, and moved back to my parents' house. I couldn't return to Proctors, not now, not with all the memories.

Daniel still waits for me, hoping I'll eventually agree to be his wife, but I can't give him an answer. I just can't find the courage or the strength of conviction to overlook his past, and in my mind, that makes me a coward. People I turn to for advice have differing opinions, which only makes things even more confusing. Last night, after a long talk with our family Rav, I think I reached a decision. I can't take the risk, I simply haven't got the guts to marry him. I, who once considered myself so brave.

It's the right decision, the best thing to do, I suppose. And yet, if it really is… why, then, am I so torn?

Having just read this story again for the anthology, I cannot remember for the life of me what made me write it. I do recall that I had been reading several of Torey Hayden's books. A psychologist and teacher who worked for years in self-contained classrooms with emotionally disturbed children, this talented young woman has written many accounts of her experiences. Maybe subconsciously that was what made me broach this topic? Why I turned it into a shidduch story, I'll never know, although the issue of what we are willing to accept or not in a shidduch is always a cause for discussion.

So, having just admitted to my bafflement at writing this story, I have to say that it generated much discussion and controversy. The story got people thinking and talking. The staff in the Hamodia office was busy discussing it and asking one another what they would have done in the protagonist's situation. And to me, that's the biggest compliment and accomplishment… getting readers to think.

Even though "Torn" is one of my earlier stories, I was actually impressed with the quality of the writing (I actually cringe over some of my older pieces). I enjoyed reading it again and actually felt a "wow" at the end. I think it is probably the most powerful story I've written!

Holding Back

"YOSSI, CAN YOU hurry up already?" Simi shouted up the stairs. "Devoiri, bring the baby, and Rochel, please tie Yitzi's shoes. If we don't get going soon the stores will be closed."

Simi rummaged through her bag for the car keys and sighed. Now that the older children were away in their respective yeshivos and seminaries, getting out of the house was like navigating the subway at rush hour. She could vaguely hear the phone ringing somewhere in the house and groaned. If they were going to go shopping for Yossi's bar mitzvah, they had to leave now.

"Ima… phone." Yossi bounded down the stairs and thrust the cordless at her.

"Tell them to call back," Simi ordered tersely. "I can't talk now."

"But it's Gitty."

Ah, Gitty. She was the only person for whom Simi literally dropped everything in order to talk to.

"Hold on, I'll tell her to phone me later. Devoiri, please give the baby her pacifier."

She took the phone from Yossi and gasped breathlessly into the receiver.

"Hi, Gitty, I'm just running out. Can I call you… Gitty, what's wrong? Why are you crying?"

Simi sank into the nearest chair. She wasn't going anywhere, and from the look on her children's faces, they knew it too.

"OKAY, GITTY, TRY taking some deep breaths, calm down and tell me what happened."

Gitty's sobs slowly spiraled down into gulps, and then shudders that allowed some words to splutter out. "Dovid's been let go."

"Really, that's awful; from where?" Simi's head was swimming with bar mitzvah suits and shoes, matching pink dresses and…

"From work, where do you think?" Gitty's voice rose like water in a clogged drainpipe and then dissolved into tears again.

"Oh, no!" said Simi, suddenly paying attention. "That's terrible. What did he do?" She scrambled to stuff the words back inside her mouth. "Um, I mean, why?"

"He's too old, that's why!" Gitty shouted in frustration. "The company had to lay off workers so the older ones got the boot first."

"But Dovid isn't old," Simi protested, genuinely puzzled. "Devoiri, please pick up the baby, she's crying again. Yossi, turn the music down."

"Of course he isn't," said Gitty heatedly. "But in the workplace, if you're over forty, it's time to sign up for a pension."

"Chas v'shalom. Yossi, I said turn it down!"

"Simi, are you with me or not?" Gitty asked impatiently.

"Yes, oh gosh… sorry; we were just about to go out…" Simi's voice trickled off. She didn't want to make her friend feel worse than she already did. "You know what, I'll just tell the kids to wait five minutes while I go up to my room for some privacy."

Upstairs in her bedroom, the family noise softened somewhat. "Okay, I'm listening now," she said reassuringly.

Gitty was crying again, her words wet and slippery. "Well, you know that we weren't exactly making it before this, especially with the wedding expenses and the girls' seminary fees, and now it looks as if we'll need to take a cheaper hall and even back out of buying the couple an apartment."

"Hold on," Simi interrupted. "When did this happen?"

"It's a few months already," Gitty answered sheepishly. "He got a month's salary to start with, but it wasn't long before there was nothing left of it."

"I can't believe it! Why didn't you tell me earlier? We've spoken practically every day and you never breathed a word! In all our conversations about the *chasunah* plans, you couldn't find a time to mention it until now? We're best friends!"

"I didn't want to worry you. At first we thought everything would work out and Dovid would get another job straight away. But it hasn't happened. And of course, we had no savings."

"I'm so very sorry," said Simi quietly. "I had no idea you were going through this."

"The worse thing is the shame and embarrassment," Gitty continued. "Dovid is quite depressed. And Simi, we're making a wedding! How are we going to pay for it all? You can't imagine the stress he's under."

Simi didn't know what to say. Gitty's distress cut into her deeply. Gitty was usually so together and in control, yet now she sounded like she was on the verge of collapse.

"Why don't you let me ask around a bit and see what I can do?" Simi offered.

"Oh, no, please don't do that. I'd be so ashamed. We'll probably take out some more loans or *gemachim*. I just needed to share it with you, that's all. I couldn't hold it in any longer."

"I understand," said Simi gently, "and I'm always here. You can call me to talk whenever you want."

SIMI HUNG UP the phone with a heavy heart. How upsetting it was to hear her friend so distraught. They'd been best friends since high school and had maintained their friendship over the years, despite living in different cities.

"I feel so bad for Gitty," Simi lamented to her husband later that evening, when the children were asleep. "There must be something we can do to help her."

Mordechai looked up from his coffee cup and eyed his wife warily. "Simi, you're not running off on another fundraising project are you? The last one took about a month to recover from, and I seem to recall that meals were rather sparse during that time. There's no way you can take anything more on at the moment. We're making a bar mitzvah, remember?"

"I know, but I have to do *something*. What if it were us in this situation, wouldn't you want someone to help you?"

"Actually, I'm not sure." Mordechai reached for a piece of chocolate cake and placed it on a white disposable plate. Simi raised her eyebrows questioningly. "Well, yes and no. I'd probably appreciate the help, but I might be embarrassed to know where it came from. It could be really awkward to face them afterwards."

Simi took a bite of cake and thought for a moment. "Um, you have a good point," she conceded. "And Gitty *is* quite proud, after all. You're probably right. I'll have to think of a way to get it to her without her knowing."

"Er, get what exactly?" Mordechai asked.

"The money, of course," Simi announced.

Mordechai sighed heavily. "What money, Simi? We're not exactly rolling in dough, either. Where do you think you'll get it from?

"Well," Simi began cautiously, using a winning smile that could thaw her freezer, "remember the savings account with the money from my Aunt Rivka?"

"Oh, nooo… you're not! That money is for you, we agreed on that. I thought you wanted to save it for the future, in case you decide to go back to school."

"I do… did, but she's my best friend. Money comes and goes, but friends… ach, you won't understand… it's a girl thing."

"Believe it or not, I do; well, kind of. But come on, aren't you going a little overboard here? I'm sure that she'll get money from somewhere else."

"Maybe she will," Simi acknowledged, "but *I* want to help her, and let's be honest, I'm not going back to school so soon." Leaning forward on her chair, she reached out to bang some cupboard doors shut. "I can't keep on top of what I'm doing now."

"Okay, maybe not yet, but one day."

"Mordechai, I really want to do this for Gitty. That's what I'd like to use the money for."

Mordechai shook his head in amazement. His wife's golden heart glowed even in daylight, but still… "And what about your own family; maybe we'll also need it eventually?"

"Yes, but we don't need it now, and anyway, I thought you wanted me to save it for school."

Mordechai laughed. "All right, you got me on that one."

"Please say that it's okay," Simi pleaded. "I'll even promise to have your shirts ironed and folded and put some food on the table."

Mordechai gave a mock frown. "Now, there's no need to go that far." He nodded his head slowly. "Look, if you're sure it's the right thing to do, then go ahead. I only hope you won't regret it."

IN THE SHOPPING mall the next afternoon, Simi wandered around in a daze. Eager shoppers swarmed around her, swinging large bags with their purchases inside. She bought things too; dresses and shoes, suits for Yossi, a hat and *davening* jacket, socks and hair accessories. Normally, she would have enjoyed a shopping spree, but thoughts of Gitty's predicament weighed on her like a lead apron, and shopping suddenly seemed less important. The children were happy, though, and they bounced through the doorway, eager to show Tatty their new purchases. In spite of herself, Simi smiled. It felt good to be making a *simchah*. She glanced at her bar mitzvah boy and felt proud. And then a fleeting thought cast a shadow on her joy. Gitty was making a *simchah* too. How would *she* be feeling?

"I'VE GOT IT!" Simi exclaimed excitedly. She'd been sitting in the armchair for ten minutes, just staring into space.

Mordechai looked up from the *mezuzah* he was checking. "Huh?"

"I've figured out a way to get the money to Gitty without her knowing it's from me. Remember Shana who was also in our class? She moved to Bnei Brak last year and they live in the same neighborhood. She comes to Yerushalayim once a week to see clients, so I can give the money to her and ask her to give it to Gitty."

"Hold on," Mordechai interrupted. "Then Gitty will think it's from Shana and she might not like that either."

"No problem, I've already figured that out," announced Simi triumphantly. "I'll put it in an envelope for her to slip under the door."

Mordechai smiled at his wife warmly. Despite his reservations, he had to admire her.

"*Hatzlachah*," he said encouragingly. "It's a really nice thing that you're doing."

SHANA CLIMBED THE steep flight of stairs to Gitty's apartment. It had been a while since she'd seen her friend, even though they lived relatively close to each other and two of their boys were in yeshivah together. Simi's envelope was tucked safely inside her pocket because she didn't want to take it out too soon. Simi hadn't told her what was in it and she hadn't asked, but she had her suspicions. Sounds of boisterous family life vibrated from Gitty's door and Shana prayed that no one would suddenly come flying out of it. She bent down and quickly slipped the envelope through the thin gap underneath the door, stood up, turned around sharply and dashed down the stairs, straight into Gitty's son.

IT WAS ONE of those precious quiet mornings, a time to treasure. The baby was taking a long nap and Simi was enjoying the peace and tranquility that accompanied rare solitary moments. She pulled up a chair and eyed the pile of bar mitzvah invitations that were neatly stacked like thin paper sandwiches on the dining room table. When the kids came home from school, she'd send them out to deliver the local ones. *Had she mailed all her out-of-town ones?* she wondered. Her eyes wandered to Gitty's wedding invitation on the other side of the table. They'd both been too busy to talk these last few weeks, but during the snippets of conversation they'd managed to squeeze in, Gitty had sounded more relaxed. Simi allowed herself a moment of satisfaction; it felt so good to have helped her friend. She was a little surprised that Gitty hadn't mentioned anything about receiving some money, though, but most likely she'd been too embarrassed. She heard the muffled sound of the phone ringing and dived to retrieve it from underneath the couch cushions.

"Oh, hi, Gitty, sorry it took so long, I was just looking for the phone."

"As usual," Gitty laughed.

"Hey," said Simi, "it's good to hear you laughing."

"Yes," Gitty agreed. "It's very exciting. We're almost there, only a week to go. But listen, I'm coming to Yerushalayim tomorrow to pick up my *sheitel*. Do you want to meet for a quick coffee?"

"Of course," Simi agreed enthusiastically. "How about our usual place, around eleven?"

THEY MET IN their favorite coffee shop in Old Katamon. For as long as they could remember, they had frequented the quaint little café, hidden beneath a camouflage of trees on a small side street. The café's sweet smelling rose garden had been privy to much of their maturation, first as giggling high school girls, then as *kallos*, each with her dreams and aspirations. After Gitty moved away and their families grew, the excursions wound down to less frequent, but cherished coffee dates, conversations centering on their children and roles as wives and mothers. It seemed particularly appropriate to be back in their old surroundings, standing before another milestone, the marriage of Gitty's eldest daughter.

"You look great!" Simi exclaimed, kissing her friend on the cheek. "A little tired perhaps, but that's to be expected. I thought you'd be..." Oh, here she was again, putting her giant size foot in her mouth.

"Stressed, anxiety-ridden and about to collapse any moment," Gitty finished the sentence for her.

"Well, yes, actually. After all, the last time we really talked, you were beside yourself with worry."

"I know," said Gitty, suddenly becoming serious, "but Hashem works in mysterious ways. *Baruch Hashem*, we got the money together, through the help of family members and *gemachim* and also," she lowered her voice and leaned forward almost conspiringly, "I received a surprise gift from Shana Kaufman. At least, I think it was her. Somebody slipped an envelope with money underneath my door and straight afterwards, my son Yehuda almost collided with her hurrying down the stairs. What a lovely thing to do. She's so sweet."

Simi's stomach contracted in an uncomfortable spasm. It was a new, disturbing feeling and she wasn't sure what it was.

"You know," Gitty continued, "she's the one person I'm comfortable to take anything from, because I know that her parents always wanted to pay me *shadchanus* for making her *shidduch*. Do you remember that?"

Simi nodded dumbly. Actually, she hadn't remembered at all. It had totally slipped her mind that Gitty had made Shana's *shidduch* with a classmate's brother and her parents hadn't allowed her to take any payment for it.

"By the way," Gitty lowered her voice even more until it almost touched the ground. "You didn't say anything, did you? I mean, how could she have known that I needed money?"

"Of course not," Simi replied quickly to the unspoken accusation. Her discomfort was growing, blowing up like an inflatable ball inside her. "I'm sure it was just a coincidence, or that Shana decided to give you a gift for the wedding. It makes sense."

"Yes, that's probably it," Gitty agreed, "although it was quite a sizable amount. What a great friend she is, though. How thoughtful!"

The ball in Simi's stomach bounced from another blow. Was she mistaken or was that another subtle accusation, delivered sweetly like an after-dinner mint? Now she was really confused. Hadn't she purposely avoided giving the gift directly, in order not to embarrass Gitty? Yet here she was, seemingly happy to have received it from Shana, raving with praise and even a little upset that it hadn't come from her. *No,* she said to herself, *she was just feeling insecure and oversensitive, that was all.* But still, she shivered suddenly in the warm summer breeze.

"Are you cold, Simi?" Gitty asked worriedly. "It's a hot day and you're shivering. Maybe you're sick?"

Simi stared at the brown sludge in her coffee cup and stirred it around in circles, this way and that, just like the circuits in her brain that banged into one another with confusion and, something else... what was it? What *was* that feeling that kicked the inflatable ball in different directions? Could it be jealousy? *Could* it? She'd never considered herself a jealous person; in fact, she'd always taken pride in her ability to be sincerely happy for others. And yet, here she was, jealous, resentful even, that another friend was getting credit for the *chessed* she had done. What did it matter anyway?

Yet it did... and she hated herself for that, for the *ga'avadik* part of her that wanted Gitty to know the truth, to shout out, "It was me! *I* gave you the money. I cashed in precious Aunt Rivka's savings in order to give it to you; me, not Shana... *me!*" But she said nothing.

"Simi, are you sure you're all right?" Gitty asked again. "You're not looking too well."

"I'm okay, really. Just a sudden headache, that's all." That was absolutely true. She felt as if hammers were knocking on her skull and flattening her thoughts.

"Hold on, I think I've got some Tylenol in my bag. Let me take a look." Gitty opened all the zippers of her pocketbook. "That's unusual. I always carry some with me. I tell you what, I'll ask at the counter if they have any, and if not, I'll just pop over to the drugstore next door and pick up a box. You really look like you're suffering."

Was her inner turmoil that physically obvious? But Simi smiled gratefully, almost relieved to be left alone for however long it would take.

"Don't go away," Gitty called out cheerfully. "I'll be right back."

AS SOON AS Gitty was out of sight, Simi whipped out her cell phone and dialed.

"Mordechai, it's me. I don't have too much time to talk, but she thinks that it's Shana."

"Listen, Simi, if you want me to understand anything you're saying, you'll have to stop speaking in riddles."

Simi groaned impatiently. "Gitty thinks that it was Shana who gave her the money and she's very happy… thinks she's a great friend, even."

Mordechai let out a loud laugh. "That's really hysterical. It couldn't have worked out better."

"Mordechai, this is not funny! If you must know, I'm jealous."

"Why, what's the problem?"

"Because she thinks that Shana gave her the money and is gushing over what a good friend she is, when it was really *me*."

Mordechai suppressed a laugh. "So you're jealous, eh?"

"I just *said* that. I'm also resentful and thinking that it's kind of not fair and… oh, I don't know… a lot of things."

"Aha, so you really did the *chessed* for yourself, to make you feel good."

"No, I didn't. At least that's what I thought." She clenched her teeth tightly. Why was he being so logical?

"Look, Simi," Mordechai turned serious, "you know that I wasn't too keen on this idea of yours in the first place, but you did it, and I'm quite sure it was for the right reason. What you're feeling is normal. You'll get over it."

"Thanks, I appreciate that," said Simi gratefully. "But listen, Gitty's going to be back soon, so just tell me what to do."

"About what?"

"About Gitty, should I tell her or not?"

Now Mordechai sounded genuinely puzzled. "Tell her it was you? Of course not; why should you?"

"But I want her to know. I want her to know what a good friend I am, to know that I care."

Mordechai fell silent.

"Nu," Simi hissed. "Quick, before she comes back."

"I'm thinking, Simi, don't rush me."

Simi started a mental countdown in her brain as she drummed her fingers on the edge of the table.

"Okay," said Mordechai, "would telling her make any difference to the outcome? Gitty got her money, right, and she's happy?"

"Yes, I suppose." There he was with his logic again.

"So, the only one who gains from telling her is you; it would make *you* feel better, not her."

"*And* I don't want her to think I'm a bad friend."

"Well, if you're worried about that, there's not much hope."

"Mordechai, this isn't helping."

"Come on, Gitty must surely have seen what a loyal friend you've been over the years. After all, your friendship isn't new."

Now it was Simi's turn to be thoughtful, while keeping one eye on the garden doorway.

"Listen, Simi, if you know what a good friend you've been, that should be enough."

"But it isn't… *oy*, here she comes, gotta go… bye."

"Golly," said Gitty, collapsing into a chair and reaching for a glass of water. "I didn't expect that to take so long, I'm really sorry. Here, let me give you a couple of pills."

"It's okay, one is fine." Simi took a pill gratefully and swallowed it quickly. What she really needed was a tranquilizer.

"You know, I have to get going," Gitty looked at her watch anxiously. "There are still those last-minute things to take care of."

So, thought Simi to herself. *It's now or never.* Should she spill the beans to Gitty, or leave her with warm, affectionate feelings towards Shana? Her husband's words reverberated in her head. "What does it matter? The only one who'll feel better is you." He was right; she knew that... infuriatingly and frustratingly right. But the urge to tell was so strong that she had to keep the words from gushing out of her throat. That inflatable ball inside her was either going to explode or the air was going to slowly seep out of it until all that remained was a shiny, flat, plastic shape that no longer bothered her. Which would it be?

The dilemma churned inside her while they paid their bill, gathered their belongings and prepared to leave. She gazed around her at the green grass and rosebushes and inhaled the perfumed scent of the flowers. There, in that quiet, unassuming café, almost unnoticeable amongst the trees, the place that had kept their secrets and observed their many milestones, it suddenly struck her. She remembered the reason for wanting to do the *chessed* quietly in the first place. She recalled the fear of embarrassing her best friend and of not wishing to cause any shame. She had wanted to do the *mitzvah* modestly and selflessly. That was it, she realized. It was all about "*shtikah*," silence. If she thought she'd been a good friend until now, she was about to take it to a higher level, way up high and beyond, to a world of peace, self-knowledge and quietness. How could she possibly have risked losing all of that?

And yet, as they walked together down the street to their respective bus stops, that persistent, destructive voice hissed in her ear, "Say it, go on, say it."

The two friends hugged warmly and parted for their separate

ways. As Gitty walked away, the voice grew louder, deafening almost, goading her on. "Tell her *now* before she goes... quickly!"

"Gitty," Simi called out urgently. Her friend stopped in her tracks and turned around.

"Yes?"

Simi stood, immobilized on the sidewalk, oblivious to the city street noises. She inhaled a long, deep, internal breath and felt the inflatable ball collapse inside her.

"Nothing... see you at the wedding."

This was a story assigned to me by my editors at Binah. *I was asked to write a fiction story where A gives B a present which B thinks was given by C. Well, it was something like that anyway... I can't even remember now. It was the first time that I'd had to write a fiction story where I was told what to write about. Initially, it was a daunting prospect. For me, creative writing in this genre was not something I could be "told" to do. I usually came up with my own ideas, and the thought of writing a story to order, about a topic that didn't exactly get my adrenaline roaring, was stifling.*

However, never one to admit defeat easily, I decided to give it a try, and the results, as I read just now, weren't bad. I was particularly amused by the character Mordechai — I must have modeled him after my own husband — and I saw that I was able to bring a meaningful message into what I thought would be an uninspiring story.

After this, I wrote several more stories "to order" and found them enjoyable. Contrary to my initial reaction, it was not monotonous or restrictive, and in fact, I discovered that one can be creative with anything and turn dust into diamonds. So, as the expression goes, "You live and learn!"

THE WORST PART was riding the school bus home. She had the whole day to think about it; in fact, it was all she thought about. School, of course, was also difficult, but the ride home was always the hardest. After endless hours cooped up in the classroom, the girls seemed to burst into the late afternoon sun to vent their frustration… on her. She wished she could walk, but the journey was much too long. She would relish that walk like a cold ice cream on a hot day. At other times, in moments of fantasy, she'd fly home, but that was impossible because her wings were caught, beating against the sides of a specimen jar. Every day she stood, staring at the open doors of the bus before making the slow, agonizing climb up the steps. She held her breath, hoping to be invisible and slide quietly into one of the shiny vinyl seats without being noticed. But once she sat down she was trapped for one whole hour; sixty ceaseless minutes at the mercy of the bullies!

WHY HER, SHE didn't know. At her last school it hadn't been like that. Sure, she was never the most popular person, like the girls who seemed to exude self-confidence in their smiles, but she'd had friends. She was pretty smart, although maybe not by her family's standards. Her super siblings sapped her confidence sometimes, although they didn't mean to. She knew that her bright, successful family loved her dearly, so why did she feel so inadequate beside them? Sandwiched firmly between them all, she felt like the least desired flavor in a multi-layered cake.

"DON'T TELL ME we're moving again!" Mindy exclaimed as she walked into the living room. Her mother and sisters were kneeling on the floor taping cardboard boxes together.

Her mother looked up, sympathetically. "Tatty has a new job. He's been transferred to another branch of the bank."

"Oh," said Mindy sullenly. "Where to, this time?"

"A suburb in New York," Mrs. Klein answered. "We've already registered you in a school there. I'm sure that you'll make friends quickly."

Yeah, right, Mindy thought to herself, *like it's so easy to start all over again.* Her heart dropped like a heavy stone and she felt herself sink.

AND SO IT went. Even though she was only twelve years old, her family had relocated four times. The other kids didn't take the moves as hard as she did; she was the sensitive soul in the family, for whom beginning again was like being reborn. None of the moves, however, had been as bad as this one.

MINDY WALKED INTO the classroom eagerly for a change. English was her favorite subject and she'd worked very hard to write a book report that she was extremely proud of.

"Well, look who's here," a familiar voice sneered from the back of the room. Mindy's stomach churned. *Oh, no,* she thought to herself the minute she heard who it was, *don't tell me this girl's been switched to my English class as well.*

"Look, everyone," Tzippy, the owner of the voice, beckoned to her classmates. "It's the teacher's pet; she fancies herself as a writer."

Mindy slid into her seat, cheeks burning, trying to tune out the snickering rippling around her.

"So," Tzippy said as she leaned menacingly over Mindy's desk. "Where's your book report? Let's see it. I'm sure it's the best... right, girls?" Turning her head, she laughed sarcastically to her friends.

Mindy fumbled nervously in her bag while Tzippy waited with her arms tightly folded.

"What's the matter? Can't you find it?"

"It... it's here somewhere. I put it in my bag this morning."

"So where is it then?" Tzippy smirked. "I bet you didn't do it. Oh boy, you're in trouble now."

Mindy was pulling everything out of her knapsack, scattering books across the table and sending papers fluttering to the floor. With no sign of the book report, she grew increasingly agitated and began to cry.

"Hey, chill out," Tzippy said smugly, "I think I've found it." A gloating smile distorted her face. She nodded her head in the direction of a wastebasket in the corner of the classroom. Mindy jumped out of her chair and ran towards it. There, stuffed inside the garbage can, was her treasured book report, crumpled and dirty and utterly useless.

FROM THE BEGINNING they'd singled her out, branded her with the mark of Cain on her forehead. Perhaps they'd picked up on her nervousness, the lack of confidence that starting a new school brings. Really, it was only one of them, but once she began her taunting many of the girls joined in, swept along like the pull of high tide. Tzippy, the ringleader, lived near her, just a few streets away, so she also had to suffer sneers and snide remarks when meeting her in the neighborhood. It seemed like Tzippy held some kind of hypnotic power over her elite group of girls, and the rest of the class, while not actually participating in the bullying and intimidating acts, never stood up to her. Her fiery black eyes flashing, Tzippy would discover yet another weak spot in Mindy, another point of humiliation to seize upon. All Mindy wanted was to become invisible, to disappear with the water down the bathroom sink.

"MINDY, WHAT ARE you doing?"

"Taking off my freckles."

Scrubbing at them was more like it, scraping with a nailbrush at the pale, brown speckles covering most of her face. Mindy, preoccupied as she was, barely noticed her mother's horrified expression in the mirror.

"Mindy, sweetheart, why would you want to do that?" her mother asked, completely confused. Mindy scrubbed harder, angrily, intent on erasing the spots.

"Because they're ugly. I'm ugly. Everyone says so."

Pulling her hand from her face and uncoiling her fingers from the brush, Mindy's mother turned her daughter gently towards her.

"Mindy, what's going on? Is there something you want to tell me?"

Mindy looked deeply into her mother's worried eyes. For a moment she felt like the swollen banks of a bursting river, ready to spill everything out. But then she remembered Bubby and how sick she was and how busy her mother was taking care of her. How could she possibly burden her with something else? And besides, there was nothing she could do about it anyway.

"No," she mumbled, slowly shaking her head. "There's nothing."

IT WAS GETTING harder and harder. Mindy appeared to have won the uncoveted role of class scapegoat. The taunts and teasing tugged at her sore, tired heart. There was always something — a shove or a kick; hurtful comments; snide remarks; damaged notebooks. The strain of it all was draining; the need to be on the alert, like a hounded animal waiting for the hunt to begin. She found her head aching constantly, a dull throb that jumbled up her thoughts.

OUCH, HER ANKLE throbbed painfully from where she'd banged into the side of her seat and humiliated tears filled her eyes.

"Watch where you're going," Tzippy jeered. She'd just pushed

Mindy down the aisle of the bus. Around her, some girls laughed. Others sat silently, pity on their faces, but no one came to her defense.

"What's wrong with me?" Mindy asked herself for the millionth time. "And why am I such a coward that I can't fight back?" As she settled wearily into her seat, the questions pounded again and again like a throbbing tooth.

WHEN SHE GOT home from school she went immediately to her hideout. She'd stumbled on this secret space a few months before, while taking a Shabbos stroll in the nearby park. At home, peace and quiet were rare, and privacy in a bedroom with two siblings was almost unheard of. So it was here that she'd found her comfort, a place to sit alone and think and escape the world. She'd come across it quite by accident after she'd crossed over the old, stone bridge that straddled the lake. It was a large lake that glistened like fine jewels when the sun caressed it, and during the winter its frozen waters mirrored the sky.

Climbing the fence with the "Keep Out" sign, Mindy had succumbed to her desire to get closer to the water, and as she pushed through bushes and undergrowth, was surprised to find a small cave-like structure hidden amongst the leaves. It was almost like a room. Soil and leaves covered the floor and the walls had been carved from surrounding rocks and boulders. Crawling inside, she'd been delighted with her find. This was exactly what she had needed — a place to get away, outdoors with nature, peaceful and serene — just hers.

Over the months, Mindy made the cave homey, even bringing an old rug that her mother had thrown away to cover the floor; a cushion to rest on if she felt like sleeping; a flashlight and blanket and a few books. But her biggest find of all was Puddles. He'd arrived almost at the same time as her, probably smelling her scent and recognizing a kindred soul. She'd presumed he was a stray cat, although he didn't behave like one when he brushed against her or lay purring in her lap. She'd bring scraps from mealtimes to feed him and they'd sit together inside the cave, her new friend a willing listener to her woes. Large pale gray splotches on his white fur had led her to naming him Puddles. She felt like a puddle herself sometimes, expecting to be stomped and jumped in, instead of being carefully stepped around without making a splash.

"COME ON, YOU'RE going to miss your stop." She felt a jab in her arm. Abruptly, Mindy jolted awake to find Tzippy hovering over her. The bus was empty; as usual, they were the last ones on.

"I said come on, you need to get off here," Tzippy repeated impatiently.

In surprise, Mindy followed the other girl off the bus. They stepped down onto the sidewalk. "Bye." Her classmate shrugged and headed on home. Mindy stood, confused, watching as she disappeared in the distance. Since when did Tzippy ever do anything nice for *her*?

THE NEXT DAY at school, Tzippy was back to her usual bullying self and Mindy thought she'd only imagined the hint of emotion hiding beneath the girl's surface. And yet, during the coming weeks, there were flashes in the darkness. Again, Tzippy woke her when she fell asleep on the bus and walked part of the way home with her, even if it was in sullen silence. In the mornings, when they were alone at the bus stop, Tzippy would attempt some feeble form of conversation. She no longer treated her as if she were an annoying insect to be stepped on. But in the classroom, Tzippy was the true intimidator, surrounded by her bodyguards like a top army general.

"WHAT ARE YOU doing?"

It was morning recess and Mindy unexpectedly entered the classroom. She was surprised to find Tzippy bent over Shevi Stern's schoolbag. Tzippy jumped up guiltily, clutching a shiny red apple in her hand. The two girls stood before one another as Mindy surveyed the scene.

"You're not stealing that, are you?" she asked.

"No," Tzippy answered hurriedly. "Shevi said I could have it. I forgot to bring food today."

MINDY WASN'T CONVINCED. She found herself paying more attention to Tzippy's behavior. Actually, it seemed like most days Tzippy didn't bring food to school, and if she did, it was very little. On several occasions Mindy heard her asking girls for something to eat. *Gosh, it looked like the girl was hungry!* Then Mindy also began noticing Tzippy's appearance. Sometimes she arrived at school with wrinkled clothes and unwashed hair. Over time, Mindy began bringing a little extra food every morning and quietly slipping it into Tzippy's bag. Why she did it, she didn't know. The two girls never said a word about it, but an unspoken agreement hung between them.

THE STRANGE ROUTINE continued; Mindy slipping Tzippy food, yet in public still bearing the brunt of the girl's jokes. They were definitely far less than before, though, and not nearly as vicious. In fact, Mindy felt intuitively that Tzippy had to keep up with her games, maybe to maintain some kind of outward appearance. A strange transformation was taking place in Mindy. She was no longer as afraid of her classmate; in fact, there were times that she felt downright sorry for her.

"WOW, YOU SURE are hungry these days," Mindy's mother said. Mindy was preparing sandwiches for school the next day when her mother walked up behind her in the kitchen. "Don't I feed you enough?" Mrs. Klein laughed. "Or are you just growing?"

"No… it's not that," Mindy replied uncomfortably. She could never lie to her mother. "Actually, it's not all for me."

"Oh," said Mrs. Klein in surprise. "So who's it for?"

All at once the whole story came pouring out. Mindy told her everything: about the bullying and the misery she'd endured; about feeling inferior to her siblings; about the strange act of giving food to a girl who had hurt her so much. Mrs. Klein was horrified to hear what her daughter had been struggling with.

"Why on earth didn't you tell me?" she asked Mindy in shock.

"I didn't want to bother you and I didn't think you could help," Mindy responded. "I was afraid that if I said anything it would make things worse for me."

Mrs. Klein shook her head sadly. "I did notice your unhappiness, but I presumed you were having a hard time adjusting to a new school. Oh, Mindy, I'm so sorry you've had to suffer through this by yourself." She hugged her daughter tightly, her eyes wet. "I'm here now, though, to help you any way I can."

Mindy thought for a moment. "You know, Mommy, I don't think I need it. I'm handling things… getting stronger. I'm changing."

Mrs. Klein gazed at her daughter with admiration. "Well, you know that I'm always here if you need me."

"Thanks," Mindy said, then wrinkled her forehead in concentration as if still trying to figure something out. "Why do I do it, Mommy?"

"Do what?"

"Why do I help a girl who hates me?"

Mindy's mother gathered her child closer. "First," she said, "the girl doesn't hate you…she hates herself. And second, kindness and compassion are your strengths. You've always had a golden heart."

AS SOON AS she opened her eyes she knew she wasn't going. Her mother had tried to wake her three times so she wouldn't miss the school bus, but Mindy just pulled the covers over her head and muttered something about a stomachache. Mrs. Klein decided to let her sleep. Her daughter deserved a day off. So the bus came and went, without her.

MINDY KNEW EXACTLY where she was headed. It had taken some coaxing to persuade her mother to let her take a walk, but she simply had to visit her cave. Lately, there'd been signs that someone else had discovered her safe haven — food other than hers had been left for Puddles; a pink handkerchief was crumpled in a corner of the rug; an old candy wrapper on the floor. A fierce feeling of possessiveness welled up inside her. Who, she wondered, had discovered her hiding place?

Last night's rain had fallen heavily, leaving huge puddles of dirty water in the mud. Carefully, she stepped over them, catching her reflection in the pools. She arrived at her cavern, began to crawl through the narrow opening… and then stopped. *What was that noise?* Suddenly, she was on alert, uneasiness gnawing at her stomach. Cautiously, she continued, holding her flashlight down by her side. *Should she turn it on or not?* There it was again, a muffled sound from inside the cave. Nervously, she moved forward, and then, as she slipped into the dark room, she saw her! Squatting on the ground, back towards her, was a girl with long black hair tumbling down her shoulders, cradling Puddles in her arms and softly crying. There was something vaguely familiar about the huddled form on the floor. Switching on the flashlight, Mindy shone it straight at her and the girl turned, startled. Their eyes met.

"What," Mindy cried, "are *you* doing here?"

Tzippy, her usual fiery eyes now glazed with tears, slumped low amongst the leaves, curling into herself like the cat she was holding.

"My parents were fighting again."

"How did you find…?"

"I've been watching, following you for a long time."

Mindy was quiet, confusion raining over her like a sudden spring shower. Tzippy, tears streaming faster now, looked up into Mindy's eyes.

"I… I've been wanting to talk to you…"

Mindy only stared in silence.

"I need you to help me, to help me stop."

All the anger that had been stored inside Mindy for months roared into flames. "Help *you*, why should I? You've made my life unbearable!"

Tzippy hung her head. "I know," she whispered, "and I'm sorry."

"Just *sorry*, that's all?"

"Yes… I mean no. I mean… I'm sorry, I really am."

Tzippy's sobs swallowed up the surrounding silence, soaking the walls of the cave.

An urge to strike back, to wound this girl's soul, surged inside Mindy. Let her carry the bruised heart that was buried inside her chest. Help her… how dare she ask? She owed her nothing!

"I was jealous," Tzippy said quietly.

"*Jealous*… of who?"

"Of you — you're smart, kind; you have parents who love you."

"So do you."

"I don't think so, I don't know. Usually they're too busy arguing to notice me. And my mom… well, she's not like other moms, keeping house and things like that. She doesn't manage too well."

Mindy focused her gaze on the girl before her, now raw and exposed, like a broken bone poking out from damaged flesh. Her usual arrogant stance was gone; she seemed so harmless now. How could she have once been terrified of her? Against her will, tiny twinges of compassion stirred inside her, that same pity that had compelled her to feed a hungry girl who was bullying her.

"Will you help me?" Tzippy asked again. "Please?"

Silence stretched between them like a long, desert road. After several strung-out moments, Mindy spoke.

"How," she asked carefully, "do you think I can do that?"

"You never told anyone." Tzippy seemed back in time now, "never got me into trouble, not even once. And you've been bringing me food every day, despite how I treated you." She paused.

"I'd... I'd like to be your friend." Her eyes were tightly closed, her forehead creased as if that would make it happen on the spot.

"You see," Tzippy continued, tracing the line of Puddles's fur, "I want to change, to be nicer, kinder; I just don't know how."

Mindy nodded towards the cat lying in Tzippy's lap. "Well," she said, "it looks like you're making a start."

Slowly, Mindy knelt down beside her on the floor. Puddles, as if on cue, stretched his legs, let out a lazy yawn and dipped his head into her lap, his hind legs still curled on Tzippy. And they stayed like that, the three of them, sheltered in the doorway, watching the glint of the sudden sun in the puddles, making rainbows.

This story was motivated by certain classroom dynamics that my young daughter was experiencing at the time. It wasn't bullying, exactly, but rather certain friends of my daughter picking up on her naivete and vulnerability and exploiting it. It felt as if my husband and I were forever trying to teach her to stand up for herself. A lack of self-confidence was embedded inside my sensitive child, though, and girls who called themselves her friends used that to the point that they could sometimes be controlling or manipulative. It pained us to no end and I wanted to write about it in an anonymous setting. Once I started writing, this is what came out... not the same scenario as ours, but similar.

Looking back on it now, I'm not thrilled with the writing. I can't say it's one of my favorites. It's definitely not one of my better stories either, from a literary point of view, but I realized that it was probably cathartic because once I had the words down on paper, I finally understood the vulnerability in the girls who were being controlling. And that made it powerful for me, too!

Beneath the Surface

"NOW REMEMBER, I'M only going this one time."

"Fine," Shani says. "But let's hurry or we'll be late."

"I don't know why I agreed to this," I grumble on the way to the bus stop. "These things are not my cup of tea, and on top of that, it's *raining!*"

Shani smiles as she struggles with the big black umbrella that she grabbed quickly on the way out of the house.

"Just think." I leap back as a car whizzes past, dousing me with water. "I could be at home now, snuggled up underneath a blanket with a book, hot chocolate and…"

"A plate of chocolate chip cookies," Shani finishes off neatly.

I glare at my soon-to-be ex-friend. "So I like eating; what's wrong with that? It doesn't mean I need to go to some meeting because of it."

"You're right," Shani agrees, giving up on her umbrella when she sees the bus arriving. "I never said you did."

SHANI HASN'T STOPPED talking about this meeting she started attending after Yossi ended up in an alcohol rehabilitation program. Honestly, I don't know why she goes; she's not the type to sit in a room with a bunch of women griping over their misfortunes, or at least that's not the way I perceive her. Still, I must admit that something has changed in her the past few months. I can't quite put my finger on what it is; she seems calmer, more relaxed. Anyway, if these meetings are good for her, I'm happy, especially with Yossi's situation being so complicated. *Baruch Hashem*, my Ariella's issues are not nearly as bad as his! But Shani's been pestering me about it for months, so I figured that I'd go this one time and finally get her off my back.

"THIS IS IT," Shani announces. "We're here."

"What kind of place is this?" I say, staring at an aging Jerusalem stone apartment building that looks as if the stones are falling out. "Is it safe?"

"Yes," Shani laughs. "It's just old."

There are several women there when we arrive, sitting around in a circle on brown vinyl chairs with armrests, chattering together in low voices. I hang back hesitantly, reluctant to go forward.

"Come, Miri," Shani beckons, "take a seat." I slip into a chair beside her, sliding down as low as I can, hoping I can disappear and no one will notice me until the night is over.

"Now remember," Shani instructs me, "when a woman 'shares' with the group, we don't respond. No questions or comments, only listening."

"Don't worry," I mutter. "I'm not planning on saying a word."

Now that I've slunk back behind Shani, I can get a good view without being seen and take stock of the participants. Like the two of us, most of the women look middle-aged, except for the lady who's wearing bright blue bohemian pants and sporting a spikey blonde haircut that's clearly dyed. She seems kind of ageless, but it's hard to tell with all the get-up. Seeing her makes me uncomfortable; she looks so… well, secular. Even stranger is that she's sitting next to a chassidish lady. I nudge Shani and motion to them.

Shani squirms in her seat. "I told you that this group is for everyone… all types."

I eye the chassidish lady suspiciously. What on earth is a woman in thick black stockings and a turban doing with this crowd? What would she know about kids or spouses with addictions? This is getting stranger by the minute, stirring up a ripple of uneasiness in the pool of my stomach.

Another woman walks in, says hello and squeezes herself into one of the chairs. She's heavier than me, which is something, I suppose, because I must admit that I've gained quite a bit lately, since Ariella started giving us trouble. Ephraim's not happy about that, although he tries not to openly criticize, but even he couldn't hide his pleasure when he heard I'd be coming with Shani this evening. Personally, I don't see the connection, other than the fact that I'm trying to keep everyone happy.

The lady on the other side of Shani is extraordinarily glamorous, dressed fashionably and wearing enough make-up and perfume to keep Estee Lauder in business for another decade. I nudge Shani again, lean over and whisper.

"Do you think that's a *sheitel*?" I ask, indicating the long, black, wavy hair cascading down her back.

Shani glances sideways, and then nods quickly.

"No way," I say in astonishment.

Shani opens her mouth to reply but another lady enters and starts taking charge. "She's the leader today," Shani explains quietly. "She'll guide the group and make sure it runs according to the structure. That way, we can keep some order."

I nod silently, feeling like a six-year-old child on her first day of school all over again: fresh faces of potential friends, a new teacher, strange rules — and desperately wanting to run back home to my warm bed and hot cocoa.

THE FIRST LADY to "share" is the bohemian woman, who I notice has a small silver ring twinkling from her left nostril. When she opens her mouth, I brace myself, because I know that I'm not going to like what she has to say one bit. Her outlook is no doubt similar to that of my liberal, non-religious relatives.

"Hi, I'm Linda," she begins, and pauses.

I nudge Shani and whisper, "Is she new here?"

"No, she's not. It's common practice for people to reintroduce themselves whenever they speak."

"Oh."

Linda continues, "I originally came here only to get visitation rights for my son. The court ordered me to attend a 12-step series after Yaron was sent to a juvenile rehabilitation program. I wouldn't have come if not for that, but now... I'm so glad I did."

I see Shani nodding her head understandingly, and I raise my eyebrows quizzically as Linda speaks on.

"I would have done anything for my son, to save him from the destructive lifestyle he's chosen. But I realize now that I can't. This group has shown me that I can't live his life for him or protect him from himself; I can only change *myself*. Each of you, in your own way, reaches out to me, sustaining me with strength and support, and I'm learning to let go and trust in G-d more and more."

Oh, please. I roll my eyes. Is she for real? And the religious stuff? Just look at her... who is she kidding?

The next person to speak is the glitzy lady with the wig, who introduces herself as Devora. She sits perfectly poised, legs crossed and hands folded neatly in her lap.

"I... I come from a family of very high achievers," she begins, with a quiver in her voice. "My mother was literally superwoman, always put together perfectly and running countless organizations and *chessed* programs while raising her ten children."

She pauses a moment to take a breath and I am momentarily taken off guard by her obvious insecurity. It's becoming clear that her clothes are not a reflection of her confidence.

"I pushed Ayala a lot," Devora continues, "to be the best in everything — the top student, the star performer... and now... now, it seems as if she's the best dropout." She sounds dangerously close to tears, and for a second I wonder how embarrassed she'll feel with all that mascara running down her face, but I quickly admonish myself. After all, she is clearly in pain.

"Coming to my first meeting was one of the hardest things I've ever done," Devora raises her head in shy pride. "It felt like an admission of guilt over how bad a mother I was." She smiles now, a soft, hopeful smile. "But from my very first meeting, I found a glimmer of hope. People understood how I felt; they didn't judge me. I am beginning to get past my guilt at being a bad parent and I'm slowly starting to understand that I did the best I could under the circumstances. Since I'm happier with myself, my relationship with my daughter has improved." Her smile brightens like a fluorescent light. "I did a lot of good things as a parent, too, and I have other children who are doing fine and don't have the same struggles as Ayala."

The sound of a buzzer almost makes me jump out of my seat.

"What's that for?" I question Shani.

"It's to let the person know her time is up," Shani explains quietly. "Everyone has to keep to her three minutes."

"Oh," I say, because that's all I can think of.

The overweight lady raises her hand and begins to speak.

"Hi, I'm Shaindy, and I'm the wife of a gambler." She takes a deep breath. "My father had a very bad temper, and I've used food to comfort myself from his anger since I was a child. I became overweight by age ten and by high school, I was obese. When I ate, it relieved the stress and tension and made me feel better, but I was just using food as a means of stuffing down the emotional pain. Since I started attending these meetings a month ago, I've lost five kilos, which is a big accomplishment for me, because I would always start a diet, stop in the middle and resort to binge eating afterwards. For the first time in my life, I'm sticking to something and giving myself boundaries — and beginning to put some on my family members, too."

Wow, five kilos! She must have been huge! I think to myself.

Shaindy talks a little more about how chaotic life is when living with a person who has an addiction, and how the 12-step program is helping her to make some order again. I vaguely hear the rest of her speech as I drift in and out of something: disdain, pity, perhaps... or confusion... But whatever it is, it's stirred up those ripples inside my stomach again.

"Is there anybody here tonight for the first time?" I suddenly hear the leader ask. Two women raise their hands. I keep mine firmly glued to my lap.

"We have some literature in the box on the table, called the newcomer's pamphlet, which you are welcome to take home. And please... don't form any opinions based on one meeting."

No problem, I think to myself, *because I'm not coming back anyway.* I turn to Shani. "Are we going home now?"

IT'S STILL RAINING outside. Funny, really, because I expected things to have changed somehow, although I'm not sure why. Shani's awfully quiet — too quiet. It makes me nervous.

"So, the bohemian woman," I begin. "How can she say she's religious? Just look at the way she's dressed. And of course her kid would end up addicted to something or other — those kinds of things are rampant in secular high schools."

Shani shoots me a quick glance. "I hope the bus comes soon," she says. "I'm cold."

"And what's her name — Devora — well, it's not surprising that her daughter rebelled, growing up with so much pressure."

Shani gives me a curious look, although it's hard to really see her face in the darkness. But I hear the tone of her voice, wounded and hurt.

"So how do you explain *my* situation?" she asks softly. "Are Yossi's problems my fault, too?"

Not for the first time this evening, I am speechless. I frantically try to find words that will erase my insensitive statement, but I know there are none.

I CAN'T SLEEP. It's nothing new, of course. How many nights have I lain awake, staring at the darkened ceiling and praying that I'll hear the sound of the front door, signaling Ariella's safe arrival home? I'm an expert insomniac nowadays, but this time is different, because Ariella's in bed sleeping for a change. I keep hearing Shani's voice inside my head. I've insulted her, even though I didn't mean to, and that makes me feel guilty. I hate that, the guilt. There's so much of it, about almost *everything*, poured over my head like sticky black tar.

I feel a wave of sadness rise up in my throat, warning that I'm close to tears. I don't want to cry… So I do what I always do best: climb out of bed, wander into the kitchen and find myself something to eat!

THE LINGERING, BITTER taste of those twilight cinnamon buns is what's brought me back again this week. That, and a sense of responsibility towards Shani, although I can't really explain that.

"This is the last time," I tell Shani. "And I'm not planning on doing any of that sharing stuff, either."

"Fine," she says, "whatever you like."

I see that the bohemian lady is back, and Devora and Shaindy. "Where's the leader from last week?" I ask Shani after we sit down.

"Over there," she nods. "She's not leading today. We rotate so that everyone can have a turn."

After the readings or whatever they're called, a young woman raises her hand to "share." I don't recall seeing her last time, but maybe I'm wrong. She's thin — stick thin, like she could snap in a second — and her gaunt face is pinched as if it's stapled together.

"Hi, I'm Ruti, and I'm addicted to pain-relieving medication," she begins.

My head jerks up. Now this should be interesting.

"Looking back," she says, "I see how easy it was to use my arthritis as an excuse to swallow another pill and another, because that's what painkillers do… relieve pain, temporarily, until they wear off."

I'm listening, sitting straight in my chair, really intrigued. Ruti's story is not what I'd expected in this group.

"The more I took, the more I needed," Ruti carries on. "And then, of course, I needed stronger medication, because the others were no longer effective. Until today, I cannot understand how my doctor kept on prescribing them, but he did."

"Me neither," I mutter to Shani. "Grossly irresponsible!"

"It's a miracle that I'm alive," Ruti gives a small, grateful smile. "I could have developed irreversible liver damage on top of my arthritis. I've enrolled in an exercise program, and the 12-step meetings have helped me understand why I developed this dependency. I don't feel as guilty over it as I once did — I know it could happen to anyone — but my sponsor is helping me dig up the deeper reason for why it happened to *me*."

The buzzer goes off. I gaze around the room, wondering who's going to share next, and the quiet moments niggle on my nerves, making me shift in my seat.

Another lady starts talking. "A few months ago I attended a couple of meetings, but stopped coming because nothing changed... my son was still using drugs. I felt angry, frustrated and depressed, and didn't want to sit around listening to other people's problems because *mine* were much more important. I can't remember when that magical moment was, but I suddenly started to listen, and I've been coming here and listening ever since. Today, I wouldn't dream of missing a meeting. Regardless of what's going on in my life, I need to be here, absorbing the positive energy and warmth from this group. It gives me the strength to continue my journey."

After she finishes speaking, silence settles over the room like a protective awning. But even though it's quiet I am still hearing, *listening* to the voices continuing to share wordlessly. It's a strange feeling, unfamiliar, unsettling... yet ironically comforting. From the corner of my eye, I see Shani raise her hand. Oh, no! She's not going to speak, is she? But she is, and if she notices me squirming at her side, she doesn't acknowledge it.

"Hi, I'm Shani, the mother of a teenage alcoholic. Before I attended these meetings I was a disaster, spiritually, mentally and physically. I couldn't concentrate on anything. Some days just getting out of bed was too much; my life was consumed by chaos and crisis, and I felt that Hashem had deserted me. From the very beginning, I felt that all of you accepted me the way I was — no judgment, only encouragement to keep coming back."

I watch Shani intently, concentrate on her words, and shudder momentarily with shame for not having realized the extent of her suffering.

"Through the 12-step program, I have changed," Shani says in a voice that's strong and steady. "I've become happy with the person I am and appreciate who I'm becoming. The way I look at the world has changed. I no longer blame my son, but see him as an opportunity for me to connect to Hashem, to grow and become the person I'm meant to be."

This is it, I realize as I listen in awe. *This is the change that I detected in her.*

"And there's something else I just want to say about the meetings," Shani goes on. "I like it that no one responds to what we share. It's not a conversation that we're having in these rooms, but something deeper, more intimate. And the silence after someone shares… I like that. It feels like there's respect in that silence, respect for my pain and confusion. There's love here, too, complete and unconditional love, that's warm and safe."

As her voice slowly winds down, Shani doesn't look at me, but she gives my hand a quick squeeze that pushes all of my undigested pain to the surface. And then it's quiet… hushed and still, with unspoken understanding and connection — far deeper than what is on the surface.

THIS WEEK WILL be number five. Who would have thought that I'd still be here, pulled by some invisible string that binds these women together? I've started to like the bohemian lady. (Maybe I should stop calling her that and use her name instead.) Really, I admire how she handles her difficult situation, how she's working on herself and her relationship with Hashem. If someone had suggested five weeks ago that I'd feel comfortable with these women who are so different from me, I'd have said they were crazy. Okay, I admit that I still struggle with acceptance sometimes — probably with accepting myself, mostly — but it's coming slowly. Maybe soon, when I'm able, I'll actually introduce myself to the group…

Shani and I take our usual seats. I give her a warm smile. She smiles back. "Good to have you here," she says.

"I'm glad you brought me," I answer, and I mean it.

Ruchie, the chassidish lady, is leading the group tonight: a fine, *aidel* woman whose insular life has been turned upside down by the harmful influences of the outside world. She's impressive in the way she carries herself, regal and refined although she's in a place she never thought she'd end up in. I didn't expect it, either — to be sitting here, I mean. But here I am, and I actually want to be here, and that realization makes me swallow hard to untie the emotional knot that's tangled in my throat.

Suddenly, I am crying. I don't want to cry, but the tears come anyway. I should be embarrassed, but I'm not. I'm crying for myself and for everyone else here, the women who may have different stories than me but whose feelings are just the same as mine. I'm crying because it feels good to finally let out the anguish, to feel it as it tumbles down my cheeks and not be afraid of it, because all of us are fighting the same battle even if on the outside we wear different armor.

I sense words forming, sitting on the edge of my tongue as if it's a cliff, deciding whether to make the leap. My mouth is like a dry, dusty desert and I reach for the cup on the armrest and gulp down some water. Ever so slowly, I raise my hand.

"Hi… I'm Miri…"

Wow, I just read this story again after two years and I found myself wondering how I wrote it. This was a commissioned story assigned to me by my Binah editors. They asked me to write a story based in a setting of an Al Anon meeting. It was meant to go into the Tisha B'Av issue, fitting into the theme of ahavas Yisrael. I remember wondering how an Al Anon group would fit that theme and how on earth I would write a story about it. My goal was to attend a group to see for myself what goes on but I didn't have the time; instead, I did a lot of research. Looking back at the story now, I see that I really did have the lingo down as well as the group protocol. Reading it again reminded me of that. As I was presenting the story based in a group setting, it had to be as authentic as possible and I hope I achieved that.

It is always challenging to write about something I'm unfamiliar with, but ultimately that much more rewarding if I can pull it off properly. There were two things that I especially wanted to bring out that were particularly connected to sinas chinam and the destruction of the Beis Hamikdash and ahavas Yisrael. First of all, the skepticism expressed by Miri in the story was a clear example of the judgmental attitudes we can have in situations where we feel different and uncomfortable. Unfortunately, this way of thinking is prevalent in our society, often breeding animosity and sometimes hatred, none of which can bring Moshiach and the rebuilding of our holy Temple. In contrast, an Al Anon meeting is a place where everybody feels welcome regardless of who they are or their level of religious observance. Everyone in the room is in the same boat, struggling together and feeling completely accepted. That is ahavas Yisrael.

So… even though I was baffled at the beginning as to how a story about an Al Anon group could fit into a Tisha B'Av theme, you can see that it did. I just had to learn to trust my editors!

Cleaning Out

"HE SOUNDS REALLY nice, Chavi, why don't you give it a try?"

"I told you, Nechama, it's too soon. I'm not ready yet."

A frustrated sigh rustled through the phone like wind in a drafty building.

"Chavi, it's been three years now," Nechama tried again. "When do you think you will be ready?"

"I don't know," Chavi said quietly. "We've been through this before. I need more time, that's all."

"And meanwhile you could miss an amazing opportunity. This could be just what you need to help you move on and rebuild your life."

"But that's just it, Nechama, I'm not sure I can."

LOGICALLY, SHE KNEW her way of thinking wasn't right, but emotionally, she couldn't let go, clinging to his memory like a crying child at her mother's leg. Maybe it was the lack of preparation that had made everything so difficult, for even though they'd both known from the way things were heading what the outcome could be, they'd never actually discussed it. His family knew, too, but nobody spoke openly, creeping around instead like covert undercover agents. Yaakov's family was like that. Things such as

Yaakov's illness could be staring them in the face like a red traffic light, yet they'd still drive right past it.

Fortunately for Chavi, her own parents were very supportive and her older sister Nechama had been like a lifeboat, picking her up frequently when she was pulled out to sea by the strong current. But it wasn't the same, somehow. She'd needed to talk to *him*; to tell him all the things one should say after ten years of marriage; to tell him what a wonderful husband and father he was; to tell him how much she loved him; to share the pain of wondering how she would carry on alone; to ask him about the "what after." She cared for him, nursed him, slept on a fold-out couch beside his hospital bed, patiently spoon-fed him the blended food she'd so carefully prepared, administered all of his many medications — and yet, they still never talked about "It."

So when "It" happened, Chavi took the disconnected pieces of her broken heart, the small holes in its chambers that sometimes made it hard to breathe… and waited. She was still waiting for the scar tissue to fade so the main arteries could open, enabling her to flow again without the anguish and unanswered questions sitting on her chest.

"SO, DID YOU think it over?" Nechama was nothing if not persistent. "You can take things very slowly, I promise. He's getting over the loss of his wife, so he's also not in a rush."

"I… er… I don't know. Who will watch the kids? And there's so much to do before Pesach; it's not a good time now."

"No problem," Nechama sprung up with a solution. "I'll send Rochel over to babysit and don't worry about Pesach; Dina and Rochel can both help you out. I have Shiftzi and Temima home from sem, so I don't need everyone."

"I don't know," Chavi hesitated, stalling as usual. "I'm not sure I can. It doesn't seem right."

"Well," said Nechama decisively, "you can decide that once

you've met him. One time won't hurt, will it? Good, so that's final then. Wednesday evening, eight p.m. at the Plaza."

"HI MOMMY, CAN I go to…" eleven-year-old Shayna stopped abruptly like a train screeching to a halt. "Wow! You look nice. I haven't seen you dressed up like that in ages. Where are you going?"

Chavi stood in front of the hallway mirror, putting the finishing touches to her make-up. Her hands wobbled so nervously it was a wonder she looked semi-normal.

"I'm just going out for a little while. Rochel is coming to babysit soon. Can you manage with the kids on your own until she gets here?"

"Sure, but *where* are you going? You *never* go out, even to *simchos*. You're always home."

"I know, honey, you're used to that." Chavi opened the hall closet and reached for her coat. She gave her intuitive elder daughter a light kiss on her forehead. "It's just this one time. Don't worry, nothing's going to change."

ONCE SHE'D QUIETED the churning in her stomach, she had to admit that getting out was nice. *He* was nice; the entire evening was nice. She and Ben Zion Weiss had much in common; two lonely souls who'd lost their spouses at a young age, who'd faced tragedy head-on yet not been broken by it. Surprisingly, despite their sad pasts, the night had not been melancholy at all. They'd talked and laughed and the atmosphere had grown pleasantly lighter over each passing hour. Their sons were a similar age so they'd delighted in reviewing the antics of energetic boys. Chavi found the hours floating by like sweet fluffy clouds on a spring day and was surprised to find it was time to go home. It had been a lovely evening, if it weren't for the guilt she'd felt for enjoying it.

"NU?"

"Nu, what?"

"Well, did you like him?"

"Nosey, aren't you, my dear sister."

"Come on, just tell me already," Nechama said impatiently. "What did you think?"

"Well," said Chavi carefully, "he's very nice and I had a lovely time…"

"But?" Nechama filled in the empty space.

"I don't know. It's too soon. It would be hard for the kids."

Nechama paused, searching for the right words. "Just try, Chavi. Give it one more chance. After that we can talk about the children."

MUCH TO CHAVI'S amazement, that "one more chance" evolved into several meetings. She *really* didn't have time for them with Pesach looming on the horizon, yet for some reason she went anyway and returned each time happier and more revitalized than before. She hadn't felt so alive in years. She pondered that briefly as she climbed the stairs late one afternoon, while simultaneously mentally reviewing her Pesach preparations. She would start the upstairs rooms first, she decided. Shayna and Ariella were old enough to clean most of their room and Yitzi could help with his and Shimon's. That left hers, the bathrooms and… and the office… Yaakov's study. She wouldn't touch that, of course. That room remained just the way it was, undisturbed and preserved like a shrine in his memory. She couldn't even bear to go in there; it was just too painful. She did need the space, though, Chavi reflected as she made her way across the landing at the top of the stairs. It would be useful for guests, as well as for Shayna who was getting older and would soon want her privacy.

She caught the faint sound of voices creeping down the hallway. Ah, the girls were back from school, talking in their bedroom; they must have come home without her hearing them. A warm feeling comforted Chavi when she thought of her two girls together like that, chattering and giggling the way sisters do. Strange, though, that they hadn't come to say hello, Chavi reflected, but never mind, she would just pop her head in and say hi. With her hand raised to gently tap on the door, she paused. The girls were talking in low voices and something about those hushed tones made her stop a moment and listen.

"So where do you think she's going?" Ariella's soft nine-year-old voice slipped underneath the doorway.

"I don't know for sure," Shayna's stronger voice answered back, "but I think she's meeting someone."

"Like who?" Ariella sounded puzzled. "You mean like one of our teachers?"

"No, silly. Why do you think she keeps getting so dressed up to go out? She's planning to get married again. That happened to a girl in my class and she's really miserable now."

"What? Another Tatty?" Ariella gasped. "How could she do that? I don't want another Tatty."

"Shush, keep your voice down or Mommy will hear us," Shayna whispered.

Chavi could hear Ariella's muffled sobs through the door and for a moment she almost went in to comfort her, to reassure her that she would never ever bring home a new father whom they wouldn't like, that their happiness always came first. But for some reason she didn't. Instead, she remained outside the doorway, a thin partition between them, as she listened shamefully to her daughters' sad conversation.

"Don't worry," Shayna's big sister voice was firm and reassuring. "I won't let it happen. No one else is coming into our family!"

"SO YOU SEE, I can't do it to the kids," Chavi explained to Nechama for the tenth time.

"Do *what*, Chavi? Give them a normal home, a father, stability?

What exactly would you be *doing?*" Nechama was growing more frustrated by the minute.

"It's too soon. They're not ready yet, that's clear. Things are fine the way they are."

"Are they?" Nechama persisted. "Are you all happy like this?"

"Happy? Well, of course we're not completely *happy,*" Chavi's voice wobbled towards the edge of tears. "How could we be?"

"So don't you think," Nechama suggested in a soft voice, "that Hashem wants your happiness, for you to have a home that's complete? And Yaakov would definitely have wanted that too."

"I… I don't know. That's the problem. Yaakov never told me… he never *said* it."

"Did he need to? Did you need to hear the words from his mouth?"

Chavi fell into a pensive silence. "You know," she said at last, "maybe the problem's with me? Maybe I need to believe and trust that's what he'd have wanted? Let me wait a bit," she proposed. "At least until after Pesach. It will give me time to think things over."

OF COURSE, WITH all the frenzied Pesach preparations, Chavi was so busy cleaning, scrubbing and polishing that she had no time for anything, let alone to think. She wanted to sit down with the girls and talk about what she'd overheard that day but she couldn't fit that in either, although truthfully, she was most likely avoiding the subject. She didn't really know what to tell them, not when she herself was so jumbled up and confused. At least Ben Zion hadn't pressurized her when she'd put things on hold, so she didn't have that to worry about. In the meantime, she placed the Ben Zion Weiss issue into a pocket of her mind until she could take it out and examine it properly. But a fleeting thought sailed through Chavi's head. Usually there was no space inside her for anyone else except Yaakov and the children, yet somehow she'd managed to squeeze Ben Zion into his own special corner.

"Mommy," Shayna's voice interrupted her contemplations, "are we going to Tante Nechama for *Leil Haseder?*"

Chavi looked up, startled, and straightened up from the couch she was cleaning. "Of course, honey, like usual. Why do you ask?"

"Oh, I don't know really. Just thought you might have other plans." She stared uncomfortably at the floor, rocking on her feet back and forth.

"What other plans were you thinking of?" Chavi asked, puzzled.

"Never mind, it doesn't matter," Shayna brushed off the question like an annoying insect.

"What's the matter, Shayna?" Chavi probed. "Don't you want to go to your cousins?"

"Yes, of course… I just wondered if you do, that's all."

The strange conversation was getting Chavi increasingly perplexed.

"Why wouldn't I want to go, honey? We've gone to Nechama's house every year since…"

The sentence remained dangling in the air like an empty light socket.

"… Tatty died," Shayna inserted the light bulb. "And what will we do when we get a new Tatty? Will we still go then?"

All of a sudden the switch flicked on in Chavi's head and she groped in the sudden glare to find the right words, calming sentences that would allay her daughter's fears, but in her congested state of mind, there were none. As Shayna swept out of the room, leaving a whoosh of cold air behind her, all the unspoken reassurance was left hanging like a giant question mark.

Chavi stared after the empty doorway, wondering who was more confused, she or her child. It was so very difficult to integrate the past and future. Would they ever combine comfortably? Her mind slipped back inside the memories of beautiful *Seder* nights in her home; Yaakov reigning like a true king at the table and the children, although young, enthralled by his descriptive narratives of the *Hagaddah* that brought the Exodus from Eygpt to life. *Emunah* and *bitachon*, the very essence of Pesach, had been a special strength of her late husband's. He'd always believed that whatever he suffered was for the best, exactly the way Hashem wanted it, and his words came from a deep, sincere place, not like a stage performance in an amateur play. A tear sneaked out of Chavi's eye and she wiped it away quickly before others could follow. No, she wasn't going there. What was the point in looking back?

She reached for the vacuum cleaner that was standing in the corner, switched it on and let herself disappear into the loud sucking noise. Maybe that thin, twisty pipe could suction her up as well?

IT HAD TAKEN every ounce of courage she possessed to make the call, but she had to do this if she wanted to move on. She couldn't make any decisions, provide any support for her children, if she didn't start making space, and here, it seemed, was the right place to start. She dialed a familiar phone number and waited for the voice at the other end. "Nechama," she said quickly, before she could change her mind, "can you please come over? I need your help with cleaning out."

"I DON'T KNOW where to begin," said Chavi, looking around the room anxiously. "What should we do first?"

"How about the desk drawers for starters and then we can move to the shelves with the *sefarim*," Nechama advised.

Agitation was aging Chavi's face by the minute. "It's… hard for me. I'm not sure I can do it."

"I know," said Nechama gently. "That's why we're going to do this together."

Nechama pulled the drawers out onto the floor and Chavi knelt down on the carpet beside her. There were piles of her husband's papers and letters to sift through, stacks of paperwork that had remained untouched except by her brother-in-law on the odd occasions he'd needed something for beauracratic purposes.

"Wow," Nechama exclaimed, intimidated too by the heap that resembled a Lag BaOmer bonfire. "Who knows what we'll find inside here?"

Chavi sighed, a long, deep, sad sigh, and then reached for some papers from the pile.

Intimate moments ticked by as the two sisters sat on the floor surrounded by the memories of a precious soul. They sorted and stacked, read and reread, discarded and saved. Chavi could never have done this alone, and only with someone as sensitive and close to her as Nechama, who could give her time to pause and remember, to reminisce and cry, to share or file away privately.

As they worked quietly together and the light outside dimmed into dusk, Chavi felt the piles of musty memories stacked within her grow smaller and smaller, as she watched the garbage can fill up with old papers. Experiences and events danced around inside her now that space existed; memories of thoughts and conversations and private moments. The sound of Yaakov's laughter pealed merrily along her emptying shelves and rolled into her inner storerooms. Who he was and what they'd had together came flooding back; all of his innate goodness, dependability, the promises he kept. How could she have forgotten all of that? And how could she not want something like it again? Inexplicably, these rusty recollections were not heavy weights that dragged her down, but rather strangely uplifting, lightening the load she'd been carrying inside.

A sudden silence roused her from her reflections and her gaze rested on Nechama, who was sitting forlornly on the floor.

"Nechama," Chavi called softly, "what is it?"

Disappointment clouded Nechama's fine features. "I thought we'd find something," she said quietly. "A letter perhaps; anything that would help you to let go."

Chavi's smile was brighter and infused with a soft glow. "We did. It's a part of the process, but for now, I think I've found what I needed."

THE CUPS OF wine stood like vases of red tulips on the white tablecloth. The *afikoman* had been hidden already and the *Seder* was well underway. As usual, it was *leibedig* at her sister's house with the younger cousins romping around together like playful puppies, except Shayna, who was unusually subdued. She would make some time to talk to Shayna during Pesach, Chavi told herself. She wanted peace and quiet for the conversation and frantic last-minute preparations had not provided that. The atmosphere at Nechama's was warm, loving and resplendent with Hashem's Presence as they recalled what He had done for the Jewish People so very long ago. And yet... something was missing. As utterly welcoming as it was, this wasn't *her* home, *her* husband leading the *Seder* at *her* lovingly prepared table... and a pang of longing tugged at her like a dog on a leash. She pushed the pangs back down; for now, it was time to enjoy the *Seder*.

All too soon it was time to search for the *afikoman* and off the children scampered, scattering in different directions of the house, each one determined to find it first. From the corner of her eye, Chavi noticed Shayna sitting alone on the porch, her usual vivaciousness dimmed by the darkness.

"Shayna," she called out softly as she walked onto the veranda. "Are you all right?"

The light of the street lamps twinkled through the trees and shone on Shayna's face, showing wet, glistening tears.

"Oh, Shayna, why are you crying?" Chavi sat down beside her daughter on the patchwork-quilted couch and slipped her arm around her shoulders.

"I want to go home," Shayna blubbered. "I want to be in my own house."

"But I thought…"

"That I wanted to come here, right? Well, I did… didn't. Oh, I don't know what I wanted. I just want to be a normal family like everyone else."

Chavi let the confused eleven-year-old thoughts settle on her shoulders and rest there a few minutes before she spoke. "Shayna, you know what that means, right? It would mean me getting married again; you having a new father."

Shayna nodded. "Yes, I know that and I don't *want* another Tatty, so I'm really stuck, aren't I?"

"No, not stuck, just frightened. I'm scared too."

"I'll bet you're not frightened of the same thing as me!" Shayna turned to her mother fiercely.

"Try me," Chavi challenged.

Shayna looked at Chavi with big, sad, fear-filled eyes. "Well, what if…?" she hesitated, the fear holding her back. "What if… another Tatty gets sick? Maybe Hashem will take him away too?"

There, she'd said it! She'd voiced the fear for both of them. Chavi closed her eyes tightly, squeezing them shut so the tears wouldn't fall. She pulled her daughter close and hugged her in the darkness, letting the freshly released fear comfort them.

"You know, Shayna," she said at last, "it's often easier to stay the same and not take chances, but that doesn't mean it's better. Look what would have happened if the Jewish People had stayed in Mitzrayim where everything was familiar, yet they were slaves. They didn't know what was waiting for them out there in the desert but they trusted Hashem when they made that enormous leap of faith to leave. It's like that with everything. We need tremendous *emunah* and *bitachon* in order to make changes… but we have to try."

"How do we do that?" Shayna's voice was barely audible.

"By preparing," Chavi answered. "By spiritually getting ready.

By looking back at all the things Hashem has ever done for us and seeing, that although they were hard sometimes, they were good. And of course, by doing our physical *hishtadlus* too."

"Are you going to marry that man, Mommy?" Shayna's voice vacillated between hope and fear.

"Ben Zion... maybe, sweetheart, but not yet. Not before you all meet him and we see how he'll fit into our family. And you need to trust me that I'll never bring someone home who wouldn't be good for us."

"Promise?" Shayna said shyly.

Chavi nodded her head and smiled. "Promise."

She took Shayna's hand in hers and together they returned to the *Seder* table. Her daughter's fingers clasped securely in hers, she sat back in her chair absorbing the freedom of *Yetzias Mitzrayim*, inside and outside of her. She looked at her girls who were growing up too quickly; at her two sons who needed a father to do with them all the things she couldn't. They would need time to adjust to any changes, of course, and she'd do her best to help them. But she had to take that giant step, to entrust herself to Hashem's loving care.

As the *Seder* slowly wound down and finished in a crescendo of *"L'shanah Habah B'Yerushalyim,"* so too, Chavi prayed, "Next year, there'll be a *Seder* in my own home!"

A few years ago my friend lost her husband to a devastating illness right after Pesach. During the previous eight months while he was sick, I watched my friend take care of him. She remained at his side constantly until the moment he passed away. They spoke often during this time about painful and significant things. One of the things they spoke about was what would happen "afterwards." My friend knew that her husband wanted her to remarry and not to remain alone. I remember thinking what a brachah *it was that she had his permission and wondered how a young widow might feel if she didn't. From this thought a story began to form.*

While cleaning for Pesach that year, I spent an extraordinary amount of time going through old letters and greeting cards, sitting on the floor reading my diaries and other things I'd written over the years. Memories of many things came flooding back to me, many of them releasing me from past things I'd held onto. I decided to combine these two ideas and then I had a story. The end of it was a natural progression from the rest and letting the pen take me wherever it wanted to go.

I don't consider this to be one of my better stories; it's probably one of my worst. But the message is important, and sometimes, even if the writing isn't top notch, that's what redeems it.

Going Out

"MICHAL, WILL YOU hurry up? We're going to miss the bus!" My friend Tova stood over me, hands on her hips and a look of exasperation on her face.

"Don't worry," I answered casually, stuffing another towel into my rucksack. "We can always hitch a ride."

"Hitch?" exclaimed Tova. "Isn't that kind of risky?"

"Yeah, but that's what makes things exciting," I said with a smile. "It's called 'living dangerously!'"

Tova let out a deep sigh as I struggled to zip up my bulging rucksack. I stood up, hoisted the pack onto my back, slung my guitar over my shoulder and flashed a quick grin.

"Well, what are you waiting for? Let's go!"

WE WERE ON our way to the Sinai for Pesach, and with our abundant sixteen-year-old enthusiasm, we couldn't wait. I was eager to hike through the wadis and waterfalls left by last winter's abundant rains; to explore hidden caves and caverns chiseled in rock faces. We'd be based in a youth hostel that was a well-known haunt of young Israelis ever since the Sinai had been given over to Egypt many years before.

We anticipated arising each morning to the freshly awakened sun winking through our open window, to the gentle sound of waves licking the shore. What better way to spend Pesach! I wouldn't have to sit through another one of our boring family *Seder* nights that went on forever, with all that wine and Abba checking that we'd eaten exactly the right amount of matzah. I was ready to explode by the end of it. And of course each of my brothers had something to say on the *Haggadah*. I don't know why everyone found their comments so interesting, because as soon as they opened their mouths I was already spacing out. Anyway, there'd be none of that this year. I was heading off to more peaceful places — no rules or people telling me what to do. I was going to free myself from the shackles of religious obligation.

"WOW," SAID TOVA, "it looks like everyone's had the same idea!"

I looked around. The hostel was pretty crowded, packed with teenagers like us, queuing up to register for a room. We signed our names, paid a deposit and lugged our gear upstairs.

"These Egyptians are a bit unnerving, aren't they?" I commented to Tova, as I backed through the door of our room.

"Sure are," Tova agreed. "And isn't it weird, having to cross the border to get here? I feel like we're in a different country."

"Well, we are," I reminded her. "We're in Mitzrayim."

I glanced at the four unoccupied beds pushed against bare, whitewashed walls and threw down my belongings on one of them.

"Come and see the view," Tova beckoned and stepped out onto the balcony.

"Mmm, stunning," I agreed, leaning over the railings and gazing at the sea in the distance. Endless rippling blue stretched out to the end of the world, bordered by soft, silky sand and majestic mountains that looked as if they could touch the sky.

"Come on," I called to Tova, "let's not waste time." I was already clattering down the stairs, heady with happiness and thirsty to drink in our new surroundings.

THE WARM WATER wrapped me in its embrace. I felt so utterly peaceful and accepted as the waves washed over me until I felt cleansed. How fortunate we were to have found this isolated spot away from the crowds. For a brief moment, I thought about Pesach and clearing out the *chametz*, scrubbing and scouring every last corner until our hands hurt and our fingers were sore. Well, I gloated to myself, there are many ways to clean out. This one was definitely liberating!

An hour later, cooled off and laughing, we raced each other back to our little hilltop guesthouse overlooking the shore. Bursting through the door in high spirits, we stopped abruptly.

"Who are you?" I asked the two girls sitting on the remaining two beds.

"Your roommates," the one with long black hair replied complacently. "It's not just *your* room, you know."

"Oh, right," I remembered, a little flustered. "Well," I gestured around the room, "make yourselves comfortable."

Tova shot me a withering glance. "I thought we were going to be by ourselves," she hissed under her breath.

"In a youth hostel? You've got to be kidding. Anyway, it might be interesting to have some company," I hissed back.

"Oh, you and your 'interesting,'" Tova sighed. "Isn't there anything you don't find boring?"

Well, no, actually, there wasn't. I'd been looking for excitement all my life and hadn't found too much of it in my small religious community. Religious life, in my opinion, was downright monotonous, strict… and black. I wanted color, flashing lights, rainbows and fireworks. I wanted storms and sunsets, sand dunes to dive into and hills to roll down. I wanted to sing and dance and wear long, flowing, colorful dresses that floated like my hair in the wind; to sit in a field of yellow buttercups and paint until dusk. I wanted to sleep outdoors beneath twinkling stars and imagine I was one of them. I wanted to be free! Instead, all I got at home were rules,

rules, rules and a depressing sea of black to wade in. It was squeezing the juice from my soul, crushing it and leaving me like the hard stone pit extracted from an olive.

Since childhood I'd been buoyant and exuberant and spent more time out of the classroom than in it. And the inevitable label of "hyperactive" pinned on me about eight years too late was useless, because there was no way I was going to take that Ritalin they prescribed. So trouble and I became good pals, successfully masking the sensitive, creative creature that existed beneath the rough exterior.

"Are you sure you really want to hang out with them?" Tova whispered, nudging me in the ribs. "They look a bit tough." I looked over at the two girls. Actually, they did look rather intimidating, especially the shorter one with the red, spiky hair and angry-looking jewelry, the likes of which I'd never seen.

"I see what you mean," I whispered back, "but we don't have any choice. After all, this isn't a hotel."

Our roommates were settling in, emptying their backpacks, laying out toiletries on the table. The tall girl with the long black hair looked nice enough; at least she didn't wear an angry scowl on her face like her friend. Maybe they wouldn't be too bad after all, as long as they didn't bother us.

Tova wrung the water from her wet towel and hung it to dry over the back of a chair. "Well," she muttered in annoyance, "this is not my idea of a vacation."

I WAS FANNING the flames, trying to get the fire going. Night had fallen and pulled us back outdoors to the large grassy area bordering the sandy beach, where barbecues were already sizzling.

"Maybe we should be friendly and ask them to eat with us?" I suggested to Tova.

"No," said Tova firmly, "we shouldn't." She turned the cooler box upside down and tipped its contents on the ground. "Don't tell me we forgot the meat!" she exclaimed in dismay. "What are we going to do?"

I looked longingly toward our roommates who were barbecuing near us, and the tantalizing aroma of chicken wings, hot dogs and hamburgers tickled my nose.

"Like I said, we could always be friendly."

"UH… THANKS FOR letting us join you. We'll be happy to pay our share or pool our food or…" Oh, this was so embarrassing. I felt almost like a beggar, and it didn't help that Tova was smirking behind me.

"No problem," said the dark-haired girl as she turned over the meat with a long roasting fork. The redhead raised a pierced eyebrow menacingly and for a moment I had second thoughts about this idea. After all, we didn't *have* to eat meat tonight, did we?

"It's fine with me," the dark-haired one confirmed. "What about you, Efrat?"

Efrat, the proud owner of all that metal, gave a grunt, apparently one of agreement.

Ten minutes later the four of us were gathered around their fire, making shy small talk, roasting marshmallows and waiting for the meat to cook. It was *Leil Haseder*!

"Are you actually going to eat bread?" Tova gasped as Efrat pulled out a packet of *pitot*.

"Of course — what's the big deal?" Efrat growled.

"Well… it *is* Pesach. I never eat bread on Pesach."

"Well I do, so mind your own business," Efrat shot back.

I could see where this might lead. Efrat sank her teeth defiantly into her pita while Tova watched in horror. I nibbled nervously on my matzah as the girl continued taking great, gulping bites.

"So," I cleared my throat, "where are you guys from?"

The dark-haired girl, whose name we knew by then was Shuli, let out a bitter laugh. "Do you mean where did we grow up or where do we live at the moment?"

"Whatever…" I really wasn't sure what to answer.

"We live in a… special hostel," the redhead said and shot up suddenly as if she'd been stung. "Our parents kicked us out." Anger oozed from her every pore; bitterness glinted from the earrings that pinched her skin. What was I supposed to say to that?

"Oh, I'm sorry."

"What did you do to get kicked out?" Tova plowed on… innocent, oblivious, like an old cart horse with blinkered eyes. Dear, sweet, sensitive Tova, who'd been orphaned of her mother at the age of thirteen. She didn't have a mean bone in her body. We'd known each other since first grade and made a great team. She was incredibly tolerant of my impulsive, energetic nature and I, deeply aware of her painful loss, protected her as much as I could.

"What *didn't* I do?" Shuli answered scornfully. "When your father's a big *Rosh Yeshivah*, you can never do anything right; nothing's ever good enough. So I did all the wrong things, got caught and then got thrown out. I stayed a while with my brother and his wife until they couldn't put up with me either. As soon as I can buy a ticket, they'll all be rid of me, because I'm going to America to make some money."

"Anyway," Efrat piped up, "the hostel's better. No fighting parents there and hardly any rules. My parents divorced a year ago and I got stuck with my father and his new wife."

"At least you *have* a mother," Tova reminded her. "You should be grateful for that. I don't."

"Can't call her a mother," Efrat retorted. "After the divorce she stopped being religious and ran off. I don't even know where she is. I'm the youngest of eight — they're all married — and I haven't heard a word from her in months."

We all lapsed into silence then. I stared into the yellow-orange flames as they licked hungrily at the ebony night. Twisting and turning, they danced toward the moon. The stars, which hung like pure souls in the sky, were comforting to me, and I grew pensive, safe inside their constellations. I found these stories, the lives of these girls, sobering. What was *my* excuse? I had loving, caring parents who accepted me anyway, despite the pain I was putting them through by not being religious anymore.

It wasn't that I didn't want to do the right thing, whatever that was. Sometimes it was just so confusing; even my teachers, whose opinions frequently changed, didn't seem too clear about it. Try as I might, I always found myself doing the opposite of what was expected, the more so as I grew older. A week without being suspended from school was rare. My mother listened patiently to the stream of complaints.

"Mrs. Fein, Michal's not dressing/behaving in a manner deemed appropriate for our school.""Mrs. Fein, Michal has an attitude problem.""Mrs Fein, your daughter is a bad influence on other girls." And so on, until one day all the complaints stopped. That's when I knew that I'd been placed permanently on the other side of their door, the outside.

"Hey, Michal!" I was startled out of my reverie. "What about you — what's your story?"

"Me? I don't really have one," I mumbled offhandedly.

MY FINGERS RAN fluidly over the guitar strings. I loved the music I could create with this simple instrument. The soft sound of singing under the open sky warmed me all over, bringing a fuzzy, contented feeling inside. There we were, four girls, strangers until that day, now sharing our food, our space, our stories, our lives. We talked on and on, deep into the night. At one point my mind flashed back to the *Seder* that was going on in my parents' home. My nephews and nieces would be bouncing with excitement at the privilege of staying up so late; little Avreimi would have chanted "*Mah Nishtanah*" and he and the rest of the grandchildren would be urgently searching for the *afikoman*. I had to admit that I felt a tiny twinge of longing, a fleeting pang of nostalgia, accompanied by a trace of guilt. Still, I reassured myself, this was much better: beautiful, calm and serene. This, for me, was more liberating than any *Leil Haseder*!

TOVA WAS ALREADY asleep. She'd faded out around two a.m., curled up like a kitten on the dewy grass. Around me I could hear low voices of all those who had streamed out of their rooms to enjoy the cool night air, and the grass and sand were soon covered with sleeping forms. The other two girls and I continued talking for a while around the dying embers of our fire. Hugging my knees to my chest, I inhaled the salty sea smell and imbibed the aura of the fading fires, flickering bravely with their last breaths. Glancing at Shuli and Efrat, I saw that they, too, had succumbed to sleep. I wriggled inside my sleeping bag and lay down, feeling a heaviness cover me like an old woolen blanket. Slowly, my eyes began to close. My mind drifted, swimming in the sea, sliding in and out with the waves. I slipped into my dreams.

WHO ON EARTH was setting off fireworks at this time of night? The cracking sounds bursting inside my head brought me back to consciousness and, groggily, I raised myself up on one elbow to check my watch. Five a.m! This was crazy. It wasn't even light out yet. The popping sounds were coming closer, accompanied by loud explosions. Suddenly, the other girls were all wide awake.

"What's that noise?" asked Tova, rubbing her eyes.

"Don't know. I thought it was fireworks." I crawled out of my sleeping bag and stood up to get a better look.

"Look," cried Shuli, "over there… someone's… shooting!" She pointed to a group of black silhouettes, now scattering in all directions.

Efrat screamed, "It's a *pigua*, a terrorist attack!"

The shooting figurers were almost upon us, the blasts so loud that I couldn't think or see or understand anything, except that the cries and screams and bullets were real, and people were running in all directions to escape the crazy Arab gunmen whose targets we were. I opened my mouth to scream too — at least I think I did. It was surreal; I couldn't be sure of anything. Dark shapes flitted across the sand, stumbling and bending low in the black shadows. We fell over one another, tripping and slipping as we ran hysterically to get away.

"*Shema Yisrael!*" Was it me who said that? I could hear the same words all around me, shooting from people's mouths like sacred arrows trying to protect us from the evil bullets. More shots were fired, more rounds of ammunition emptied into the bodies of innocent people. And then… there was nothing.

WAS I DEAD? Was this how it felt to die? It was so quiet I thought my heart had stopped beating. Questions dangled above my head like funeral notices. But I was still alive! I checked myself carefully. Nothing hurt, no signs of bleeding. I could move all my limbs. Had I really escaped without a scratch? What about the others? Where were they? Why was everything so quiet?

"Michal?" I heard a whimper. *Tova!* It was Tova. *Where was she?* I scrambled over live bodies too frozen to move, their belongings strewn everywhere. Shell-shocked people were beginning to move. I heard cries, moans, and some weeping. Pushing and elbowing, I crawled my way through until I found my friend.

"Tova!" a strangled scream left my lips. She was sprawled awkwardly on the sand and her pale, clammy complexion suggested that something serious had happened. Opening her eyes, she smiled faintly.

"Michal," she whispered weakly, "I'm hurt."

Quickly, my glance took note of her bloodstained clothes. Her left leg was spurting red like a fountain. In a flash, I whipped my scarf from my neck and wrapped it tightly around her limb above the wound. At least I knew to do that much. *Think, Michal, think!* What had I learned in first-aid class? Apprehensively, I lifted Tova's shirt and gasped. The wound was so deep that it momentarily stunned me. I started to cry.

"Help, help!" I shouted through my tears. "Over here! My friend is badly hurt!" I pulled off my sweatshirt, drenched it with clean water from a bottle I found nearby and pressed it to her side to try and staunch the bleeding.

"Help, somebody… please. My friend is badly wounded!"

Arabic voices pierced the crowd like daggers, and I realized they were coming from Egyptian soldiers. Frantically, I grabbed a soldier's sleeve.

"Please!" I pointed. "My friend needs help. She has to get to the hospital quickly."

The soldier gave a curt nod and continued walking.

"Please!" I ran after him. "Call an ambulance! She'll die if you don't."

He answered with a string of Arabic, so utterly foreign, so totally incomprehensible that I felt dizzy from despair and helplessness. Why didn't he speak to me in Hebrew, even English? He must have known a little of those languages.

"Michal!" a voice rang out shrilly, like a wrong note in an orchestral symphony.

"Shuli!" We wept and fell into each other's arms. "Where's Tova?" Shuli asked after a minute.

"She's over there, badly hurt. She needs to get to a hospital fast. Where's Efrat?"

"With me, over here. She got shot in the leg." My feeling of dread deepened.

"Are you all right?" I asked Shuli quickly. She nodded her head affirmatively. "I must get back to Tova; I can't leave her alone. See if you can move Efrat over there and we'll stay together."

Tova was breathing shallowly when I returned. A young woman sat beside her, holding the sweatshirt to Tova's side and speaking gentle words of encouragement.

"Could you stay with her," I pleaded, "while I go for help?" The woman, just a stranger until now, gave a warm smile and nodded.

I ran like a frightened rabbit. I ran, darting in and out of the crowd of confused people, back and forth from soldier to soldier, begging, pleading for assistance. Some people wandered around in a daze, others were screaming at the soldiers, beseeching them for help, for medical supplies, for helicopters to fly us back across the border. But the only answers we received were harsh, guttural, abrasive shouts in Arabic. I was crying so hard that my tears sucked the air out of me, leaving me gasping for breath.

Where are our soldiers? I asked myself, looking around. *Where are our Jewish soldiers who care about us like brothers?* "Oh, Hashem," I *davened* desperately, "please get us out of here."

SHULI HAD MANAGED with difficulty to bring Efrat over to the place where Tova lay. Efrat's leg looked bad, and despite a brave attempt to hide it, her strained face showed she was obviously in great pain. I stroked her hand and tried to reassure her that help was on its way. Well… I hoped it was. I sank down on the sand beside my friend, noting her dusky gray color and the beads of sweat that glistened on her forehead.

"Tova," I shouted fiercely, "don't you dare give up, you hear? Come on, you're strong; you're going to fight."

Tova opened her glazed eyes. "Michal," she beckoned me closer. "If I survive this, I promise to come back."

I stared at her, puzzled.

"To Torah and *mitzvos*; to getting along with my father… for my mother's sake, for Hashem."

I was weeping now, distraught from her words. "Stop it, Tova," I shouted. "Don't talk that way. Of course you'll survive."

Shuli and Efrat sat next to us quietly, listening, tears streaming silently down their cheeks. She was going to make it; she *was*… if only we could get her out of there. Desperately, I surveyed my surroundings again, searching for signs of rescue. Someone nearby, who knew Arabic, was saying that the soldiers were bringing help, that we should all hold on and wait patiently.

"Wait!" I railed angrily. "My friend is badly hurt. There's no time to wait!"

In the meantime, the Egyptians were circulating among us, collecting our passports, and I felt the walls closing around us. Well, I wasn't going to give them ours, I decided, in a valiant effort to regain control.

"I want to go home," a small voice moaned from behind me.

"We all do, Efrat, we all want to get out," Shuli tried to calm her. Efrat was suddenly soft and vulnerable, afraid and homesick like us; her piercings seemed to fade away with her hard edges. Shuli clutched her friend's hand tightly. "Don't worry," she soothed, "we'll be out of here soon."

"I… I have an idea," I suggesting cautiously, unsure of the response. "We could say *Tehillim*."

Cradling my best friend's head in my arms, I began to sing softly. I'd always loved putting those inspiring, holy words to song; I could sing them for hours. So I sang the sweet words from memory, all the Psalms I'd ever known that spoke of trust and faith and hope; and I turned my face Heavenward to the now brightening sky, which seemed to bring with it the promise of a new day.

"Please, Hashem," I prayed, "give Tova — and all of us — another chance. Take us out of here; take us back where we belong."

Two shaky voices began to sing *Tehillim* with me, awkwardly, as they reacquainted themselves with the words.

"Michal," Tova was calling me again. "I want to talk to my father; can you call him?"

"It's Yom Tov," I gently reminded her, "he won't answer his phone. But when we get back, I'll call him."

"Thank you," her voice was thin and raspy. "Tell him..." it was getting harder to hear her, "that I'm sorry."

"No," I stated resolutely, "you can tell him that yourself!"

EVERYTHING AROUND ME became rosy from the rising sun, whose golden glow now glazed the whole sky. The steaming panic of the crowd had settled down into a slow simmer. We were quiet now, cowed into fearful silence, except for the low moans and cries of the wounded along the seashore. I stroked Tova's hair and prayed she'd hold on, that she'd cling to the fraying rope of her promise. I yearned to talk to my parents, to see their faces, to feel safe. I wondered if they'd heard of the attack, if the news had spread rapidly like it always does in Israel. They would be out of their minds with worry, and I thought I'd drown in guilt from all the pain I'd caused them.

So this was freedom? Who was I kidding? I was running away, that's all. Running from myself, making excuses, convincing myself that more and more excitement would bring me happiness. Life, I suddenly realized, was as tenuous as walking a tightrope. We could fall off at any moment, events could change in a second, snap like a broken bone, requiring complicated, painful surgery to repair the once-healthy limb. I could have been at home, sleeping safely in my own bed instead of sitting on the grass in Sinai with so many casualties. I yearned to be back among my people, to hear our holy Hebrew language, to return to the Land that we'd finally redeemed.

I found myself thinking about *Leil Haseder* and *Yetzias Mitzrayim* and how Hashem had taken us out from the very place we girls had returned to for a taste of temporary pleasure. Back then, the one-fifth of our fellow Jews who were found worthy chose to leave Eygpt at G-d's command, unlike us, who'd gone to Egypt on a whim and would have stayed on if not for the disaster that had befallen us. Suddenly, everything seemed as clear as if I was looking through a glass-bottomed boat and seeing my reflection in the water. I knew without question that I had to make changes. My shame went so deep, was so agonizing, that I wanted to crawl out of my skin and leave it behind in the dry desert.

Suddenly, I heard in the distance the drone of helicopters. Soon the rotary blades were blowing up clouds of sand and shaking the leaves on the trees as they landed all around us. Israeli soldiers and doctors with medical bags were spilling out onto the sand.

"They're here, Tova — they've arrived." I shook her awake urgently. "Tova, open your eyes, you're going to be fine now. Hang on a little bit longer."

Tova smiled bravely. I wanted to hold that smile, carry it with me forever. I clutched her hand tightly, willing my newfound spiritual energy to enter and surge through her veins.

"We're leaving Mitzrayim," I told her, and the irony was not lost. "They're taking us out — back home... to Eretz Yisrael!"

Many years ago, when I worked in the pediatric surgery unit in Hadassah Ein Kerem, we admitted several children who had been shooting victims of a terrorist attack in the Sinai. It was a cruel, vicious attack and these children suffered painful, life-changing injuries.

Fast forward a few years. I'm sitting at my Seder table with my family and reminiscing on the different types of Pesach experiences that I'd had. One of them was a week spent with friends in Taba, a small strip of land in the Sinai still under Israeli sovereignty (the rest of the Sinai had been given back to Egypt in a peace treaty with Israel negotiated by then-Prime Minister, Menachem Begin). As we related the story of yetzias Mitzrayim in the proper way, I pondered how I could possibly have spent Pesach on the beach in such "foreign" circumstances. Then, as a non-religious Jew who'd been raised with little Yiddishkeit, it felt normal; that's what all the young people did. Years later, though, as a baalas teshuvah *fully committed to a Torah life, I was quite horrified that I did that. I began thinking about all the young people who leave Israel for this holiday to go to the very place that Hashem took us out of and I became sad. Suddenly, I remembered those little children who'd been shooting victims of terrorists and then I had a story.

"Going Out" was my first story to appear in the Hamodia Story Supplement, so that was a milestone for me. Appearing in the supplement had been one of my goals and I was happy to have achieved it. There was one comment that stuck in my mind from the feedback on this story. A very clever, educated man in my neighborhood called me up especially to thank me for the story. He said that it had given him a whole new perspective on yetzias Mitzrayim that he'd never thought of before.

The Decision Maker

"SHE HAS A few days at the most." The air froze into a sheet of ice.

"A few days!" A middle-aged woman stood before me, wringing her hands in distress. "What are you saying? She's always been so healthy… until recently. How could this happen?"

"It happens," I said knowingly, straightening my already straight white coat and slipping my gold-plated ballpoint pen into the top pocket. "I see things like this all the time."

The woman turned away and began to sob. Her daughter lay amidst a tangle of tubes and wires, and it was easy to forget that beneath the lifesaving equipment a person still existed. A respirator forced her chest rhythmically up and down, pushing in breaths and letting them out with deep sighs. Irregular graph lines flitted across the heart monitor above her head, but the girl remained cold, unresponsive and outwardly oblivious. Besides for her mother's sobs, the only sounds in the room were the beeps and whooshes that pierced the sterile silence.

"Isn't there anything more you can do? Maybe a different antibiotic… something?" the young woman's mother pleaded desperately, like a condemned prisoner before sentencing. Her husband sat by their daughter's bed, his head slumped forward in his hands, crumpled up with grief.

"No," I stated authoritatively, "there isn't. This kind of bacterium is almost always fatal, and it has already attacked her major organs. They are beyond healing. I'm afraid she's not going to make it."

Okay, I suppose I could have injected a little more compassion into my voice when I announced the prognosis, but in my experience, it's better to tell it the way it is, and I've had lots of that… experience.

I remember the first time I had to deliver bad news as an intern. We'd lost a young, newly married woman after a car accident, and when I placed my arm around the husband's heaving shoulders, I suddenly realized I was crying, too. I must admit it was embarrassing, because young men are not supposed to cry. And my tears — then, and on several other such occasions— didn't earn me any points with the other interns.

"Come on, Levine," they'd say, punching me playfully on the shoulder. "You Jews are too sensitive… gotta toughen up a bit."

And I did. Many years have passed since then and I've seen it all. Over time, you can get used to anything.

The distraught mother clasped her daughter's limp hand, holding on for as long as she could. She inclined her head toward me.

"Thank you," she said gratefully, "for everything."

I stared at her, dumbfounded. Why on earth was she thanking me? For coldly delivering the verdict like a courtroom judge? No one had ever thanked me for that. Relatives would either be angry and shout or grow numb and detached, depending on their emotional state at the time — but thank me? Never!

Strangely, I did something that I always tried to avoid doing — I actually looked directly into that mother's eyes, where I saw such goodness mingled with pain that I turned away for fear of drowning in it.

"Er… you're welcome," I stammered. "I… I didn't do anything. I… I'm very sorry."

Courteously, I excused myself, quickly stepped out of the ICU and made my way to the surgical ward for general rounds. But my stomach felt like a lone boat adrift at sea without an anchor.

Half an hour later the young woman in intensive care no longer occupied my mind. It was amazing how easily I could empty it out, clear a space that others would quickly fill, like emptying the garbage bin only to have it fill up again. There was so much to do and so many patients to worry about that the bin overflowed more quickly than I could keep up with it. I was always running out of "room."

I entered the surgical ward with my flock of medical students and interns and stopped by Mr. Edwards's bed. I had recently returned from an overseas conference so I was a little out of touch with my patients.

"Case history, anyone?"

Broderson piped up eagerly. He was a smart one, that boy. We would make a fine physician out of him.

"Sixty-eight-year-old Caucasian male; history of type 2 diabetes and hypertension, probably due to obesity. Blood pressure controlled with medication. Current problem gangrene in the right foot, which isn't responding to —"

"How long has he been here, Broderson?" I interrupted.

"Er —" The intern leafed through the file hurriedly. "About six weeks.

"Six weeks and still no improvement?"

I pulled back the bedcovers to reveal a highly inflamed, swollen foot, dotted with numerous black spots tracking dangerously toward his knee.

"Have we tried those new X-type dressings?"

"Yes."

"Antibiotics?"

"Yes again. Both intravenous and topic."

"What about his sugar? Regulated?"

"Well, no, but that's the problem — he doesn't cooperate.

At home he forgets his medications and won't stick to his diet; even here, his family members sneak in snacks all the time."

For the first time, I looked at the patient sitting up in bed.

"Is that right, Mr. Edwards, that you're not cooperating?"

Mr. Edwards rested his hands on his swollen stomach and grunted loudly. *Hmm, not a communicative chap,* I thought.

I turned back to Broderson. "I assume the diabetics nurse is on the case?"

"Yes, but she's not really getting anywhere."

"Social worker?"

"Yes, also involved."

I looked at Mr. Edwards and back again at his leg. Bending over, I examined his foot carefully, noting the advanced, spreading necrosis. The leg was a mess.

"We need to amputate," I announced, straightening up. "Broderson, make sure you book the operating room for tomorrow afternoon."

There was a loud, collective gasp from the entourage surrounding me. I patted Mr. Edwards briefly on the arm. "Don't worry, we'll soon have you back on your feet again." Based on the sniggering behind me, it must have been a good joke; unintentional, of course. As I moved on to the next patient, I heard Mr. Edwards mutter under his breath something like, "Go jump, you pompous young twit!"

It wasn't always like this. Believe it or not, I had once been an idealist with high hopes, grand ideas. I'd give my parents such *nachas.* Their only son, a doctor; it was every immigrant's dream. I remember my days as a student. I can still recall being shocked to the core at the callousness of my colleagues, the insensitive comments and stream of black humor. I was going to be different, or so I thought. People would see that Jewish doctors were better than the rest, more compassionate and humane.

When did things start to change?

My thoughts were interrupted. "Dr. Levine, what would you like to give Mr. Atkins for pain?"

"What's he had already?" I was slightly irritated.

The nurse read a long list from the patient's chart. "Well, he's had codeine, morphine, Percoset, Optalgin, Valium —"

"So he can't have anything else."

"But he's still in pain, and he's unable to sleep."

"He's way over the limit. Will you take responsibility if he becomes addicted?"

"Well, no… I understand… but perhaps another type of sleeping pill, then?"

"Like I said," I repeated firmly, "he's way over his limit. Give him another dose of IV Optalgin. That should be enough."

IT HAD HAPPENED slowly, the gradual deadening of my emotions, so I could relate to Mr. Edwards's gangrenous foot. My heart had withered from its diminishing supply of empathy until it had been removed and replaced with an impenetrable plastic prosthesis. I was good at amputating; as a surgeon, that was my job.

It's kind of hard to imagine that I had once been a highly sensitive man, one who rejoiced in situations with happy endings and was deeply saddened by people suffering pain and loss. It was my residency in pediatrics that finally broke me. I'd go home physically and emotionally drained from the cries of those suffering children, and when little Liam succumbed to his valiant fight against leukemia, I realized that if I didn't toughen up, I'd never make it as a doctor.

Becoming a surgeon seemed like the best option; I didn't have to connect with the patients' suffering when they were asleep. As I climbed the professional ladder, I built up a protective wall without realizing it, cementing the bricks with ego. When I swept through the wards, announcing my prognoses like royal proclamations, I felt power surge inside me like an electric current. The world was at my feet; nothing was beyond my grasp. I could reach for the stars, pull them down beside me and change creation.

I worked hard. I knew I was a good doctor — except for the emotional aspect, of course, but I was known for my thoroughness, efficiency and skill as a surgeon. And I did care about my patients. Many a night would find me sitting up until the wee hours, grappling with a difficult diagnosis or wracking my brain to devise an optimal course of treatment.

The hospital consumed my days and nights, though, swallowing it up until there was little left over for a social life, marriage or a family. I guess I wasn't giving my parents *nachas* in that area, especially as the years rolled by with no sign of grandchildren. Still, practicing medicine was everything to me. One day I would have it all.

"HOW DARE YOU just give up on my father?" the woman said, turning on me angrily. "Who do you think you are, anyway … G-d?"

I eyed the woman and her husband warily. From the way they were attired, I knew that they were Orthodox Jews. *Um*, I thought, *this is going to be tricky.*

"Look, Mrs. —"

"Pearlstein," she interjected, her brown eyes blazing.

"Yes, uh, well, Mrs. Pearlstein, it's like this. You see, your father has had a serious stroke and has already developed pneumonia, and of course his age is against him."

"Eighty-eight is not old, Dr. Levine, not by our standards. He's got a few good years left, *b'ezras Hashem*. My grandmother was 102 when she was called home by her Maker." The woman was raising her voice higher and higher, like an opera singer, and attracting so much attention that others in the emergency room came out of their cubicles to investigate.

Feeling uncomfortable, I spoke softly, in my most professional manner. "Your father, I'm afraid, is going to be paralyzed on the left side, unable to talk or swallow, and on top of that he has a serious lung infection with respiratory failure. Do you really want me to put him on a respirator and prolong his suffering? Even if he survives, which is highly unlikely, what kind of life will he have?"

"That, Dr. Levine," she replied, glancing at my identity badge, "is not for you to decide. There's a G-d Who makes those decisions."

I stared at her blankly.

"You are Jewish, Dr. Levine?" Mrs. Pearlstein asked.

"Well, yes…"

"A Jewish doctor ought to know better than to decide when a patient's life is no longer worth preserving. Only G-d can decide that. When it's time to go, we must accept His decision, but until then a person has to use every single second he has left in this world, even while he is in a coma."

I looked at her and asked cynically, "How exactly does one use his time if he's in a coma?"

"The soul, Dr. Levine, the soul." Mrs Pearlstein shook her head in exasperation. "While the body is alive, the soul inside it still has a purpose."

Whoa, now… this was really not a conversation I wanted to have. My eyes moved back to her father, lying in bed, frail, unconscious and struggling to breathe even with an oxygen mask.

"I… uh… still think we should just keep him comfortable — no heroics or anything like that."

"Mendy," Mrs. Pearlstein said, beckoning to her husband. "Can you call the Rav, please?" And then, turning sharply to face me, she added, "You don't know my father! You've absolutely no idea who you're writing off. I demand that you put him on a respirator… right now."

IT WAS STRANGE how her words stuck in my mind. I mulled them over and over, unable to forget them. I'd done what Mrs. Pearlstein had requested — intubated her father and placed him on a respirator. That was over a week ago, and even though he wasn't my patient, I kept tabs on his progress. Of course, I was expecting to hear of his demise any minute, but no, he was still holding on.

I pondered this as I prepared to leave the hospital late that Friday afternoon to visit my parents. On my off weekends, they insisted I eat Friday night dinner with them; it was all they asked of me, the one thing they had preserved from the Old Country.

On my way out, I stopped by the ICU to check on Mr. Pearlstein. He wasn't in his usual place, so I immediately assumed the worst. In disbelief, I soon realized that he'd been moved out of intensive care to the recovery section. There he was, propped up on pillows and breathing on his own. He reclined like a king, surrounded by smiling relatives who obviously adored and revered him. I quickly stepped back out of sight, and then, winded as if I had received a punch in the stomach, I stumbled out the door.

So I'd been wrong. It happens. But that incident kept intruding into my thoughts like the first cut of a surgical scalpel as I exited the densely populated city and hit the winding country roads. I tried to keep my mind focused on the road and the long drive ahead.

But I'd been wrong! Inexplicably, this nagged at me like an aching tooth, and I couldn't understand why. I'd made mistakes before; after all, I was only human, so why was this different? Maybe because the elderly patient was Jewish. Or was it something about his daughter's speech on ethics? *That's not your decision, young man.* Her words echoed in my head like a shout in an empty auditorium.

I had always been skeptical of the Orthodox stance on prolonging life. I'd heard that in Israel it was standard procedure to do the maximum, even if it meant treating a hopeless condition aggressively, and I was relieved that this wasn't the accepted practice in the United States. It wasn't that I didn't value life; after all, I was a doctor. It was just that my definition of life was more… well, physical.

And yet I was startled to realize that with the wave of my hand I could snuff out someone's life just like… that! I — and so many other professionals like me — made such decisions often. How many flames had we extinguished over the years? But more important: What had I become?

My eyes grew heavy as the silt of self-doubt settled over my eyelids. The last few weeks of intensive work must have caught up with me. I was so tired. In front of me, the road stretched ahead dizzyingly, and above my head the sky darkened, with ominous black clouds threatening a storm. As I shot forward in my luxury automobile, the rain swiftly lashed down, beating furiously against my windshield, determined to melt my frozen heart until I couldn't tell whether it was the rain or tears that were blurring my vision.

I knew it was going to happen but was helpless to stop it. No one could drive safely with such a clouded perspective. I needed to see more clearly, to unclutter my mind. In slow motion, I found myself flying, spinning in the sudden chill of the night air. It felt so good up there, outside my car, outside of myself, floating weightlessly like a soft silk handkerchief held aloft in the wind. But then, suddenly, I was free-falling, faster and faster, plummeting, lower and lower, until I hit rock bottom.

"THERE'S NOTHING MORE to do," a voice rumbled. "He's not going to make it."

"Pity," chimed another voice. "He's a young guy. From his ID it appears that he's a doctor."

"Yeah, but he's not from around here. I've never seen him before. I've also never seen anyone survive injuries like his. We need to contact his next of kin."

Who were they talking about? Could it be me? Wait! This was me!

Where was I? Here, there, somewhere in between? I looked down at my inert body on the hospital bed, watched the white-coated miracle workers shake their heads with finality, and I wanted to stop them before they turned away, to tell them they were wrong, that I still existed.

"Okay," said the chiming voice, "I'll go make the call."

"And nurse," said the rumbler, "there's nothing more to do here except keep him comfortable."

I heard the words, my words, coming back to haunt me. I had uttered those words all the time. Was that how I sounded?

"Nooo…" I screamed from wherever I was, up high in that lofty place. "Hold on… I'm here… I've not gone yet!"

Suddenly, I began to feel my body reawaken, though heavy and weighted like a sunken ship, and a strange, indescribable sensation washed over me, swimming like a fish in and out of the wreckage. It felt as if I existed in two dimensions. And in that moment I understood, clearly, all my mistakes, all my misconceptions. I had just been introduced to my own soul.

"Nooo," I cried, "wait! Ple-e-ease! I promise I'll never say those words again!"

And as I fought to come back, to have another chance to do things over, for the first time in my life, I prayed.

"Please, G-d, don't let it be too late!"

This story is a jumble of several different medical situations I've encountered over the years, but I think the main thing that inspired it was the feeling of helplessness many people feel. Baruch Hashem, I haven't had that feeling myself in medical situations (I count my blessings that I'm fortunate to have medical knowledge), but unfortunately, I have met people who found themselves totally at the mercy of medical personnel. One case in particular stands out in my mind: when my friend watched her father lie in a coma for weeks, completely unable to express his needs. His family performed the task admirably, but still, it wasn't the same as her father being able to speak for himself. This made me aware, more than ever, how dependent we are on the medical staff to make vital decisions. I imagined my friend's father lying unconscious yet able to hear the conversations around him… and feeling completely helpless to react. How much more careful those doctors might be if they were to experience this themselves!

At the time of my writing this story there happened to be a news item about a family who had requested that their son, in a coma for eight months, be taken off life support. I was flabbergasted that they could make that decision using the rationale, "this is what he would have wanted, etc.," and all the more appreciative that, as Orthodox Jews, we have strict guidelines regarding how to behave in this area. How lucky we are that we don't need to make these decisions by ourselves.

During the many years that I worked as a nurse in NICU, I cared for babies who spent months and months on respirators. There were those babies who we knew would not make it short of an open miracle, but our instructions were to treat them "until the end." It wasn't always easy to do this and I'll admit that there were times when I had questions if a baby was really suffering. And yet I knew that we were following halachah, our instruction manual for life. In our world there would be no disconnecting respirators, leaving patients struggling with their last breath.

All of these things made me more aware than ever of Who is the real Doctor — and not the ones in the white coats who often think they are G-d.

FEBRUARY 1995

Mom's behaving like an icicle again. I don't know what I've done wrong this time, but it must be something. When she gets that frosty look on her face and her lips set into a thin line of disapproval, I know what's coming. She'll pile the ice around her until she's inside an igloo and I, Shayna Kirsch, will have to strain and strain, like I'm hacking away with a pick axe, to get her out. Usually, it's the word "sorry" that makes her agree to exit her frozen dome. Not just saying it once, though, but over and over until I'm truly repentant for whatever I did to send her there in the first place. As if I know! How do any of us in our family really know? We occupy ourselves with guessing games. Maybe it was because Dad forgot their wedding anniversary or because I didn't get a high enough test grade or because Dovid didn't thank her for making his favorite supper?

I'm getting married in two weeks, so I really do need to thaw her out as soon as possible. I'd better just apologize for whatever I'm supposed to have done or not done. I hate myself for thinking it, but honestly, I'm beginning to wish more and more that she'd just stay inside.

Dear Father in heaven, please don't let me be the same way as her when I'm a mother!

MARCH 2011

It was raining! Great globs of it pouring like runny custard down the windows of the café where Shayna waited. She checked her watch again and sighed. Layki was late, as usual. Inside the café it was hot and stuffy, in contrast to the wetness outside. Just as she was getting up to order another chocochino, her sister stumbled in through the door.

"Whew," said Layki, shaking herself off like a wet dog and dropping her shopping bags onto the table. "It's really rough out there. Sorry I'm late. I had some last minute errands to finish and traffic was bad… because of the weather, I suppose."

Shayna stared, her face looking like a fruit out of season.

"Hey, I said I'm sorry," Layki repeated. "Like I said, I got held up in traffic. It wasn't my fault." She pulled out a chair to sit down on and moved the dripping bags onto the floor.

"You're always late," Shayna grouched. "Couldn't you have been on time just this once? You know how much it means to me."

Layki sighed. "I suppose you're right, but now I'm here, so shall we get started?" She unzipped her pocketbook and pulled out a notepad and pen. "What about the guest list, for starters?"

"Maybe," Shayna said sulkily.

"Oh, come on," Layki said. "Cheer up. You look so glum. Let me order you a coffee."

"Chocochino," Shayna said.

"Fine, chocochino it is."

She turned back to Shayna after placing her order. "Ready to start now?"

"Oh, I don't know. I'm not really in the mood anymore."

"Because I came late?"

"I guess so. The thing is, I was so excited and enthusiastic about planning everything, especially with you, my favorite sister, but the waiting… it put me off already."

Layki stared, her mouth open in disbelief, although in truth she shouldn't have been so surprised. "Shayna," she said pointedly, "what time was I supposed to meet you here at The Rimon?"

"Ten o'clock," Shayna mumbled into her glass.

"And what's the time now?"

Shayna looked up and briefly glanced at the wall clock behind the serving counter. "Ten fifteen."

"And I've been here for about five minutes already, so do you realize how late I actually was?"

Shayna stared back into the empty glass as if it was a crystal ball that would reveal her future. "Ten minutes."

"THE LEAST SHE could have done was come on time," Shayna complained later to her husband. She passed by some open kitchen cabinets and banged them closed. "I mean, it's the principle involved here. Come on, show a little interest. Why should everything always be on my head?"

Ephraim groaned inwardly, knowing what was coming. He turned to the bowl in front of him, lifted a large spoon of butternut squash soup to his mouth and took a long slurp. Shayna turned around sharply.

"Can you please stop making that noise?"

Ephraim nodded and dipped his spoon back in the soup. "Good soup."

"Did you hear what I said?"

"About the slurping? Sure, I'll try not to do it again."

"No, not that." Shayna wiped her hands irritably on her apron. "I was talking about Mom and Dad's fiftieth anniversary. It looks like it will be me doing most of the work, as usual."

"But you like it that way, don't you?" Ephraim said after a toned-down slurp. "That way, you can take all the credit."

"And what's that supposed to mean?" Shayna crossed her arms and stood, glaring across the table.

Ephraim tried backing out of the corner he'd slipped into.

"Well, you never really let anybody help you, even though you say you want it, so it seems as if you'd rather do everything yourself."

"That's because I'm the oldest daughter, I suppose," Shayna said with more than a hint of resentment in her voice. "I'm expected to organize all these affairs."

Ephraim wiped his mouth with his napkin and leaned back in his chair. "Quite frankly, I don't know why you're going to so much trouble over this. It's an anniversary party. Why do you need to make it in a hall when we can have it here in our house?"

Shayna shook her head firmly. "It's only the shul hall, nothing fancy, and I'm catering most of it myself. That's what Mom would want. You know how she is."

"Yes," Ephraim nodded knowingly, "I do." For a moment he was quiet, thinking of his mother-in-law and "how she was" and of his wife's countless efforts to please her over the years.

"She'll never appreciate it anyway," he mumbled.

"Sorry?"

"No matter what you do, it will never be enough."

Shayna stuck out her chin and pursed her lips together until they looked like one long line across her face. Ephraim knew that look well: the coldness in her eyes as she retreated, her mouth covered in frost. She was halfway into her icy dome and he knew just what it would take to keep her out.

"It doesn't matter, though, because you'll do an amazing job." He smiled warmly and noted a slight melting in her eyes. "It will be stunning as usual, and we'll all be so proud of you."

Shayna stepped back from the igloo doorway. Ah, he'd caught her just in time! Warm compliments and platitudes had thawed her, at least for now. Inwardly, Ephraim sighed. Sometimes, meeting his wife's emotional needs was so very exhausting, it was easier to tune her out than deliver what she required. For today at least, he'd managed to come up with the goods, although he had no idea how long they would sustain her. Whatever he offered was usually never enough.

EDNA KIRSCH BENT down slowly and opened the lower cupboard doors of her display cabinet. Photo albums, stacks of them, lined the shelves. Edna gave a little yelp of pain and clutched her back. Age was catching up with her, winning the race against youth. Panting for breath slightly, she managed to withdraw a worn, dusty album and limped painfully with it to the dining room table. Next time Shayna came to visit, she would have her put all the albums in a more accessible place.

She turned the pages and gazed at the old, musty pictures that lay before her, calling her to connect the pieces of her family history puzzle... yet somehow she couldn't. Naturally, she remembered her parents, standing stiffly at some kind of *simchah*, Tatty in his long black coat and Mama in an elegant, navy blue taffeta gown. Two children stood on each side of them like little stick soldiers lined up for roll call. Edna was one of them, standing straight to attention, her empty eyes as remote and distant as her mother's. They looked like a strong, well-disciplined army where there was no room for mistakes or emotion. Edna's eyes strayed briefly to her mother's arms, which hung woodenly by her sides — arms that had seldom held or hugged Edna, or wiped a tear from her face.

Uncharacteristically, Edna felt herself choking up, an unfamiliar feeling of something wriggling its way up her esophagus, entering her throat and wetting her eyes. *Silly*, she thought, dabbing at her eyes quickly. Her parents had been good, decent, moral people, even if they hadn't been particularly warm. And that wasn't their fault, either, each of them traumatized the way they had been, from the war. Yes, they'd educated her and her siblings well and raised them with strong Torah values, and she'd known they cared about her, even if they were critical and hard to please. And anyway, that wasn't a bad thing, was it? Having high standards and lofty goals built character and elevated a person.

She flipped through more pages as quickly as her aching fingers allowed her. Ah, here were some pictures of her brothers where they were all laughing, and even Mama had a smile on her face. Edna smiled, too, remembering. Her eyes felt wet again, and she shook her head as if she could shake the tears away into oblivion. Why was she being so ridiculously emotional?

"Sidney!" she called out to her husband. "*SID!*" Nothing… only an ear-splitting silence. Where was he? How come he was never around when she needed him?

"RIVKI, ARE THE lemon meringues ready yet?" Shayna yelled from the hallway.

"Yes, Mom, I'm almost finished wrapping them; they'll be there soon."

"Well, hurry up, please. We have to get the food to the shul and I don't have much time."

"Here." Rivki held out a box of saran wrap to her friend, Tova. "Hold this, will you, and help me cover the pies."

"Wow," Tova marveled. "Did you make these? They look good enough to be professional."

Rivki nodded proudly. She absolutely loved being in the kitchen playing around with recipes, which she never really followed, and coming up with new creative ideas. Tova sunk her teeth into a chocolate brownie.

"Mmm, these are delicious."

"Hey, will you get your fingers out of those!" Rivki cried, grabbing the cake away from her. "We need them for the party."

"Aw, just this piece. It's…"

"Rivki, come on!" Shayna yelled again. "We're going to be late."

Rivki made a face at Tova and handed her a brown box. "Go give this to my mother and stay out of the cakes."

Tova held the box and smiled. "My mother would love it if I could make things like this. Your mom must be really proud of you."

"Yeah, maybe she is," Rivki said offhandedly. "Who knows? Come, let's go."

The two friends carried box after box outside and filled up the car until the seats were completely hidden. Shayna barked out instructions. "I'll take this load first, so be ready for me when I come back for more. Oh, and Auntie Layki and Auntie Esther should be here soon, so tell them what to do, and the little ones need baths and *please* make sure that you look respectable."

"Phew," said Tova after the car had zoomed off. "You've got your work cut out for you. It's making me tired just thinking about it."

Rivki flashed her friend a small smile. "That's why you're here to help."

All afternoon the girls worked — shlepping boxes, cutting up fruit and arranging platters, setting tables at the hall, shooing the little ones away from the chaos and keeping them out of trouble.

Finally, the modest shul room was ready. It had been transformed to look like a *simchah* hall. Lavender-colored napkins were folded into half-open fans next to each place setting, scented candles flickered in the middle of the tables, and balloons dangled on strings from the ceiling. Soon, everybody would be arriving, and then Bubby and Zeide Kirsch, the guests of honor, would be brought to their surprise party.

Rivki was tired — no, actually, exhausted was more like it. She had been on her feet nonstop since early morning, and despite knowing she was supposed to be a strong, energetic fourteen-year-old, her legs really hurt. Wearily, she made her way to the restroom to clean herself up a little. She gazed at herself in the bathroom mirror. Her hair, which she'd pinned neatly back earlier, was already hanging in strands across her face, and the "respectable" dress she'd donned was… *dirty!* Rivki stared, horrified, at the two greasy brown stains on her beige wool dress. What was she going to do? Mom would be furious. Frantically, she grabbed one of the hand towels from a nearby sink, thrust it under the tap and began rubbing vigorously at the marks with the wet cloth. After a moment she stood back and looked in the mirror, squelching a rising panic as two wet blotches, even bigger than before, stared out at her. She rushed to fix her hair. Maybe Mom wouldn't notice the dress if her hair was tidy. She was just tucking a stray strand inside her ponytail when the restroom door opened.

"Rivki!" her mother cried out. "Here you are. I've been looking all over for you." She quickly took in her daughter's straggly hair and the stains, spreading like ink spots, across her dress. "Goodness, whatever happened to you? You look like such a mess! Tidy yourself up quickly and come outside to help."

Shayna swept back out through the doors and Rivki laid her head wearily against the cold, tiled wall... and wept.

"JUST ONE MORE picture, then we'll be done," Layki waved everyone into position. "Rivki, sit over there so you don't block Bubby's face. Shmuel, kneel down on the floor by Zeide's feet. Where's Shayna? Shayna, come and stand next to Esther. Okay... everyone ready... SMILE!"

The flash on the camera went off, snapping the crowd permanently into a picture. It would be another one for the album, another memory to be laid out stiffly on crisp white paper.

"*Mazel tov, mazel tov!* A beautiful evening!" Shayna received the hugs and blessings graciously. The words wrapped themselves around her. "A great job, Shayna, as usual! Stunningly done... very tasteful!" She accepted the compliments eagerly, lapping them up like a cat with its milk. The thanks and appreciation warmed the cold winter night and yet still, she shivered, for even though she welcomed the sincere embraces, there was something missing, something that the hugs could not provide.

She should have been used to it by now; after all, there were rarely surprises in her family performances. The script of decades could not be rewritten. And yet it hurt.... No, it ached — a long, ceaseless, inescapable hurt that gnawed at her insides, maintaining an open wound. Because out of all the people in the room, the only person not to hug her, the only one who didn't utter a word of thanks, was… her mother.

SHAYNA RUBBED HER eyes tiredly and made her way to the shul kitchen, where mounds of clean-up awaited. As she surveyed the mess, she could hear the laughter and lively conversations in the hall, and suddenly she felt separate from it all, like a single goldfish swimming around in circles in a glass bowl. Alone in the kitchen surrounded by the spoils of her hard work, a surge of resentment hit her like a tidal wave. She had worked so hard to make her mother happy. Her sisters had pitched in, of course, but still, she was the one who had organized everything, as usual.

All of a sudden, a thought struck her. *Why?* Why did she keep on doing it? Year after year, month after month, still striving, always seeking her mother's love and approval. She had tried, and was still trying, to find something, anything that would make Mom happy with her, but nothing ever really did.

The door burst open and Layki bounced in, stopping abruptly when she saw the look on Shayna's face.

"Are you okay?" Layki asked anxiously, eyeing her sister carefully.

Shayna turned away towards the countertop. "I'm fine," she said tersely.

"Really? Are you sure?"

"I'm just tired. It's been a long day."

"Yes," said Layki, "it has." She hesitated a moment, seemingly unsure of her next words. "You're still trying to please them, aren't you?" she said quietly.

Shayna gripped the countertop tightly, fighting the pressure in her chest.

"It's okay, you know, it's nothing abnormal; we all wanted that, once." Layki's voice was soft, almost hesitant.

Shayna tilted her chin slightly. "What do you mean?"

"Well, Esther and I also yearned for the warmth and affection, praise instead of criticism, but we realized we would never get it the way we would have liked, so we distanced ourselves, threw ourselves into our own families instead."

"Oh, three cheers for the two of you... hip, hip, hurray!"

Layki flinched from her sister's sarcastic jab, then recomposed herself and continued. "Esther and I have both been in therapy for years about this. It's been hard, but we've learned to accept what we can't change. We've learned to develop ourselves independent of Mom and Dad... and to still keep a connection with them." She paused to take a deep breath. "I've discovered that patterns can be changed, even if it seems like they can't. It *is* possible to break the cycle of generations. It's hard work, but it's better than living with the conflict... with always feeling lacking and unsure of yourself."

"I don't know what you're talking about," Shayna snapped, a fearful look in her eyes. "I don't feel unsure of myself, I feel — angry. I feel spent. I'm tired of always trying to make everyone happy, to keep the family together, to please Mom!"

An insecure quietness crept into the kitchen. Layki watched as her sister grabbed a sponge and began wiping down a dirty tray with frantic motions. Suddenly Shayna stopped and whirled around. "What about *me?*" she cried angrily. "If you two had some coping mechanism, why didn't you include *me?*"

"We tried," Layki admitted, "but you seemed unable to let go..."

"You could have tried harder... you could have cared more. What was so difficult about approaching me?" A searing hot bolt of pain shot across her chest when she realized that even her own sisters had left her out in the snowstorm. Shayna felt like a swollen dam ready to burst its banks but fighting valiantly to keep the sluice-gates closed.

"It's not as if we wanted it this way," Layki continued, trying to keep the defensiveness out of her voice. "We really did try... but you were... unreachable...so cold." She looked down uncomfortably at the floor."

That was it! The gates finally yielded to the pressure from behind them and the water gushed out, pouring in painful torrents down Shayna's cheeks.

Layki watched her sister in silence, twisting her fingers together and making small movements with her feet as if she wanted to walk over and hug her but was unsure if she could. So she left her in the silence that throbbed with the pitiful sound of Shayna's cries.

Thoroughly exhausted, emotionally and physically, Shayna sat down on a kitchen stool and buried her face in her hands. It was almost a relief to let it all out after so many years of fighting, battling herself and her old hurts… fighting, fighting.

The two were startled by the sound of the kitchen door.

"Mommy, do you need… what's wrong?"

Shayna looked up into her daughter's panicked eyes.

"Your mother isn't feeling very well," Layki explained gently to Rivki. "Don't worry, she'll be all right and then she'll come out to talk to you. Could you just give us a moment?"

"Er, yes… sure." The young girl glanced quickly between her mother and aunt before carrying her slumped shoulders out of the door.

"What have I done to her?" Shayna whispered as if speaking to herself. "How can I ever fix the damage?"

"You can and you will." Layki pulled up another stool and sat down next to her sister. "You're very strong."

Shayna raised her eyebrows skeptically. "I am?"

"Of course you are. What do you think you've been using to fight your pain all of these years? You have an incredible amount of strength. You can use that in order to change."

A flicker of hope shone in Shayna's eyes but was quickly extinguished as she burst into tears again.

"It… hurts… too much," Shayna gulped, while clutching her chest. "The pain… I can't stand this pain." Her face was screwed up in agony. "I… I've done everything I can to avoid feeling it."

"I know," said Layki. "I know all about the pain." She placed her hand tentatively on her sister's shoulder and Shayna didn't bristle or brush it off.

"I've turned out just like Mom, haven't I?" she sobbed. "Retreating into the igloo just as Bubby once did and like Mommy still does… a generation of icicles."

"Except that it's not quite the same," said Layki gently. "You see, icicles don't cry. They stay stuck to the walls of their stalactite caves or hang rigidly from the ceiling."

Shayna's crying grew louder and more desperate, as if her heart was opening for the first time, exposing the frantic beating in her chest. "At… at least it doesn't hurt," she gasped. "Ice… doesn't feel the pain of rejection."

"I know," said Layki again, and the pain in her eyes showed that she really did. "But it doesn't do anything else except make sure that things stay cold."

She wrapped her arms around her sister in a comforting embrace. "These… are the things that keep us warm."

"Icicles" was another assigned story from Binah. Somebody had approached a member of the staff with an idea she had about patterns of behavior that repeat themselves throughout the generations. For example, if a key family member like a father or mother was unable to show warmth and express love, this trait was likely to be passed down to each generation and the behavior continued. The person presenting this idea had experienced this herself in her own family. Because this lady did not want to write up the account herself lest any family members recognize themselves in it, the Binah editorial staff decided that writing it as a fiction story was the best way to go — and gave me the assignment. I have learned that often the most effective way to convey a message can be through fiction and this instance was no exception.

First I interviewed the woman in question and was able to form a picture in my mind of the kind of family life she'd experienced. Then, when I had all the pieces together, I wrote the story. Baruch Hashem, the woman was thrilled with the way it came out.

I don't think her situation was unusual and that was reflected by the subsequent feedback to the story after it was printed. So many people related to it and the way that patterns of behavior are passed down almost like a legacy, without us being aware of it. In this woman's case the circumstances revolved around the inability to express emotions and the fallout of that, which leads to criticism and manipulation. But it can be any kind of behavior, some things more damaging, some less. I believe this story has an important place in bringing this issue to light, making people more aware of their destructive patterns and therefore able to take steps to change them.

Measuring Up

"WHY DON'T YOU try this?" Naomi asked, holding up a black tunic dress.

Dina pulled a face. "Ugh, Mom, it looks like a sack. And why black? I'm only ten years old. Girls my age wear bright colors."

Because it's slimming, that's why, Naomi thought as she hung the garment back on the rail. She sighed to herself. Her Dina was growing… and growing. In fact, it seemed as if she was getting bigger every month. She smoothed her own narrow skirt with her palms. Where was her daughter's weight problem coming from? No one else in the family had that issue. As Dina emerged from the dressing room dressed in a snugly-fitting brown skirt with a fiery orange top, Naomi suppressed a smile. Well, at least she wasn't self-conscious yet; that was good.

"What do you think, Mom?" Dina paraded in front of her.

"No," Naomi shook her head. "I'm afraid you need something much looser."

"I WAS THINKING that I should take Dina to the doctor," Naomi said as she placed her husband's breakfast plate on the table.

"Whatever for?" Aryeh asked, preparing to tuck into his scrambled eggs and thin slices of toast.

"About her weight," Naomi said, sitting down beside him.

"It's not normal how she's growing. She's twelve years old and wears a size sixteen already. There must be a medical reason for it. No one else in our family is heavy."

Aryeh swallowed a mouthful of eggs. "Ach, leave her be," he said, shrugging his shoulders. "You're just going to give her a complex about it."

"But what if she *does* have a problem?" Naomi persisted. "I've been watching her gain more and more weight these last few years. Maybe she has something that can be treated?"

"Maybe," said Aryeh, finishing his coffee. "Or maybe you're going to drive her crazy." He reached for a *bentcher*. "Look, take her if it will make you feel better. Sorry, I can't talk about it now. Gotta *bentch* and go."

Naomi waved her husband good-bye, scanned through the local phone directory, picked up the phone, and dialed.

"ANY UNUSUAL TIREDNESS?" Dr. Glazer asked Dina, peering over his metal-framed glasses.

"Like what?" Dina answered, puzzled. "You mean sleeping a lot? Sure, I like to sleep, especially on Shabbos."

Naomi cleared her throat. "No, sweetheart, he means *excessive* tiredness, like lack of energy, falling asleep at odd times… those kinds of things… right?" She glanced at the doctor.

"Right." Dr. Glazer nodded.

"No," Dina said abruptly.

"No, what?"

"No, I don't have *excessive* tiredness," Dina said impatiently.

"Okay, good. Now, how's your appetite? Do you eat a lot?"

"I don't know," Dina replied, staring at the thin, gray-haired man behind the desk. "I eat when I'm hungry. Does that mean I eat a lot?"

Naomi gave Dina a withering look. "Just answer the questions properly," she instructed.

"I am," Dina retorted through gritted teeth.

But the list stretched out forever, like a road with no end. What do you eat? How much? Do you snack between meals? Any exercise? Shortness of breath? Dizziness? Ever fainted? Finally, Dr. Glazer finished his interrogation, printed out some forms, scribbled some hasty signatures, and handed them to Naomi. "It doesn't sound like there's any medical problem but have her do these blood tests anyway, and then come back to me," the doctor advised. "And in the meantime, here's a recommendation for a dietician."

"I'm not going!" Dina declared once they'd left the office. Her face was a swirl of angry red embarrassment.

"Oh, yes, you are," Naomi stated firmly. "We are going to get this under control!"

DINA SHUFFLED INTO the kitchen and leaned against the countertop. "Mom," she began hesitantly, running her hand over the marble. "Do you remember I told you that Liora's having this big sleepover?"

"What's that? I can't hear." Naomi switched off the mixer and picked up a carton of low-fat milk.

"I said that Liora's having a slumber party for her birthday and I'd like to go."

"Sounds good," Naomi said, pouring some milk into the mixing bowl. "I like Liora, she's a nice girl… and I can pack up your food for you."

"Well," Dina cleared her throat. "That's just it. It's getting kind of embarrassing to take special food measured out in portions with me, everywhere I go. And I… I'd like to take some nosh like the rest of the girls."

"Nosh!" Naomi swiveled around sharply. "Absolutely not! You can't afford to have any of that junk. Look, I'm making some delicious diet ice cream and if you like, I'll bake some sugar-free cookies as well."

"No!" Dina slapped her hand down on the counter. "I… I mean, it's good of you to make it and all that," she stammered when she saw the look on her mother's face, "but I just want to be the same as everyone else."

Naomi looked at her daughter and sighed. "But you're *not* the same as everyone else," she said, placing her hand gently on Dina's shoulder. "You've got a weight problem."

"It's not a sickness!" Dina cried, shrugging off Naomi's hand. "So why do you treat me as if it is?"

"No, sweetheart, it's not an illness, but it's not healthy to be too heavy. It can cause all kinds of medical problems, you know... and of course, there's *shidduchim* to think about."

Dina grimaced. "Mom, I'm only sixteen and you're worrying that I won't get married."

"I didn't say that," Naomi replied brusquely, turning back to the recipe book. "But it's definitely easier for a girl if she's not overweight."

Hot, frustrated tears burned Dina's eyes. "I'm going to take some nosh anyway," she said fiercely.

Naomi's finger hovered over the button on the mixer. "Look, the diet you were given is keeping your weight under control. Why ruin it?"

"Oof," Dina stamped her foot on the floor like a two-year-old. "Do you know just how embarrassing it is to shlep all this... *stuff*... with me?" She waved her hand disdainfully over the counter. "Just for once, I don't want to think about everything I eat."

Naomi flicked on the switch and the mixer roared into life, drowning out all of Dina's pleas, whipping up her increasing resistance into another perfect portion of dietetic ice cream.

NAOMI STEPPED OVER the scattered cushions on the floor. As she waded through Dina's bedroom, she picked up some wet towels, a robe, a couple of shirts, and two hairbrushes. Naomi smiled to herself. Today, the mess didn't bother her. She had actually been a messy teenager, too, although there were no traces left of it now.

Naomi sat down on Dina's bed and took in the little touches that her daughter had added to make the room hers… the pictures on the wall, the stuffed toys, including her old, one-eyed teddy, jumbled together on her pillows, the fluttery curtains on the windows that she'd sewn from scraps of leftover material. Naomi sighed nostalgically. Soon the room would be empty. Another week and Dina would be off to seminary in Eretz Yisrael. She was going to miss her youngest child terribly. She'd fought tooth and nail for her not to go but Aryeh had won the battle with unusual tenacity. His argument that Dina needed her independence, to get away from home, had been a sharp jab in her side and she was still feeling the pain of it.

Blinking back tears, Naomi stood up and went to open the closet doors. She browsed through Dina's clothes, mentally noting what she needed to buy her before she left. Actually, it was quite a lot of things because Dina had gained some weight lately. Naomi frowned. How would Dina manage her diet portions without her mother's supervision? Now *that* was a worry.

Choked with emotion, Naomi closed the closet doors and lay down on her daughter's bed. She stared up at the ceiling fan that whirled like the thoughts in her head. Her Dina was leaving home! She couldn't wrap her mind around it. It wasn't empty-nest syndrome because Shani was still in the house, but something more, something deeply enmeshed that tied the two of them together with thick twine. She'd always had a soft spot for Dina, even if that wasn't nice to say. Maybe it was because Dina had always been a little different than her siblings? Maybe it was because she'd invested so much in Dina; the special preparation of her food, the careful watching of her diet, the worrying about her health and future. Yes, she was going to miss her. Naomi turned her head and lowered her eyes to look at the floor. Even the mess, she'd miss that, too.

She sank her head back on the pillows and heard a crackling noise underneath them. The candy wrappers that she pulled out made her gasp. So that was it! Dina was cheating, sneaking candy. That's why she'd gained weight. Naomi sprang off the bed. Where was the principal's phone number? She had all the evidence she needed that Dina could not go to seminary without strict supervision!

"SO IT LOOKS like they'll be making a decision any day now," Naomi said breathlessly. "I can hardly wait. You can't imagine what it's like to have to keep my mouth closed every time Shani walks through the door. But those were her instructions. She said she's talked to us enough and now she has to think things through by herself."

Naomi tucked the phone into the crook of her neck while she mixed cake batter. "I'm making some brownies... you know, just in case."

"I hope they'll be used the way you'd like but if not, I'll come help you eat them," her sister laughed.

"Not with me, you won't... I'm on a new diet," Naomi said teasingly. "Just hold on a sec... I'm getting another call." She pressed the button to check the number. "I'll call you back soon. I think it's Dina phoning from Israel."

Naomi hung up and took the incoming call. "Dina, is that you?" she said hurriedly, while trying to stir in the egg yolks.

"Good afternoon, Mrs. Gordon, I hope I'm not disturbing you. This is Mrs. Elinger, Dina's principal."

Naomi's heart took two quick beats. "Is everything okay?" she asked anxiously.

"Yes, yes," Mrs. Elinger reassured her. "I only wanted to update you on Dina's excellent progress. She's truly a wonderful girl with the finest of *middos*. The school is very happy to have her."

"That's great," Naomi said, a little taken aback. She felt as if someone with a hot air balloon had just landed in her living room. "It's so nice of you to call."

"Oh, you're welcome. I always like to keep mothers abreast of what's going on, especially when it's good things. You can be very proud of your daughter, Mrs. Gordon."

"Oh, believe me, I am," Naomi replied quickly. "Tell me, though... how is her weight doing?"

"Excuse me?"

"Her diet... is she sticking to it? I called especially at the beginning of the year to make sure she'd get her low-calorie food and measured portions. If she doesn't keep up with it she'll have serious weight problems."

Mrs. Elinger was quiet, as if she was thinking. "Ah, yes... I remember now," she said at last. "But I really don't think there's an issue. In fact, Dina doesn't look heavy at all."

"It doesn't sound as if we're talking about the same girl," Naomi laughed nervously. "That's not my Dina... she's been overweight almost her whole life."

"Well, not anymore," Mrs. Elinger said in a sure voice. "You don't need to worry."

NAOMI STOOD ON her tiptoes to look over people's heads in front of her.

"When is she coming already?" she muttered to Aryeh impatiently. "It seems like everyone's come through from that flight, except her."

Aryeh smiled indulgently and nodded at Shani. "Your mother just can't wait," he said, ruffling his daughter's hair affectionately.

"Dad," Shani slipped out from under his hand. "I'm not a little girl anymore... I'm getting married."

"You'll always be my little girl," Aryeh grinned. He moved forward to stand next to Naomi and stretched his neck out like an ostrich, in order to see. "I think that's her," he said, pointing to a young girl wheeling an airport trolley with a giant suitcase on it. He strained further. "Yes… yes… it is Dina."

Shani shot off like the gun start of a 100-meter race and was soon embracing her sister, smothering her in velvety warm hugs. Naomi merely stood, staring.

"What's the matter?" Aryeh asked.

"Dina… she's changed."

"Well, she's lost a bit of weight, yes."

"A bit!" Naomi exclaimed. "She's lost a lot!"

Shani was pushing the trolley and walking Dina over to them. Naomi quickly took in her daughter's neatly layered blonde hair and her beloved, if somewhat pale face. She absorbed the smaller-sized clothes that covered her now-slender frame and she smiled. Her face burst into a radiant sunbeam as she took Dina's hands in hers.

"Welcome home, sweetheart… you look absolutely wonderful!"

"ARE YOU SURE you don't need anything else to take back with you?" Naomi asked as she watched Dina struggle to close her case.

"Where do you think I'd put it?" Dina answered, her face creased in irritation.

"I don't know… just asking." Naomi tried to sweep away the hurt.

"Sorry," Dina said, without looking up.

Naomi sat down on Dina's bed and played absently with the clothes that were piled on it. Her daughter had been awfully irritable since the wedding, snapping like a crocodile at every little thing. On more than one occasion, she'd needed to move away from the jaws.

"These will have to go into another bag," she said, lifting up the pile.

"Yes, Mom… I know that."

Ouch, another snap.

"It's been lovely having you home," Naomi began, hoping to keep the reptiles at bay. "And I hope you understood that we couldn't fly you back for both Pesach *and* the wedding."

"Yes, we've talked about that already."

Naomi reached for a small case on the floor and began to pack the clothes in it. "It was fun shopping together," she remarked, nodding toward the items, "especially now that you're much thinner and we could find things to fit you. I couldn't believe how we found matching gowns for all of us so easily this time."

Dina finally zipped the suitcase to the end and flopped back on the carpet. "And at least I didn't ruin the perfect family photographs this time, either," she muttered while leaning over to pick up a stray sock.

Naomi stiffened. "What do you mean by that?"

"Oh, come on, Mom, you know. I was always the giant smudge on the otherwise spotless window. Now you don't have to be embarrassed by me anymore. I'm finally looking the way you wanted."

"I… I'm not sure what you mean…" Naomi felt the words stick to her tongue. "I've… I've always wanted what's best for you. How could you say that?"

Dina looked briefly at her mother. "Never mind… it doesn't matter," she said, and turned away.

Naomi stared at her daughter, watching as she folded her belongings into neat piles, like those on carefully-filled department store shelves. What had happened to the easygoing, messy girl who had merely tossed her clothes into a suitcase before she left? Her Dina had changed. And whatever that seminary was doing to her, Naomi didn't like it… at all.

"A MRS. ELINGER called from Dina's school today," Aryeh said to Naomi casually at suppertime. "She said she's spoken to you a few times already."

"Oh," Naomi said, twisting spaghetti around her fork while her own stomach coiled tightly. "She's Dina's principal. Was she calling to sing Dina's praises again?"

"Not exactly," Aryeh said, his eyes straying towards the newspaper on the edge of the table. "She seemed kind of worried."

Naomi poured some orange juice into two glasses. "Really… what about?"

Aryeh took a drink. "Mrs Elinger thinks that Dina's getting too thin… she's concerned that she may be developing an eating disorder because she's not eating enough and losing more weight."

"Oh, nonsense," Naomi said as she speared a meatball with her fork. "The principal's just nervous. She's been calling me about this as well. Personally, I think *she's* making Dina anxious. Did you see how irritable she was when she was home?"

"She was a lot tidier, I can say that," Aryeh grinned. "What do *you* think?"

"What do I think? I think that Dina is finally getting herself together after all these years and taking control of her life. You saw how good she looked when she came home. I think Mrs. Elinger is exaggerating… that's all."

Aryeh stroked his beard thoughtfully. "Did you notice if she ate while she was here?" he said finally.

"I'd say she was being careful," Naomi replied, "which she wasn't before she left. All in all, considering the amount of food floating around during that week, I think she was very responsible."

"Hmm," Aryeh wiped his mouth with his napkin. "So I guess we'll just have to be on top of it."

THE NEXT PHONE call came when Naomi wasn't even home. It found its way to her mobile while she was over at Shani's, helping to organize her apartment. Somehow, she knew who it was before she answered and her stomach began to twist into familiar knots.

Shani burst into the living room but pulled up sharp when she saw her mother's chalk-white face. "What happened?" she asked with concern.

Naomi let the phone slide out of her hand and stared, glassy-eyed, straight ahead.

"Mom, what's wrong?" Shani shook her mother urgently.

"It's Dina," Naomi said dully. "She's in the hospital."

"Why, what's the matter with her?"

"She collapsed," Naomi said flatly, the words coming out like an automatic voice message. "She's not been eating enough so she's malnourished and dehydrated."

"Oh," Shani said, and looked away, avoiding her mother's eyes.

"The doctors say she may have developed… a… anorexia," Naomi said woodenly. She turned to Shani, scrutinizing her daughter's face, as if hoping it would tell her the information wasn't true.

Shani rocked from one foot to the other. "I… I was afraid it would happen."

Naomi jerked out of her robotic state. "You *knew*?"

Shani sighed. "Well, I could see it coming, let's put it that way." She sat down on the couch and fiddled with the tassels on the cushions.

"Why didn't you tell me?" Naomi cried. "I could have helped her!"

Shani said nothing, reaching instead for some unopened wedding presents that were on the floor.

"I don't understand why nobody alerted me to this." Naomi stood up and paced like an anxious relative outside a hospital recovery room. "It's that bad that they're going to start tube-feeding her and I didn't even *know*?"

Shani took a small, square-shaped gift and began to unwrap it.

"Put that down, I'm talking to you," Naomi ordered, standing in front of her daughter like an army general.

Shani chewed her nails. "I did try to warn you," she mumbled. "We all voiced our concern… but… you didn't take it too seriously."

"Of course I'd have taken it seriously. I'm her mother! I have worried about Dina all her life. I knew that she shouldn't have gone away to seminary and I was right!"

Shani began playing with another package absently. "It's… it's not the seminary, Mom. I… think they're trying to help her."

"Of course they are. Look what's happened since she went there. She needs to be home with me where I can take care of her and make sure…"

"… that she doesn't eat too much," Shani blurted, immediately covering her mouth in horror.

Naomi gasped, clutching her stomach as if she'd been kicked. In a daze she lowered herself to the sofa, perching on the edge of it, as if unsure she was welcome.

"It was such a busy time when Dina was here, Mom. Nobody could blame you for not noticing," Shani rushed to ease the pain. "And you were thrilled that she looked so good… that this time she could wear the same style of gown as everyone else."

Words were echoing in Naomi's head, as empty and hollow as they'd sounded at the time.

"*Now you don't have to be embarrassed by me anymore. I'm finally looking the way you wanted.*"

That silent accusatory sentence turned around in her mind, the words wound together like barbed wire, each twist of the rope cutting into her heart and sending searing pain across her chest.

"And anyway, it wasn't for sure, then," Shani was saying, trying to pour balm over her mother's wounds. "Dina didn't actually *say* anything to me, it was just kind of obvious, you know… the way she behaved."

Naomi did not react, caught as she was by the memory of Dina's words, pinning her down and stopping her from running to a safe, ignorant place.

Is that what Dina really thought... that only her looks had mattered? Of course it wasn't about that. She just wanted her daughter to be healthy and find a good husband, that's all.

"I'm finally looking the way you wanted."

Dina's words twisted again, sending more jabs into Naomi's side. Just who was she kidding? Yes, she *had* wanted all those things... but she also wanted Dina to be thin.

"Well, *now I am*," that familiar voice reflected back.

Naomi dropped her head into her hands and leaned forward, trying to unravel the knots and straighten the wire, but her heart was still bleeding and sore. Had her concern for Dina really been something more self-centered? Was the way Dina *looked* more important to her than the way she'd *felt*?

Suddenly, the thick twine that had bound the two of them so tightly together was nothing more than an ugly, twisted barbed-wire fence. How she wished she knew how to straighten the kinks so that the love she felt for her daughter would be a balm for her spirit rather than the cause of her pain.

At first glance it might seem that "Measuring Up" is a story about eating disorders. Actually, it's more about the demands and expectations that mothers can place on their daughters, even to the point of living "through them." The eating disorder was merely a setting in which to address these issues although it morphed into a topic in its own right.

This issue of demands and expectations was something I had personally been grappling with. My oldest daughter was an extremely talented classical ballet dancer. She studied with a frum dance teacher, along with other religious girls, and performed for women and girls only. I took great pleasure in watching her and was transported back to my childhood when I also danced, on skates! I greatly encouraged my daughter to dance as much as possible and was willing to invest all the time and energy necessary to enable her to do this. Her dancing was like me dancing. Although I wasn't aware of it at the time, I was living my own dream through my daughter. The result... she stopped! There were other reasons for this, but the pressure I unwittingly added did not help. Today she no longer dances.

I learned the lesson the hard way. In contrast, my other daughter (who has inherited the same talent) does dance. She takes classes three times a week and also practices and performs with a religious girls' dance ensemble. And I leave her alone! I don't push or pressurize because her dancing is for her, not for me. I want it to be hers, just to enjoy and do whatever she wants with it; no pressure, no expectations. When I watch her perform I get great pleasure; for her sake, not mine. And she loves it!

I believe that on some level all parents live through their children and place demands on them to "perform," even if only a little. "Measuring Up" was a format to show how dangerous it can be when we do that. This example was more extreme but the message is still the same. We have to let our children be who they are even if it's not always to our liking. We have to let them live their own lives — which might be very different than our own — and accept them anyway. If not, the damage can be great.

Against a Wall

"WE SHOULDN'T TELL the kids yet," said Sara sadly, a lump as big as a baseball forming in her throat.

Rafi was sitting at the kitchen table, rummaging through upturned drawers of documents.

"Do you know where the passports are?" he asked distractedly. "I can't find Rivki's."

Sara sank down on a chair beside him. "I said we shouldn't tell the kids yet," she repeated. Rafi abruptly stopped his search and regarded his wife's dejected face.

"I know," he said gently, "but we have to."

SINCE THEY GOT married, she'd known that this could happen. But as the years rolled by, she secretly hoped her husband's dream to be a *kiruv* Rabbi in *chutz laAretz* had faded. Of course, she felt guilty about that. What kind of wife wouldn't follow her husband to the other side of the world? It was just that, well, her soul was embedded in the spiritual soil of Eretz Yisrael; she had felt that way ever since she arrived as a seminary girl a long time ago. How could she possibly live anywhere else?

Rafi had been hesitant to tell her about the wonderful opportunity he'd been offered.

"Just think, Sara, of all the amazing things we could do over there," he tried convincing her. "All those Jewish souls we can bring back to *Yiddishkeit.*"

"No," she stated firmly.

"You can work with the women… teach, like you love to."

"No."

"Sara, please just think about it. I don't have to give an answer yet. Just think it over."

"No, I'm not going." With the determination of a two-year-old, she'd clenched her mouth tightly shut, turned her back and continued doing the dishes.

OF COURSE SHE couldn't stay that way, like a frozen statue of ice in the middle of a lake. She had to thaw. Actually, it was impossible not to, with all the people who tried to encourage her to let her husband use his gifts for *Klal Yisrael.* Then there were the Rabbis he'd taken her to see.

"Go," they all said. "Do your work and come back."

So her icicles melted, slowly sliding down her until they surged like waterfalls. She never knew she had so many tears.

"I THINK," SAID Rafi thoughtfully, "you might even like America." They'd just settled the children to sleep after the Friday evening meal and were relaxing in the living room, enjoying the Shabbos peace.

"I hate America."

"Sara, you've only been there once. How can you tell?"

"Once," she declared, "is enough. Besides, I don't like Americans."

"Well," said Rafi, grinning, "you're married to one."

"You know what I mean. It's not my culture."

"Yes," Rafi smiled. "I used to say the same about Australians, and then I married you."

"That's different," Sara argued. "Don't try to persuade me. I know I'm going to hate it."

She curled her legs underneath her on the recliner and appraised her cozy surroundings, familiar to her as a second skin. Over there she'd have a big house, bigger than anything she could imagine. And a garden! Oh, how she yearned for a garden; a place to spend long, lazy summer nights with the children. But she didn't want to go there for that. She'd have lived in a box just to stay in Eretz Yisrael. She closed her eyes, trying to imprint the image of her humble home within her heart.

"DADDY, WHY IS Mummy crying again?" seven-year-old Shloimi questioned, an anxious look creasing his young face.

"Yeah, she always cries these days. Why is she so unhappy?" ten-year-old Rivki wanted to know.

The four-year-old twins, Shishi and Shevi, were snuggled comfortably on Rafi's lap. They looked at their father. "Is something hurting Mummy? Does she have a tummy ache?" asked Shevi.

Rafi smiled and drew the children closer. "The reason Mummy's sad," he began, "is because Daddy got a new job as a Rabbi in America, so we're leaving Eretz Yisrael once school is over."

All four of the children squealed at once.

"You mean we're going to live there?"

"Are we going on an airplane?"

"What about my friends, can they come, too?"

Rafi held the children tightly. "Soon," he said, "I'll tell you everything — where we're going to live, the names of your schools. But first, there's a lot to do."

"But Daddy," Rivki queried again, worry clouding her wise eyes, "why isn't Mummy happy?"

"Well," he explained gently, "your mother *is* happy for me, but she loves Eretz Yisrael so much that her heart is breaking."

EVERYWHERE SHE WENT, she cried. Each small outing anywhere in her neighborhood, in her Land, was, for her, the last.

She tried not to count the days, because, like counting the *Omer*, doing so would bring her closer to the end — and, unlike *Sefiras HaOmer*, she didn't anticipate the end. She would never be ready. The good-byes, she knew, would be terrible; her heart ached with the thought of it. And, oh, she was so jealous. Why did her friends get to stay behind, while *she* had to leave? She felt like she was being spat out, like she was unworthy of living in the Land, undeserving of the precious gift.

Knowing that Rafi's family was over there waiting for them brought her no comfort, either. America was vast, and they were settling in some hick town far from the city, so it seemed unlikely that they'd see the family very often.

But the worst thing was the guilt. More than anything, she wished to be a loyal, devoted wife, standing staunchly by her husband's side instead of drowning in pools of tears all day. She wanted to be happy, but she just couldn't. She *was* proud of him, of his successes and talents, but her heart had shrunk, too small now to hold anything other than her pain, too contracted to let anything else in. How much more crying could she do? She was making everybody miserable.

"SARA?" RAFI TIPTOED softly into the girls' bedroom. Night had slipped in soundlessly and his wife was sitting on the floor in the dark, sorting through toys and clothes. The hallway light lingered in the doorway, casting a soft glow around her head. She seemed lost in thought, as though her mind had already flown far away.

"Sara," he said again, "can I talk to you a moment?"

Wearily, she sighed, resting her hands on top of the carefully folded clothes in her lap.

"Yes… of course."

Rafi knelt cautiously down beside her. It seemed like an entire ocean had opened between them, and he wasn't sure how to swim across it. He paused, struggling for the right words.

"I can't do this to you, Sara," he finally said. "I can't see you in so much pain. I'm breaking your heart."

She raised her deep, dark eyes to his, giant question marks flashing inside them.

"I've changed my mind, Sara — we're not going. I won't take you away."

Slowly, he stood. With heavy steps, he walked out of the room and quietly closed the door, taking the last remaining light with him. She stared after him, stunned, wrapped inside the darkness where he'd left her. What had he just said? They weren't leaving after all?

She should have been happy... but she wasn't.

EARLY THE NEXT morning, Sara found herself riding the bus to the Kosel. The spring air was fresh and inviting with the promise of a new day. She watched the world go by through the window as she gathered her scattered thoughts. She wasn't sure where to put them anymore; everything was so confusing.

The Kosel plaza was unusually quiet, except for the sentry of circling birds singing their welcome. The emptiness around her felt hollow, like the gaping hole inside her. She hoped Hashem would fill it with His wisdom, with His truth. Entering the square she passed some elderly, arthritic ladies collecting money for *tzedakah*, and as the sun winked its way through the clouds, she dropped coins into their withered palms.

Soon she would go to the Wall to *daven*, but for now she wanted only to look, to capture its holiness in the lens of her heart and carry it close to her forever. She sat down on a stone ledge facing the ancient stones. When, she asked herself, would she be back here again? If they did leave, she'd never be able to visit whenever she liked. But then, she realized, how often did she actually come, anyway? Suddenly Sara saw all the missed opportunities pass before her eyes, times she could have, should have taken advantage of living in the Holy Land, but didn't. There were so many of them — scores of those missed opportunities.

Out of the corner of her eye, Sara noticed a young girl walking towards her. She looked about eleven years old and had the sparkling freshness of a first-time visitor.

"Excuse me," the girl began, in a thick American accent. "Do you think you could help me find the right page in my *siddur*?"

Taking the leather-bound, Hebrew-English prayer book gently from her, Sara turned the crisp, gild-edged pages until she found the morning blessings. She turned back to the girl and smiled. "What a beautiful *siddur*. Is it new?"

"Yes," the girl answered excitedly. "It's my first one… for my bat mitzvah. I don't really know how to *daven* properly yet; I'm still a bit new at all this."

"Really." Sara's curiosity was aroused. "Have you recently become religious?"

"My whole family has," the girl replied, with the eager enthusiasm of someone who has discovered gold. "We arrived in Israel yesterday for a visit, and I couldn't wait to come here… Do you think you could show me what we're supposed to do here at the Kotel?" she asked shyly. "I mean, if you have the time?"

Sara stared at the sweet, idealistic girl standing before her and was inspired. In a flash, all those missed opportunities were there again, as if on a screen, reeling back and forth like a slide show. Time… of course she would make the time! She wasn't going to miss this chance. And probably, she conceded, her husband shouldn't miss his, either.

She drew in a long, deep breath and tried to find courage within herself. No, it was not going to be easy.

She tilted her head toward the girl and smiled. "What's your name?" she asked.

"Becky."

Sara stretched out her hand.

"Come," she beckoned.

And they walked together toward the Wall, pressed their faces to the precious stones… and prayed.

This story was almost mine and my husband's, though some details were changed. For example, my husband was not a kiruv Rabbi, but he did dream of moving back to America during the early years when making a parnassah was difficult. I am from England, not Australia, and I did not like Americans, let alone want to marry one, because I'd had negative experiences with the Yanks during my time at the one-year Overseas Program at Hebrew University. I was, and still am, passionate about Eretz Yisrael and did not want to entertain the idea of leaving. However, when money became tight and the chances of getting a new job were slim, that's exactly what hubby wanted to do… go back to the U.S. I resisted for as long as possible until I could hold out no longer. It was too painful to see him so stressed and unhappy. So, reluctantly and miserably, I gave in and agreed to go.

The search for jobs in America began. In the meantime, I walked around with a heavy heart and constant tears at the thought of leaving. I honestly did feel that I was unworthy to be here, that I was being spat out of the Land, and I was insanely jealous of all my friends who I was leaving behind.

(I have to add here that my children reacted exactly the way I described in the story when we told them we were going.)

It seems that my tears melted Hashem's heart; that and the fact that my husband displayed tremendous mesirus nefesh by turning down a good job offer in a small American community because of the lack of Yiddishkeit. A job did not materialize over there but one did pop up here; a job he is fortunate to have until today. So we were staying after all. Hodu laShem ki tov!!

Whenever I read this story, I remember those difficult years, my agonizing decision to leave and our rejoicing when we found out we didn't have to. I am forever grateful to live here in eretz hakodesh. And my husband is, too!

Opportunities

I WATCHED. THAT'S what I do best. In my quiet way, I see things that you probably wouldn't even notice. I see sounds, emotions, lines etched on faces, crinkled corners of mouths; whatever it is that I need in order to know someone's story. So, on that cold wintry evening, coming home late after art class, I stood silently on the corner of the darkened side street and observed Ginger Harris and his group of friends robbing old Mr. Jacobs's grocery store. Except for the pounding of my pulse, I couldn't feel anything as I watched the boys smash windows and climb inside, hurl cartons of fruit and vegetables like hand grenades; throw apples and oranges back and forth like baseballs. It was really awful. Believe me, there are some things you just don't want to see!

Suddenly, my schoolbag slipped from my hand and crashed onto the pavement. Ginger, on alert like a trapped animal, turned his head sharply in my direction. Shrinking back into a nearby doorway, I wished that the shadows would swallow me.

"Hey, you, deaf girl!" The redheaded ringleader strode towards me and jabbed his finger painfully into my shoulder. "You didn't see this, okay? You'd better not say anything… or else!"

With my frightened eyes, I read the lips on his flushed face and felt his angry vibrations jolt my body like aftershocks. Fearfully, I nodded vigorously, praying that he'd release his tight grip on my arm. With a quick shove, he pushed me forcefully out of the alleyway and into the street.

"Get out of here," he commanded. "Run." And I did. I'm a good runner, the fastest kid on my block, so I didn't look back until I spotted the red-tiled roof of our corner house and burst through the gate like I was crossing a finishing line.

NOBODY REALLY LISTENS to a "deaf girl" anyway, so Ginger and his gang needn't have worried. Some people think I'm a bit on the slow side, even mentally disabled, but I'm used to it by now. Sometimes when people talk to me they shout, or they stick their faces so close to mine that our noses are almost touching; or even worse, I am ignored completely, insignificant as a speck of dust in the atmosphere. But that's life, I suppose, or my life, anyway. Don't get me wrong, I'm not complaining or anything. I've got a fabulous family and friends and at least the people in my small town know me, so most of them are more understanding of my situation. But there's always somebody...

When I slipped into the house, I was welcomed with a warm aroma wafting from the kitchen. Mmm, it smelled like my mother's famous tomato soup with *kneidlach*. After what I'd just seen, though, I wasn't too hungry, so I raced upstairs to my bedroom before anyone could notice me. I needed to put myself back together before going down for supper.

"YOU'LL NEVER GUESS what happened," exclaimed my father when he walked into the house from shul the next morning. "Poor Mr. Jacobs had his store vandalized and robbed last night. What a mess it is. Everything's smashed up, his merchandise is all over the street and the town is in an uproar!"

My mother laid his breakfast plate on the table in front of him. "How awful," she empathized. "Whoever would want to do that to a helpless old man?"

As I looked between my parents, reading their lips, my stomach began to bubble with a sickly feeling. "I'll bet it was that Ginger and his friends," my father continued. "Can't think of anyone else in town who'd do something like this."

"Maybe it was *goyim?*" my mother suggested while flipping over a fresh cheese omelet.

"No, I don't think so," he shook his head. "How many *goyim* do we have here?"

My mother nodded. "What a waste," she said sadly. "Ginger was such a good boy until his father became sick with that awful illness... what's it called?"

"Multiple sclerosis," Abba answered.

Ima shook her head again. "What a terrible disease and especially for such an active man. I don't know how Mrs. Harris copes with all those children and a bedridden husband."

"Well, that's just it, she doesn't; despite the help the community is giving her," my father confirmed.

"Good morning, Tamari," my mother suddenly smiled, turning towards me so her face was directly in front of mine. I'd been sitting quietly, trying to blend in with the wallpaper. "Abba was just telling me about the destruction to Mr. Jacobs's store last night."

I squirmed; oh gosh, I hoped they wouldn't ask me any awkward questions.

"Yes," my father continued. "You're lucky you didn't run into it, because it seems like it happened around the time you'd have been coming home from art class. You really need to be careful."

Uh huh, it was time to make my escape! I slipped my sleeves into my warm, wool winter coat, picked up my schoolbag off the table and painted on a smile. "Don't worry," I enunciated my words clearly, just like they'd taught me in therapy. "I know how to take care of myself."

AND THANKS TO my parents, I did. What a shock they received eleven years ago to find out that their only child was deaf.

Actually, I wasn't born deaf, my parents always remind me; not that it helps too much. I've heard the story over and over like some kind of family folk legend; how it was the strong intravenous antibiotics I was given for a life-threatening case of bacterial meningitis that did the damage when I was six months old; how my parents cried when they brought me home because I would never hear their lullabies or laughter or the lilt of their voices.

I've got the best parents. Really! It wasn't easy for them, as you can imagine, but they're very strong, so I'm lucky. Initially, my mother took a leave of absence from her job as a social worker. She took me all over the country to tons of doctors, looking for the magic man to appear in silver sprinkles and gold dust who would help me hear again. Well, he never arrived, so then my parents began researching things by themselves. My mother's always reading, even now; looking for new methods and techniques that can help me.

I communicate by lip reading. My parents decided that was best, because sign language would have kept me isolated from the hearing world, comfortable only with others like myself. I've been reading fluently since I'm six years old and that's highly unusual for someone in my situation. I love reading; I can really disappear into those books. Sometimes I think my parents taught me so well, I could read the whole library. You see, for them, I was always a child first and foremost, and had a hearing impairment second, and if you ask me, that's a pretty healthy attitude. Like I said, my parents are amazing.

"DID YOU HEAR what happened to Mr. Jacobs's store?" my friend Mally asked me as she slid into her seat next to mine in class.

"Yes," I answered, and left it at that.

"I wonder who did it," she continued while I busied myself taking out my schoolbooks. Mally is hearing impaired too, although unlike me, her hearing aids give her some sounds. She's a year older than me and we're like sisters, which is great, because it can get lonely sometimes on your own. Our mothers are really good friends, too, so that's really neat, and they've raised lots of money for our special class in the mainstream school. You wouldn't believe how many therapies and how much expensive equipment we need, but my mother says that soon I'll go to a regular class and have someone sitting with me all the time to help me.

"Mari," Mally used the affectionate version of my name, "is something wrong?"

Well, I guess you could say that. Should I tell her or not? We usually shared everything with each other. And maybe I was even going against the Torah by not speaking out? Ginger, however, was not someone to start up with. For a start, he was twice my size, much older-looking than fourteen, already tall and muscular. And boy, was he strong! I'd seen for myself how he'd hurled those heavy cartons one-handed, like a discus thrower. No, I didn't want to make him angry. Inside myself, though, I smiled ironically; after all, keeping quiet had never been my difficulty. I turned my head slightly to Mally, unable to meet her eyes.

"No," I replied. "Just got a headache, that's all."

GINGER WAS WAITING for me after school. In the long, wintry evenings, daylight disappeared early into darkness. I've always hated the winter when, coming home from school, the side streets were already draped in black shapes that lurk in corners, ready to leap out at me; and now I had to worry about Ginger Harris as well. Here he was, blocking my path as I made my brisk walk home.

"Remember, deaf girl," I could feel the heat of his breath on my face like a panting dog. "You're not to say anything… understand?"

Yes, I understood… loud and clear!

"MARI," MY MOTHER motioned me over to her on the couch, "I want you to rest as much as you can before your operation next week. And don't make a face about it." I gave my mother one of my looks. "I know you're nervous about the surgery," she said understandingly, "but it will all be worth it in the end. Won't it be amazing to finally hear?"

Of course it would, what a silly question. Wouldn't it? Actually, I wasn't sure, and what's worse, I wasn't even sure why I wasn't sure. How could I answer that question? How *would* it feel to hear? I had no idea. All I'd ever known was the quietness. Yes, I was excited about the new treatment that would hopefully change that, but I was also so terribly frightened. I guess my intuitive mother understood, because suddenly, I found myself in her arms, wrapped inside one of her special hugs.

MY PARENTS WERE more enthusiastic than I was about the cochlear implant. They'd read up loads about this new medical breakthrough and managed to find some top doctor to do the procedure. Dr. Simon, the ENT specialist, does this kind of stuff all day long, so he really knows what he's doing… I hope. I've been going to him for months already, and he's a very nice man, also Jewish like us, so that makes me feel better. Anyway, he explained it all to me and said that I'd be able to understand because I'm so smart and grown up for my age. Funny, people say that about me all the time. Well, I *am* almost bat mitzvah and anyway, I guess you have to grow up pretty fast in my situation.

"It's like this," Dr. Simon said as he printed a strange diagram off the computer. "Here's your ear (*My ear*, I thought in amusement, *how did it get there?*) and here's the part inside it called the cochlea; that's where the nerves are."

He could have been speaking a foreign language for all I knew, but as he rattled along, I did get a reasonable idea of what he was talking about. My cochlea was damaged, so it couldn't send signals from outside sounds to my auditory nerve. The new cochlea would bypass mine and send electrical signals to stimulate the nerve that would then enable me to hear. Dr. Simon continued with his explanation while I chewed the top of a pencil I'd found on the desk. "This part," he pointed with his finger, "will be inserted under your skull (uh oh… I thought I'd faint when he said that), and this part," he pointed again, "is the speech processor which can be worn behind your ear like a hearing aid, in a pocket or on a belt."

"Great," I thought to myself. "I'm going to look like some sort of alien." I briefly pictured antennae sticking out of my head, wobbling as I walked and looking like one of those bobbing toy dogs perched in the back of car windows. Dr. Simon beckoned with his hand to get my attention.

"Basically," he pronounced the words slowly and clearly so I could read his lips, "you'll be getting a new, bionic ear."

Oh cool, I thought. *Now* that *part sounded good.*

WHEN I CHECKED into the hospital a few days later, the robbery at Mr. Jacobs's store was still the talk of the town. I've never seen the neighbors so upset and they all pitched in to clean up and get the shop back in order. Poor Mr. Jacobs was heartbroken. "What do they want from an old man like me?" he'd wailed. "I'm only trying to make a living." Plenty of suspicion rested on Ginger and his friends but no one could prove anything. Meanwhile, I ate myself up with guilt, for I could have handed them all the necessary proof on a plate, but I didn't. What would you have done in my position?

WHEN I AWOKE, I wanted to go right back to sleep. Even though I was lying down I was dizzy and my head was heavy and covered on one side with a bandage that smelled like hospitals. It took a few moments to remember where I was until, wincing with pain, I looked up into my parents' anxious eyes.

"I can't hear anything!" I cried in alarm.

"You're not supposed to, honey," Ima reassured me. "First you need to recover from the surgery and in three or four weeks the device will be switched on."

Oh, of course, I'd forgotten about that. Well, I guess I'd waited this long. What were another few weeks?

"GOOD NIGHT, MARI, get some sleep now," Abba kissed me gently on the forehead.

"We'll be back in the morning to take you home," Ima said. "Are you sure you'll be all right by yourself?"

I nodded my head affirmatively. "That's my girl, independent as usual," Abba laughed. "But if you need anything, just have the nurse call us."

I waved them out of the doorway and into the corridor, and then sank back onto my pillows, exhausted and ready to fold for the night. As I closed my eyes, slowly drifting off, I felt a vibration on the floor next to my bed and jerking upright, I looked into the face… of Ginger! My eyes darted around the room in panic, searching for the nurse call button, but until I found it, it was just the two of us, alone in my hospital room. I felt like a bird was caught inside my rib cage.

"This is just a reminder," he said clearly, making sure I could read his lips. "You didn't see anything, right? I… I could go to jail, you know."

I stared at him in silence and I found a flicker of something, fear maybe, within his troubled, sea-green eyes. He looked kind of nervous underneath all that toughness. Still, it didn't really matter, did it? I had no energy for all this. Why couldn't he just leave me alone?

"Er, can you hear anything yet?" he asked hesitantly. I wondered how he knew about the implant, but then again, in our small town, people know what you eat for breakfast. I still didn't answer. In that instant, Ginger retrieved his swagger and wrapped it around himself like a steel cloak.

"Understand, deaf girl? Just keep your mouth closed!"

The next minute he was gone and I thought that maybe, in my post anesthetic, drowsy state, I'd dreamt the whole thing. But I hadn't. Why had Ginger come? What had made him travel all the way to the hospital just to deliver another warning? What was he afraid of? The questions ran up and down in my mind like an escalator until I stepped off with the answers. Could it be that he thought hearing and talking go together; that if I could hear then I'd spill everything out? Now that was funny. Did he really think that I couldn't have told by now if I'd wanted? I had no problem making myself understood, and besides, I had a good, strong hand to write with. No, it had to be more than that. In his eyes, being "deaf" meant that I was vulnerable; he could intimidate me. Hearing meant my being the same as everyone else... "normal," strong, independent... and maybe that's what Ginger was afraid of. When I looked at it like this, I felt a bit better... less afraid of him. Turning my head slightly, something made me gaze at the slightly open door Ginger had left behind and I caught a glimpse of a familiar black shape in the hallway. As I drifted back to sleep, I wondered fleetingly who it was.

"AM I REALLY going to hear?" I questioned my mother again as we entered the revolving hospital doors.

"Well, that's the plan," she answered, smiling. "That's why we're doing this. After you're switched on today and finish the mapping, you should be able to hear sounds."

"I wonder what it's going to be like." Anxiety and excitement danced around each other inside the ballroom of my stomach.

"I believe that it's strange at first; the sounds may be somewhat uncomfortable but the settings will be adjusted until you get used to them." My mother pressed the elevator button for the sixth floor and we squeezed ourselves inside. I was ready to burst with my mixed emotions before the doors even closed.

"TAKE IT OFF, take it off!" I clapped my hands over my ears and screamed.

"Mari, it's okay. There's nothing to be frightened of. It's just a little loud for you, that's all." My mother was holding me tightly and trying to speak above the racket I was making while the hospital audiologist adjusted buttons and other devices on her machine. I broke free from her and bolted like a runaway horse, bucking and rearing its legs in fright. I didn't know where to put myself. What was this *noise?*

"Stop it, stop it; make it stop!" I opened my mouth and screamed over and over again from the deepest of places. Strange, guttural, animal sounds escaped from somewhere within me, and the weirdest thing was… I could hear them.

"NO, I TOLD you, I'm not going to use it." I turned my head sideways so my parents couldn't talk to me, a power that I knew I had, but seldom used.

"Please, Mari," my mother pleaded, pulling me towards her. "Just give it a chance, even for just a few minutes a day, until you get used to it."

I shook my head resolutely. I can be pretty stubborn when I want to, let me tell you. No. If this was the hearing world, they could keep it. Give me the silence and softness, not the ear-splitting sounds that felt like explosions inside my head. My world was quiet, calm and peaceful like a cool forest where lush leaves on thick trees protected me from the harsh rays of the sun. True, I could only really communicate properly with others like myself, or people who understood me, but so what. Things were just fine before I had this contraption drilled into my head.

"Mari, please," my parents tried again to convince me, while I in turn tried not to notice their worry and pain.

"I'm sorry," I said to them, "but I just can't."

IT HAD BEEN over three weeks and still I wouldn't use the implant. At times I almost caved in, thinking that maybe it wouldn't be so bad after all, but then I'd remember the shrill, invasive screeches that had rained down like missiles and I'd shake off my doubts like water from a wet dog. That had happened again yesterday evening until I'd made myself walk downstairs to the living room to distract my thoughts. As I reached the bottom of the stairs, I caught a brief glimpse of a boy entering my father's office and stopped abruptly in my tracks. Was that Ginger who'd just walked into my father's room? It sure looked like him, with that mop of auburn hair. Actually, since all this implant business, I'd forgotten all about him. Come to think about it, I hadn't seen him since that visit to the hospital. No, I said to myself, it couldn't be him here in my house. Lots of people always came to see my father for advice so it could have been anyone. I turned the knob on the study door slightly. It was locked.

I WAS SWIVELING on the garden swing enjoying a crisp, sunny Shabbos afternoon. It had been another hard week, batting back and forth with my parents, teachers and therapists on the same subject. Even Mally had joined forces with everyone. I was isolating myself, they all told me, disconnecting myself from the "normal" world, and missing out on an opportunity to reach my potential. At times of frustration when I remained unresponsive, words like stubborn, strong-willed and headstrong were thrown in my direction, but I just lowered my head and let them fly over me. I was weary... we all were. The truth was that all of it was chipping away at the wall I'd built around myself; stones were crumbling, more bricks tumbling out every day. And yet, something was holding me back.

I SENSED HIS presence before I saw him. The vibration of his feet, his smell, and the feel of him, all matched to one person...

Ginger. His shadow arrived with gray clouds that briefly blocked the winter sun and I shivered in the sudden afternoon chill. I looked up from the ground where I'd been gazing at tens of tiny new shoots poking their heads through the soil in preparation for spring. Ginger shifted uncomfortably, rocking back and forth from one foot to the other, hands stuffed in his jean pockets.

"Er, um… Tamari," he looked straight at me so I could read his lips. "Can I talk to you?"

I looked at him sharply. Talk to *me*? Now that was a good one. Since when did Ginger Harris *talk* to anyone? He gave his orders and that was that; I couldn't recall him ever being polite enough to use my name. I tried to read his face and wondered what he wanted from me this time. To tell you the truth, I was getting pretty sick of his sudden appearances in my life. On the top of his curly auburn hair, I noticed a small leather yarmulke, sitting on his head like an upturned saucer. *Interesting*, I thought, *that was something new.*

"What did you come for?" I raised my eyebrows questioningly.

Ginger hesitated and I kept staring at him, the boy who'd been so full of himself, the leader of the gang. Well, he didn't seem like that now. He pulled a small notepad and pen out of his pocket.

"I just wanted to say sorry about all that stuff that happened," he wrote.

"Maybe you should say sorry to Mr. Jacobs instead?" I wrote back.

Ginger stopped writing and looked at me intently. "I already did. I'm even working in his store. Your father arranged it."

I took the notepad again. "What's my father got to do with all this?" Things were getting more confusing by the minute.

"He knows everything," Ginger explained, continuing to talk directly to me instead of writing. "That night, at the hospital, he saw me go into your room and waited outside afterwards. Since then he's been helping me. He straightened things out with the police so I could have a chance to get my life back together, and he got me a job. He's a great guy, your dad."

Slowly, like dissipating early morning mist, it dawned on me that the boy who'd entered my father's study *had* been Ginger after all. I hadn't imagined it. Ginger Harris, who had never taken help from anyone, had allowed *my* father to do so. I was so very proud, warmed inside, like when I drink a hot cup of cocoa on a snowy white night.

"There's something else, though," he paused, taking a deep breath. "What about that thing they stuck on your ear? Why aren't you using it?"

I stiffened. Weren't we talking about him, not me? I didn't like where this conversation was going. "Did my father send you?" I asked suspiciously.

"No," Ginger answered, "he didn't. But he did mention that you don't want to use it and… well, I owe your father a lot.

"Why didn't Abba tell me that he knew?" I persisted.

"Well, I asked him not to… things were uncomfortable at first… and I had to work through some stuff… you know."

I nodded. Yup, I sure did.

"You're just scared, that's all," Ginger continued. "So was I… frightened of new things, like I'd fail or something; I know all about that. Kinda like a waste, though, isn't it? You must be crazy not to use that thing that won't make you deaf anymore."

Well, he was certainly blunt; nothing like saying things straight! I wanted to be angry with him, but couldn't. I lowered my head, so he shouldn't see the tears welling in my eyes. Ginger was gesturing animatedly, lest he lose my attention, and I looked up reluctantly.

"So watcha gonna do about it then? Look at me… I'm pulling things together now and it's pretty neat. Shoulda done this ages ago. All you're doin' is hurtin' yourself."

I knew he was right. My tears spilled over, full of my fears and anxiety over joining the "hearing world" and leaving the safety of mine. Whatever confidence I had thought I had was only familiarity; soft cushions inside my comfort zone. Really I was a coward;

too scared to move on, to make changes. And now, here I was, crying unashamedly in front of this boy who, until today, had only ever called me "deaf girl." I felt like a jumbled-up jigsaw, straightening out the pieces.

Ginger started writing again and pressed a note into my hand. "If I can do it, so can you," it said. "Just got to jump in, that's all; it's like learning to swim."

I wanted it! Yes, I did! I knew it, really. Despite the difficulties I'd have to face, I still wanted it. I stared at Ginger and marveled over his plain, simple understanding, his newfound capacity to care and my father's role in that, and with deliberate, precise movements of the lips, I mouthed, "Thank you."

I glanced down again at those delicate shoots peeking through the soil and thought about all the beautiful new beginnings. Suddenly, a strong gust of wind tugged at the clouds, clearing the sky. Together, Ginger and I looked up at the horizon and I realized that we were both seeing the same sun. I smiled. A bright and wondrous world was waiting for us!

I wrote this story while in the throes of incapacitating medical treatment. When I say "wrote," I mean that I somehow managed to throw out a few sentences at a time, a paragraph here or there. In the terrible physical state I was in — where I could barely keep awake for too long or walk up a flight of stairs — it was hard to be creative. That required energy and an active mind, which I didn't have. How I managed to write this story is a mystery to me. But on some level, it was a victory!

The story begins with the protagonist, Mari, talking about how she watches what's going on around her quietly. That has always been a trait of mine, too, but during my illness this behavior was heightened. I was in a "seeing" position most of the time, forced out of the "normal" world and thrust into a different one. This new world with a different way of seeing things became a place I didn't want to leave. There was a beauty and safety to it that the outside world didn't have and I wanted to stay there. Mari's fear of change, of going out into something so alien to her, was mine, because that's what the "real" world had become to me. My world was now the real one, and even though I have rejoined society, I still believe that the place I "lived" in for that year was the true reality, a glimpse of life beyond the physical one down here.

The sounds that were too loud for Mari to cope with were the noises I heard when "venturing out." I found the world abrasive, jarring, horribly uncomfortable. It literally made me squirm. On my occasional trips out (usually to the hospital), the sound of peoples' voices, unashamed conversations on cell phones, music blasting in stores in the mall, made me physically ill and sent me running back to the safety of my four walls. After I finished my treatment I encountered major resistance to rejoining society; like Mari, I was terrified. It was only after I grew stronger and had several conversations with my Rav, where he explained that I had a responsibility to put back into the world what I had learned, that I was able to make the transition. However, like Mari, I still have a feeling of being different until today.

I'm not quite sure why I chose a hearing impaired girl as the protagonist for my story. Maybe because I had a friend with a hearing impaired grandchild and she would tell me about both her struggles and triumphs. I did a lot of research about cochlear implants and the pros and cons of lip reading versus sign language. Of course, I wanted to transmit the message that we should make the most of every opportunity and not be afraid to change, but perhaps most of all, I wanted to present the possibility that a way of living that can seem disabling, pitiful, even, can actually be very beautiful.

The Shelter

"CHECK!" I MOVE my Knight into position.

"Mate!" Tuli quickly places his Queen in front of mine.

"I'm not playing with you again; you always win," I sulk, scooping the pieces off the chessboard.

My brother leans back on his chair, puts his hands behind his head and laughs. "Gila, you're a sore loser."

I throw him a dirty look and snap the board closed.

"When are we gonna get out of here?" Tuli asks. "I want to start building the *sukkah* already."

"What *sukkah*?" Mr. Amsalom grunts from his seat near us. "Are you mad? Who's going to be sitting in a *sukkah* this year?"

He's always like this, Mr. Amsalom. Grouchy and dry with a face like a shriveled prune. Ima says that he used to be religious once, before he lost his wife and children in a tragic traffic accident. Since then he's closed himself off from his family and lives alone with his dog, Oblix, who is really cute, although he can sure kick up a sandstorm when he's upset.

"About five minutes," I say.

"What?"

"We have to wait five minutes from the moment we get the all clear."

"Well," Tuli says, glancing at his watch, "I think that passed already."

"Wait a bit longer, son," Abba says, looking up briefly from his *shtender*. "Just to be sure."

"Humph," Mr. Amsalom snorts again. "I'm telling you, there won't be any *sukkahs* this year; we're going to be stuck inside this…" he opens his arms in a wide gesture "… *miklat!*"

"Well," says Tuli, standing up and heading towards the door, "we'll see about that."

SINCE THE ROCKET attacks have resumed we've adopted a routine in a weird sort of way. When the air raid siren wails we have less than a minute to race down the three flights of stairs from our apartment and run to the communal shelter. My friend, Hadassa, tells me that the Goldsteins from the top floor are really fast. They always get there first, grab thick mattresses and stake out their usual corner. Our family usually arrives last, because we pick up elderly Mr. Kastlebaum on the way. He's a Holocaust survivor who lives alone and Ima wouldn't dream of going without him. We're quite lucky, I suppose, because our *miklat* isn't too crowded — unlike some, which have to host occupants from several buildings all at once. I don't mind the shelter, really. Now that it's *bein hazmanim* and Tuli and Abba are home, we all go together, and that helps me feel safer.

The first time I heard the loud rise and fall of the siren, I jumped up and down shrieking, "Shabbos! Shabbos has come on Tuesday!" until my mother told me to stop being silly, it wasn't Shabbos. We were being attacked, and we would probably also have to get used to it in Ashdod like our cousins have in Sderot.

Anyway, getting back to the shelter, it's actually not so bad down here. We've tried to fix it up a bit; I painted some pretty pink flowers on the walls with Shiffy and Devora, the two Cohen girls whose father wheezes like Mr. Amsalom's dog and clutches his chest saying he can't breathe while their mother fans his face with a handkerchief and screams, "Get him his medicine quickly!" I'm pretty proud of these walls, because they make our shelter warm and welcoming and brighten up the gloom that's in our hearts.

I CLIMB UP the basement stairs and out into the blinding glare of sunlight.

"I'm afraid to turn on the radio again," Ima says. "The news is never good."

She's right, of course. Once the rockets used to land in open fields, but lately they're exploding in residential areas, causing many casualties and much damage. Two weeks ago a rocket landed near Aunt Rivka's house in Be'er Sheva, and she's still in a state of shock. Tuli says she can't stop shaking and is afraid to leave the house, which is really sad because she's really such a happy, sociable person.

We trudge upstairs to our apartment, Ima, Abba, my younger sister Sari and I — without Tuli, because he's already off in the yard downstairs building the *sukkah*. Nowadays, Sari cries in her sleep from dreams that are filled with ear-splitting wails. When she wakes up like that, I reach over from my opposite bed, hold her hand and whisper soothing words that reassure her and comfort me, too. I feel important when I do that, like it's my job to take care of my nine-year-old sister because I'm a whole two years older.

Mr. Amsalom shuffles up the stairs behind us as Tuli bounds past on his way to collect more tools.

"*Meshuggeh*," he mutters. "You really believe that you'll sit in the *sukkah*?"

"Yes, Mr. Amsalom, I do," my brother calls cheerfully over the railing. "And if you like, I'll build one for you too!"

I'M SO BORED. Today has been really bad. We've hardly been out of the shelter at all because there have been too many rockets. According to the news, there have been eighty-two attacks so far in the last two days, but, *baruch Hashem*, nothing has landed near us. I should be frightened, but I'm not… well, maybe a little, but nothing that makes me scream at night like Sari. Maybe I'm too busy trying to be strong for her?

Hadassa wanders over to me. "Want to play Rummikub?" she suggests.

I groan. "Not again."

"We could say more *Tehillim*,'" she says.

"We've already said the *sefer* twice."

"How about we play with the Gutman twins?" Hadassa nods towards the two little girls coloring picture books on the other side of the room.

"Done that already."

I glance at Ima, who is preparing test papers for her fifth grade students even though, the way things are going, there won't be school anyway after the Yamim Tovim are over. Tuli's getting restless. He's beaten me at chess three times and is having a hard time concentrating on his learning. Mr. Amsalom calls to him from the mattress he's resting on. "See, I told you there won't be any *sukkahs*. How can we sit in a *sukkah* when we're cooped up here? You can't even finish building it."

"You'll see, Mr. Amsalom," Tuli replies confidently. "Just wait."

"IT'S BEAUTIFUL," IMA says, a warm, satisfied smile lighting up her permanently worried face. "Really lovely."

"Sari and I decorated it," I say proudly, pointing at the glittering lights, pictures and paper chains that are strung from one side of the ceiling to the other. Tuli and Abba stand behind us, hammers and screwdrivers still in their hands, wearing huge smiles. It wasn't easy to finish the *sukkah* while running in and out of the shelter in between sirens, but with Hashem's help we had succeeded.

"Let's *daven* that we'll be able to use it tonight," Ima says longingly, touching the walls almost reverently.

"Of course we'll use it!" Tuli and Abba declare together. "In fact, let's go upstairs and bring down the Yom Tov dishes right now."

"*NU*, WHAT DID I tell you?" Mr. Amsalom chides, an unlit pipe hanging from his mouth. "A waste of time building it, if you ask me." He wraps a piece of salami in a tissue to feed Oblix when he gets home. "Why don't you just face it already?" he drones on like a low flying plane. "It's the first night of Sukkos, and look where we are. We're going to be stuck in here for the entire week."

"Better than the camps," Mr. Kastlebaum says, and we all look up at the sound of his voice. "Food, beds, good neighbors, no Nazis beating you… it's not so bad."

Abba nods gravely while I avert my eyes from the tattooed number on Mr. Kastlebaum's forearm. Tuli leans forward until he's so close to Mr. Amsalom that their noses almost touch.

"Mr. Amsalom, we *are* going to use our *sukkah*, even if it's only for a minute to make a *brachah* before running off to the shelter. Every available minute we'll be in there, and you're invited to join us."

Mr. Amsalom gives Tuli a cynical look while chewing on the end of his pipe.

"Dovi from the building next door told me that their family is going to stay in the *sukkah* all the time," says Hadassa.

"What, even when the siren goes off?" Sari asks curiously. "Isn't that dangerous?"

"It's foolish!" Mr. Amsalom spits out. "And irresponsible! Those kinds of parents should have their children taken away from them."

Ima shifts uncomfortably in her chair as Hadassa stares wide-eyed at the older man.

"When your time is up, it happens wherever you are," Mr. Kastlebaum says, so quietly that we have to strain to listen. There isn't much we can say to that, because if anybody would know, it's Mr. Kastlebaum, so we sit in silence for a few seconds.

"Well," Mr. Amsalom says eventually, "it doesn't mean deliberately putting yourself in danger, does it? That's why we have a *miklat* to keep us safe."

"And maybe the *sukkah* can protect us too?" Tuli says, looking up from his *sefer*, and Mr. Kastlebaum nods his head in agreement.

To be honest, this conversation is really confusing me, and I'm no longer sure why we're in the *miklat* to begin with.

"Yes, but we're not meant to rely on *nissim*," Abba joins in. "There's a basic *hishtadlus* we need to do; it's a question of finding the right balance of *hishtadlus* and *bitachon*."

Mr. Kastlebaum nods to that as well, which only confuses me more.

"So which is it?" I ask Ima. "Do we go to the *miklat* or just stay in the *sukkah*?"

"Both," Ima replies, stroking my hair gently. "We'll stay in the *sukkah* as much as we can, and if we need to go to the shelter we will, taking lots of *tefillah* with us wherever we are."

"Hey," says Tuli, quickly jumping up. "We got the all clear." We listen to the special station on the radio that is kept open throughout Shabbos and Yom Tov. "Let's go up now and make *Kiddush*. Anybody who wants to is welcome to join us." He turns to Mr. Amsalom. "Are you coming?"

"No," Mr. Amsalom says. "I'm not. Those flimsy *sukkahs* don't offer any protection."

OUR *SUKKAH* IS special this year. No, *all* the *sukkahs* are special, simply by existing. We eat the delicious *seudah* that Ima has prepared for us, and Mr. Kastlebaum, Tuli and Abba sing so loudly. It seems as if there is singing everywhere, an orchestra of finely tuned voices thanking Hashem for being able to do this *mitzvah*. I feel so safe and cozy in here with my family that for a brief time I forget the dangers lurking outside of our little wooden hut.

Abba stops singing and leans back in his chair. "Ah, Sukkos," he says, his face shining with pure joy. "A particularly powerful time for trusting Hashem and knowing Who really takes care of us. It's a true *Shehecheyanu* this year!"

Ima closes her eyes and nods dreamily. "I feel so blessed to be here."

We all agree with that, including Sari, who is still nervously jumping up at every sound in case it's the siren. If we finish the meal without rushing off to the *miklat*, we'll be lucky. I wonder what Mr. Amsalom is doing all alone in his apartment, and I feel sorry for him and everything he's missing. Does he really think he's safer up there than down here?

THANK GOODNESS FOR Ima's foresight. She set up grape juice and challah in the shelter in case we don't make it out in time. So far, we've had tremendous *siyatta diShmaya* and made it to many of the meals, although obviously we can't have any guests from out of town (except the *Ushpizin*) because nobody's traveling. Ima is always prepared with food and drinks, though, just in case we have to eat in the shelter. Yesterday, we did that. Abba arranged the tables and chairs so everyone could sit together to eat and sing, and even Mr. Amsalom looked as if he was enjoying himself. We felt so close and connected with one another. I've never had that feeling before. Ima says that's what happens during war, that we all forget about our differences and the things that bother us about each other and we unite together as one, which is how Hashem wants us to be all the time. I hope things will stay this way after all of this is over.

"I wish Dovi's family were down here with us," Sari says suddenly. "It scares me that they're outside in their *sukkah*."

Mr. Amsalom is still shaking his head in obvious disapproval, but he joins in our *tefillos* for the safety of Dovi's family.

"OKAY," ABBA SAYS, "this time you're coming, and we're not taking no for an answer." We are in Mr. Amsalom's apartment, trying to convince him to join us for the Shabbos evening meal. After a lot of persuasion, Mr. Amsalom has been spending quite a bit of time with us in the *sukkah*, and he is surprisingly good company. One day Chol Hamoed he even played lively songs on his old red accordion while Abba and Tuli sang along, creating a happy, festive atmosphere. He's really a nice man deep down. Ima has always said that. Now, while we're urging him to join us for the meal, she tells him that his heart is soft as butter, if he would only let us have some of it. Mr. Amsalom gives his usual grunt and then smiles. "I think that's an offer I can't refuse."

Mr. Kastlebaum has gone to his niece for Shabbos, so we are getting Mr. Amsalom all to ourselves. Abba treats him like a king, and he loves that. The table is beautifully set with special china dishes and sparkling silver *Kiddush* cups, and we stand behind our chairs while Abba prepares *Kiddush*. Carefully, he pours wine into the largest cup, raises it up and takes a *bentcher* with his other hand. His powerful, melodic voice sings the *Kiddush* praise when suddenly I hear another noise rising up and down with my father's, and I'm confused.

"The siren!" Tuli yells. "Let's go!" Ima grabs my hand and Sari's and we race for the door, but when I look back over my shoulder, Abba is still standing with the *Kiddush* cup in his hand, eyes closed, reciting the *brachah* word for word, and Mr. Amsalom is right there beside him.

"Come on." My mother pulls me towards the steps of the *miklat*.

"But, Abba is still…" the sentence doesn't make it out of my mouth because in a flash I am flung to the ground by the force of a blast that is bigger and deadlier than anything I've ever heard in my life.

WHEN I WAKE up, I'm not sure if I ever went to sleep, but I must have, because there's a heavy weight on my arm and leg and a bandage covering my eye that wasn't there before.

"Gila," I hear my mother's familiar voice hovering above my head… no, it's floating over my face; where is it exactly? I turn slightly, trying to catch it.

"Gila, I'm here. Open your eyes and look at me."

Slowly, I open my good eye and find Ima leaning over, her tight, tired face the first thing I see. And then I remember.

"Abba, Mr. Amsalom, everybody, where are they?" I try to pull myself up in bed, but it's hard with the thick white casts that I've been plastered into, and Ima gently pushes me back down.

"Tuli's fine," she says. "Some shrapnel wounds, but he'll be okay. Sari is all right, too. She wasn't injured physically but she's in shock."

"Oy, poor Sari," I say, overwhelmed by a deep feeling of love and concern for my sister. "What about you?"

"*Baruch Hashem*, I'm also fine," Ima answers quickly. "I was very lucky."

"And Abba?"

Ima sucks in her breath. "Abba was the most seriously wounded of the family. He's still in intensive care because he had complicated surgery two days ago, straight after we arrived."

I gasp. "Two days… I've been here that long?"

"I'm afraid so. You've had surgery, too, so you've been heavily sedated."

"Never mind, just tell me about Abba," I continue hurriedly. "Can I see him?"

"Not yet." Ima stands and busies herself fluffing up my pillows. "You're not well enough to go anywhere right now. Maybe in a couple of days."

"I can't wait that long," my eyes fill with tears. "And what about Mr. Amsalom? Where is *he*?"

"He's in intensive care, too," my mother says quietly, and my heart lurches because I know what she's thinking, or at least I think

I do — that it's all our fault he got hurt because he was with us in the *sukkah* and not in the shelter.

I'm getting tired. The strain of talking and absorbing all this information is sapping the little energy I have. Yet as I drift drowsily away, there's still one more thing I need to know. "Dovi's family," I murmur, my voice slurring. "What happened to them?"

"Ah," Ima answers, "*baruch Hashem*, nothing, they are all right."

I WANT TO go, but I'm so nervous.

"Are you sure Mr. Amsalom isn't angry?" I ask Ima again while she drapes a blanket over my knees.

"Yes, and he's waiting to see you, so let's get going."

Tuli pushes my wheelchair, skillfully guiding it through the maze of hospital corridors until we reach the department that houses the ICU.

"Wait," I say, before we go inside. "Tell me again what he said."

Tuli parks my wheelchair next to some seats in the waiting room and quickly disappears while Ima and Sari sit down. "He said that he's happy he could do what he did and doesn't regret anything; that the times he spent in the *sukkah* with us were some of the happiest moments of his life, and that he's never been *moser nefesh* for anything before like he was when he stayed to say *Kiddush* with Abba that night."

I'm still not convinced, although it sounds very nice. Did he really say that? It's hard to believe. I ponder this, and also a question that's eating away at my insides. I've been trying to push it out of my mind because I'm ashamed of the lack of *emunah* that causes me to have such a thought. I see Ima glance over my head, her eyes lighting up, and I turn around.

"Abba… what a nice surprise!" I was planning to visit him later, on the internal medicine ward he's been moved to, but here he is, walking slowly towards me, supported by Tuli at his side.

"Abba!" I lift up my unplastered arm to hug him. "Why did

you tire yourself like this? I was going to come and see you as usual."

Abba looks down at me and smiles his sweet, dear smile that belongs only to him. "Just thought you might need me before you go in," he says, inclining his head to the ICU doorway and sitting down. How did he know? But that's Abba, he always knows things, and that gives me a warm, secure feeling that covers me like my childhood comfort blanket.

"You want to know why we got hurt and Dovi's family didn't, right?"

I nod and lower my eyes to the floor.

Abba squeezes my hand gently and sighs. "Ah, these are difficult things, Gila, and not everything can be understood, but do you remember Mr. Kastlebaum's words… 'When your time is up, it happens wherever you are?'"

I look up from the floor. "Yes, I remember."

"Well, it's true," Abba continues. "I guess it wasn't meant for Dovi's family to be injured in the attack, but for us, it was. And the one Shabbos that Mr. Amsalom ate with us, we got hit… just look at the *hashgachah pratis* there… it was clearly from Hashem."

I nod again, although there's still something bothering me. "But what about *hishtadlus*? Why do we need to make any?"

"Because Hashem told us to," Abba answers simply. "It's one of the reasons that we're here in this world… to make an effort. The end result is not in our hands, but we still have to try our best."

It's getting hard to sit so long, and I shift uncomfortably in my wheelchair. I still don't really understand everything properly, but I imagine I will understand more when I'm older. Meanwhile, I know that I have my father to help me whenever I have questions.

I try to squeeze Abba's hand, although I'm very weak, but at least I'm making the effort, kind of like my *hishtadlus*, I suppose.

I glance anxiously at the door of the ICU. I'm still nervous about seeing Mr. Amsalom because I'm not sure what to say to him, but I have to try with this as well.

Abba lays his hand on my shoulder. I feel his strength seep through me and I smile. "I think I'm ready now… to go inside!"

The idea for "The Shelter" developed as a result of the continual barrage of rocket fire on communities in southern Israel at that time. After the expelling of Jews from Gush Katif, Sderot became the first city in the firing line for militants from Gaza and they suffered nonstop kassam attacks. These transformed a vibrant and bustling city to a virtual ghost town. My husband and I visited Sderot before Purim the year that the attacks escalated. We wanted to see firsthand how the people were living and show our solidarity, even if it was only in the minor way of buying our Purim supplies from businesses that were suffering. While there I had the strange desire for a rocket to fall. I'm not sure whether it was out of a sincere wish to not just be an "outsider" or because of an immature yearning for excitement. Needless to say, no rockets fell, but they did start falling in other cities like Ashkelon and Ashdod, longer-range missiles that could reach farther and cause chaos throughout southern Israel. It was then that I began to appreciate the fact that I lived in relative safety near Yerushalayim.

When thinking up an idea for the Sukkos supplement (usually the writers are asked for their pitches several months in advance), I remember wondering whether residents in the South would be able to enjoy their Sukkos that year and a story centered around this began to take shape. Years earlier I had experienced the first Gulf War with the fear of chemical warfare from Saddam Hussein, citizens walking everywhere with gas masks on their shoulders, the sealed rooms, curfews, sirens that wailed while on the bus or in the shower, running for shelter in the most unlikely places and the waiting for the all clear on the radio. And all of this was carried out in the finest of spirits, with a unity amongst Am Yisrael that always appears in times of crisis. I had all the personal ingredients for a story of this nature.

As usual, discussion often revolved around how much hishtadlus one should do. There were those who didn't even prepare a sealed room, others who took great care to prepare one. Some people did not pick up their gas masks, others queued for hours to get them. There were differences of opinion and hashkafah on how to approach the looming war. For some, it was very confusing.

In "The Shelter," I raise these issues. It is a story designed to make readers think and provide a possible answer to the questions raised. How much hishtadlus to do is a question pertaining to just about everything in life, but especially in life and death situations. But that is the beauty of the Jewish People. We don't just run to use the protection the physical world provides but turn to Hashem as our Protector.

Just a few words about the literary style of this piece. It is written in first person, present tense, in the voice of a child. I happen to particularly enjoy writing in this style. My early stories were almost all in third person, past tense and somehow they feel less powerful. It's fun to play around with styles, to "feel" what is best suited to each story. Only recently I began writing stories with a male protagonist. I've always felt more comfortable with the female but I'm enjoying getting into the role of the male character. For me, so much is about feeling and sensing the best style to make my piece powerful.

Within These Walls

"DO YOU *HAVE* to go?" Mom asks, her forehead creased in a worried frown. "Can't they ask someone else instead?"

"No, Mom, they can't," I say as I stuff another towel and some pairs of socks into my backpack. "This is what I'm trained for. There's no one else at my level to do it."

Dad sits on my bed and leafs through one of those little tour-guide books that he's picked up from the local bookstore. "It looks like a beautiful country," he says, nodding his head in approval.

"She's not going for a *vacation*," Mom reminds him, clasping her hands together tightly. I'm used to this nervous habit of hers; it is as old as my very first day in school, but today it feels as new as if I'm seeing it for the first time.

"How long do you think you'll be gone?" Dad asks, without waiting for an answer. "Don't forget Jenny's bat mitzvah party. David is expecting all the family to come. He's rented a hotel especially for this."

Yes, well, that's David's style… lavish and extravagant. I wasn't going to change my brother now after all these years. "I don't know when I'll be back," I answer. "A few weeks maybe… it depends how things go over there." I zip up my luggage, roll up a sleeping bag, strap it onto the back frame of my backpack and straighten myself up.

"I'm sorry, Mom and Dad, but I have to get going now. I'm flying with the rest of the team to Geneva, where we'll connect with the other doctors and then continue on to Africa."

"Will you call as soon as you arrive?" Mom grabs my hand so hard that I'm afraid she'll break my fingers.

"I'm going to a remote village in the forests, Mom, so I can't promise. From what I understand, there's no radio contact coming out of any towns in surrounding areas at the moment."

Mom's eyes filled with tears. "So how will I know if you're okay?" she blubbers.

"I'll be in touch the first opportunity I have," I reassure her.

My parents accompany me to the door, seeing me out of my own apartment as if I'm a little girl leaving home. Dad kisses the top of my forehead and tells me to take care, and then Mom grabs hold of me as if she's afraid she'll never see me again. I gently pry her fingers off me and give her one last hug.

"I'll be all right… you'll see."

I climb into the car that's been sent for me and open the window.

"Lisa, wait!" my mother cries. "Hold on, there's something I want to give you." She runs inside the house for her pocketbook, takes out something square and flat and presses it into my hand. "Bubby's bracelet," she says breathlessly. "I know she would have wanted you to have it."

I open up the little brown box and stare at Bubby's gold charm bracelet. As I fasten it onto my wrist, tears well in my eyes. The driver is pressing his foot on the accelerator impatiently. I stretch out my arm as the car drives slowly off.

"Don't worry, Mom, I'll be back soon!" I shout as we pick up speed.

My words are caught by the wind, whispering the faint echo of, "I'll be back." I bite my lip hard and feel an inexpressible fear drop to the pit of my stomach and wonder whether I really will be back.

ONCE WE LAND in Africa, we continue our journey in an American military plane that belongs to the Zaire Air Force. As I look out of the window at the endless tracts of rain forest and the wide, winding river, I wonder how I've ended up here; one of two female doctors amongst a specially chosen medical team assigned to treat villagers infected with a rapidly spreading virus. Viruses are my thing. That's what I do for a living... isolate them and try to find cures. They have always fascinated me. When I look under an electron microscope at an especially deadly virus like Ebola or Marbug, there's a beauty there amongst those particles that rise up like cobras, twisting towards me. As I gaze at them, many times alone at night in the special lab where I've been trained for this work, I'm overwhelmed by a feeling of something so much bigger and beyond me that can reduce me to nothing at any moment. I'm in awe of their power and deadly life force.

I lean closer to the window, watching the terrain unfold beneath my feet as I am taken deeper into the heart of Africa, and suddenly, I'm consumed with terror. Before we embarked on this trip, I was pulsating with adrenaline, but now that we're here, I want to stay on the plane, up in the air where it's safe and we won't need to worry about breathing in dangerous particles. It's one thing to look at these things through a microscope; face to face is a different story.

"You okay?" Carol, my colleague, nudges me.

"Not really. And you?"

Beads of sweat glisten like silkworms on Carol's forehead. "Petrified," she nods.

I grasp her hand tightly as the plane begins its descent. Like me, Carol has been sent on this mission by the Center for Disease

Control. She is an epidemiologist; I'm here as a virologist. We've never laid eyes on each other before this trip.

"We're in this together," I say tensely, watching the ground rise up towards us.

Further along the Congo River we can see the small town of Bumba. Our flight crew is so frightened to breathe the air that they practically push us off the aircraft, tossing our bags and equipment after us and taking off again like a terror-stricken bird. And that's when we're left, the group of us, all alone, standing by the side of the river, more frightened than we've ever been in our lives.

AS WE TRUDGE into the center of town, I am immediately struck by how different my life is from what lies before me. There's an eerie quietness to the place, a deathly silence that's closed shop doors and boarded up windows, leaving just remnants of a town ravaged by a particularly virulent strain of *something* that's emerged from the villages. We make our way to the governor's office to pick up our jeeps, drivers and translators, and we set off north toward the Ebola River, deep into the African forest. It's the rainy season, so the road is just a string of mud holes and running streams that the wheels get stuck in. By nightfall, we finally reach some rows of round, thatched African houses, and I wonder once more what a nice thirty-year-old American Jewish girl is doing amongst all of this.

Carol sighs. "I wish it were Friday night, and I was home with my parents having our usual dinner."

I lift my head sharply. "You're Jewish?"

She nods. "You too?"

"Yes," I reply. "We don't do much, though… you know, the traditional things… fasting on Yom Kippur, a *Seder* on Pesach, that kind of stuff. My grandparents were religious, but I didn't grow up with it."

Carol smiles thinly. "I suppose you could say we keep a little more than that. In fact, I was raised quite religious, but after my grandfather died, I kind of slipped away from it. When I went to medical school, I pretty much gave everything up… except for Friday night."

Suddenly we are interrupted by loud, frightened shouts coming from behind a barrier of trees that have been placed across the road to stop people from going in or out of the village.

"Reverse quarantine," Carol explains. "It comes from the times of the smallpox virus, when the village elders found their own way to control it by cutting their villages off from the world."

"Wow, pretty smart," I marvel.

"Who are you? What are you doing?" the anxious voices shout out again. "Why did you come here?"

"We are doctors! We came to help!" our translator calls back.

Once the villagers see they can trust us, they clear the trees, and we press on deeper into the forest until, after what seems like an eternity, we arrive at the main village, supposedly the place where the devastation began. Like the town, the place seems deserted, but as we take a look around, we find sick people ensconced in huts. Some have been put in isolation at the edge of the village; other huts have been burned down to prevent the virus from spreading. I wander between them and know that we have lots of work ahead of us. But first… we need to sleep.

CAROL AND I are assigned to a hut together with some of the village women who appear not to have been infected. We are given thick straw mattresses over in a corner, and even though I'm so exhausted that I expect to spiral into oblivion, I cannot sleep. The rains continue throughout the night, and I wonder how the roof keeps them out.

"It's like a *sukkah*," Carol whispers in the dark.

"What's that?" I whisper back, my eyelids finally drooping.

"They're kind of like this," she says. "Little booths that we build outside every year after Yom Kippur. We'd build ours in the garden. I remember feeling cozy and safe and inhaling the grainy scent of the wood."

"What was the point of that?" I'm beginning to get drowsy.

"It's to show G-d that we trust Him to take care of us," Carol explains, appearing to grow more animated as I grow sleepier. "We go out of our houses and live in the *sukkah* for a week, eating all our meals there as if it's our home. Some people even sleep in it."

"A whole week," I say, waking up slightly.

"Yes," Carol says wistfully. "It was great. I think out of everything I've given up, I miss Sukkos the most."

I turn on my side to look at her, but I can only make out a shape in the darkness. "So why are you remembering it now?"

"Because," she says thoughtfully, "*this* is just like that — living in a little hut and relying on G-d to keep us safe."

I WAKE UP in the morning to see the sun reaching through the gaps in the wood like outstretched fingers. For a moment, I'm disoriented, and it's only when I turn and see Carol sprawled out on the mattress next to me that I remember where we are.

"Come on, get up," I nudge Carol gently. "We need to get started."

After politely declining whatever delicacy the village women offer us, we breakfast on our dried food, gather our equipment, and set out on our mission of mercy. It must still be early morning because the air is cool and the ground glistens a silvery green. I can hear the hee-hawing of monkeys shaking the trees as they leap back and forth on gnarled branches, and I shudder because back home there is strong evidence that the virus is carried by these creatures. There are all kinds of noises that I'm not familiar with, and there is a feeling of vulnerability from the raw, inhospitable nature. The sun is getting hotter and I am already tired, thirsty, and afraid of what we're going to find inside the primitive dwellings.

"Ready?" Carol turns to me as we stand outside an entranceway. I take a deep breath. "Yes."

What we find in the first hut are rows of sick people lying on straw mattresses or cots. They've been left there in isolation — the rest of the villagers are afraid to enter for fear of contamination. We quickly get to work, assessing situations, administering medicines to reduce fever, inserting intravenous lines for fluids to those who need them, and all the while taking blood samples to take back to our laboratories in America. The decision back home was not to bring the pressurized space suits we usually use when working with a virus on this level, so we don't have much protective gear — just some surgical masks that we hope will prevent droplets hitting our faces, rubber gloves, gowns and disinfectant. But I don't have time to think about that as I move quickly from patient to patient, trying to stifle my horror at the pitiful results of some unknown predator.

One elderly man is particularly confused and aggressive when I approach him. "Carol, I need your help to hold him while I draw blood," I call over to her.

She finishes what she's doing and comes to keep the man's arm still while he thrashes about. I wind the tourniquet around his forearm and search for veins that have collapsed from dehydration.

"There's one here," I say to Carol. "You've got him?"

"Yup."

I insert the needle as gently as possible, but even that seems too much for the old man because in a surge of unnatural strength, he jerks forward and grabs the syringe from my hand. While I look on in frozen horror, he shoots the needle into my arm. I feel the stab vaguely, like the quick, tongue-lashing sting of a venomous snake, but all I can do is stare at my arm as if it no longer belongs to me.

Carol shakes herself out of her horrified stupor. "Quick, get the antiseptic!" she screams. "Water, we need water," she shouts wildly to anyone who can understand.

I watch, like a spectator at an underwater observatory, offering my arm like a sacrifice as she throws a bucket of water over it and scrubs frantically at the injection site with whatever cleaning agents we have. I'm no longer inside myself, but looking down from above at me, the Lisa Ellings that was... who's now very likely going to die.

WHEN I FINALLY lift my head out of the murky water, fear-filled adrenaline surges through my veins.

"What am I going to do?" I ask Carol. I feel my heart thumping in my chest and have this strange sense of relief that at least it's still beating.

"Quarantine," Carol says slowly. "You'll have to go into isolation for ten days."

"No!" I cry. "Not that... I'll go crazy!" I lower my voice, even though there's no one in the hut who can understand me. "Maybe... maybe, we can just not say anything?"

Carol shakes her head. "That wouldn't be right. It's not fair to the others."

"But not everybody who comes into contact with the virus gets sick from it," I plead weakly.

"We can't take that chance." Carol's logic is making me insane, but I figure that one way or another, that's going to happen anyway.

They prepare a hut for me at the edge of the village, away from both the sick people and the remaining healthy ones. Inside is a thick, straw mattress and two pails, one empty and another full of water. There's an odd looking wooden table with a kerosene lamp, but other than that, there is nothing at all, except me. Carol carries my belongings and a bowl of oatmeal from one of our packages with gloved hands.

"I'm not sick," I say sullenly to her masked face.

Carol remains silent while she arranges my things as best she can on the table. She leaves a metal cup with tea and some old magazines she's brought with her on the trip and then turns towards the rickety door.

"Don't!" I clutch her hand desperately. "Please don't go!"

Carol gently unfolds my fingers from hers. "I'm sorry," she says, her eyes wet. "I really am. I'll be back to bring your meals, so I'll talk to you through the gap."

She is standing in the entranceway, half hidden in the shadow that obscures the descending sun. As she turns to leave, she pauses. "Try to think of this as your *sukkah*," she says slowly. "Inside it, you'll have G-d's protection."

AT NIGHT, THE rains come again. The thunderstorm hammers my little hut, and I lean against the wall and pray that it will soon pass. Inside my temporary dwelling it is dark, cold and unfriendly. In the daytime the air is heavy with a sultry heat that sucks the strength from my bones and leaves me listless and dull. Carol comes quickly to the door with my meals, as instructed, and except for an elderly village woman who takes care of the pails, I see no one.

I have never been so lonely in my life.

I think about Mom, who is probably sitting by the phone in her rambling ranch house, waiting for it to ring. I think about Dad, who is most likely telling her not to worry and thinking up creative ideas to distract her. I think about David, who I've never seen eye to eye with, and Jenny's fancy bat mitzvah party. Will I ever see any of them again?

My days are marked by the rains that never fail to arrive, reminding me just how frail and vulnerable I am inside this little hut.

"Think of it as a *sukkah*," Carol says each time she delivers my food. "You are under G-d's protection."

I've never thought much about G-d, although deep down inside, I feel there is One. Now, in my timeless, nothing-less state,

I begin to think more about Him, to wonder if there is something else beyond these fragile walls… something else that's within *me?*

On day three, I wake up feverish and start to panic. Is this it? Have I got it? I check myself for other signs, feeling for lumps on my glands and gaze repeatedly into my small compact mirror, looking for the tell-tale redness in the whites of my eyes. I pull my sleeping bag over me, shivering in the heat. When will Carol come? Maybe by the time she gets here it will be too late?

I want to get married, have children, live a meaningful life and enjoy the rain again. I want to eat real food, sleep in a normal bed and make a difference in the world.

I want to live.

When Carol arrives, she looks at me in horror from the doorway, tries to hold her face together and mumbles, "I'll bring you some Tyenol®," before rushing off. Afterwards, I swallow the two white pills gratefully and fall into a fitful sleep.

By morning, the fever has broken. When Carol pushes the door open and tentatively peers around it, I want to pull her inside and dance with her until I'm dizzy.

"It's not the virus," I whoop, even though I'm weak. "Look at me…I'm fine!"

Carol stands there, her arms twitching as if she wants to hug me. But she can't. Although this time the fever was nothing, there are still six more days to go until I'm all clear. "It's the *sukkah*," she mumbles, looking up at the roof. "G-d's protecting you."

I don't know about this *sukkah* thing or about G-d, but Carol seems to believe it. I wish she was allowed to sit and tell me more about it. I am so bored that even an ant crossing the floor would get my attention. The new bag of magazines she's brought me is a relief. I tip the bag upside down and rummage through the magazines scattered on my mattress, when suddenly my fingers touch something hard and flat. I lift up the object, open it up, and stare at Hebrew words on stained, yellow pages… Bubby's Book of Psalms!

What is Bubby's Book of Psalms doing *here?* For a moment I am disoriented, still inside my hut by the river, but passing through months and seasons and years of a different life.

"Bubby, where are you?" I whisper, looking upwards.

I feel as if I'm holding an oyster with a precious jewel in my hands. Turning to the inside cover, I read the black, spidery writing. "My dear Carol…"

So it's not Bubby's!

My mind must be playing tricks on me, after all these days by myself. But I begin to read the English translation anyway. Time seems to stand still, and the only sound I hear is the African weaverbirds outside and an occasional elephant in the distance, moving through the forest making cracking noises as it peels bark and breaks limbs off trees.

"Hashem is my shepherd; I shall not lack. In lush meadows He lays me down, beside tranquil waters He leads me."

I am back with Bubby, a little girl, sitting by her feet as she tells me stories and reads words that sound like songs and ripple like music in my ears.

"Though I walk in the valley overshadowed by death, I will fear no evil, for You are with me."

Bubby's eyes are dreamlike, coated with a fine film as she recounts G-d's kindness and thanks Him for her liberation.

"May only goodness and kindness pursue me all the days of my life, and I shall dwell in the House of Hashem for long days."

I clutch the book close, pressing it against my chest the way Bubby used to hold *me* as she recited these psalms in Hebrew, and I can hear her voice, taste the salty tears on her cheeks, touch the sadness she feels when I don't understand what she's saying.

I continue reading. I read all the way through the rains and past mealtimes, and when I've finished, I start all over again.

"Hashem is your Guardian; Hashem is your shade at your right hand."

Bubby's hand is gently caressing mine.

"By day the sun will not harm you, nor the moon by night."

Someone else is holding my hand, too.

"Hashem will protect you from every evil; He will guard your soul."

My soul! The spark that I know is there inside me when I take the time to feel it.

"Hashem will guard your departure and your arrival, from this time and forever."

I don't know where I'm going... if I'll make it out. I don't know anything except that instead of being humbled by the viruses I once loved, I'm in awe of the One Who created them. And what I do know, is that out here, deep in the African jungle where nature is not benign... I am not alone!

This was a fun story to write... not too heavy, more focused on the rich descriptions of Africa rather than a deep message. The idea was generated from reading a book called "The Hot Zone," a true account of deadly viruses that seem to originate from certain breeds of monkeys in Africa. The viruses, all under the group known as the Ebola family, are considered level four "hot" viruses by the CDC (Center for Disease Control) and require anyone working with them to wear a space suit in a highly protected area. The book describes a fascinating but terrifying scenario of crate loads of monkeys from Africa delivered to a research facility in America who began dying from the Marbug strain of Ebola. The ramifications of this were enormous. With the sophisticated travel possibilities we have today, all it would take is for one infected person to board an airplane, infect a few others who would all subsequently change flights for different destinations, and you've killed off half the world. The monkeys in Westinghouse needed to be euthanized immediately and the entire building fumigated. It was a huge job placed in the hands of the army and which was, baruch Hashem, *successful.*

In the book a team of scientists venture to Africa to try to find the origins of these deadly viruses. There is one cave in Sudan that has strong evidence that the host recipient is stemming from there. The hunt for the source of these viruses fascinated me along with the rich descriptions of Africa. As I was reading I envisioned the huts inside the villages and it occurred to me that they could be like sukkos, providing protection despite their flimsy outer structure. In fact, I realized that we could make a sukkah out of anything provided it had the right amount of walls.

MAMA SAYS IT'S good that we live in the City of Hope!

"If we'd stayed where we were, who knows what situation we'd be in today," she repeats over and over, like a mantra that puts us to sleep. Papa, who never says much of anything, just nods wisely from his corner in the little stone house of ours that is a block of ice in the winter and a furnace in the summer.

"Yup," he says curtly. "It's always good to be the builders... the first ones to settle the land."

My brothers and I have heard this all before, of course. It's a family legend that we have to listen to continuously, usually on Shabbos when we're gathered around the wooden table the older boys carved so beautifully from the sturdy trees in the nearby forest. I love the forest; the huge, old oaks that cover me with arms full of leaves, protecting me from the harsh sun. I spend hours soaking my feet in the cool water of running brooks, stretching out on the grassy banks until the light begins to fade and I hear the anxious cries of, "Pessia! Pessi, come home!"

The cries are never really worried ones, though, because in the City of Hope, nobody worries about anything! In our town, *everything* is good, even when it isn't, if you know what I mean. Even one small negative word has no place here, lest it mushroom into a black cloud of despair. The people of Hope have already had enough of that… the hopelessness, the despondency, the depression. And that's why they built their enclave; the reason they broke away from all the rest, to live a safe and isolated lifestyle, dedicated to their lofty ideals. And that's how I, twelve-year-old Pessia Mankoff, became one of those fortunate elite!

"Mama, Mama!" Yankel comes running into the house. "Mama…" he can hardly catch his breath. "There's a new boy in my class."

"That's nice, Yankel." Mama looks up from the pail of soapy water where she's scrubbing the curtains for Pesach and smiles.

"No, you don't understand." Yankel flops down on the floor beside her. "He's not from here… he's from the City of Despair."

Mama gasps and stops scrubbing. "How can that be?" she asks worriedly. "Nobody from Despair is allowed in."

This sounds interesting, so I sit down on the dusty ground to listen.

"His parents are changing, or so I heard," Yankel explains with an air of self-importance. "Rumor has it that they want to move their entire family to Hope."

"It will never work," says Mama, shaking her head. She coughs, a deep rattle that shakes her rib cage.

"You must see the doctor, Mama," I say, but she brushes me off with a wave of her hand.

"It cannot happen," she repeats. "The reason we left Despair and built Hope was to escape those harmful influences."

"But what if they're doing *teshuvah*?" I ask, puzzled. "Anyone can do that, can't they? And anyway, aren't we supposed to think only positive thoughts in Hope?"

Mama looks at me curiously. "Go inside, Pessia, and set the table. Soon I shall call everyone in for supper."

Tears sting my eyes at my dismissal. It's not fair that I cannot be included in adult conversation. I'm plenty old enough now. But then

I wipe my eyes with my sleeve and push down the "not fair" until it's sitting in a City of Suppression in the seabed of my being. I'm from the City of Hope and I must never think this way.

MAMA HAS BEEN in bed all week because of her cough, so it's up to me, the only girl, to make sure the house runs properly. One of the healers has been summoned. He makes some kind of potion for Mama to drink, gives her special leaves that smell like mint and garlic to take down the fever, and says he'll come back in three days. Papa is smiling, thanking Hashem that soon his wife will be better. Aunt Machla, Papa's unmarried sister, cheerfully stirs a pot of broth on the stove and the younger boys run around, giggling. I sweep the floor, waiting for the lightheartedness to infect me, but Mama rests with her eyes closed and a thin layer of sweat covering her forehead and I really don't understand why I'm supposed to be happy.

Three days later, as promised, the healer is back, this time with another healer who waves his hands over Mama's head, declares her healed, and rushes out as if afraid he will catch something. I sneak a peek at her through the doorway while Aunt Machla and Papa and Uncle Hershel gather around her bed. I know I'm only twelve years old and I'm not supposed to know much, but Mama doesn't look better to me. Her breathing rises up and down, gurgling noisily like the water pump, and she's as white as our Shabbos tablecloth. Papa turns slightly and I slip away fast, back to the parlor, where I start getting the boys ready for bed. As I'm putting Dovi's arms in the sleeves of his pajamas, I can still hear Mama's breathing in my head and the bubbling sounds from her mouth, and when I tuck Dovi under his blanket and say the *Shema* with him, I start to cry.

"Whatsamadder?" my brother asks, thumb in his mouth.

"Nothing, Dovi, go to sleep now. Mama will be here for you in the morning."

Once I see that his little form is still and his breathing even, I step outside into the night, hoping it will comfort me with its quiet state of knowingness as it silently absorbs every passing shadow. I sit on the rocking chair on the porch, fireflies and the crackly conversations of the crickets my only company. Suddenly, Aunt Machla appears, sits down beside me and says nothing, only stares into the darkness.

"Auntie…" I begin falteringly. "Is… is Mama going to get better?"

Aunt Machla turns to me abruptly. "Yes, child, of course she is. You heard what the healers said… she's already fine."

"So why, then, are you so sad?"

Aunt Machla gives me one of those strange looks like Mama's, leans over and takes my hands in hers. "Pessi, dear, you and your questions… I am just sad to see your poor mother suffer so until she recovers."

I grasp my aunt's hand tight, as if I can pass my strength through her and into Mama. "B-but what if she *doesn't* recover?" I whisper, my voice trembling.

Aunt Machla releases my grip and puts her arm around my quivering shoulders. "Child, you must not think this way, let alone say it. We live here in Hope, where there is no room for doubts or negativity. At the weekly meeting on Tuesday, I shall put your thoughts to the Elders and we'll see how to help you."

I smile gratefully, even though I don't feel grateful at all.

"Now go and put up the kettle of water for your mother's tea." Aunt Machla pats my knee. "I'll be in soon."

I boil the water, pour the tea into a pretty cup and saucer, and give it to Papa to take into Mama's room. Once the house is quiet and everyone's asleep, I take my feather quilt and lie down on the floor at the foot of Mama's bed, listening to her trying to breathe. I must have eventually nodded off into a fitful sleep, because when I wake up it is quiet; not a sound, not a trace of the rattling respirations that shook the walls. All that remains is an eerie silence with a huge absence. And that's when I know that Mama has gone.

I AM ANGRY! Red hot, spewing lava angry!

"You lied to me!" I rail at Papa, Aunt Machla, the Elders... anyone who will listen. "You said she'd get better!"

Aunt Machla, who has moved into the house to take care of us, looks at me with grief-filled eyes. "We did not lie, my child. Where there is hope, anything is possible."

"But that's not the same, is it?" I shout. "And hope didn't stop her from dying!" I hurl out my accusations like stones, jagged pieces of rock that hurt *hard*.

"Pessia, dearest, at Hope we do not think this way. We have to always believe until the very last moment and never give in to despair."

"You don't understand." I beat my fists against the wall, drawing blood from my broken knuckles, and I cry, hot, angry, confused tears, because all I know is that *hope* did not save my Mama and therefore, it does not exist.

"Child... this is not the way." Aunt Machla puts out her arm to catch my next fist before it hits the wall. She pulls me close and I collapse against her soft frame, for a second thinking she's Mama, and feel the frustration and pain hiss out of me, collapsing like deflated challah dough onto the floor.

"Come..." My aunt lifts me up gently. "You must wash your face and drink something. Later, I will take you to the Sages. You can ask them your questions."

SPRING IS IN the air... the pale pink blossoms on the trees and the sweet smell of freshly cut grass. Even though it is six years since Mama died and I don't have the same questions I once did, I still cannot face this time of year without a sense of mourning, as if I'm sitting *shivah* all over again. The Elders tell me this cannot be. I must move on, they say… look towards the future instead of reliving the past. But even though I *can* enjoy the warmth of the sun after the long, hard rains, I am still stuck somewhere in the frosty earth, before it has thawed.

Papa is very busy. His new wife, Hindy, is nice enough, I suppose, but I'm not the one to ask. He couldn't have stayed alone, though, so when a suggestion was made for a match with a widowed woman from Hope, it was perfect for him. Lately, Papa has been busier than usual, receiving visitors in his tiny study, men who come and whisper in low tones until late at night. One evening after I finish my chores, I linger a little by Papa's door, the hushed voices drawing me closer.

"Come on, Yisrael, why won't you consider it?" one of the men says.

"No," Papa says, and I hear him slam something down on his desk. "No child of mine is going to take someone from Despair, and that's that!"

"But Gideon is from Hope now. His whole family moved over years ago," the man with the huskier voice replies. "He is one of us."

Papa's voice rises as if he's getting angry. "So go take him for one of *your* daughters and leave me with mine."

The husky voice, which I think belongs to the local *shadchan*, Moshe, is softer. "You should think about it again, Yisrael. After all, your Pessia is not what we would call… standard."

"Pray tell, what is *that* supposed to mean?" Papa asks indignantly. "Pessia is a fine girl. She will make a wonderful wife for a deserving boy."

"Yes, yes, of course. Of that there is no doubt. But surely you agree that she's a little… different. You know… all those questions she used to ask."

"Pessia has lived through much in her short life," Papa says softly, and I can sense his sadness seeping underneath the door.

"Exactly!" Moshe the matchmaker cries, banging his fist on the table. "And Gideon has been through plenty also. That is why this match is so perfect!"

I feel my cheeks burn with shame as a flame of embarrassment whips my face. Papa is losing his strength, I can feel it.

"I… I don't know," he mumbles. "I came to Hope to get away from this… to begin a new life."

"And so did they," declares Moshe triumphantly. "Gideon's family is really no different from yours."

Papa is silent, running out of words I wish I could give him. The other man speaks up again.

"Yisrael, my friend, you will see that this idea makes sense. Your boys, *iy"H*, will go quickly, but a girl, with only a small dowry and no mother…"

I have heard enough! Humiliated tears sting my eyes and I jump back from the door as if there's a hornet's nest behind it. I run to my room and fling myself onto my bed, pulling the pillow hard over my head while over in Papa's office, three men decide my future.

So I am engaged to be married to nineteen-year-old Gideon Tessler, formerly from Despair, but now settled in Hope. He appears to be a fine boy with good *middos* and I'm told that he's reliable, hardworking, and will take good care of his family — and really, that's what counts. After the wedding we shall live in Hope, of course, although Gideon still has some cousins and uncles in Despair, so we will need to visit there occasionally. At first we shall live with Gideon's parents, until our own house is built. Gideon has a dream to build us a home made only from wood, unlike the regular stone structures they have here. Hopefully, if he's successful, he'll then be hired to build more houses for other residents.

So how do I feel? I'm almost afraid to ask myself that question. Frightened, excited and ashamed that I have to take a boy who was once from Despair. My good friends tell me that I shouldn't care about that because Gideon and his family are fine people, but still, when I walk through the streets, past the old women sitting on their stools, I can almost hear them clucking with a *tsk, tsk* of disapproval.

On the other hand… I'm getting married! Yes, I really am! It's every girl's dream, every mother's… no, I cannot go there, to the thought that Mama won't be with me on the most special day of my life. Yet how can I go through all of this without her? Aunt Machla is so excited to take me to the *chuppah*, almost as excited as she was when she got married herself a few years ago. Actually, there's a warm, festive atmosphere in our house. Even Papa has softened his usual stoic stance to smile and let his eyes twinkle. Gideon is welcomed into the family like another brother and the air is alive with eager anticipation. Maybe there will be *simchah* here after all, despite the gaping hole. And if truth be told, I am proud that I can make everyone so happy.

"MAYBE WE CAN move into the house by the summer?" I say casually to Gideon one evening when we're sitting by the fireplace.

"No, I don't think so." Gideon shakes his head and moves closer to the fire to warm his hands. "I cannot see it being finished by then and when we move in, I want it to be perfect."

I keep my eyes fixed on the blanket I'm knitting for Gideon's baby sister. "But it only needs to be livable. It is good the way it is."

"No," Gideon says again. "I shall not be responsible for moving my wife into something unsafe. What if something happens?"

I glance at my husband sharply. "Unfinished does not mean unsafe," I say firmly, but he refuses to budge.

We are so different, the two of us. Sometimes, in chillier moments, I feel that those differences are like a huge chasm that can never be crossed. His tendency to think of the worst is a remnant of his childhood in Despair, something that I am not used to in Hope. Often it is frustrating and depressing and reminds me of the reason my parents started Hope in the first place. Gideon straightens himself up from the fire and turns to me like he's absorbed the glow of the embers on his face.

"Do not worry, Pessia," he smiles. "I shall do my best to have it finished before the hot winds come."

And I smile too, no longer cold, but warmed by the depth of my husband's dedication.

Gideon is true to his word and we are in our home as summer slips in stealthily. I cannot stop thanking my husband for our beautiful house, carved from our very own forest trees that have now been transformed into our indoor fortress. Even now, two months later, I can still smell the varnish on the logs that have been stacked up in perfect precision to provide our walls. The neighbors stream in and out, all curious to see the new kind of house that Gideon Tessler has built with his own hands. The orders come pouring in. Yes, more and more people want to replace their ugly stone houses for one of these beautiful, modern homes. Soon, Gideon has to hire some workers to help him with the construction and he is out most of the day, straggling home once the sun sets, hot, dirty and tired. But he is happy... very happy... and so am I.

IT'S ON ONE of those comfortable evenings when Gideon has freshened up after a grueling day and we're sitting down to supper that I notice it.

"Do you smell burning?" I ask, tilting my chin upwards. Gideon rubs his eyes tiredly and sniffs the air like a dog.

"No," he says, going back to the vegetables on his plate. "It is nothing."

But that night, somewhere in the early hours, it is unmistakable. I am still deep in my sleep when the flames come, licking at our door, hungry to consume whatever is inside, and somehow, I'm standing at the open window and Gideon is yelling, screaming, "Jump, jump... jump *now!*"

Surprisingly, I am out then, watching my home be devoured by an insatiable enemy. I find myself not far from Gideon, who is writhing on the ground in pain, tears streaming down his blackened face, watching his dream disappear with the smoke that, once dissipated, leaves nothing but ashes.

"WE SHALL REBUILD," I say again, although I don't know why I bother. "Gideon, it's been a month now. It's time to move on."

My husband says nothing. He lays his head back on the pillow and closes his eyes as if I'm not here and the irritation that's been festering inside me comes to a head. "How long can you remain like this, day after day, in bed?" I accuse angrily. "You need to get up, to go out to work."

"I have no work," he says flatly, with no bitterness or accusation in his voice, just fact.

"But not everybody canceled their orders, did they? There is still the Herskowitz family, and the —"

"Nobody wants a house that can go up in flames. And even if they do, I shall not build them one."

"So then you must do something else," I insist.

"Like what?" Gideon turns on me angrily. "There is nothing for me to do."

I shake my head, "No, that is not true. There is always something. In Hope, we do not think this way."

"In *Hope*..." Gideon laughs bitterly. "That's all I hear all day! In Hope we do this... in Hope we don't do that."

Hurt, I stand up and back away. "That's not fair," I shoot back. "At least in Hope we *do* things with our pain and don't let our sadness destroy us like in Despair." My hand flies to my mouth. That was mean of me to remind him about his past. "I... I'm sorry."

"Sadness," Gideon drops his voice down, like the low ceiling in the room his parents have provided us. "What sadness? In Hope, there is no place for sadness."

"What is that supposed to mean? One could say the same about Despair, that *there*, there is no place for happiness," I counter defensively.

"Perhaps that is so, but it does not have to be one or the other," Gideon says. "Neither way is right."

I sit down again, suddenly tired and heavy from the weight of the child I am carrying, but mostly from the other burdens that are bundled up on a long stick across my shoulders.

"You must let me grieve, Pessia. Stop pushing me... I need time."

I feel shunned, ashamed, as if I've just been turned away from a family gathering, an unwelcome guest pushed out into the cold. "I... I have only tried to help you," I say, fighting back my tears. "This is the only way I know."

Gideon nods. "I realize that." He stops, looking thoughtful. "What about your Mama?" he asks me suddenly. "Where is your sadness over your Mama?"

"I..." the words are stuck, shocked, in my throat.

"What did you do with it, Pessia?" Gideon persists. "Where did you put it?"

Ever so slowly, I feel a stirring in the City of Suppression, a light kicking up of the silt in the seabed as tiny fish flit in and out of holes buried in the sand. "Please... don't..." My voice comes out pleadingly like the small child I was, the twelve-year-old girl who, despite the rest of the voices, knew her mother was going to die. "Don't bring it back," I beg my husband. "In Hope, we can only be positive..."

My words are empty to my own ears. I don't believe them myself, I realize. They're just a collection of vowels and consonants rolling off my tongue, and I bite down hard on my lip — as if that will stop the tears.

"Pain and hope *can* go together," Gideon says gently. "It's okay to cry."

"But… but… if we give in to our pain we shall fall into the sink-hole of despair," I say desperately. "Surely our way is better?"

But Gideon remains silent, just giving me the space for my tears, room for the grief that's been stuck in Suppression, to come out. And out it comes… rising up like a tsunami from the bottom of the cracked seabed, leaving me gasping for breath, fighting for oxygen, finally washing me up, exhausted but safe, on dry land.

"So you survived," Gideon says afterwards, his soft, compassionate words warming me. "And we will survive this, too."

IT HAS TAKEN time for Gideon to put himself back together. On occasion, he slips back into the negativity he learned in Despair. And I, too, sometimes revert to the ways of Hope, pushing him to move past his feelings and to think only positively. But in general, as a team, we synchronize well, each one passing the ball to the other until we reach our goal. Sometimes he runs faster than me or vice versa. Mostly, we try to work together, but if the old methods creep in, we stop and point them out to each other and are grateful for that. More than anything, we are learning that one can fall into the depths of despair, not cling to hope, and then climb out again, and that this, in fact, is *emunah*.

Papa is sitting in his usual chair, puffing on his pipe, when Gideon and I go to say good-bye. He looks up at us, and I can see that he knows without us even opening our mouths. Wistfully, he ruffles little Yehudit's hair, our baby who carries Mama's name, and her huge, dark, hopeful eyes.

"Where will you go?" Papa asks haltingly, without taking his eyes off Ditti.

"Not too far away," Gideon replies. "There is some land on the other side of the forest where we can build."

"You can come with us," I say softly, pleadingly. Papa says nothing. He will not come, after all that he's invested in Hope.

"We shall be back to visit often," I say, taking Papa's hand in mine. "But we have to do this… you understand."

"Yes," says Papa, rising up from his chair slowly. "Come, I will walk with you."

The four of us make our way through town, down the steep hill on Main Street and around the bend to the gate. Other families are waiting, the women sitting on top of their belongings, the men impatient to get moving.

Gideon and I lower our heads so that Papa can give us a *brachah*, saving his last blessing for Ditti. My husband looks at the group and nods and there is a flurry of activity, the wives gathering their children onto the carriages, the husbands mounting the horses, and then we're off. We travel away from Hope until Papa is only a small speck of goodness standing on the dusty road.

I am still waving.

"You can come, too!" I shout into the wind. And I mean it. Everybody's welcome. There will be no rejection, only warm, wide-open arms. Whoever wants can bring everything, *all* of himself, whatever he is or has — whether it's hope or despair, pride or shame, happiness or sorrow — and all of his questions… into our City of Emunah.

There are some stories I have written that simply astound me afterwards. "Cities" is one of them. Throughout my writing life I have always thanked the Almighty profusely for giving me the gift to write, to have a talent I can share with the world. It is stories such as these — that seem to have come from nowhere — that make me look back and ask, "How did I write that? Where did the ideas/words come from?" And I know without a doubt that they could only have come from Hashem.

"Cities" is a story that even I as the author can read over and over and still find messages which I wasn't even aware I was giving. Often, I think writing can be a totally subconscious experience if I just let myself go when I write. Thoughts and feelings and ideas can come out easily when I don't try to control them. That process is incredible; watching a story unfold like the gradual uncurling of ones' fingers. When I read "Cities" today, I see things that I'm sure I didn't see then.

Looking back, I recall that I was going through a painful time in my life. There were many things happening at once. One day, I remember standing, gazing out of my kitchen window, enjoying the birds pecking at the vines on my lattice, all the while tears streaming down my face. And that's when I realized I could be happy and sad at the same time, that one was not mutually exclusive of the other. I found this a revelation of sorts. So often we think that we can only feel one emotion at a time, and sometimes the emotions warring within us are bipolar opposites of each other. Well, at that moment, standing by my window, I knew that I was a happy, content person even if my heart was breaking at the same time, and somehow I wanted to get that concept out into the world. In addition, due to certain things that my children were going through, I realized the importance of addressing issues and not sweeping things under the rug. A child of mine had made certain choices for which she was ostracized. The ramifications of that have affected her until this day. Accepting others with their differences and not being afraid of them almost became a mission for me.

So now, when I read "Cities," I see that the story is a cholent pot full of all these things. Acceptance of others, whether it be the difference between "frum from birth" or "baalei teshuvah" or the diversity in peoples' personalities or character traits; the importance of not suppressing one's feelings, especially a child's; and the ability to stretch and expand to accommodate conflicting emotions… it all somehow ended up there in that story.

I love the story, the style, the backdrop. As I said before, I particularly like writing in first person. First person narrative, while not actually me, could be me; it is not outside of me like third person. When choosing a genre for a story, I have to feel the piece, to know what it needs. If I'm writing about a character who does something I don't like it would be difficult to present that in first person. Right from the onset this story "worked" in the "I" form. I hope you enjoyed reading it as much as I enjoyed writing it.

Fitting In

"OKAY, I THINK we're just about done."

Shulamis appraised the refurbished room while feeling the caress of billowing curtains on her face. The fresh, invigorating air from the open window brought the sweet promise of new beginnings.

"Do you think he'll like it, Mommy?" five-year-old Brachie asked anxiously.

"Why shouldn't he?" eleven-year-old Shmuel retorted. "I wouldn't say no to a room like this."

"Me neither," said Sruly, curling his lanky nine-year-old legs on a pouf in the corner.

"I think it's beautiful, Mommy," Ruchama, the oldest, said approvingly. "I'm sure that Zvi is going to love it."

"Good." Shulamis made a decisive movement towards the door. "Shmuel, please go tell Tatty we're ready and Ruchama, could you get everyone in the car?"

The ride to the airport was boisterous, bubbling with mixed emotions as each family member anticipated Zvi's arrival. For Shulamis, her oldest son's year off in Israel had flashed by like the click of a camera.

"Mommy," said Brachie again as they entered the arrivals lounge. "Do you *really* think he'll like it?"

"Aw, Brachie, give it a break," Shmuel rolled his eyes. "If he doesn't, then it's too bad."

"Of course he will." Ruchama ruffled her little sister's hair and glared at her brother.

Shulamis was standing on tiptoe, straining to see over the heads of people in front of her. "Can you see him?" she asked her husband, without turning around.

"Not yet," Aryeh answered, lifting Brachie onto his shoulders so she could get a better view.

Shulamis could barely contain herself as she watched new arrivals spill out of the arrivals tunnel like apples from a torn sack. Where *was* Zvi? Trust him to be last, as usual. Actually, that wasn't really fair of her; after all, she might not even recognize him, adolescent boys could change a lot in a year.

"Brachie, keep still," Aryeh told his daughter. "You're hurting my neck." Brachie bounced up and down on his shoulders, kicking her legs as if her father was a racehorse she was urging on. Throwing her arms in the air enthusiastically, she waved and shouted her brother's name at no one in particular. Suddenly, a young boy disconnected himself from the crowd and started walking over to her.

"Brachie!" the boy called out. "Is that you?" He glided towards her, lifting her off her father's shoulders and spinning her in the air like a circus performer. "Hello, Mom… Dad…" the boy broke out into a wide grin.

Shulamis stared at the stranger before her; gaped at his gelled hair and piercings, especially the one in his eyebrow that glinted at her amidst the artificial lights. His scruffy pants looked as if they hadn't seen the inside of a washing machine in months; in fact, the guitar bag on his back looked cleaner. But the most shocking thing of all, the very worst that could be was… his bare head! Shulamis unwittingly brought her hand to her mouth. Why hadn't he warned them? Yes, she knew that he'd gone to Israel to try to "find himself"… but was *this* what he'd found?

ON THE JOURNEY home, the inside of the car felt like a throat with a huge bone stuck inside it and raspy sentences gurgled out of everyone's mouths. At least Brachie's curious questions warmed the frosty atmosphere as she bounced in her seat next to her brother.

"Zvi, what's this?" she pressed her small finger to his eyebrow.

"It's a ring, Brachie," Zvi replied cheerfully.

"What's it for?"

"Nothing, really… I just like it."

Shulamis coughed uncomfortably. "So, how was the weather in Israel when you left?"

"Hot, Mom… and sunny! It's summer, remember. In Israel it's *always* hot in the summer."

"No need to be flippant," Aryeh reprimanded. "Please be respectful to your mother."

"Well, it was a stupid question," Zvi mumbled to himself, staring out of the window.

"We have a nice surprise for you when we get home," Ruchama announced chirpily.

"Oh yeah, what is it?" Zvi brightened a little, as if the cloud blocking the sun had shifted.

"Wait and see… or it won't be a surprise!"

"WELL, AT LEAST he liked his room," said Ayreh, sinking wearily into the lounge sofa.

"Mmm," Shulamis clutched a couch cushion closely to her chest as if it was a comfort blanket.

"It's a bit of a shock, isn't it?" Aryeh attempted feebly.

"You could say that," Shulamis muttered.

A strained, uncomfortable silence covered them like a mosquito net, trapping all of their tangled emotions, and Shulamis felt hot, angry tears bubbling to the surface like lava.

"He could have prepared us, at least," she fumed.

"Right."

"How could he do this; turning up looking like some kind of punk? Who knows, maybe he's violent?"

"He's still our son, Shulamis," Areyeh said quietly. "He's still Zvi."

"Is he?" The tears spouted out, almost scorching Shulamis's cheeks with their heat. "Is he?" she asked again. "That… that lowlife-looking creature is not my son! That's not my Zvi… my child!"

"I know," said Aryeh soothingly. "And I know he seems like he's changed, but maybe he hasn't?"

"Of course he's *changed*! Anyone can see that! He didn't look like this a year ago!"

Aryeh struggled to explain himself. "What I mean is… that on the outside he *is* different, but…"

"He certainly is," Shulamis declared. "And it's utterly embarrassing."

SHULAMIS DUCKED DOWN quickly behind the canned pickles, her face flaming as red as the tomatoes in the vegetable section. This was all she needed now, to bump into Ruchama's homeroom teacher. Cautiously, she peeked over the top shelf while slowly making her way down the aisle towards the stacked cereal boxes. A hand clamped down on her shoulder like an iron tarantula.

"Gotcha!"

"Yaagh!" Shulamis jumped up in fright, crashing forward into the cereal stand and sending the tower of boxes toppling over.

"What are you *doing*?" her friend Tirtza choked, in between laughs. "You look as if you're on some undercover mission."

""Shssh," Shulamis whispered, looking around her suspiciously. "I don't want her to see me."

"Who…?"

Shulamis grabbed Tirtza's hand and pulled her outside to the parking lot.

"Hey, hold on, I haven't paid for my groceries," Tirtza giggled. "You're going to get me arrested!"

"Quick," Shulamis beckoned. "Just get into the car." She fumbled for her car keys, aimed them towards the door and pressed the automatic lock opener. "*Nu*, come on… why isn't it working?"

"Here, give me those." Tirtza grabbed the keys from Shulamis and pressed. The locks clicked open. "You'd never make a criminal," she gasped, collapsing into the passenger's seat. "That was some performance in there; what's going on?"

Shulamis slid lower in her seat and cast a nervous glance out of the window. "Mrs. Berger was inside," she gestured towards the store without turning around.

"Huh?"

"She was Ruchama's homeroom teacher this past year."

"I think I'm missing something," Tirtza shook her head in confusion.

"I don't want her to see me," said Shulamis.

"No kidding!" said Tirtza. "And you also haven't answered any of my calls for the past week. What's with you, are you having some kind of nervous breakdown?"

Shulamis turned in her seat to face her friend.

"You know, now that you mention it, maybe I am!" She stared down at the pedals beneath her feet. "Zvi came home."

"Hey, that's wonderful. Weren't you expecting him only at the end of the summer? That must have been a nice surprise."

"Yes, he threw this on us as usual, but that wasn't the biggest shock, though."

Tirtza stared at her friend expectantly.

"Well," Shulamis started, "he came home looking rather different than when he left. It appears that he's… no longer religious."

Sympathetic brushstrokes painted Tirtza's face. "Oh… I'm so sorry. That must be devastating. So *that's* why you're hiding!"

Shulamis briefly recalled Tirtza's words after she'd dragged her out of the supermarket. "You'll never make a criminal," her friend had said. It was funny, because for some strange reason, that's exactly what she felt she was!

"MOM, I'M BORED." Zvi wandered into the kitchen, swiped his finger into the jar of chocolate spread and licked it.

"Zvi, will you stop that!" Shulamis shrieked. "Nobody can eat from that container now."

"But I'm bored." The finger found its way back into the chocolate jar.

"So what do you want me to do about it?" queried Shulamis, quickly snatching the jar from his grasp.

"Can I come with you to work… like, to hang out?"

Shulamis looked at her son incredulously. "Certainly not! My office is not a hang-out place and anyway, all the company secretaries are going out for lunch today for a good-bye party."

"What should I do then?" Zvi asked dejectedly.

"Don't ask me," Shulamis answered impatiently. She picked up her briefcase off the chair and headed towards the door. "Oh, I have an idea," she said before going out. "You could always go back to yeshivah and learn Torah!"

The sting from that parting comment stayed with her all morning and made her eyes prick with water as if she'd just peeled an onion. She leaned forward over her desk and surreptitiously brushed the tears away so that no one would notice. She cried a lot these days, so much more than usual that she sometimes wondered if she had leaking tear ducts. Zvi's hurt face when she'd fired her final shot hovered before her angry one. It wasn't nice of her, she knew, but she didn't know how to talk to him anymore; they no longer spoke the same language or enjoyed the expression of a familiar vocabulary. *He* had tried though, hadn't he? The trouble was that she could barely look at him, let alone spend time together. Those hard, metal piercings had created an impenetrable shield of armor between them and she lacked the words or weapons to break it down.

Miriam, her coworker, tapped her lightly on her arm. "Are you ready? It's 12:30."

Shulamis gathered her belongings and walked towards the elevator with the older woman. A group of about ten secretaries was waiting downstairs in the lobby when they arrived and they exited the cool building into the harsh glare of the midday sun. Outside in the street, there were youths who were not in summer camp for whatever reason; boys kicking a ball in the park, teenagers outside a pizza shop.

"Ugh," said Miriam as she walked beside her, "just look at those hooligans over there." She narrowed her eyes. "I don't know how their parents let them behave like that; it would never have been allowed in my day."

Shulamis followed Miriam's gaze to a group of bareheaded boys across the street. They reminded her of…

"Hey, Mom," a hand waved above the boys' heads like a frond swaying in the wind, and Shulamis turned her face away quickly.

"Shulamis," Miriam said in shock. "Is one of those boys waving at *you?*"

Shulamis felt a fire in her cheeks that she'd become familiar with during the last weeks.

"No," she continued hurriedly along the sidewalk. "You must be mistaken."

And an unwelcome companion called guilt accompanied her to the restaurant.

"I THINK WE should move!" Shulamis suggested a few weeks later. "I don't like it here anymore."

"Why would you want to do that?" Aryeh asked. "This has always been your favorite neighborhood."

"Not anymore. Things have changed."

Aryeh tried to concentrate on the winding road ahead of him. "Things?" he threw out.

"Zvi's changed… so have I. We don't fit in anymore."

Aryeh stared out of the windshield into the still, summer night. He'd been looking forward to a relaxing evening with his wife. For a while he was silent, fumbling for the right words to say and not even knowing if he had them.

"Things change all the time," he said at last. "It's meant to be that way; even each day is different. Look at these trees," he pointed at the sturdy branches through the window. "They change constantly with the seasons but that doesn't mean they have to uproot."

"People are *talking* about us," Shulamis ignored her husband's poetic recital. "We've lost our good reputation."

"Do you know that for sure?" Aryeh persisted. "Or is just your imagination?"

"Of course not," declared Shulamis hotly. "Everybody knows what it's like when you have a child off the *derech*. You'll see… Ruchama won't get into a good high school and it will affect her *shidduch* chances."

"Hmm, I don't think I agree," Aryeh mused. "Things *have* changed, like you said, and unfortunately, that includes most families having at least one child who is struggling these days. People are less judgmental than they used to be."

"Well, maybe you don't notice so much; it's probably the women who feel it more."

"Now, that's not fair. Don't you think I'm pained that my eldest son doesn't come with me to shul or to learn, that it's uncomfortable for me when other men ask about him?"

"So you do see what I mean then!" Shulamis said pointedly.

"Yes," Aryeh agreed, "I do. But I'm not picking up and running!"

"I WAS THINKING about a more modern community," Shulamis told the estate agent. Aryeh raised his eyebrows. "I mean, something less closed, you know… more accepting…" her voice trickled off weakly like a drying up stream.

"Pardon me for saying so, Mrs. Krauss, but do you really think your family would fit into a modern town? You are *chareidi*, aren't you?" Stella Blum was a well-known estate agent amongst the religious circles and although not observant herself, knew her clientele well.

"Yes, we are. My husband learns half a day," Shulamis said proudly.

"So what else is available?" Aryeh interrupted hastily.

"Let me see," Stella scanned her list. "Do you want a house or an apartment? I have a lovely apartment here in this neighborhood." She pointed at one of the pictures on the third page. "Nice neighborhood for what you're looking for, I think. Pricey, though. This apartment is on the fourth floor."

"No," Shulamis shook her head. "Definitely not! The last thing I need is all the neighbors staring into my living room. I need my privacy."

"So you wouldn't want an apartment *anywhere* then?"

"That's right."

Stella flashed a questioning glance at Aryeh.

"Yep, right… whatever."

"Fine, so no apartments," Stella scribbled down the details. "Not too modern… husband learns. Not *chassidish* either, I presume?" She looked up.

"Correct," Aryeh confirmed.

"You never know," Stella continued, running over the list. "You can't always tell. Ah, here's something nice. It's in your community but on the other side, at the far end of town."

Shulamis frowned. "It depends where. Can I see the address? Oh, no," she turned to her husband. "Waterstone Drive… that's right near the boys' *cheder*."

"Convenient," Stella smiled. "No carpools."

"Er, no, we don't think so," Aryeh smiled back. He looked at his watch and sighed. He hated to miss *shiur* for this, especially when the whole exercise seemed so futile. "Mind if I go?" he asked Shulamis. "You don't really need me, do you?"

Shulamis nodded her head slowly. Actually, at that moment she wasn't quite sure what she needed.

An hour later, she weaved unsteadily through the main street and along the suburban sidewalks towards her home. Her head was reeling with the myriads of impossibilities and unsuitable suggestions. She hadn't expected it to be so difficult to find the right neighborhood. When she got in the house she headed for the kitchen, opened the freezer and tossed some frozen cutlets into the microwave. An open jar of chocolate spread with telltale signs of Zvi's fingers winked at her from the table. She checked in the vegetable rack for potatoes; nothing. At least Mr. Rozen would still be open, so she could send Ruchama to get some. She opened her purse to take out money and groaned; none of that either. What was with her today? But then she remembered that Mr. Rozen would let her write down whatever she owed him. A small smile spread across her face. They were lucky to have such a *mentch* as their local grocer and that reassuring knowledge warmed her.

Later that night when Shulamis had some quiet moments with Aryeh, he hesitantly asked her, "So how did you get on with the real-estate agent in the end? Does she have any ideas for us?"

"Yes, actually, she does," Shulamis said wryly. "She suggests that we stay where we are!"

SLAM! THERE WENT the door again. Angry shouts tumbled down the stairs and crashed into the living room. She sighed. Another fight, argument, disagreement or whatever they called it. Shmuel had always been highly strung, but since Zvi had come home, he was impossible. Well, they'd just have to work this one out because she wasn't going to get involved. Shulamis went back to the brochures she had brought back from the new real-estate agent. She wasn't giving up so fast; there were more Stella Blums out there waiting to do business.

"Mommy, can I talk to you?"

Shulamis looked up, startled.

"Sure," she smiled at Ruchama and patted the couch. "Come, sit down."

Ruchama sat next to her mother. "Sruly, can you leave us alone for a few minutes?" She nodded at her brother who was deep inside one of his latest jigsaw puzzles at the dining room table. She picked up a maroon cushion and started pulling at its tassels and looked uncomfortably at her mother. "I'm sorry to bother you."

"That's all right," said Shulamis, stealing a furtive glance at the brochure. Hmm, that one seemed interesting.

"Is it true that you're thinking of moving?" Ruchama peeked over her mother's shoulder.

"Um… maybe." Yes, this was definitely worth looking into.

"Oh." Ruchama stared down into her lap. "So… when?"

"When what?" Shulamis took out a pen from her pocketbook and started scribbling down details.

"When are we *moving*?" Ruchama asked with exasperation. "Mommy, you're not listening to me."

"I'm sorry, honey," Shulamis put down her pen and faced her daughter. "I'm just a bit preoccupied, that's all."

"I know," said Ruchama, "but we need to talk, because none of us want to go."

Shulamis suddenly sat up straight like a soldier called to attention. "What do you mean? And who's we? What do you know about it?"

"It's obvious, Mommy. It's all you talk about these days. But we don't want to move and I wanted to tell you that."

""Look, the change will be hard at first but you'll get used to it. It will be much better for us in the long term."

Ruchama twisted the tassels around her fingers. "Better than what? We're happy here. We have our schools, friends and Shmuel…"

"What about Shmuel?"

"Well, he's really angry. He says that everything is because of Zvi and it's not fair that he needs to leave all his friends behind because of him." Ruchama's voice wobbled close to the edge of tears and fresh water welled in Shulamis's eyes.

"Yes," said Shulamis sadly, "things are different since Zvi came home."

Ruchama tucked her feet underneath her and wrapped her arms tightly around the cushion. "I know, but he's not the only child at home… what about the rest of us? Why do *we* have to suffer?"

"You don't!" a voice called from the doorway. "Because *I'm* leaving instead!"

HE LOOKED AS if he was going, with his huge, bulging duffle bag and his trusty guitar. Actually, he could have just been going away for a long weekend but there was more than that in his stance, something thought out and final.

"G… going where?" Shulamis stammered.

"To Uncle Yaakov first, until I decide what to do," said Zvi. There were thin cracks in his stone face, threatening to widen with every movement of his mouth. "It's better for everybody like this."

"Don't be silly," Shulamis's voice wavered. "Of course it's not." Her words were hollow, ringing with falsehood.

"Mom, I don't fit in here anymore and I'm just causing trouble for all of you."

This time the empty words didn't come. They remained inside in simple understanding and acknowledgement of what was, and nothing more.

"Please… don't go," she offered weakly… but the space where he'd stood… was empty.

A FAINT CHILL was left behind. Ruchama wept quietly next to her and Shulamis put her arm around her shoulders.

"I'm sorry," she said softly, although she wasn't sure for what. She was just sorry… for everything… for losing a son, for the crumbling of a family, for the confusion within herself and the shakiness of her foundations.

"I'm going after him," said Ruchama, jumping up quickly and running out of the room.

Shulamis rose from the couch and stared after the swinging doorway, feeling displaced and wobbly as if her hinges were broken. On the table was Sruly's unfinished jigsaw puzzle, pieces scattered over the polished surface like fallen leaves. She walked over to the table, pulled out a chair and sat down, gathering pieces in her hand, fingering them carefully along their edges, feeling the round connecting parts that stretched out like butternuts. Silently, she started searching for spaces, looking for homes where they all belonged. Scooping up more and more shapes, Shulamis pieced the puzzle together, some pieces slipping into their spaces effortlessly, others less so, and while she connected them, she found herself thinking of her family.

There… this piece was for Sruly; that one for Ruchama; another for Aryeh. There were so many pieces and it took time to fit them all together but there was a place for them all. As a picture began to emerge, Shulamis struggled to remember what it had looked like when it was whole, frequently glancing at the image on the box that showed her how it was supposed to be. How hard it had been to see the complete picture when pieces were missing. For a while now, she had been that broken jigsaw, filled with holes and empty spaces, but instead of trying to fill them with her own parts, she'd looked instead for a different puzzle.

A piece was missing and the empty space where it belonged looked out longingly for its occupant. Shulamis slipped off her chair and crawled under the table, sweeping her hand over the carpet in search of that last piece. And then she found it! Teasingly, it poked its head out from underneath the trim and she leaned over to take it, climbed back out and carefully inserted it into place. This one… was for Zvi!

Suddenly, she jumped up and dashed for the front door, frantically pulling it open. She ran outside into the night, feeling the sharp air sting her face. She called his name, despite knowing that he was long gone and wouldn't be able to hear her.

Still, she did it, because one day he *would* hear, once she talked to him, once she listened to her child and understood his pain of not belonging. *He* had to find a place where he felt comfortable, not *her*. She wasn't going anywhere, except to that sweet promise of a new beginning that carried love and acceptance and to a place she called home. And that's… where she'd be waiting for him!

This was another fiction story assigned to me by Binah. Unfortunately, I can't actually remember what the assignment was. I recall that it was something to do with neighborhoods and moving but that's about it. So, sorry about that… blame it on my having a "senior day."

When I read the story just now to try to jog my memory (alas, it is well and truly clogged), I found myself enjoying it, which is pretty good considering I don't know why I wrote it in the first place!

The messages in the story are very real and pertinent to the struggles taking place in contemporary society. One thing I do remember is how years ago, friends of mine with older children were often harassed by them into moving out of the neighborhood. As their children morphed into teenagers, my friends were deluged with statements like, "It's boring here," "Let's move to where the Cohens have gone," "Anyway, none of us go to school here anymore," and so on. I remember listening to these exchanges with amusement and confusion, never dreaming that my time would come, too.

Now I hear these persuasive arguments all the time.

"Let's move up north… we can have a big house and a horse." (That's the horsey daughter speaking.)

"Chen's family is really happy in Givat Ze'ev… let's go there."

"We're not coming back here when we're married so you might as well move."

"It's sooooooo boring in this town… there's nothing to do here."

Although the dynamics in "Fitting In" are a little different from my scenario (it was the mother wishing to move, not the children), I believe that the message is the same. How many times do we think things will be better somewhere else? How often do we think our problems will magically disappear if we leave them behind? No matter what the reason, whether it's having a child no longer "fitting in" to the neighborhood or some other thing, running away is never the solution. Sometimes moving can be the answer, but only once it's well thought out and discussed with other family members and not carried out on impulse like the protagonist in this story.

When my older kids gripe and kvetch about the place they live and implore us to move, this is what I tell them: "Im yirtzeh Hashem, you will all get married one day and build your own homes. Abba and I need to be happy where we are living, and we are. We have our shul, our Rabbis, our friends and kehillah. We have a house that we love (at least I do anyway) and we're in a perfect location... twenty minutes from Yerushalayim, thirty minutes from Tel Aviv. Nowhere is perfect. You can move and find you have nasty neighbors or you can buy a house with a spectacular view and a year later the tractors arrive because an eight-story apartment block is on the horizon."

In short, we remind our kids that it's better to stick with what you know (unless it's absolutely unbearable of course) and to work with it.

Now, you could say that the boy in the story should have stayed and worked with it, too. This is different. Although it was his home, he would move out of it anyway one day and he was in fact suffering by living in a place he no longer felt part of. The mother, however, was about to uproot everyone else in the family because of her embarrassment over this child. Moves like this can rarely be successful because when the bags are all neatly packed, they'll be picked up and transported to the "new" place!

Lost

DEAR TARA,

I miss you! Even now, a whole year since you've gone, I'm still missing you. Can you hear me wherever you are? Are you lonely too? We were inseparable, weren't we? Friends since kindergarten, bound together like sisters... I thought it would be like that forever... but it wasn't.

Tara, how could you leave me like this? Whatever happened to all the thousands of tefillos I cried for your recovery? Where did they go? Did you take them with you?

I wish you would talk to me, tell me where you are and what it's like "up there." Ima says I should talk to Hashem but I don't do that kind of thing anymore. What's the point when He doesn't listen?

Dear, dear Tara, I am lost without you. No... I am simply lost!

Love,

Rikki

"I'M GOING TO India!"

Six pairs of wide eyes stared at me out of frozen faces.

"Why don't you say something?"

"Um," Mommy cleared her throat. "Well... er..."

"When are you thinking of going, *zeeskeit?*" Tatty asked casually as if inquiring about a trip to the zoo.

"In about two weeks. Alice has to arrange the tickets."

"Alice…" Mommy murmured and let out a strangled sigh. "If Alice said sneeze, you would do it."

"Where's India, Tatty?" little Chesky piped up.

"It's a very, very big country, a long way away," Tatty answered him. "So," he turned to me, "how long are you planning to stay for?"

"Dunno," I shrugged. "For as long as we feel like it."

"What's in India that you don't have here?" Dina asked in that know-it-all, sixteen-year-old voice.

"There is *nothing* here," I answered angrily. "Only empty promises… that's all!"

"What about us, Rikki?" ten-year-old Adina looked at me beseechingly across the table. "Don't you like your family anymore?"

I felt myself swaying like a tall flower bending in a strong breeze and my lip quivered.

"Of course I do, Adina," I reached over to squeeze her hand. "I love you all… it's just that… I need to get away." I stood up abruptly. "Thanks for supper. I'll see you guys before I leave."

My parents rose from the table; Tatty, tall and stately in his long, black rabbinical coat, Mommy his immaculate queen beside him, and the tears that welled in their eyes were deep enough to drown in.

DEAR TARA,

I can't believe I'm going. It's a strange feeling because I've never left Israel before. I wish you were coming with me. Maybe you are. Mommy and Tatty don't like Alice but she's been a good friend to me since… since you're gone. Of course she's got issues, but who doesn't?

Tara, I still see you in my dreams. Do you remember when we went to buy you a wig after you lost your hair and you wanted some goofy-looking black thing that made you look like a gollywog and we laughed until our stomachs hurt? And then there was the day we ran away from the hospital because you'd decided you'd had enough. You were still in

your pajamas with your IV pole so we didn't get very far, but it was
great fun trying.

Oh, why did you have to go? Everyone was davening for you,
taking challah, trying different segulos, but nothing helped. I don't
understand it. All I know is that the pain scratches my heart every
time I take a breath and I don't believe in anything anymore.

Do you think I'll find some peace in India?

Love,

Rikki

I CARRIED MY family's good-byes like pictures in my pocketbook. I hadn't expected the departure to be so hard, especially
when I'd been waiting for this moment, to open my wings wide
and fly. Alice found my inexperience amusing.

"What, nineteen years old and you've never been abroad!" she
exclaimed incredulously as she fastened her seat belt. "I had already
flown to five different countries by the time I was ten."

"Fun for you," I said enviously.

"You religious people never go anywhere, right?" It was more of
a statement than a question.

I bristled. These occasional jabs at Judaism were the one irritating
thing about my friend. "Well, I wouldn't say that exactly. It's expensive to travel with large families but we always have a good time."

Alice raised her eyebrows skeptically and played with the head-
phones on her armrest.

"This will be my third time in India and it's quite a culture
shock, but stick with me and you'll be okay."

"Of course," I eyed her strangely. "Why wouldn't I?"

"No reason, I suppose. Just that people have a tendency to get
swept up with the crowds in that country."

"Oh," I said, biting my lip.

"By the way," Alice nodded towards the notebook on my lap,
"are you going to be writing in that the entire time?"

Instinctively I clutched my notepad tightly as if afraid someone would snatch it off me.

"Yes," I declared resolutely. "Wherever I go, it goes too."

DEAR TARA,

We arrived in Mumbai a few days ago and it's been such a whirl-wind that I haven't had time to write. How do I describe this place? The first thing is the smells; there are so many of them that they over-load my senses. The second I stepped off the plane I was assaulted by a smell of dirt and grime that seems to have stuck with me along with the heady scent of fragrant blossoms and wafting incense. It's a combina-tion that doesn't really fit.

Guess what? Alice and I checked into one of those hostel places with squat toilets and a shower that's only a cup and a bucket of cold water. Believe it or not, even that was a refreshing respite from the intense heat and humidity. But the worst thing is the bedbugs! Alice doesn't have any but I woke up bitten all over. It's horrible. Alice is good company, bouncy and fun... the main reason I was drawn to her. She takes life so easily, nothing seems to faze her. We don't talk about anything too serious, which is just fine with me for now. Of course, she's very differ-ent than you.

I don't know if you'd like it here. I don't know if I like it here... it's too soon to know. Alice is infatuated with this place, which is why she keeps coming back every year. I am looking for peace and solitude but everything is so noisy. I have enough of that already... the noise, I mean, inside my head.

Missing you, as usual.

Love,

Rikki

"WE NEED TO earn some money!" Alice announced. "I'm going to find us a job."

"What do you have in mind?" I asked curiously.

"I'll check out the hotels in Mumbai," Alice answered confidently. "They hire tourists to work there all the time as waiters or cleaners. I've done it before."

"Ugh, cleaning," I wrinkled my nose in disdain, thinking about the Indian sanitation standards, or lack of them.

Alice chuckled. "My, are you spoiled. What's the matter, afraid to get your hands dirty?"

"Absolutely not!" I replied indignantly. "I could teach *you* a thing or two about cleaning. I used to help get the house ready every Erev Shabbos and you should have seen what I did for Pesach."

Alice rolled her eyes and swung her bag over her shoulder. "Honestly, sometimes I wonder how you and I ever became friends. We are so different and come from such opposite backgrounds. You're kind of sweet, though; I love you anyway."

"Gee, thanks, I'm highly honored."

Alice grinned and headed for the door. "Are you coming or not?"

Of course I was. Was there a choice? I was completely dependent on her in this foreign place and she knew it.

DEAR TARA,

I have so much to tell you but can't possibly get the words out fast enough. What can I say about Mumbai? It's a city of paradox, a place filled with opulence and unbelievable poverty at the same time. The hotel where I work is one of the most magnificent buildings I have ever seen, yet in a shanty town nearby, thousands live in squalor. I can't get my head around the suffering I see here. Barefoot children tie sweet-smelling flower garlands on our wrists while they beg for coins. Others kick balls in the streets, their swollen bellies sagging on stick legs. Sometimes the suffering saddens me so much that I just want to give away everything I own and cry in the gutter with the homeless.

Tara, this world of ours is so confusing. I don't know why people have to suffer so. If only you were here for me to talk to. Would you have any answers? Do you remember when Mrs. Sherkin once said I should stop asking so many questions because I'd never find the answers in this world, only the next...? I envy you, now that you don't have questions anymore, but I'm angry that you left me with mine.

I would love to know if there really is a G-d in this world. With everything that's happening in the world, I don't think there could be.

Love,

Rikki

"BUBBY KEEPS ASKING for you."

"I... I'm sorry."

"Sorry? Is that all you can say?" Mommy's voice sounded as distant as I felt and just as bruised.

"I'm not done yet, Mom."

"And what's that supposed to mean? What do you have to *do* exactly in that pagan country? Your grandmother is deteriorating. Don't you realize that?"

"Yes," I whispered, "I do."

"So what are you waiting for? Just come home already."

"Mom... I can't." Quietly, I started to weep and I hoped the crackle on the line would replace my words for a moment. I couldn't let Mommy hear me cry, I just couldn't.

"Why not? Bubby wants you. Isn't that more important?"

"I will come, but not now. Alice and I are taking a trip to Alleppy very soon, to the backwaters."

"A trip... a trip!" Mommy spluttered. "Instead of coming home to Bubby, you're taking a *trip!*"

My weeping grew stronger, no longer hidden by the static down the wire.

"Rivka? Are you there? I can't hear you!" Mommy shouted in frustration.

"Neither can I," I mouthed wordlessly, as I dropped the phone and watched it dangle from the receiver and sway back and forth in the stagnant air.

DEAR TARA,

I did the most terrible thing to Mommy; I put the phone down on her. I've never done anything like that to her before but hearing the pain in her voice was simply too much for me. How can she possibly understand that I can't return home yet? Alice and I have made enough money to leave Mumbai and head out to the country where we can hike. I'm hoping to find my peace there; a chance to empty my lungs and breathe a cleaner air that's not polluted with my problems. Do you think that's possible? I think it is.

We traveled the first leg of the journey by train. Tara, you would have loved it! Trains in India have lives of their own. There were about four people sitting in my seat and a constant flurry of activity in the aisles where people seem to sell anything they can lay their hands on. And that's just the inside. You should see the hundreds of people clinging to the outside, holding on for dear life like mountain climbers afraid to lose their footing. As we rattled along through the Indian countryside, everything looked like a jumble of houses, slums, shanty towns and apartment buildings. There were people squatting near the train tracks and kids even threw stones at us while the passengers just smiled and wobbled their heads. Their heads are always wobbling; it's a wonder that they don't fall off.

Oh, and I forgot to tell you about some other things in India that are really beautiful, like the dragonflies that dip and dive over the water, as vibrantly colored as kingfishers and with wings as wide as small birds. Like I've told you before, India is a land of great contrast; fascinating and utter beauty and total, devastating poverty.

I find it humbling here. I guess one learns to appreciate what she has… running water, flushing toilets, a warm, comfortable bed, family and friends. You realize what's important. And that's why I feel so bad about Mommy and Bubby and not going home because they and everyone else mean so much to me. But I can't go back yet. I still have things to do. You do understand that, don't you?

Tara, would you think badly of me if I told you that I'm fascinated by the religious culture here? Actually, that's not completely true because I'm also uncomfortable with it. Just a few days ago, the Hindus were celebrating a festival across the street with a noisy parade and loud songs blasting over loudspeakers. I am both drawn and repelled by it at the same time.

Oh, I don't know what to think anymore. I wish Hashem would bring me clarity.

Did I really say that?

Love,

Rikki

"HOW LONG DO you think we'll be out there?" I asked Alice while adjusting the straps on my backpack.

"I've no idea. Depends how far we hike... could be a week or two." Alice rolled up her sleeping bag into a compact ball.

"What about food and stuff?" I asked nervously.

Alice rolled her eyes. "We take it with us," she said in a condescending tone, "and there are always villages along the way where we can pick things up."

"Okay," I said, although I couldn't really quell the queasiness in my stomach. My slow-growing dependency on Alice was turning into a malignancy, causing me much discomfort and making me wish I could excise it. But what could I do? This was her territory, not mine, and I was clueless as to how to navigate it alone.

"Before we leave the city," Alice was saying, pulling the string on her sleeping bag tighter with her teeth, "I've mapped out some amazing temples for us to visit."

I inhaled deeply to try to settle my nausea. "Wha... what kind of temples?"

Alice raised her eyebrows. "You don't know what a temple is?"

"Of course I know. But what do people do there?"

"Ah, now I understand. Still a good little religious girl at heart, aren't you?"

I felt my cheeks burn as a hot flame brushed over them. "What's the connection?" I shot back quickly. "I'm just asking, that's all."

DEAR TARA,

Alice and I are getting on each other's nerves. We are arguing more and more, the longer we're together. Yesterday, she blew up at me because I refused to go inside one of those temples they have here. Don't ask me why I couldn't go in, but for some reason, I just couldn't. Alice says that underneath it all, I'm still brainwashed and unable to think for myself. I've thought about that and I don't think it's true; if anything, I think too much. Maybe… maybe, I'm more connected to Judaism than I thought? Or perhaps it's just habit?

Up here in the mountains where the only sound is the rustle of grass in the wind and the calling of the birds as they swoop down low and soar back high in the sky, I have found the silence I've been seeking. And yet, there's still so much noise clanging around inside my head.

I wish I could just scrub out my brain matter and start all over.
Struggling,
Rikki

TARA,

Alice has gone! Just like that! We had another fight and she dumped me to join another group of Israeli hikers we met on the way. I don't know what to do… don't even know where I am! How could she drop me like this in the middle of nowhere? I thought we were friends.

I am so terribly frightened. I am so alone. I am lost!

DEAR TARA,

I've been walking for two days by myself, trying to find my way. I'm looking for signs of civilization or anything that can guide me. My water is running out, so I'm trying to ration it and to drink only sips but my mouth is so dry that my tongue sticks to my palate. Where am I? What am I? I feel completely abandoned. Did I really want all this… the so-called solitude, the peace? Help me, somebody… help me, because I am lost! Hashem, please don't leave me!

Rikki

TARA,

I have had no strength to write. It's been days maybe, I can't keep track of time, since I arrived at the village. I was delirious from dehydration when the villagers found me. The people here are very kind. Even though we don't speak the same language and I am not one of them, I see the warmth and compassion in their eyes and I am grateful that Hashem delivered me into their care. I cry a lot. Sometimes I sob in my sleep like a baby and yearn to be held and soothed like one. Even though I am drained from crying, I know that it's good. These are the first real tears I have shed since you died. I think they washed away my anger. Today I actually said some Tehillim. I'm not sure what to think about that. Maybe I'm only turning to Hashem because I'm vulnerable and there's no One else?

I'm too tired to write more.

Love,

Rikki

DEAR HASHEM,

Here in this tiny village amongst these simple peasant folks who never stop smiling, I've had plenty of time to think while regaining strength. I've started talking to You again… will You forgive me for not having done that sooner? My words are so pitifully inadequate to express what's in my heart. I realize that I was angry, confused, vulnerable and too dependent on people around me… Alice, even Tara. Looking back, I honestly cannot understand what I saw in Alice. She seemed so vibrant and alive, as if nothing in the world would ever bother her, indestructible almost, and I liked that, needed it even. I'm sure she sensed my weakness, my broken self, fragmented into tiny pieces that I couldn't connect together and still can't. But now I understand that the peace I desperately seek has to come from within me, a vessel that's healthy and complete.

Hashem, I know from a place deep inside, from a storehouse that's been filled for years with lessons in emunah, *that the only One I can depend on is You… but it's really hard for me to feel it sometimes. I would like to try, though.*

There is still so much I need to work out in myself and my relationship with You and I have many, many questions, but in my heart, I know where the answers lie and it's not here, in India.

I am a stranger in this land… this is not my place, never was.

Hashem… I'm coming home!

"Lost" was a Rosh Hashanah story. It seemed appropriate to use India as the background for this piece because it is where so many Jews, especially Israelis, go to "find themselves." I once worked with a young woman, a baalas teshuvah who had spent many months in India, and her descriptions of the place were both fascinating and disturbing. My colleague had adopted Chabad as her expression of Yiddishkeit, mainly because it was they who had been mekarev her in India. Chabad has a big presence in that country, and hundreds of Israelis, thinking they are on a mission to find whatever they're missing, find it within their own religion after all.

So that explains the setting for my story. The plot was inspired by certain questions my daughter used to ask me and also questions I had of my own. As a child I questioned constantly, much to my parents' frustration, so it did not come as any surprise to me when my daughter did likewise. There was a young girl in her school who was very sick, and after outpourings of Tehillim and learning in her zechus, sadly she passed away. My daughter came to me extremely troubled.

"Ima, what happened to all the tefillos that were said for Mindy*?" she asked. "Where do they all go and what was the point of them when they didn't help?"

I tried to explain that tefillos are never wasted, that they are stored in Shamayim to use for someone else and that the most important thing is to have a connection to Hashem.

I think we all have times when we are "lost," not only after a tragedy. There are moments when we are less connected to Hashem and other occasions when we are more. I speak for myself when I say that whenever I feel far away from Hashem, I am lost. I drift around, floundering, with no one to guide me. It's very simple to reconnect again. All I need to do is TALK to Him, in my own words, straight from my heart. Simple, right? I just have to remember to do it.

Those heartfelt, personal prayers can be said anywhere, not only and even in India. I pray that we don't have to travel so far to find them!

A Matter of Pride

HONESTLY? I DON'T know what my mother was thinking of when she named me Olivia! It's not like we were high society or anything — not even close. Maybe it was delusions of grandeur or an innate sense of intuition that I would become the female namesake of the famous Dickens character, Oliver Twist? Whatever it was, she was right, because I did in fact end up roaming the streets just like that wretched pauper.

I had never known anything different from the slums I was growing up in. We were just the three of us; Mom, me, and my younger sister, Victoria — another high-minded name from who knows where.

Dad had long gone, leaving us a legacy of overdue rent, unpaid bills and moldy bread in the broken cupboard above the sink. Not that it was better when he was around, or so Mom always told us. But then, she told us a lot of things, like how she'd been disowned by her wealthy family when she'd married him, because he had no job or money and would never make anything of himself, unlike she, who had been groomed for better things, like medical school or a law degree.

If you ask me, I thought she had made a huge mistake! I mean, imagine having all that money and giving it up to live like a bag lady! Mom got real mad at me whenever I said that. She said I'm not allowed to talk that way, and that Victoria and I wouldn't be here if she hadn't married Dad.

I used to think about that in the middle of the night, when I couldn't sleep from the cold that burrowed into my bones. While I lay shivering beneath my thin blanket, I would wonder if I'd have simply been born to a different set of parents if Mom and Dad hadn't married each other. I used to dream about it — growing up in another family, like the ones on the other side of town, where the dads wore suits and ties and the moms smelled of freshly-baked bread and perfumed soap.

Mom and Victoria were always yelling at me for asking questions and thinking so much, but I couldn't help it; my head was the place I liked best. Inside my imagination, I wasn't cold and hungry and rummaging through the alleyway garbage cans for something to eat.

"OLIVIA!"

I heard my name, rumbling through the fog like a train approaching in a dark tunnel.

"Olivia, can you put that book down and come and help me?"

I was just about to find out if Anne Frank's hiding place would be discovered, and the cruel clattering of steel-tipped shiny boots was slow to fade away.

"Olivia! I said put the book down." My mother whisked it out of my hands, hoping that I'd blink back to reality, no longer a girl called Anne, huddled in fear with her family in a secret room, spilling out her hopes and dreams into her diary.

"Hmm," my mother frowned. "Where did you get this from?"

"I found it near one of the garbage cans on the other side of the bridge."

Mom leafed through the pages nostalgically. "I read this too, once." She looked at me and sighed. "I wish there was money for your books, Olivia."

"That's okay," I said lightly. "Somehow, I always manage to find some."

"Honey," my mother sat down on the edge of my bed. "I need you to go across the river again… to sell this." She held up a diamond ring that glistened in the dimly-lit room. "There's a family in that big house on Woodborne Grove that deals in jewelry."

I gasped. "Isn't that your grandmother Sadie's ring? I thought it was meant to be passed down!"

"It is," Mom said sadly, "but there's no longer any choice. I have to let it go; either that, or we'll be evicted, because Mr. Smith is running out of patience for the rent money. Our welfare payments simply aren't enough."

I took the ring and fingered it gently, tracing the exquisite, delicate stones that clustered together in a diamond shape, imagining each little stone falling away one by one, and felt some kind of deep connection roll away from me too. "Is… isn't there anything else to sell?"

"No," Mom shook her head wearily. "There's nothing left anymore." Her voice quavered on the edge of tears. "I saved this for last."

I nodded in tired resignation. "Okay… I'll do it."

"I'm sorry, Olivia," Mom said simply.

"For what?"

"For always asking you to do these things. You know that I can't ask Victoria because she's too young, and I don't have time for anything else except my cleaning jobs."

"It's fine, Mom," I smiled weakly, while pulling on my worn winter jacket and heading for the door.

"Just one thing, though," I paused before leaving. "When am I going back to school?"

My mother sighed heavily again. Sometimes, when I thought of her, it was as one long sigh, a wistful expiration of breath, on hold — just like her life.

"Soon, honey… soon."

I REMEMBERED THAT posh house on the corner of Woodborne Grove. The lady who lived there had once bought some pretty beaded necklaces that I'd made, and had kind green eyes that sparkled like the diamond inside my purse. I hummed as I walked along, hands stuffed in my pockets, kicking occasional stones from my path and holding onto that purse for dear life.

It was always strange to be on the rich side of town. I felt like Alice in Wonderland, transported down the rabbit hole to a fairy-tale place where nothing is as it seems. How many times had I made these trips already? At the tender age of eleven, I had lost count.

Across the street, a group of giggling girls tumbled out of a school bus, and for a moment I was jolted by jealousy. Sure, I was envious of their laughter and carefree chatter, but more than anything, I was envious that they went to school.

I, too, wanted to learn, instead of babysitting my five-year-old sister and hocking our wares like a street peddler. So often I found myself praying to G-d that Mom would get into trouble for keeping me out of school, and then I'd have to go. But G-d never seemed to listen (which was only reasonable, because I wasn't even sure if He was there in the first place).

Anyway, whether He was listening or not, it just wasn't fair! Why could all those other girls go to school and not me? Not for the first time, I wished I'd been born into a different family.

Mrs. Kind-Eyes' mansion was right around the corner and, grand as it was, for some reason it wasn't intimidating. Maybe it was the garden with the tall, willowy trees and rhododendron bushes that softened it, or the flowers in the window boxes and vines of twisted ivy that crept up the walls. I made my way along the garden path to the front door. There was a funny, narrow stick-shaped thing on one side of the doorway and a nameplate written in a strange language.

Mrs. Kind-Eyes answered the door so fast that I was practically knocked off balance, but her face was the way I'd remembered it, friendly crinkles around her eyes and a smile that said "welcome." She was way older than my Mom, but somehow less worn.

"Hello," she said, in a voice that didn't sound like proper English. (Maybe she hadn't gone to school either?) "How can I help you?"

"Please," I held out Great-Granny's diamond ring. "Would you like to buy this?"

Mrs. Kind-Eyes looked down at me and then at the ring, wearing one of those troubled expressions that only adults know how to dress up in.

"What's your name, child?" she asked gently.

"O… Olivia," I gulped.

"Well, then, Olivia, why don't you come inside?"

I THOUGHT I'D faint from embarrassment when my stomach growled like a hungry dog and my legs shook so badly that my knees knocked together. Mrs. Kind-Eyes led me down a hallway of thick, velvety carpet that looked like purple grass just begging to be cartwheeled upon, and then we came to the biggest kitchen I'd ever seen in my life.

"Wow!" I exclaimed, gazing around. "This is like a palace! Your cupboards even have handles on them!" I leaned forward into the sink. "Hey, I can see my face in your faucets!"

My new host gave a half-smile that looked as if it hadn't decided to become a full one and pulled out a chair from the kitchen table.

"Here, Olivia, sit down. Would you like a cold drink — maybe some lemonade?"

Lemonade! I'd have drunk dishwater at that moment. My mouth started salivating at the thought of it. She served it in a tall glass with ice that clinked against the sides, a slice of lemon, and a straw. For a moment I simply stared, hesitant to drink, because then it would be all gone, and maybe I'd have only imagined its existence.

"Go ahead," Mrs. Kind-Eyes nodded. "Drink it up; there's plenty more."

She pulled up a chair for herself and sat down at the table opposite me.

"So." Her smile was a full one this time. "Where do you live?"

"Across the river," I spluttered between gulps. "I'm eleven years old, have a sister called Victoria, and I really want to go back to school."

Mrs. Kind-Eyes looked at me curiously.

"In the mornings I have to take Victoria to kindergarten and then watch her in the afternoons, and my mother needs me to help her make money to pay the rent, but I really want to go to school and study so that I won't end up becoming a cleaning lady like my Mom."

Mrs. Kind-Eyes nodded slowly. "And the ring... where did you get that?"

"It's my great-grandmother Sadie's, but Mom says we have to sell it now or we'll get thrown out of our house for not paying the rent."

"May I?" Mrs. Kind-Eyes stretched out her hand towards the ring and I dropped it into her palm like a gold coin. She held it carefully between her fingers while holding it to the light and examined it this way and that. I wasn't exactly sure why, because anybody could see it was a ring.

"It's very beautiful," she said at last. "Much too precious to sell."

My heart must have stopped for a moment, because I found myself feeling lightheaded and faint, and once I read that's what happens when your heart stops beating or something like that. Mrs. Kind-Eyes pulled out her purse from her pocketbook and counted out some dollars.

"Give this back to your mother," she passed me the ring. "And here's some money for the rent."

I guess my heart had restarted because I felt it pounding so loudly inside my chest that I thought it would plop out right there on the floor. I didn't know what to say, so I said nothing (it's usually better that way), and I followed Mrs. Kind-Eyes out in silence. Suddenly, an open door on the right-hand side caught my attention and I stopped in surprise. What I saw inside the room threatened to make my heart stop again — wall-to-wall shelves, straight up to the ceiling, each with row upon row of books!

MRS. ROSENGARTEN, OR whatever her name was (she'd always be Mrs. Kind-Eyes or Mrs. K. to me), was Jewish, or so my mother said, after she went to her house to thank her for the generous gift. Really, Mom had wanted to send me back to do that because she was mighty embarrassed, but I refused to go, which was probably very mean of me. The way I see it, though, is that adults have to face up to their own responsibilities and not keep sending their kids to do things for them.

Mom said that Mrs. Rosen-what-not came from a country called Hungary, and that's why she had a funny accent. I remember hearing about that place in geography lessons back when I still went to school. Mom returned from Mrs. K. very happy and contented, and for the first time ever I saw a little sparkle in her eyes, like one of those stones in Great-Granny's diamond ring. And my mother had a message for me that lit up my eyes, too. "Tell Olivia," Mrs. K. had said, "to come whenever she wants to read the books."

MY KNEES WERE knocking again, but this time from excitement. The thought of those books was like ice cream on a sizzling hot day, and I was positively drooling over the thought of them.

"Olivia, how lovely to see you," said Mrs. K. when she opened the door. "Come and have some lemonade. Then I'll take you to the library."

I didn't know where to start. There were hundreds of books

that smelled of musty leather, and I wanted to press my face into them until I was completely transported into an imaginary world of hopes, dreams and better days — and yes, even a different home...

"Please don't touch these," Mrs. K. said, pointing to the shelves on the right-hand side, which were filled to bursting with volumes of old, dusty books and the same strange letters on the spines as those on the front-door nameplate.

"What are they?" I asked curiously, impressed by a certain importance they possessed up on those shelves.

"They are holy books, written in Hebrew and Aramaic," Mrs. K. replied, "books that the Jewish People have studied for centuries."

"Wow," I said in amazement. "You know," I pumped myself up a little taller, although I didn't know why, "my mother says that we're Jewish, too."

"Really?" Mrs. K. seemed surprised. "Are your mother's parents Jewish?"

"Yup, as far as I know," I replied, and proceeded to tell her the story about Mom's marriage to Dad and how she ended up as a cleaning lady living in a lousy neighborhood instead of enjoying the comfortable lifestyle she'd been born into.

Mrs. K. listened carefully. "Being Jewish," she said when I was done, "is something to be proud of."

"Aw, I don't know about that." I shrugged nonchalantly. "Mom says that we're Jewish in name only." Mrs. K. only nodded; she looked disturbed about something, but I couldn't imagine what.

AFTER THAT, I spent every spare moment there. Mrs. K. even let me take books home, although Mom didn't like it, because then I lay in bed reading instead of doing my chores. She even threatened to send me back to school, which normally I would have jumped at, except that I didn't want to give up Mrs. K. for anything in the world. Her stories were real, not from the history books; tales of being smuggled out of the ghetto in a large duffle bag on her mother's back when she was three years old; running from place to place to hide, in constant terror of being discovered throughout the war — although I wasn't quite sure which war, because there seemed to have been so many of them. And she taught me Jewish stuff too, interesting things about the Sabbath, and lots of complicated things about keeping kosher and not putting cheese on a hamburger, not that I ate too many of those. When I asked Mom if she could separate milk from meat, she told me not to worry, because we didn't have that much food anyway.

One day, when Mom told me that the education authorities were coming to check why I wasn't in school, I slipped quickly out the back door, tripping over the garbage cans and sending them clattering down the alleyway until I was racing like an Olympic runner across the bridge to Mrs. K.'s house. Mom was so furious, because she thought she'd be in trouble if I wasn't there, maybe even get arrested or something.

Anyway, I thought I'd be grounded for a year, but she couldn't stay mad for long, because Mrs. K. went and got her a new job as a secretary in a Jewish elementary school, of all things. I think she'd almost have let me move in with Mrs. K. after that.

Towards autumn, I showed up at her house one afternoon and found her husband and sons building some sort of wooden hut in the backyard. Even after I helped decorate it with bright, shimmering lights and helped to hang up pictures and tinsel things that looked like the stuff I see in stores during the winter, I was still confused. I mean, it was pretty and all that, and I guess kinda cozy, but it just didn't make sense to me that someone would move out of a house that size and live in a hut for a week. Some of this Jewish stuff was downright weird.

SHE DROPPED THE bomb in my lap during the meal we'd all been invited to. Mom and Victoria were sitting in the *sukkah* (I'd learned its name by then), engaged in lively conversation with some of the Rosengartens' married children and grandchildren, while I was in the kitchen helping with the dishes.

"So," said Mrs. K. casually, as she handed me another plate to dry, "you're twelve now. How would you like to go and learn how to be Jewish in more than name only?"

The plate almost slid through my fingers. "Wh… what did you say?"

"There are schools," she explained, while fishing out spoons from the dishwater, "for girls like you, who want to learn and ask questions; I think you'd love it."

"Where… where are these places?" I stammered, glancing around nervously. It sort of felt as if we were conspirators, although I had no idea about what.

"Well, the one that I think will be best for you is in New York. There's a special school there for girls who haven't grown up religious."

"New York!" I spluttered. "In the city? How will I get there? I don't even have the money for a bus ticket."

Mrs. K. laughed. "That's the last thing you need to worry about. You wouldn't be traveling every day; it's much too far. You'd have to room there with other girls."

"You mean like all living together and stuff?"

"Yes," she chuckled again. "That's exactly what I mean."

"Ugh," I wrinkled my nose. "What if I don't like someone, or her feet smell, or she pops bubble gum in my ear?"

"I'll tell you what," Mrs. K. smiled brightly. "Why don't you ask your mother if you can come with me to see the school first, and then we can take it from there?"

I STILL COULDN'T believe that Mom had agreed. Yikes… she'd said yes! Yes, yes, yes! Maybe it was because she knew I'd have to go back to school anyway, or because she didn't need my help as much, seeing as how she was earning more money with her secretarial job; or maybe the full scholarship being offered had something to do with it... Or maybe it was simply because she knew it was what I desperately wanted.

I kissed Victoria and my mother good-bye the day after I'd helped them move into a modest apartment further down the river, where the stairway smelled of pine cleaner instead of dead animals, and the communal yard had real grass, and not just lonely blades poking through the concrete. Sometimes I felt like one of those lone blades, pushing myself up, trying to force my way out into the sunshine.

Our good-bye was awkward and prickly, as if in preparation for the thorny ground ahead. Victoria was sulking, saying that I was running away and how she just knew that I'd never come back. The truth was, I couldn't wait to get away; to pick up my tattered suitcase and race to the car, where Mrs. K.'s driver was waiting for me. I walked down to the main road, waving behind me as I went, so absolutely bursting with excitement that I just wanted to pick up and run as fast as I could, but I forced my legs to slow down instead, which wasn't easy, let me tell you. I gave a last, lingering wave as the car started moving. I was going to a new place, a new life — new horizons, far, far away from the slum I'd called home. But despite efforts to hide my eagerness to leave, the look in my mother's eyes said that I hadn't disguised it at all.

SO I LEARNED all about being Jewish! I learned about Hashem and being His chosen people and how He loves us so much that He gave us His Torah. I learned and learned 'til late at night, *Tanach* and *Tehillim*, *halachah* and *hashkafah*, until my eyes were red and I couldn't keep them open for a moment longer. I learned — no, experienced — Shabbos. I learned about the unique role of the Jewish woman and about building a Torah home. I had fun and made friends with other girls like me (some of them even came from Russia without their parents), although

I never met anyone who had grown up quite the way I had. Olivia slowly became Ahuva, and eventually ceased to exist. Gone was the poor, hungry girl who'd grown up with threadbare blankets and blue-tinged toes. When, after five years, I went to Israel to further my studies, Olivia stayed behind in America, buried in the garbage bins in the alleyway with the cats.

"OLIVIA, I THINK you should come home. We miss you."

"It's Ahuva now, Mom. That's my Hebrew name." Hearing the old name made me cringe.

"Whatever. I think you should come home for a visit."

I breathed a small sigh of relief. For a moment I thought she was suggesting I return for good. Honestly, though, I didn't really want to go there at all, not even for just a few weeks.

"You haven't been back in America for over two years now," my mother continued. "And during your time in New York we hardly saw you either."

"I know, Mom. I'm sorry."

"Mrs. Rosengarten isn't very well, I hear."

"Really?" My ears pricked up at that. We'd remained very close while I was in New York, before she sent me to Israel, but since then our contact had dwindled somewhat.

"Yes, I heard it from someone at school. Seems like her husband passed away, and she's had a very hard time."

A pang of guilt shot through me for not knowing about this, for no longer being involved in the life of the woman who had given mine a new lease.

"So, Olivia" — I cringed again — "are you coming home?"

IT WASN'T THE same house, of course, but they were the same stale memories. We embraced awkwardly and I observed how much Victoria had grown, trying to ignore her cut-off denim shorts and T-shirt. There was a hint of hostility in her eyes;

resentment, perhaps, that explained why she'd never answered my letters. Mom had aged more, dark roots dirtying her dyed-blonde hair, but the small apartment was at least clean and tidy and even had air conditioning.

"So," I said, quickly surveying the surroundings. "Are you guys happy here?"

"I'm very grateful for everything, Olivia," Mom answered.

"Ahuva... My name is Ahuva now."

"Oh, yes, I'm sorry — I keep forgetting. Come, why don't you put your things down and I'll show you to your room."

I hesitated a second, my stomach tightening, and I found myself wishing that the next conversation had already happened before I'd left Israel. "Um, there's a bit of a problem, Mom, like with food and that kind of stuff."

"Oh, that's okay, I've thought of that," Mom answered brightly. "Here, let me show you." She led me into the kitchen like an excited schoolgirl and flung open a cupboard. "Look, I bought you kosher food," she said proudly, and indicated the pile of plastic utensils that was next to it. "One of the teachers at school told me what to buy and where to get it all."

"Thanks, Mom, that's so nice of you; I really appreciate it." I smiled gratefully. Another guilty pang ran through me at the thought of her going to so much trouble on my behalf. I was having a lot of those pangs lately.

I followed my mother out of the kitchen and into a bedroom with a freshly-made bed, and a small bowl of fruit and a book on the night table. I picked up the book curiously. "The Diary of Anne Frank," my mother announced. "I remembered that you liked it."

"Yes," I fingered the worn pages carefully. "I did."

"It's good to have you home, Oliv... Ahuva, even though you're quite different now."

I smiled weakly, touched but troubled in my unsettled state of mind; moved by my mother's care and concern, yet yearning to be back in a normal religious environment where I'd feel comfortable and understood. My mother touched me tentatively on my shoulder as if afraid that she'd be stung.

"I… I just wanted to tell you that I understand."

I looked at her quizzically.

"You wanting to leave and get a better life; I'm happy for you." Her bottom lip quivered with unaccustomed emotion. "You had a hard time growing up. I know I wasn't such a good mother… I messed up a lot."

Tears sprang to my eyes and a lump lodged in my throat, so I squeezed Mom's hand lightly to replace the words.

"By the way," Mom quickly retreated from her discomfort, "Mrs. Rosengarten doesn't live in the same house as before." She scribbled something on a piece of paper. "Here's her new address."

IT HAD TO be a mistake! I looked at the note in my hand to check the address again. Yes, this was it. I hadn't even known this part of town existed. Gazing up at the brownstone apartment building burrowed among the rest of the row, my hands started shaking as I wondered what I was going to find inside. Fortunately, I was young and healthy enough to tackle the four flights of stairs, but I still found myself panting when I stood before the door with the familiar nameplate.

"Who is it?" a faint voice called out when I rang the bell.

"Ahuva — Olivia," I answered.

The door flung wide open with a strength that the elder Mrs. K. didn't look like she had, and the next minute I was wrapped in her warm, sturdy embrace.

"Olivia!" she cried, holding onto my hands and stepping back. "Let me look at you!"

As she led me down her narrow hallway into her kitchen, I felt as if I was traveling back in time, once more the hungry little girl who had come to sell her great-grandmother's diamond ring.

"Sit, sit," Mrs. K. beckoned, and there was a spring in her step despite an obvious weakness that she hadn't had a few years ago.

Once again I sat before a tall glass of iced lemonade, in shock from the surroundings — but not for the same reason.

"What happened?" I asked with deep concern.

"Ach, never mind about me; let's hear about you. What a fine *meidelah* you've become!"

"No, please — I want to know."

"Let's go into the living room," Mrs. K. settled herself wearily onto the couch. I recognized it from the other house and wondered with the simplicity of my once-eleven-year-old mind how it had ended up in that apartment. Mrs. K patted the seat next to her.

"My husband became ill suddenly," she began, as if too tired to tell the story again. "*Baruch Hashem*, the end came quickly, so he didn't have to suffer much." Her eyes glistened with tears.

"I'm so sorry," I said quietly.

"It's fine, really… everything's good. Hashem was very kind."

I blinked in astonishment. "And this?" I gestured to the living room with both hands. "Why did you move here?"

"There were medical bills and debts, lots of them. Things I hadn't known about, that needed to be paid off after my husband passed away. There was no choice but to sell the house, and most of the things in it."

I sat quietly, feelings and thoughts crashing into one another as I tried to comprehend what she had just said. I reached for one of her mouthwatering, home-baked pastries that had always been my favorite and made a *brachah* loud and clear.

"*Amen!*"

I didn't know what to say to this wonderful woman who had sent me off to a better life while she now struggled with her own. How had my gracious, elegant hostess been reduced to this? I wondered if she was the same person, now that she was no longer surrounded by the safe, majestic walls of her mansion.

"You should be in touch with your mother more," Mrs. K.'s caring voice interrupted my thoughts.

I bit the nail on my right thumb nervously. "It's not easy, with her not being religious."

"Is that the only reason?" Of course, Mrs. K.'s mind was razor sharp as always. "I know she made some bad decisions in her life and you suffered the consequences, but she did the best she could under the circumstances."

All at once, the shame and humiliation was upon me and I was that little girl again, wandering from house to house, door to door, like a little Oliver Twist, dreaming, yearning to have a full stomach and a warm pair of socks or to fall asleep at night despite the cold. Normal... all I ever wanted was to be normal.

"Did she? Was sending her daughter out into the streets to make money doing her best?"

Mrs. K. sighed. "You're angry, Olivia dear, and that's understandable; I think I would be, too. But just think... we'd never have met one another if things had been different. Nothing ever happens by chance; Hashem doesn't make mistakes."

I thought about that for a minute, how Hashem had brought us together and how I was where I was because of her and all of a sudden I was aware of a Presence in the world so much bigger and greater than me and my opinions.

"I was always so envious of you; I thought you had everything," I whispered softly.

"I do."

I lifted my head in surprise. "But isn't it degrading to live like this, now that you've lost it all?"

"Oh, no," Mrs. K. smiled. "Everything is right here; look around. I could have moved in with my children if I'd wanted to, but I preferred to stay here on my own."

Was I mistaken, or did I detect a slight tilting of her chin, an understated pride? I saw the family photographs in frames on the walls; the pictures made for "Bubby" that decorated her fridge; crystal vases, silver *Kiddush* cups and spice boxes in the glass breakfront... The *sefarim* — they were there, too. I saw all the love and warmth and happiness that Mrs. K. had taken with her to this modest apartment. She had transplanted herself into this humble home, and now it was she who was majestic, not the splendid stones that once surrounded her.

I searched for even a trace of shame or embarrassment but found none; just a royal woman, content and complete. And then I thought about my mother, of whom I was ashamed for not being religious, for being uneducated and poor — for simply being who she was. Yes, me, the pious one, who kept her collar tightly buttoned and could shout a *brachah* so loud it could shake the heavens, but who had tried desperately to disown her family, and this time I felt a different kind of shame... for myself.

"She did the best she could," the sentence rang in my head. Come to think of it, I had never heard my mother complain, even though her family had rejected her completely, leaving her to suffer alone. She just carried on, continuing with whatever she needed to do at the time, with a calm acceptance. I never saw her depressed either; she always thought up new solutions for her troubles, even though I usually didn't like them. But she was a fighter, my Mom, dodging the many minefields placed in her path, and when the time had come to let me go, she'd set me free and let me fly. They weren't so different, Mrs. K. and my mother; both had faced their hardships with courage, strength and a quiet dignity.

"I'm sorry that I haven't been in contact lately," I muttered, my head lowered.

"You should spend some time with your mother," Mrs. K. replied, as if she hadn't heard me.

"Yes," I nodded. "I think I'll go to her now."

My mind was like a channel of shipping lanes, each vessel filled with shame... for my mother, for myself, of myself. As I traced my footsteps back, it covered me like the leaves of a plant that had ripped itself up from the ground in order to take root somewhere else. I owed Mom and Victoria a big apology. The first thing I had to do, though, was find Olivia, who was still shivering behind the garbage cans in the alley next to our old house. I had to tell her that it was okay to meet Ahuva, that she needn't be ashamed; she could hold her head up high and be proud of who she'd become.

We had turned out just fine, after all!

I wrote this story when I was in America for my first book release ("The View from Ninveh," Israel Book Shop Publications). It was my first time in New York and only my second visit to the United States (I went to Los Angeles once with my husband to visit my in-laws). As a special treat, I took my fourteen-year-old daughter along with me and we stayed by my dear friend, co-star of "The View from Ninveh," Mrs. Debbie Schechter. For those of you who have already been to Ninveh with me, you'll recall that Debbie and I first made each other's acquaintance in a professional capacity as editor/writer at Binah. After Debbie stopped working for Binah our relationship morphed into something incredibly meaningful and we became very, very close. Our connection was, and still is, something unique.

So it was Debbie's home in Flatbush where my daughter, Tovi, and I stayed for two weeks, feeling like part of the family. And it was at Debbie's house where I created "Olivia" for this story. I'm not quite sure how or why she came about, but looking back I can see how much I reflected on relationships during that time, particulary the relationship between Tovi and myself. The trip to America was a great opportunity for the two of us to bond and that's what we did. I so enjoyed being with her, just enjoying her company with no stress or complications, and I remember feeling extremely grateful that we could have that time together. More than anything, I was happy that we both shared the same lifestyle and values, that we didn't have the difficulties that arise when there's a discrepancy in one's way of life. As a baalas teshuvah, I knew those differences could be problematic, even with a patient, accepting mother like mine who went out of her way to accommodate me and my family whenever we'd visit.

It was with these reflections that "Olivia" came into being. I think I'd recently finished Charles Dicken's classic, "Pickwick Papers," so the character, Oliver, was in my head. It just goes to show how influenced we are by what we read. I liked the "girl" Olivia. The image of a young child with her head in her books always asking questions was someone I related to. I wasn't too thrilled with Ahuva, although I totally understood her behavior. Although the protagonist in the story had justifiable reasons to distance herself from her mother, the idea of looking down on her once she became frum is something that many baalei teshuvah go through. I felt it important to show what having respect for one's parents really means and how the baal teshuvah has to search for that in situations where it isn't always easy to find. Separating ourselves from our child and adult selves, from the past and present, is something that most of us do and it isn't healthy. From my own experience, I can say that it's only when we can integrate the different aspects of ourselves that we will be whole human beings.

"When it Rains..."

IF I COULD, I'd trade this job in a minute. Not that it's possible, because one in my position never has any say in the matter. One fine day, I just kind of found myself here like I came into existence from nothing and that was a real shock. Come to think of it, how *did* I get here? I suppose if I knew the answer to that question, I'd be much happier with my lot. Ach, here I go, getting all philosophical again.

Anyway, back to this job of mine. I bet you wouldn't do it… just hang around all day waiting to be dispatched on a mission. I haven't been sent anywhere since the last rainfall, and who knows when that was, for I don't count time or space or seasons; didn't even know they existed until recently when I met a season called Autumn for the first time. I guess you could say that I'm not very worldly because I'm always home and only get the news from my friends who get sent out regularly while I continue to float in this enormous sky, biding time until I can rain.

SNOWFLAKE IS TRAVELING again. How come he gets to go meet up with his mates and make a jolly good snowstorm while I can't squeeze out a single drop of rain?

"Hey, Empty, what's doin'?" Snowflake yells to me above Wind.

Now that's a job I'd like… to be Wind. He nearly always has

something to do and boy is he powerful. He can down trees in a second, and not just any old type of tree, either, but some of the sturdiest old oaks. When he's really riled up he can swoop down on wooden houses, lift their roofs off and tear down the walls.

"Empty, you're up in the clouds again." Snowflakes laughs when I don't answer, proud of himself for the pun. He's a witty one, that Snowflake. He's the one who thought up my lovely name and told it to all the others. I watch as he floats around in his usual flaky manner.

"Don't be so down; you'll get your turn soon," he tells me. Yeah, well, that's easy for him to say when he's always off globetrotting.

"We'll be seein' you," Frost waves. "The Boss is sending us to somewhere called Canada where we're gonna whip up an awesome storm. Just wait and see... all of those mortals over there won't be able to open their mouths, they'll be that frozen."

Hmm, sounds mean to me, but what do I know? Like I said, I'm not exactly experienced about life, stuck as I am here with nothing to do. I pull a face. "Have a good time and don't come back too pleased with yourselves."

"Hey, you can always come with us," Snowflake suggests ridiculously. "Just ask The Boss."

"What's the point of that? I'm a rain cloud... I don't do snow, and anyway, it never helps when I talk to The Boss. All he says is patience... lots of patience...everything in its right time."

I have to hand it to Frost that he manages to flash me a lukewarm sympathetic smile before heading off. Ice, though, is a lost cause. Nothing can chink through *his* armor; I don't think he ever *feels* anything so I definitely wouldn't like to be him.

In a whoosh, they are gone, leaving me alone as usual with my tears that aren't enough to produce so much as a sprinkle. Let's face it... Snowflake's name is perfect for me. I'm as parched and dry as a dusty desert.

IF YOU REALLY want to know, the worst feeling is that I'm not fulfilling my purpose. After all, what's a rain cloud supposed to do when he doesn't have rain? I know deep down, in the bottom of my cloud belly, that I have so much potential. It's all there, just waiting to come out, and it's downright frustrating that I can't use it. Being jealous of the others doesn't help, either. All it does is make me more shriveled than I already am, and then for sure I won't have any water. That's when my soft, fluffy edges go all brown and brittle like the leaves I used to see on the ground in the days when I was working harder. Back then, I would find the leaves, heaped in piles on the pavements, all dry and crunchy, but after a good burst of rain from me they'd turn soft and squelchy and people had to be careful not to slip on the sidewalks. Ah, those were the days. I know, I know, you don't have to tell me there are ups and downs in life and things can't always be rainy, but lately, I just feel as if I'm living in a long, endless drought.

So what am I to do? How can I not be envious when I see my friends always out at work and moving on in life, while I'm just stuck up here doing absolutely nothing? Honestly, if there was a roof on the sky, I think I'd be glued to it.

TODAY, WHEN IT'S particularly hot, I decide to go visit Sun. I have to pull in my woolly sides real close so I won't get burned and end up one big scorched mess. Sun is beaming away as usual, shining his brilliant rays upon the earth and having a thoroughly good time watching the mortals sweat out enough water to fill *me* up, or even pass flat out in faints. Personally, I think that's rather nasty and taking advantage. If I had that job, I wouldn't do that. I'd send my rays down gently, not too much or too little, just enough to keep things pleasant. But then again, if I had that much power, maybe I wouldn't?

"Hello, Empty," Sun says cheerfully. "You bored again?"

"Always," I scowl.

"Yeah, well, you're not the only one," says Sun, swiveling around slowly so he can shine in a different direction.

"You?" I ask incredulously. "What do *you* have to be bored about?"

"Humph," Sun grumbles as he sends a quick laser-like blast into the atmosphere. "You think that it's fun, forever sitting up here and *shining?*"

"You're kidding!" I say, thoroughly amazed. "But you've got such an important job. Are you saying that you don't *like* it?"

"Nah, I didn't say that. Just that even the best jobs can be boring."

I scratch my head with my spongy cloud fingers. I don't get it at all. "I'll do it," I say impulsively. "Really, let me have a go. I won't be bored."

Sun stares at me with his bright, burning eyes. "*You?* You're a rain cloud! You couldn't do my job." He laughs so hard that I'm afraid he'll wobble over and light up the wrong side of the world.

"Yes, I can," I retort, deeply insulted. "Try me. You be me for a day and I'll be you."

Sun is still roaring his head off and every time he opens his mouth I'm hit by his hot breath.

"You're just scared," I say mockingly. "A big, bold sun like you, but really, you're a coward."

"Huh? Who are ya callin' a coward?" Sun suddenly sobers up and turns serious. "I ain't havin' anyone say that Sun doesn't rise to the challenge... get it... *rise*... oh, never mind."

"So, does that mean yes?"

"Sure. You're on! Be here tomorrow morning before I... no, *you*... come up."

BRRRR, IT'S MIGHTY cold before Sun gets himself going in the mornings. As I float downwards to where he's spent the night, I find myself shivering and I wrap my cloudy arms around myself. The truth is, now that this is for real, I'm getting cold cloud-feet. If The Boss catches us, we're in big trouble because I heard that he doesn't like it when we change jobs because he has everything planned out just right. I don't know why He likes things that way. From my cloudy perspective, I can't see what's wrong with having a change every now and again; that way, we'll all have equal opportunities.

"Ready?" Sun booms. I jump and take a tiny tumble before righting myself again.

"Whoa, you startled me," I say. "Yes, I'm ready."

"Good, because you need to start now. You're a little late and you've got to get yourself up there so that the mortal folks down below will have some light. Now, remember not to rise too quickly. It has to be slow and graceful. Don't hit people with a blast all at once or they won't like it."

I gulp. This sounds like a work of art and I'm not sure that a silly little cloud like me is up to the craft. But then I remember that this was my idea and I really want to see if I can do it.

"Off you go. Good luck." Sun gives me a gentle push and I'm on my way.

"Don't worry about the cloud stuff," I call out as I move upwards. "It's not difficult. All you have to do is float around and look fluffy."

Sun smiles, gives a wave and then I'm all alone, left with this enormous responsibility of warming the world. Right from the start I run into problems because I can't keep my lightweight body from floating up too fast and I have to force myself to slow down and it's a real struggle because it's so against my nature. After a while, I get tired so I stop and just hang out where I am. Wow, I never realized how controlled Sun has to be, and that's before he's even risen properly and begun a days' work.

Okay, I think I'm in the right place now. Gosh, that was hard… phew… I just need to catch my breath. I try to remember the rest of Sun's instructions. Ah, yes… I'm meant to hover here for the entire day and to turn around ever so slightly, not too quick and not too slow. Here goes…

"YOU CAN KEEP your job," I say to Sun later. "Just let me get my strength back."

"Ha, I told you it was no fun, didn't I?" Sun says, gloating. "Still, it's better than being an empty rain cloud. I don't know how you just float around all day long and I really couldn't get the hang of that curvy shape of yours."

Right now, all I want to do is float effortlessly, to glide through the sky and drift across Moon or even Sun. Actually, come to think about it, even from a distance I can cover Sun and Moon whenever I want and block their light, so I suppose I do have some power in me after all.

"Agh, my back hurts," I groan. "I'm really not cut out for this."

"And me neither," Sun agrees. "I'd rather do what I do best even though it's not always easy."

We shake on it and Sun rolls off while I wend my way back to the cloud center. I'm happy to just be floating again, suspended in the air, and yet I still feel pangs of regret that all I am… is just an empty rain cloud.

THERE ARE STIRRINGS of rebellion in the camp. From what I understand, things are getting a bit out of hand. Snowflake, Frost and their friends have taken things too far in Canada and they've dumped so much snow there that electricity has been off for more than a week and mortals are trapped, freezing, inside their homes. I wouldn't want to be in their wellingtons when they come back because I hear that The Boss isn't at all happy about it and they'll probably be severely punished. I don't really understand that, because if The Boss has everything planned out exactly the way things are supposed to be, how can He be angry? Moon, who's very wise, explains it like this. He says that The Boss knows what's going to happen but we don't, which is how we have free choice. I don't quite get that either; after all, I can't choose to rain, can I? And does that mean that Snowflake and co. could have decided not to blast Canada or not? According to Moon, that's exactly right. He says that even though there were meant to be storms, they didn't have to be the ones to bring them. This is all mighty complicated for an air-headed rain cloud, but if there's one thing I think I'm learning, it's to take responsibility for my actions.

One of the perks of being unemployed is that I get to spend much more time with The Boss than everyone else who are so busy rushing around with barely a moment to breathe. I never actually *see* Him of course, nobody can do that, but it's an awesome experience and one I'm privileged to have. It's like a feeling, knowing that He's there; sensing His majestic Presence all around me. I talk to Him constantly, even complain, which I know I shouldn't but I do it anyway because after all, I'm only a cloud and I sometimes get angry and frustrated. The Boss reminds me that everyone has their time and I have to be patient, and just because I'm small without a fancy title it doesn't mean I'm not important. Everyone is important, He tells me, otherwise He wouldn't have created us in the first place. When I remember to remember that, I feel warm and fuzzy all over, but when I forget, I'm wrapped in my loneliness and inadequacy, convinced that there's no one else who has it as hard as me.

Meanwhile, I'll admit begrudgingly, even though it's hard to be hanging on the horizon so to speak, I'm learning a lot. I guess I don't always have to be out amongst the masses in order to gain cloud clarity. Take Fire, for example. I was always envious of his super power and he was forever taking the credit for another house he'd burned down or a forest he'd set on fire. Recently, though, he's seemed a little under the weather. The other day, I wandered over to the Elements camp and saw Fire slipping away unescorted, which is against the rules because clouds like me can get badly burned if we get too close.

When I saw him coming I immediately headed off in the other direction, but Fire called out, almost pleadingly.

"Please, Empty… don't run away from me. I won't hurt you. Almost all my fire has gone."

I peered at him curiously and guess what? He did, in fact, look quite damp, as if he'd received a good dousing of water that had extinguished his flames.

"What happened to you?" I asked, not as frightened of him like I usually was because now he looked pretty harmless with only the dim glow of his embers burning.

"I lost my flames," said Fire miserably.

"What do you mean, you *lost* them?" I was really confused, because as far as I knew flames weren't something you could lose, like money, for example, which the mortals misplaced all the time.

"The Boss took them off me," Fire explained, lowering his head in shame. "He said I wasn't using them properly so I'm not allowed to have them for a while. He said that fire can be a good thing, even very beautiful at a safe distance, but I've only been using it to destroy things. Recently, a little girl got severely burned when I lost control and licked my flames over her. So now, I haven't got them anymore and I'm all empty just like you."

Ouch, that hurt for a moment until I realized that it wasn't the same kind of emptiness he was talking about at all.

EVEN THOUGH I remember that I did have work once and probably will again, I am running out of patience. How much longer can I go on? When will I see the light instead of spending my days huddled in a bleak corner of the cloud camp? Lately, I've been feeling some strange rumblings that make me shake and stop in mid-float when I do go outside. I wonder if I'm getting sick but The Boss says no, it means I'm almost ready and He's very happy about that. One day the rumbles get really strong and they're so powerful that I'm almost propelled downwards towards Earth, but after a while I float back up again because I have nothing inside to keep me there. All of this feels weird but it's also exciting, the anticipation of something huge about to happen.

Eventually, The Boss summons me through Malach, one of His right hand aides.

"Empty," He says, "The Boss says it's time for your mission."

A flurry of excitement ripples through me, creating a slight breeze that pushes me slightly away.

"Come closer," Malach beckons. "Let me tell you about your job."

I puff up my cloud wings and float back towards him.

"The Boss is sending you to a place called Eretz Yisrael," Malach says seriously. "It's a very special country, not like all the rest."

"What am I supposed to do there?" I ask, confused.

"You're going to rain, of course," Malach says impatiently. "It hasn't rained in Eretz Yisrael in more than forever. The Kinneret, the biggest supply of water, is drying up, crops are dying and there's not enough water for the mortals to drink or bathe in."

"Wow," I say in amazement. "How did things get that bad? Why didn't The Boss send rain there sooner?"

"Like I said, Eretz Yisrael is no ordinary place. Over there, the rain doesn't come by itself but through the mortals' actions and by praying for it. Yesterday, there was a massive *tefillah* gathering for rain that finally stormed *Shamayim*."

"You mean… are you saying that's what the shaking was…? *That's* what I've been feeling?"

"Yes," Malach smiled. "And that's what The Boss has been waiting for… *their* prayers and for *you* to feel them. Not every cloud does, you know."

I wrap my cloud arms around myself and don't know what to say because I am humbled and afraid at the same time. "H… how am I going to rain?" I ask hesitantly. "There's nothing inside me. I'm all dry."

"Don't you think The Boss hasn't thought about that already? You must trust Him."

"Right." I brighten slightly. "Anyway, I won't be alone. There will be lots of other rain clouds with me as well."

"No, actually, there won't. It's just you." Malach delivers that last sentence like a death sentence.

"Only *me*? How can I do it alone? This is a job far too big for just one empty cloud! What are you doing to me? I'll never survive it!"

"Yes, you will," Malach says knowingly. "Just trust, Empty, and believe you can do it. Has The Boss ever made a mistake before?"

And the next thing I know, he's given me a polite shove and I'm spiraling downwards, growing heavier and heavier until I'm hurtling full speed towards Earth.

WHEN I ARRIVE, I feel it instantly. It hits me like a spiritual bolt of thunder. Clearly, this is no ordinary place. I can smell The Boss's presence in the ground even through the dry, dusty soil. I can taste it in the fruit trees that stand threadbare and forgotten; I can touch it in the shriveled riverbeds and wadis. There is something in the air here that tells me this land is not living by chance but from some eternal spring that keeps it alive. I have never, in all my cloud life, been anywhere like it.

Suddenly, while I'm cruising through the surroundings, I see crowds of mini-mortals pointing up to the sky and shouting, "Look, Mommy… rain!" I swivel around to look behind me when all at once I realize they are talking about *me*! Sure enough, my belly is swelling with water and huge drops of rain push themselves through my fluffy white cloudiness until I turn gray, then black, as I expand. With a loud clap from Thunder who is hovering above me, I let go; all the water gushes out and I rain and rain and rain until I'm spent.

Down below, mini-mortals are squealing as they jump in

puddles and maxi-mortals seek shelter, broad smiles on their faces even though they are soaked to the skin. Water runs in rivulets in the gutters, streams down hillsides and drips through leaking roofs, but everyone is saturated with such joy that they turn their faces upward and even open their mouths to drink it. Never before have I felt so needed.

I take a short break in order to replenish my water supply. Honestly, I don't know where it's coming from; certainly not from me. No, it's coming from something far higher and greater; I could never produce this on my own. I glance around with my cloud eyes that are clear enough to see from one end of the land to the other, and that's when I notice that the only rain cloud in the sky *is* me. Just like Malach said, I am doing this alone. All it's taking to water this land is one tiny, unimportant rain cloud.

I am ready to rain again. I pelt it out, emptying and refilling, sending it down in sheets until dried up mud holes turn to lakes and the mortals can sail ships in the streets. I rain and rain until I'm all empty… but oh, I'm so eternally full!

I absolutely love this story! It's not only refreshing and funny (I laughed when I read it), but the messages run deep (did I really write it?). I thoroughly enjoyed reading it again and can say that it's up there with my favorites.

It was the first time I'd written an allegory (in my adult life anyway) and I had such a good time with it. Allegory can be a very potent means of expression like it was with this story (can't you tell I'm a fan?). The story was inspired after an excessively heavy rainfall in Eretz Yisrael one winter. The weather had been warm and dry for weeks and the decreasing water supply in the Kinneret was becoming very worrisome. After a few months of this there were intense tefillos at the Kosel. Shortly afterward, we got our rain. And how! It pelted down for about three days. High winds toppled trees and roof-tops, torrents of gushing water flooded the Negev, surging into people's living rooms through their balcony doors. The water level in the Kinneret rose at an astonishing rate. Within just three days we got enough water to no longer worry about our supplies anymore. It was incredible!

I thought a lot about this wondrous thing. Apart from the clear evidence that rain in Eretz Yisrael is pure "gishmei brachah," the fact that it finally came after waiting patiently for so long and davening gave me chizuk in other areas of my life. Everything and everybody has his time, and when things are difficult because nothing seems to be changing, it's important to remember that.

"When it Rains" is essentially a story about emunah and bitachon; trusting Hashem and believing that no matter how insignificant we may feel down here, we all have our "moment" even if we're not aware of it. It's not about yichus and titles, but about the purpose for which Hashem created us. We never know what little ole' us can achieve.

Just a word about the part where "Fire" loses his flames and the ability to burn things. His "gift" was taken from him because he didn't use it properly. This is the way I feel about my writing. It is a gift that Hashem gave me and if I don't use it the way He wants He can take it away from me whenever He likes.

When I read my "Cloud Story" again, as I always referred to it, the messages jumped out at me. I wondered where they came from. They must have been deeply imbedded within me, not always accessible but there, nevertheless, waiting to be tapped into. I don't know… I must have been on a spiritual high when I wrote this story!

The Change

I FIND HIM sitting on the end of the creaky wooden jetty that is slowly sinking into the sea. Where else would he be at six a.m. on a crisp summer morning in Maine?

"Hi," I say softly, sitting down beside him. He tilts his head towards the tin of worms over to his left. "Want to give me that bait?"

I reach over and pick up the tin gingerly, trying not to look at the wriggling creatures inside.

"Ugh," I say, and he chuckles. It's the thirty-six-year-old laugh that has pealed throughout our marriage when we're in Maine but also when we're inside the walls of our Brooklyn house, with its well-worn wallpaper.

"Want to cast off?" he teases me.

"Sure… why not?" I go along with his game, the one we always play because he knows how much I hate fishing. How anybody could just *sit* hour after hour waiting to catch fish is beyond me. But that's my Mordechai, patient as ever.

"Am I disturbing you?" I ask, shielding my eyes from the emerging sun.

"Never," he says, and casts off, slowly winding in his line until he has it where he wants it.

I gaze at the little orange float bobbing up and down in the water and feel a strange affinity with it.

"Are you ready?" I say, lifting my face upwards to feel the sting of the sea spray on my cheeks.

"Yes," Mordechai nods. "I am." He stares out to his beloved ocean as if looking for something out there in the vast, deep water. This trip was my idea, to come away to his favorite place, just the two of us; a chance for him to do what he loves, before...

"I'm not," I say as a few stray tears slip out to meet the sea spray.

Mordechai turns and looks at me seriously. "Leah, whatever happens, it's the will of Hashem," he says with his warm, believing eyes, "and I accept it."

"And I don't," I say only to myself and the seagulls that sweep down and back up again to the freshly painted blue sky. "I'm frightened," is what I say instead, "and I'm not ready."

"Yes," Mordechai says thoughtfully. "I understand that... and I'm sorry."

Oh, this is just too much... my husband apologizing for my fear, as if it's his fault. My tears pour freely. If ever I'd suspected I'd married a *tzaddik*, now I know. In two more days I'll drive him to the hospital, one of those big, fancy medical centers where there are surgeons ready and waiting to cut out the big, fat, overgrown tumor that sits inside his head, bulging onto his brain stem.

And he's ready!

I sit beside him, trying to hold onto whatever I still have left of the man I married, wondering if, and how much, I'm going to lose. And as my tears dry in the hot wind, I wonder how in the world he can just sit there, waiting for something to bite.

THEY SAY THIS tumor is benign, but as far as I'm concerned there's something malignant, even hostile, about it. It's been growing slowly but stealthily for the past few years, stealing more and more from Mordechai's rhythm of life. First it was the strange hiccupping that wouldn't stop and then the shaking of his left hand and weakness in his legs. Lately the headaches are so bad that when I'm next to him I can almost feel his brain throbbing against his skull. He seldom complains, though. And that annoys me.

"Aren't you just a little bit frightened?" I ask him on the way to the hospital.

"No," he says, and then grins. "Well, a drop, if it makes you feel better."

I turn to look out the window, trying to calm the churning feelings inside me. It's hard being married to someone who makes me feel like I'm a complete *apikores* with all my questions because he has none. But that's why I married him, of course... that and his gentleness. He's not perfect, mind you, but all in all, he is an excellent reservoir of water for keeping my flames at bay.

"HERE WE ARE," Mordechai says, pulling into the huge, multi-story car park. "Where are we meeting the kids?" He fumbles with the keys as his hand begins to shake and he can't get them out of the ignition. I do nothing to help him, because that's the way he wants it.

"They should be waiting in the lobby," I say. "They're all coming."

"There was no need for that," Mordechai grumbles.

He walks around the back of the car and lugs his suitcase awkwardly out of the trunk. "It's as if we're going on vacation again," he laughs.

"I prefer Maine," I mutter. I look around for signposts to the hospital. "I told you it would have been better to drop you off at the entrance," I grumble, when we finally stagger out of the elevator.

"Ma, Pa!" Suddenly the familiar voices of our children are calling out to us and we are hugging one another tightly, like we're at a family reunion.

Mordechai is still mumbling that there's no need for all the fuss even when he's installed in the hospital bed and dressed up in a green cotton gown.

"How do I look?" he asks, grinning.

"Very handsome," laughs Eliyahu, our oldest.

Making small talk is unbearable while we wait for Mordechai to be taken down to the operating theater. The forced cheerfulness is only causing my hot blood to bubble even more. And when the surgeon stops by and runs over the pre-op list, just to make sure my husband knows the risks involved, I think I'm going to boil over. Of course, Mordechai *knows*. He's the one who agreed to this operation, while I fought with all my might against it. There is no longer any choice, the mighty specialists said. If he didn't do it now the damage would be irreversible. Well, there's not much to say to that, is there? After all, I'm not a doctor or a Rabbi, just a worried wife who seems to be severely lacking in *emunah*.

Finally, they come for Mordechai, and we escort him downstairs, as if he's the guest of honor. I continue on alone to the preparation area with him. There's so much I want to say, but strangely, the words get stuck in my throat.

"Leah," Mordechai says suddenly, "it will be okay."

I look at him closely. Maybe it will or maybe it won't. Nobody knows which way the scale will tip. But for the first time I see a flicker of fear in his eyes and I wonder if that reassurance is for him as well as me?

"Yes," I say with false enthusiasm, "it will." And these are the last words on my lips as I wave good-bye.

"HOW MUCH LONGER?" I ask again, pacing up and down the waiting room. I've said the entire *Sefer Tehillim* twice already and I don't know what to do with my pent-up energy.

"Ma, could you sit down?" Eliyahu says, his head lowered in embarrassment. "It's not going to bring Pa out quicker if you pace and I think it's making people nervous." He nods towards the other "waiters" like us.

"Pa's in the recovery room," my daughter Goldie shrieks as she watches the computer screen. "Here, look… number 4, Mordechai Greenbaum."

"I'm going in," I say, about to charge off like a battering ram, but then a man clad in green scrubs, a blue paper hat on his head and paper covers over his shoes, walks through the door.

"Mrs. Greenbaum," he says, pulling off his mask, and that's when I recognize our surgeon. "Good news," he smiles as we all gather around him. "The operation was successful. We got most of the tumor out and it was much easier than expected."

"And complications?" I ask, barely breathing.

"Look, no one can say for sure, but based on the way the surgery went, I do not foresee any problems. We'll know more when he wakes up properly. Right now he's sedated but responsive. You can go into him as soon as the nurse calls you."

Until then I'm like a caged lion. When I'm finally let out, I bolt towards the door and almost leap into the recovery room. There, in the middle bed in front of the nurses' station, is my husband, barely recognizable with all the tubes and wires dangling over him. I pull up a reclining chair next to the bed and wait as patiently as possible, the way he's tried to teach me over the years.

As night creeps up, I doze fitfully in the chair. The hours slip into one another and time doesn't exist until Mordechai finally opens his eyes. There is nothing more beautiful to me than the turning of his head, the weak raising of his hand as he tries to gesture hello before falling asleep again. I place his fishing rod against the wall where he can see it, put his weary smile in my pocket, and go home.

"DO YOUR REALLY expect Pa to eat that?" Goldie says, eyeing the blueberry and cream pie that's in my hands.

"He'd better, because I slaved over this," I laugh.

Goldie smiles. "If I know you, you'll spoon in every last piece." She presses the elevator buttons and we wait for one of them to arrive at the ground floor and sweep us up to the seventh. I put my arm around her shoulders and give her a hug.

"Thanks for staying on after the others left. It means a lot to me," I say, gratitude and warmth mixed together like a soothing cocktail.

"I'm just happy I'm able to do it," Goldie replies. "I don't have to rush back to a job and, *baruch Hashem*, the children are old enough to manage. I wouldn't dream of leaving you home alone."

And I'm glad she hasn't, I reflect while I step inside the elevator. With Goldie in the house I don't feel the void that Mordechai's absence has left behind. I don't hear the silences left by the lack of his voice.

"Hopefully, it won't be for much longer the way Pa is progressing," I say, unable to hide the beam spreading across my face. "Who would have thought he'd be up and about after only four days?"

"Yes," says Goldie, "it's incredible."

The last few days my heart is singing, beating out melodies of thanks and appreciation to Hashem for keeping my husband safe. All the fears, the worries that kept me up well into the night, obviously weren't necessary. Next time, and I hope there won't be one, I shall try to have a little more faith and trust in Hashem instead of paralyzing myself with anxiety.

We walk into Mordechai's room in high spirits.

"Shh," I say to Goldie, putting a finger on my lips. "He's sleeping." I put the pie on the top of his bed table and at the same time gather some of the clutter to put in the garbage. Mordechai must have fallen into a heavy sleep because even this slight sound would normally wake him, and it doesn't. I open the cupboard doors and remove dirty laundry that I'll take home to wash.

"Ma," Goldie says, frowning a little. "Pa's making some strange noises."

I straighten up and glance at Mordechai's sleeping form and suddenly feel icy cold. There is something about the way he's lying there that tells me my husband is more than just asleep. His eyelids seem to flicker open, but when I lean forward to look, I see that they are not... his eyes are rolling back in their sockets as if they are seeing something up there that we cannot.

"Pa, wake up," Goldie begins to shake her father frantically.

But he doesn't move at all. The only sign of life is the viscous, white saliva that bubbles out of his mouth. The bags in my hands drop to the floor like dead weights as I run out into the corridor and scream, "*Nurse! Anyone! Come quickly! Something is wrong with my husband!*"

SO I WAS right after all! There *was* reason for me to be so worried that I almost went out of my mind. Maybe I even knew somewhere in the crevices of my bones, like one of those wise, ancient Chinese men who have premonitions. The "wise ones" over here in the hospital deny there being a connection between the surgery and Mordechai's stroke. But that's the way the Western doctors always work, separating things, treating each body part like one has no connection to another.

I may not be wise, but I know different. Everything flows into everything else, a life-giving energy that runs through meridians like rivers into the sea. There's nothing flowing about Mordechai now, though. There is no gentle lapping of the waves around him and the sound of seagulls calling as he waits for the fish to bite. No, his life is stagnating; his left arm that won't straighten at the elbow; the rubber feeding tube that snakes out of his stomach because he cannot swallow; his legs that can no longer carry his sturdy frame, which seems to have withered away so quickly. But the very worst thing is when he opens his mouth to talk and nothing comes out except the squawky cries of the seagulls that circle the skies in Maine, the ones that swoop down and gather pieces of raggedy wet seaweed in their beaks... and now remind me of my husband.

"HOW'S HE DOING today?" I ask a little too brightly, painting the usual smile on my face.

Shirley, the physiotherapist, looks up from the reclining chair she's bending over. "Oh, hi," she says, as if we've just bumped into each other at the supermarket. "I'm about to take him for his walk."

I glance at Mordechai, whose face is full of thunder and warnings of an impending storm. "Um, I don't think he wants to go," I say, watching her position the walker by his feet.

"Of course he doesn't, but he has to," Shirley says as she begins to raise him up. "It's important. He won't progress otherwise."

I stand by, watching helplessly as my husband shakes his head furiously from side to side, his face growing redder and his eyes bulging like the veins in his neck. I can feel the fury rising in me too, but I zip my mouth firmly closed the way I've been subtly instructed by the staff. We shuffle down the corridor together, step by painful step, until I don't know who's more exhausted, him or me. Suddenly he's swaying like a tree in the wind.

"He's going to fall," I yell at the therapist. "Catch him!"

Shirley steadies his arm until he doesn't look so uprooted and glares at me. "Mrs. Greenbaum, I have told you before, it's not helpful to interrupt me while I'm working. You must trust that I know what I'm doing."

"But… he was losing his balance," I protest. "He's too tired to continue."

"I think I can judge that," Shirley says, leading Mordechai back to his bed. I look at him and am totally puzzled. How can she possibly know how he feels when he can't speak? He swings his good arm wildly, white frothy secretions coming out of his mouth.

"You see, I'm right," I declare, facing Shirley with my hands on my hips. "He's angry and frustrated. You're pushing him too hard."

"Am I?" she says, turning to Mordechai. It takes me a moment then, in the ensuing silence, to realize that my husband is still swinging his arm like a shot putter, and the one he's aiming for… is me.

"THE HARDEST THING is the change. He's not the man I married," I say to Rabbi Hillman while sitting in his warm office one chilly morning. "He's angry, aggressive, frustrated... Mordechai was *never* like that. *You* know... he is one of the most gentle people you could meet."

The Rabbi leans back in his leather reclining chair, stroking his beard thoughtfully. "Yes," he says, "he was."

I don't know why, but those few words light up fireworks inside me as if my husband is being written off, sent up to the sky with one of those shooting stars and never coming back. My jaw tightens and I bite my tongue without realizing it.

Rabbi Hillman looks at me closely. "All of this must be very hard for you," he says, "especially when you were against the operation in the first place."

"Oh, but there's no connection between that and the stroke," I say cynically, my lip curling in a small sneer. "I guess it's easier that way because nobody needs to take responsibility."

Rabbi Hillman pauses, letting my bitter accusation hang in the air. "You're angry," he says at last.

One doesn't need to be a genius to figure that out, I say only to myself. It would be disrespectful to say it out loud. "Of course," I say instead, "and with good reason."

Rabbi Hillman leans forward and puts his elbows on his desk. "Who do you think is angrier... you or your husband?"

"I... I'm not sure I know what you mean..." the question flusters me, sends my firecrackers off in conflicting directions.

"What would you like from me, Mrs. Greenbaum?" the Rav changes track. "What are you looking for?"

"I... I don't know. Answers, maybe... to know why this happened."

"And so you came to me... the Rav who said to go ahead with the operation?"

"Yes," I stare down at the floor. "I came to you."

"I'm sorry," he says, shrugging slightly. "I wish I had answers for you, but I don't. Not everything is meant to be understood."

I look up sharply. "But… but you said Mordechai should do the surgery, and he listened to you."

Rabbi Hillman shakes his head. "Unfortunately, I do not have *ruach hakodesh*," he says softly. "I don't make promises. All I can do is take the doctors' recommendations to the Rabbis on the medical committee and give my *psak*, based on the facts; the outcome is in G-d's hands."

Tears are welling up in my eyes. I know all this. I've learned the *hashkafah* a thousand times in drafty classrooms, from books, and around Shabbos tables, but I don't want to hear it now. This answer is fine for *shiurim*, but it's not good enough for my present situation.

"There *is* something that I might be able to help you with, though," the Rav says quietly.

I take a tissue from the box on the table and dab at my eyes. "Oh, what's that?"

"It's about why you really came here… What you're hoping for… to find peace of mind."

I stare at him through narrow, confused eyes. "I have no idea what you're talking about," I protest. "All I want is to understand what happened."

"And to let me know that you're angry because if I hadn't said to go ahead, you'd still have your husband the way he was."

"No! I… I'm not angry at you. I'm angry at them, the surgeons, the doctors, physiotherapists… everybody… even Mordechai!" I can almost feel my blood getting hotter and hotter until it's going to melt my veins and then there will be a confused mess of myself blowing off poisonous gasses.

I look at Rabbi Hillman, a small man, dwarfed by his huge chair, and his calm understanding infuriates me. "Yes," I say, anger and frustration all mingling into one. "I'm also angry at you."

My embarrassment covers me in a red cloak of shame. I have never said such a thing to a Rabbi before… it's almost like saying it to Hashem himself!

I hang my head. "I… I apologize… that was disrespectful of me."

"But understandable," Rabbi Hillman says quietly.

The tears bubble up then, spewing like molten lava down my cheeks. They pour and pour, unable to stop, and I no longer care that I'm sitting in a Rabbi's office, because this is where volcanoes are allowed to erupt. For a moment I *am* a volcano, my pain forming the base and the middle, but the opening is too small to let it all out without a mighty explosion. And as the boiling water from my tears spills over the sides, that's when I realize what it is that I want.

"I… I want Mordechai to get better," I sob. "I… I want the man I married back."

The Rav's face folds into pain and compassion and he nods his head. "I know."

"I want Hashem to heal him," I almost howl. "I want Him to give me back my husband."

Rabbi Hillman just listens as I rant and plead and beg, and when I'm all spent, he slides the box of tissues across the table and waits while I blow my nose loudly.

"Mrs. Greenbaum," he says hesitantly, "we all want your husband to recover, but…" and the air seems to quiver reluctantly, "… what if he doesn't? What will you do then?"

I gaze at the floor with my watery eyes. "I… I don't know. It's not a place I want to go to."

"Perhaps you should?" Rabbi Hillman suggests gently. "Then, maybe, it will be easier for you to handle."

I raise my head and stare at him in amazement. How could considering the possibility that Mordechai might not get better make it easier for me? What is he talking about? I drum my fingers on the tabletop.

"Usually, the only thing we can change is ourselves," Rabbi Hillman continues. "When we find ourselves powerless and unable to get what we want, the only choice we have is in the way we think."

I'm trying to process what he's saying, but my mind is mostly cloudy, with little patches of light peeking through. I want to hold onto that light, to push the clouds away so that the sky is clear, but I don't know how.

"Acceptance," Rabbi Hillman says, "is the key to true *menuchas hanefesh*. And we can't have that while we're angry."

I listen intently. Could it be that some clouds have moved slightly, letting in some more light?

"Stop fighting, Mrs. Greenbaum," I hear him say softly. "It's exhausting you."

My eyelids start to droop and suddenly I am so very weary that all I want to do is go to sleep.

I WALK A lot. The exercise is good for me, especially at my age; I don't know why I haven't done it before. The best time is early morning before I go visit Mordechai in the rehabilitation unit, when the air is bitingly fresh and reproductive. At first I would stroll through the park, relishing the crunch of the fallen autumn leaves underfoot until the winter rain made them slippery and soggy and I had to be careful not to fall. Today the rain is icy cold and I know I have to change my pace if I'm to stay warm. Its sharpness stings my face as it stimulates my mind and helps me to think.

But I love it! Once I would have run from this rain, grumbling all the way home until I stumbled, relieved, into the hallway. I guess I've changed. Actually, I was always changing, even if I didn't realize it; every single second, every DNA replication, each rejuvenation of a cell… I look up at the bare trees, their branches hanging like snarled arms over my head, and at the flowers lying limply in the wet soil. When spring arrives everything will come to life again; a new cycle will begin. Sometimes I'm amazed that for so many years I've been stuck in the same place, never noticing the continual growth around me, ignoring the small things. My daily encounters with nature are the best lessons.

Reluctantly, my walk is over for the day, but as I drive to the hospital an idea is budding in my mind and I'm impatient to get there. When I push open the doors to the unit, I see Shirley accompanying Mordechai down the corridor for *his* walk and I smile. He is changing too... slowly.

"Hi," I call out, and wave. They both smile, and Mordechai waves back with his crooked left arm.

"I'll wait here until you finish," I say, settling into the recliner by the bed. "And then, I'd like to share my idea."

MORDECHAI FUMBLES WITH the bait. It slips repeatedly out of the fingers of his bad hand, but he doesn't give up. Thankfully, there are some things that *don't* change. I watch him struggle, not daring to offer help. I think my frustration is worse than his. Along with the feeling of utter helplessness, I find the fury rising up inside of me again. Sometimes this acceptance thing is hard to juggle with my natural tendency to take control.

"You okay?" I ask, because I can't help myself.

Mordechai nods and scoops up the fallen bait off the deck. I turn away because I can't bear to see this, even though I should be used to his stubborn persistence of doing everything by himself. I stare out at the ocean, watch the sea smashing against the rocks, and pull my coat tighter around myself. At least it's stopped raining. It's not Maine, and it's not summer, but Sheepshead Bay is the best we can do right now. The light that shone in Mordechai's eyes when I suggested the trip makes it all worthwhile.

I turn back. "Are you warm enough?" I ask, and when an elongated "yeees" comes out of his mouth, my anger is gone and I want to sing. It takes him time, but he does it. In a moment he'll be ready to cast off. He raises himself up shakily out of the folding chair

I've brought for him, and with his good arm he throws the rod back over his shoulder before swinging it out to sea. Ever so slowly he reels the line in until he has the little orange float bobbing up and down just where he wants it, and then he sits down again. He turns to me and smiles and forces the most beautiful words out of his mouth that I've ever heard.

"Th... thaaank y... you."

Tears sting my eyes, but this time they're ones of happiness. It starts to rain again, the drops splattering thickly on the wooden pier. But it doesn't matter. Nothing matters except that I'm here together with my husband, who can stand on his own, prepare a fishing rod, and make some magical, musical sounds.

I hate fishing; always have. I cannot stand the monotonous waiting for a fish to bite. But right now, I'm willing to stay here forever!

This story was inspired by a situation of a young girl to whom my family is very close. Unfortunately, her father has a serious, chronic illness for which there's no cure and watching his deterioration is excruciating for her and the whole family. The feeling of helplessness that arises when watching someone you love suffer and being unable to do anything about it can often balloon into a ball of frustration and anger.

There was something this girl said that got me thinking one day. She mentioned that it was hard for her to daven because the tefillos didn't seem to help — in a nutshell, she wasn't seeing any results, or at least the ones she wanted. How often do we throw in the towel when we don't get the answer we would like?

Perhaps even harder, though, is the situation where the Rav says that everything will be okay, that the sick person will have a refuah sheleimah… and he doesn't! I happen to have a hard time with that, and for that reason I don't go to a Rav with the expectation that he'll guarantee health, wealth, shalom bayis, *etc. Asking for guidance is one thing, but expecting reassurance that all will turn out the way I'd like it to seems wrong to me.*

The main message in this story is that we all change throughout our lives. Some of those changes are forced upon us and we have to choose how to accept them. Other changes we make ourselves from our own desires. And then, of course, there are the changes that occur naturally as life progresses. Nothing ever stays the same.

A close friend of mine mentioned something her mother had said after her three-year-old son was diagnosed with leukemia with serious life-altering complications. "You will never be a normal family again," her mother told her.

"Well, today, we are a normal family," my friend says. "It's just a different normal."

She could not have reached this understanding if she'd continued to cling to the child "that was." She needed to change her way of thinking in order to accept her new reality. This is what Leah did in "The Change." By changing her attitude she came to acceptance of the change in her husband and was ultimately able to open herself up to the possibility of happiness.

From a literary point of view, I like the way I wrote this story very much. It worked well in the first person. I'm not sure why I chose Maine as a setting for it at the beginning and I have no idea why I used fishing as a form of expression. One thing that's really true, though, is that I hate fishing! And I don't think that will ever change!

ON THE DAY Zalman Tenner's father was buried, the heavens cried. Water gushed out of the sky, sloshing down the sides of Zalman's big, black umbrella and making a big, muddy pool by his feet.

Zalman stood dry-eyed next to his father's grave, watching the funeral proceedings in slow motion. Protectively, he pulled his younger brothers close to him, putting an arm around each of their slumped shoulders. *How was Ma managing?* he wondered. He'd told her not to come to the *kevurah*, but rather to go back home with Aunt Simi and the girls, out of the biting cold that gnawed at her toes and made her arthritic bones ache. Suddenly, he felt the weight of his brothers who were leaning against him as if he were a brick wall, and his heart was as heavy as all the headstones in the cemetery.

"NO," MRS. TENNER said. "I won't hear of it!"

Zalman sighed. "Well, what choice do we have?"

"We'll get help. The family will pitch in. I'll get a widow's pension."

"A pension," Zalman snorted. "And what will that cover? The food maybe, the utility bills if we're lucky. I checked into it. Your medical bills alone are a fortune."

"Maybe... maybe I could get a job," Mrs. Tenner said. "I really don't want you to stop learning."

Zalman sat down on the edge of his mother's bed. "And what would you do, Ma? You've got dialysis three times a week, and your legs are very bad now."

"I don't know. Perhaps an office job where I could sit down? I could do it in between —"

"No, Ma," Zalman said firmly. "I'm the oldest *bachur*, and supporting the family is my responsibility." He forced a lump back down his throat. "So long as Aunt Simi can get you there and back from the hospital each time, I'll be fine. And don't worry. I'll find the time to learn."

ZALMAN WANDERED AROUND with a perpetual knot in his stomach. How was he going to support his mother and siblings at the tender age of twenty-two? Sometimes, when the burden felt overwhelming, he found himself angry at his father for having abandoned them, succumbing to a heart attack at age fifty-three, leaving them to fend for themselves like lion cubs lost in the jungle. But even with all the anger and the missing and the pain that suddenly shot up out of nowhere, there was no place for self-pity. The family was depending on him. He had to find work.

Very quickly, though, Zalman realized it was not going to be easy for a *yeshivah bachur* to find a job.

"I guess I could clean houses or stack shelves in a supermarket," Zalman moaned to Chezky, his *chavrusa*. "But what I want is to use my head and my heart. I want to make a difference." He sighed. "Not that I have any choice in the matter."

"You could always tutor," Chezky said. "Maybe the *Rosh Yeshivah* can find you some students."

"Maybe," Zalman nodded.

"Hey, I just thought of something!" Chezky's face lit up, then dimmed again. "No, on second thought, it's not for you."

"What? Maybe it is. What is it?"

Chezky looked pensive. "Well," he said, "my brother delivers kosher food to the Jewish boys in the juvenile detention center, and he mentioned that they're looking for security guards."

"You mean, like, to watch criminals?"

"Not proper ones. They're just boys who've gotten into trouble."

"I don't know," Zalman said slowly, mulling over the idea in his head.

"I heard it pays well," Chezky said.

"So does being a stunt man, but I wouldn't do that."

Chezky shrugged. "Just saying."

"So what is a detention center, exactly? Is it a prison?"

"Dunno. Fortunately, I've never been to one. From what my brother says, it's like a school with a dormitory, but much stricter than a regular one. And of course they're not allowed out alone, and stuff like that."

"*Nebach*," Zalman said, his voice soft with compassion. He twisted his *tzitzis* strings while he contemplated. There was a stirring inside him, a sudden curiosity and sense of adventure. "Sounds interesting. Why don't you give me the phone number, and I'll give them a call. They probably won't take me, anyway."

"IT'S TOO DANGEROUS," Ma said the first day that he donned his pale blue security officer shirt with its black epaulettes. She buried her head in her hands. "*Oy!* My son working in a prison. What will be?"

"It's not a prison, Ma. It's a school for troubled boys."

"Same thing," she muttered.

"Look, I promise you that if it's not safe, I'll quit."

Before Zalman left the house Ma hugged him hard as if they were back in the 1800s and she was sending him off on a sea voyage.

"Don't worry, Ma," Zalman said, wriggling out of her embrace. "I'll be fine. I'm a bit nervous, too, but it's okay."

Mrs. Tenner smiled weakly as she watched him walk down the driveway.

"Don't worry!" Zalman called again before turning the corner. And then he was gone.

The bus was long in coming. He could feel people's eyes sweeping over him. He supposed he looked rather strange — an Orthodox Jewish boy dressed up in what looked like a police uniform instead of his usual black and white one. Zalman looked at the ground, suddenly self-conscious.

The bus arrived and he climbed on, finding a seat by a window that looked as if it hadn't been cleaned in months. He peered through the glass as the bus sped on. Maybe it was the stains or the sticky imprints of fingers on the pane, but to Zalman, life looked different through that lens. Pedestrians rushed by; children sucked on lollipops as they walked next to their mothers; drivers honked their horns; trucks left clouds of dirty fumes from their exhaust pipes. It was all so… normal. But not for Zalman. He had on new spectacles now, and different clothing. He no longer belonged in that world. His world was one where fathers died without warning and sons exchanged their snow-white shirts for a shade of melancholy blue.

DINING ROOM DUTY! It was better than standing outside the school entrance, blowing on his hands and stomping his feet to keep warm. Besides, the clatter and banging at lunchtime exhilarated him. The high-pitched chatter punctuated with whistles and shouts brought him temporarily out of his sadness. Today, though, the boys seemed particularly rowdy. They had their moments when all of them literally buzzed with nervous energy, like a swarm of bees ready to attack. Zalman looked around nervously, hoping there'd be no trouble on his shift. Outbursts were understandable, of course, but even after a few months on the job, he still had a hard time breaking up fights.

"Whoa, be careful!" Zalman put his arms out to catch a boy who charged into him. He held the boy's shoulders to steady him.

"Wow, you must be really hungry," Zalman said.

"Starving," said the child with a mop of coal black hair and eyes so dark they could melt into the night.

"Come on, Billy, let's go. The French fries will be all finished." The boy's friend tugged at his sleeve.

"Umm, sounds good," Zalman said, licking his lips.

"Come *on*." The boy's friend pulled on his shirt again. "I'm hungry."

"Just a minute," Billy said, shaking him off. He stood before Zalman, staring up at his head. "You're Jewish, right?" he asked.

Zalman nodded. "Right."

"You're one of those religious geeks. I've seen people like you knocking around my part of town."

"Really?" Zalman smiled. "Which neighborhood is that?"

"Queens," Billy said, sticking his hands in his pockets and puffing out his chest slightly.

"Is that so?" Zalman exclaimed. "I have some relatives in Queens. Which area do you live in?"

"Doesn't matter." Billy shrugged. "Anyway, I live here now."

Zalman opened his mouth to speak. "Not for…"

"I'm going!" Billy's friend announced. "If you want to stay and talk to the Jew guy, you can."

Zalman winced. "Nice to meet you, Billy," he said, giving him a pat on the arm. "Off you go, and enjoy your lunch."

He stood, watching the two boys as they walked away. Then a sudden thought occurred to him. "Billy!" he called out.

The young boy turned.

"Are you also Jewish?"

Billy lowered his eyes to the ground and nodded. "Yeah."

SPRING WAS ON its way. The first blades of grass were pushing their way through the cracks in the concrete, and people appeared again on the park benches. Mrs. Tenner's legs were not so swollen anymore, and she ventured outside for short walks up the block. Zalman was no longer so anxious when he guarded the entrance to the center, and some days he even lifted his face to the sun and smiled.

But despite the thaw in the weather, Ma wasn't happy.

"Enough is enough now," she said as she clutched Zalman's arm during one of her brief excursions. "We have to find a solution to the *parnassah* problem. You can't keep working in that prison place."

"It's not a prison, Ma. I already told you."

"Whatever." Ma waved her free arm. "All I know is, it's not suitable for a *yeshivah bachur* like you."

"Actually, I like it," Zalman mumbled, looking out across the street.

Mrs. Tenner stopped abruptly. "You what?"

"I like it. I'm getting to know the boys a little, and they're really special. There's even a Jewish boy there."

"*Oy, vey!*" Ma slapped her forehead. "A Jewish child in such a place! What is the world coming to?"

"They're basically good kids who've had a rough start in life," Zalman explained. "And that can happen to Jewish children, too."

Mrs. Tenner pointed toward a bench. "Let's sit down a while. I need to rest."

Zalman steered her slowly over to the bench and sat down beside her.

"So," Ma said, gathering her breath, "you were saying."

Zalman shivered slightly in the cool breeze and watched a boy in a suit and hat, around bar mitzvah age, his arm linked through his *zeidy's* as he accompanied him down the street.

"Billy is probably the same age as him," Zalman said, nodding in their direction. He sighed. "There'll be no bar mitzvah for him, though."

"Who's Billy? The Jewish kid?"

"Yes. He's from a poor section of Queens. His parents are totally cut off from *Yiddishkeit*, and all he knows is that he's Jewish. The family is very problematic and dysfunctional."

"*Oy*, that poor boy," Mrs. Tenner's face looked pained. "What can you do for a child like that?"

"Support him, give him love, help him feel listened to."

Ma looked at Zalman curiously. "Aren't you just a guard there? How do you know all this?"

Zalman blushed. "As I was saying, I like the job. I'm getting to know some of the boys. They come and shmooze with me, especially in the evenings." He leaned forward on the bench, resting his elbows on his knees. "I… I don't know. I feel I can help them, be a big brother to them, or something. I don't know how to explain it, just that I feel more alive than I've felt in years."

Mrs. Tenner nodded. "I understand."

Zalman's head jerked up. "You do?"

"Sure. You're saying that you feel useful, productive, needed."

"Yes, that's it!" Zalman resisted the urge to jump up. "And it's exactly what I need right now, you know… for the pain."

Ma patted Zalman's hand. "Of course I know. I'm happy for you even though… even though I wish that the circumstances were different, that you didn't have to do this."

Zalman said nothing, just sat there next to his mother on the street bench, noticing the newly blossoming trees and the flowers budding in front gardens.

"In my younger days, before I got sick, I had that same energized feeling," Mrs. Tenner said, a faraway look in her eyes. "I taught a class of special-needs children. Even though it was hard, I thrived on it."

Zalman turned. "You'll get back to that again, Ma," he said.

"We'll see," she replied.

"You still learning with Chezky?" Ma asked suddenly.

"Yes. It's going well. We learn great together."

Ma took Zalman's hand in hers. "Thank you for everything," she said. "You have my blessing." The strength of her hand squeeze startled Zalman. There was still so much life in her ailing body.

"By the way, why's that child in there?" Ma asked. "What did he do?"

"Arson," Zalman replied. "He tried to burn his parents' house down."

"COME ON, YOU can do better than that," Zalman said, bouncing the ball around the court.

"It's not fair. You're much taller and faster than me," Billy grumbled.

"No excuse. You have to try. Here, come get the ball off me."

Billy ran up to Zalman and stood in front of him, moving from side to side to stop him from getting past.

"That's it," Zalman panted. "Run faster. Raise your arms higher so I can't shoot."

Billy jumped up, knocked the ball out of Zalman's hands and went racing off down the court.

"You've got it, boy. That's right! Keep going."

Zalman headed after him, trying to ignore the small stitch in his side. Just as he caught up, Billy was in the air sliding the ball into the basket like a real pro.

"Gooooooaaaaaaal!" Zalman screamed. He swallowed the boy in a huge hug.

Billy slipped out of his embrace. "You let me win," he said sulkily.

"I did not!" Zalman retorted. He strolled over to the sidelines to take a water bottle out of his bag. "You want some?" he asked, tossing it in Billy's direction.

"You let me take the ball off you," Billy persisted, catching the bottle and sitting down on the ground beside Zalman.

Zalman turned to look at him. "I'd never do that, Billy. I want your accomplishments to be real."

Billy took a swig of water. "Where did you learn to play like that, anyway?"

Zalman smiled. "I played a lot when I was a kid, before I went to *mesivta*."

"To *what?*"

"The school where religious boys learn Torah. That's G-d's instruction manual for how to live our lives."

"That's stupid. What do you need that for?"

Zalman regarded the child closely. "We all need it, Billy. It's like a book of rules. If we don't keep them, we can make big mistakes."

Billy snorted. He took some pebbles off the ground and skimmed them across the court. "Are you hungry?" Zalman asked. "I could get permission to take you out for pizza."

Billy skimmed another pebble. "Maybe." Suddenly, he looked up. "Why do you do this, anyway… you know, like come visit me after work and stuff? What's it to you?"

Zalman picked up the water bottle and passed it back and forth from hand to hand. "I like you, Billy. Is that so strange?"

Billy scowled. "You wouldn't like me if I wasn't Jewish."

Zalman felt like he'd been hit with the basketball in his stomach. He caught his breath for a moment before answering. "It's true," he said, "that there's a special connection because we're both Jewish. But I like you anyway, for who you are."

"That's not what Skip says."

Ah, Billy's friend Skip. Zalman was forever hearing about him.

"He says you're not a real friend… that you only feel sorry for me."

"Well, I think that's something you can decide for yourself."

Billy tugged at the grass he was sitting on, ripping out clumps. "Do you ever shout?" he said suddenly. "I mean really yell, like my Pa does?"

Zalman shrugged. "I guess I do if I'm very angry."

"Pa yells so loud it hurts my ears."

"I'm really sorry to hear that."

This time it was Billy who shrugged.

Suddenly, there was a loud crash. Zalman's water bottle went flying and tiny stones scattered in different directions. Zalman grabbed the basketball that had invaded their space and stood up. "Hey! Who threw that? Be careful."

No sooner had he spoken than another ball went whizzing past him. Skip appeared from the shadows. "So sorry," he said, sarcasm slipping off his tongue like melted butter. He glanced at Billy. "Are you gonna spend all night with the Jew guy, or what?"

Billy's eyes darted back and forth between Zalman and Skip. And then he slowly rose and walked away.

"SO," MR. DALEY said, leaning back in his swivel chair, "I hear that you're making connections with some of the boys."

Zalman fiddled with his fingers under the desk and tried to avoid the superintendent's stare. "Umm, yes. I am getting to know a few of them."

"Especially Billy Jacobs," Mr. Daley said, as if stating a fact.

Zalman squirmed in his seat. This was it, then. He was going to be put right back in his place, which was at the door entrances he was supposed to be guarding. He swallowed. "Y... yes, that's right."

Mr. Daley eyed Zalman carefully. "Do you think you're getting through to young Billy?"

"I think so; I'm not sure. I lost my father recently, so I guess I feel for him."

Mr. Daley frowned. "Billy *has* a father," he said. "Not a good one, but a father nevertheless. At the end of the day, nothing can replace that."

Zalman blushed. "Yes, of course."

"Billy's had a hard life, like all of the boys here. But he's very disturbed. He can be extremely volatile. You have to be careful."

"Yes, yes. You're right. Thanks for reminding me." Zalman's heart hammered in his chest. It was coming, he knew it. Any minute now Mr. Daley was going to tell him to keep away from the boys and thus extinguish the one flame of light in his dark life.

Mr. Daley leaned across his desk and scrutinized the young man's face. "It must be frustrating to just be a security guard."

Zalman nodded.

"I see that you're talented in this line of work, so let me give you a suggestion. How would you like to take a course?"

"A course!" Zalman spluttered. "In what?"

"To learn how to be a counselor. It's a good course, very professional. You'll get certification in the end."

Zalman brought both hands to his chest. "M… me? How could I do that?"

"I will send you," Mr. Daley said. "All I need to do is recommend you."

"And you'd do that?" Zalman stammered.

"Yes, Zalman, I would do that," Mr. Daley nodded. "So, are you up to it?"

"You bet I am!" Zalman exclaimed. "I mean, sure, I'd love to do it."

"Well, then, that's settled," Mr. Daley smiled. "I'll be in touch soon with more details."

"Thank you, sir, really, thank you." A wide smile spread across Zalman's face. He stood up, propelling himself out the door and down the corridor, trying not to trip over his feet that were going too fast. He exited the building into the bright glare of the midday sun, took a running leap into the air, and whooped.

THE DAYS WERE growing longer, and it was so hot you could cook supper on the sidewalk. Even the trees seemed to sweat in the sweltering heat, their leaves droopy and dull. Ma only went for her walks in the evenings which, while still sultry, offered a brief respite with their slight breezes.

Zalman roasted for hours outside. Indoor guard duty was now a special treat, something to savor like a soft vanilla ice cream that swirled like a shell on top of the cone. He couldn't wait for the summer to end and for school to start. He was going to be a counselor! Yes, he, Zalman Tenner, was being given the opportunity to make a difference.

Meanwhile, Billy was slowly uncurling his clenched fingers and allowing Zalman to take him by the hand. Sometimes Billy pulled back, as if Zalman's grip was too tight, but he then tentatively reached out again. His face looked less sultry, his eyes less thunderous. The hours on the court shooting baskets were therapeutic. *Try, Billy, try.* That was Zalman's mantra. *Don't give up! Just keep trying!* And it was spilling over to other things, like schoolwork and even trying to control the anger that raged inside him.

The thorn in Billy's side was Skip. The two boys were stuck to each other as one. Often, when Zalman went somewhere with Billy, Skip was there, taunting, until eventually Billy sidled back to Skip's side.

ONE EVENING, ZAMAN and Billy were sprawled on the grass after one of their basketball games. Thirsty and tired, they drank in silence. The air was hot and humid, the sky cloudless.

"How are things at home?" Zalman asked casually.

Billy's mouth grew tight. "Pa's gone away again." He stretched out his leg and kicked at a rock. "He won't be back for my birthday."

Zalman was quiet for a moment. "I can make you a birthday, if you like."

Billy looked away. "You're not my father."

Zalman nodded. "I know. But I know what it's like not to have one."

Billy suddenly turned and stared at Zalman curiously. Zalman opened the zipper on his backpack and withdrew a small package.

"For you," Zalman said.

Billy stared at the object in Zalman's hand. "What is it?"

"Open it and see."

Billy tore off the wrapping paper and found a shiny brown leather book. He opened it, then closed it again. "What's this? I can't even read it!"

"It's a Hebrew prayer book… for your bar mitzvah. It's got an English translation."

Billy scowled and handed it back. "What do I want one of these for?"

"Keep it," Zalman said, pressing it into Billy's hand. "You might want to use it someday."

Out of nowhere, Skip swooped down like an eagle and snatched the *siddur* out of Billy's hand. And with a sweeping movement, he took off, with Billy running after him.

ZALMAN HUMMED AS he entered the detention center. He could already feel the relaxed Sunday atmosphere. He worked a lot of Sundays; that way he didn't have to work on Shabbos. Today he was on indoor duty. He nodded to one of his colleagues and made his way down the corridor to the visiting area where he would guard during the afternoon. As usual, Billy had no visitors. Not even one family member had shown up for his thirteenth birthday.

Zalman stood thoughtfully, reflecting on this. He sniffed. "Hey, do you smell smoke?" he called to one of the youth officers overseeing the visitors.

Suddenly, a group of boys burst through the doors, their eyes bright with fear. "Come quickly! Billy's setting fire to the sitting room!"

Zalman raced along the hallway and into the sitting room, pulling the lever on the fire alarm as he ran. The heat hit him head on, and he could hear the crackling of flames as he pushed his way through a large group of boys who were standing in a circle.

"Get back," he shouted. "Everybody out!"

The air grew foggy with thick smoke and it was difficult to breathe. Coughs, sputters, shouts and screams sizzled with the blaze as staff members tried to herd the boys outside. Zalman continued pushing forward to the center of the room.

There was Billy, kneeling on the floor, a pile of his belongings heaped in a bonfire that danced wildly in sunset orange flames in front of him. The color swam before Zalman's eyes. He lurched forward, grabbed a fistful of Billy's shirt, pulled the boy toward him, and ran.

"YOU MUST GET up and go back to work," Ma said again.

The lump under the covers didn't stir. Ma shuffled over to the window and opened the shades, flooding the room with sunlight. "Come on," she said. "You can't lie there all day."

Zalman lay as still as a log. "Nu!" Mrs. Tenner tugged at the covers. "Get up, I said. Moping around won't do you any good."

Zalman groaned. "Leave me alone, Ma. I can't go back."

"Of course you can. Just take your two good legs and get yourself over there."

Zalman pulled the covers back over his head. "I'll go tomorrow."

"That's what you say every day, but it's been a week already. You're going to lose that job."

Zalman shrugged. "So I'll lose it."

Mrs. Tenner pulled up a chair next to the bed and sat down. "It's not your fault, you know," she said. "You mustn't take it so hard."

Zalman didn't answer.

"Billy is a very troubled boy. You knew that."

Zalman shot up in bed. "But I was getting through to him! I was reaching him! Why did he do it?"

Ma shook her head. "Like I said, he's far too complicated for you or me to figure out."

"I… I failed." Zalman's bloodshot eyes bored into his mother's. "Don't you understand? How can I learn to be a counselor now?"

"*Ach*, you're already giving up," Ma said sternly. "What do you think, that you'll never have challenges, that you'll never meet failure? Welcome to life!"

"I have my challenges. You know that."

"Right! And you've faced them valiantly, head on." Mrs. Tenner clutched Zalman's hand tightly. "And that's why I'm sure you'll get over this one and try again."

Zalman looked at his mother carefully; a woman scaling insurmountable mountains but continuing to climb. Maybe she could throw him a rope to hang on to?

HE WENT BACK; in body, not in soul. He returned to what he'd been hired as: a security guard. Billy had been transferred to a psychiatric unit and was refusing to speak to him and he, in turn, spoke to no one else. Mr. Daley had been surprised and disappointed when Zalman had said he was withdrawing from the course and told him to take time to reconsider. But Zalman's mind was hardened like steel.

Meanwhile, summer was suffocating with its sticky heat, and he yearned for the fall, when he could breathe again. On several occasions it had seemed like Skip had tried to catch his eye, almost as if he wanted to talk to him, but Zalman had just looked straight ahead like a British guard outside the royal palace, stiff and unflinching.

One lunchtime when Zalman was on dining room duty, Skip suddenly appeared at his side, coming from nowhere like he always did. Zalman set his jaw firmly, watching the boys as they passed by.

"Here," Skip said, thrusting something at him. "I suppose you'd better have this." Skip's arm was outstretched and he held something in his hand.

Reluctantly, Zalman glanced down. He let out a gasp. It was the *siddur* he'd bought Billy for his bar mitzvah. He looked up at Skip curiously.

"Billy tried to burn it with his things, but I stopped him," Skip shrugged, slipping his hands into his pockets and gazing up at the ceiling.

"You? Now why would *you* have done that?"

"I…" the boy stammered, the words not coming out.

Zalman took the *siddur*. "Thank you, anyway," he said.

Skip nodded and began to walk away slowly. After a few hesitant steps, he turned around. "You wanna teach me some of that Hebrew stuff?"

"What?" Zalman jumped in shock. He scrutinized the boy carefully; his ginger-colored hair and his pale, freckled face. "You're *Jewish*?"

Skip nodded. "Sure. Why not?"

Zalman stared, his mouth open in shock. "I don't understand."

Skip paced back and forth nervously. "You were giving Billy all that attention and not me. And anyway, I never liked Jews, until…" his voice trailed off.

Zalman swallowed. It had never occurred to him that this youngster could be Jewish, too. "What's your real name, Skip?"

"Stuart… Stuart O'Reilly. My Dad's Irish; my Mom's Jewish… from Russia."

Whoa! Zalman felt as if he was trying to stand upright on a swaying boat.

"In any case, I'm sorry," Skip muttered, rocking on his heels awkwardly. "I acted like a real idiot."

"That's okay," Zalman said, still finding his feet.

"So… you'll do it then… teach me?

The boat came to a sudden standstill and Zalman no longer wobbled. "No," he said. "I'm sorry. I'm just a security guard here… that's all."

THE STORM WAS keeping Zalman awake. For days he'd been tossing thoughts around in his head, trying to process Skip's revelation and the responsibility that came with it. His Rav had said that if Skip really was Jewish then he should teach him. He could be helping a lost Jewish soul trying to find his way back. Ma, of course, had agreed, going even further and encouraging him to take the counseling course.

The letter he'd recently received from Billy had buoyed his spirits somewhat. In his messy scribble on a dirty piece of paper, Billy had told Zalman he was doing better; the hasty thank-you at the end had made his heart contract.

But as he lay in bed, listening to the deafening symphony of lightning and thunder, he battled with himself. He couldn't do this again, he reasoned to no one in particular. What if it didn't work out? It would be too painful. And yet a young boy was reaching out to him. How could he not?

Zalman could hear the wind howling outside, the rain beating against his window. A sudden shot of lightning lit up his darkened room. *Come on, Billy, you can do better than that*, he heard himself saying. *Don't give up… try harder*, rang his mantra.

Visions of a thin, small boy leaping upward toward the basketball net appeared before his eyes. Images of his mother hooked up to the dialysis machine and a young man standing by his father's grave, ready to fill the role of head of the family, rolled past like scenes on a video screen. *Come on, Billy, try again.* The words came back to him. And so it went, back and forth, throughout the night. Sometime during the twilight hours the storm retreated into the dull thud of drumming rain, and finally, he fell asleep.

In the morning when he awoke, the sky was a clear, expansive blue and the sun streamed through his window. Droplets of rain hung off the tree branches, shimmering like diamonds. Zalman washed *negel vasser* and went to open the window. He stood a while, inhaling the fresh scent of a world made new again. The cleanliness held a whisper of hope.

Again, Billy… you can do it! In his mind he saw Billy leap into the air with the ball in his hands. But this time it was him being cheered on, to reach for that goal. *Come, on Zalman… don't give up!* He was dribbling the ball, his feet barely touching the asphalt.

All he needed to do now was to take the leap.

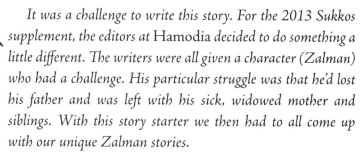

It was a challenge to write this story. For the 2013 Sukkos supplement, the editors at Hamodia *decided to do something a little different. The writers were all given a character (Zalman) who had a challenge. His particular struggle was that he'd lost his father and was left with his sick, widowed mother and siblings. With this story starter we then had to all come up with our unique Zalman stories.*

For starters, the name "Zalman" was hard for me to get my tongue around. It's not a name I would have chosen for a protagonist and it was difficult to use it because I have to like the names I give my characters. Names conjure up an image in my mind and I need to connect to that image.

Then there was the story starter. I had to rack my brains to come up with a good plot. In addition, I rarely write from the male viewpoint so that was challenging. I had to get into a man's head and I wasn't used to that.

I submitted two story outlines to the editors and both were rejected. By the time I sent in my third attempt I was ready to throttle Zalman and leave him for dead in the street. But, baruch Hashem, *my perseverance paid off and Zalman number three was inducted into The Hamodia Hall of Zalmans.*

I did actually like the story in the end. Don't ask me where I got the idea for it, though, because I haven't a clue. Often I just daven *that Hashem will infuse some inspirational thoughts into my head. If I wait long enough He does, and that's what happened here.*

I am happy that I managed to rise to the challenge and not throw in the towel like I occasionally wanted. It's always a good feeling to conquer the mountain. And interestingly enough, the protagonist in my next supplement story was also a male!

Swimming Lessons

SHE CLINGS TO me like I'm a lifeboat in a stormy sea.

"Don't let go," she says, even though it is *she* who is wrapping her arms around *my* neck.

"I won't," I say and hold her hands tightly. "Not until you're ready."

Tanya kicks her legs like flippers, creating whirlpools in the water. "I'm scared," she cries. "I want to go back."

"Just a bit longer, and then we'll get out and go for an ice cream."

But she's had enough already. I can tell by the way she hangs limply against me.

"Come, sweetheart," I say gently, wading back toward the pool steps. "I think we're done for today."

TANYA HASN'T LEARNED to swim yet. I first began to teach her when she was six years old, but she still prefers dry land. I really want her to learn, to overcome the fear of water that made bath time a battle and even a family hike through riverbed trails something to think twice about. I want her to have fun with her friends at summer camp, frolicking in the pool on the long, hot, humid days. Instead, Tanya just sits on the side, laughing at the other girls' antics.

I don't know why it's so important to me that Tanya know how to swim. Maybe it's because somewhere deep down I feel she's not safe otherwise, and I desperately want to protect her.

TANYA WAS FIVE years old when she came to us. I was hypnotized right from the start by the huge, haunted brown eyes that flooded her thin, little face. I knew that if they could speak, those eyes would tell a story that would be difficult to hear and even harder to understand. I remember Tanya standing on our gravel driveway with the social worker, Mrs. Phillips. One hand clutched Mrs. Phillips's arm; she sucked the thumb of the other. Her spindly legs stuck out from under her dress like two matchsticks, and I was afraid that they'd snap in two and she'd crumple down right there on our driveway.

I knelt in front of her. "Hi," I said. "My name is Mindy. What's yours?"

Tanya burrowed into the social worker's side, thumb still in her mouth. I looked up at my husband, asking for his help wordlessly.

Chaim bent down as well. "Would you like to come see our house?" he said. "We have a big slide and swing set in the garden."

The little girl nodded shyly, and the next thing I knew, she had let my husband take her by the hand and lead her around the back of the house.

"Amazing," I said to Mrs. Phillips as we followed them. "That's my husband, though… always good with children." I sighed wistfully, wishing that our own children and grandchildren lived closer.

"It's a good sign," the social worker said. "Although it will obviously take time for her to settle."

"Of course." Chaim was already pushing Tanya on the swing.

"If you have any questions you can always call me," Mrs. Phillips continued. "And I'll be coming once a week to see how things are going."

"I… I hope we'll manage," I said, suddenly overwhelmed by the tremendous responsibility that Chaim and I had taken on.

"It helps that you've raised children of your own," Mrs. Phillips said, giving a small smile. "The main thing is to be patient, establish boundaries and to give love… lots of love."

"Right." I continued to watch my husband and the sweet little girl who was now going down the slide. I turned to the social worker. "Aside from what you've already told us, is there anything else we need to know?"

"Not really. There's the physical and emotional neglect, of course. The therapy will help her with that."

"And her mother? Will she be coming to visit her?"

"Highly unlikely," Mrs. Phillips said. "As far as I know, her family is taking her back home to Chicago. Apparently there's a good psychiatric hospital there."

I sighed. "Poor woman."

Tanya was actually laughing now… her high-pitched squeals sounding like the chimes that tinkled outside my kitchen window.

"Indeed," Mrs. Phillips said. "And it seems this last breakdown came after learning that her husband's missing in action."

"Does… does that mean he's probably dead?" I asked hesitantly. I didn't even know the man, but still, the thought that this little girl's father had died fighting in Afghanistan was disturbing… another tragedy in her young life.

"Probably," Mrs. Phillips said. "Unless a miracle happens."

Chaim and Tanya walked towards us. Maybe I was imagining it, but I thought I already saw a spring in the child's step, a little hop here and there.

"Did you have fun, Tanya?" Mrs. Phillips smiled.

The thumb went back in the little girl's mouth, and she tilted her head down to her raised shoulder.

"Come," I said, taking Tanya by the hand. "Let me show you the special room you'll be sleeping in. We just painted it recently so it looks new. Do you like dolls? We have lots of those. And teddy bears? We also have a giant stuffed dog called Clarence."

I couldn't stop talking. The words rolled off my tongue. It was like if I kept talking I could prevent her from nestling into Mrs. Phillips's side again. Maybe, if I didn't leave gaps between the sentences, Tanya would choose what was already solidly built and decide to stay with us.

SHE CALLS US Mommy and Daddy even though we're not. I suppose after five years it's only natural. And anyway, we're hoping that very soon she'll become our real daughter, if the adoption goes through. Mrs. Cooperman, who's replaced Mrs. Phillips, has started the process. She says that there are some things to work out, but hopes there won't be any problems.

Tanya bounces into the house after school. She's invited some friends to sleep over tonight, and even though we usually only allow that on Shabbos, we've made an exception because it's her birthday. She drops her backpack onto the floor.

"Hey, Miss… pick that up," I say with mock sternness.

"Sorry," Tanya says hurriedly. Her eyes dart around the kitchen. "Where is everything? Did you bake the cake? What about the balloons?"

I laugh. "Take it easy. Everything's set up in the living room. Go take a look."

Tanya bounds off, flings the door open wide and lets out an excited squeal. "It's beautiful, Mommy," she says, jumping up and down. "Where is everybody? I want them to come already."

I laugh again and glance at my watch. "Another hour," I say. "Maybe you want to go upstairs and get dressed in the meantime."

She takes the stairs two at a time, and smiling to myself, I go back to the kitchen. The kettle is still warm, so I prepare a cup of coffee and sit down at the table. *Look how far she's come*, I think to myself. Who would think that she'd been a frightened waif of a child who shoveled food into her mouth with her fingers and banged her head against the wall whenever she was angry? My heart is warm and spongy when I see her now, looking and behaving like a normal ten-year-old. All the love and patience and hours of therapy have, *baruch Hashem*, paid off.

I hear Tanya calling me from upstairs and for a brief moment I glow inside, lit up as I am by this little girl's presence.

"Coming," I say.

"I don't know which dress to wear," Tanya says, pointing at a few she's taken out of her closet.

"I like this one," I say, picking up the azure blue jumper with the white collar that makes her jet-black hair shine.

She looks at the dresses carefully for a few moments. "I think I'll wear this," she finally declares, pulling a cream and brown two-piece off the hanger.

"As you wish," I say, wondering why she'd even asked my opinion in the first place. I start to exit the room.

"Mommy," Tanya calls after me, her voice smooth like a glossy wedding invitation. "Can I ask you something?"

"Sure," I say, turning around.

"Well…" She sits down on her bed and I sit next to her. "I really don't like my name. I want a Jewish one like the other girls."

I rub her back gently, tracing my fingers along her spine. "It's great that you want a Jewish name, sweetheart. Hopefully you'll have one once we become your proper mommy and daddy."

Tanya breaks into a wide smile. "And then I can choose?"

"Yes, my darling… then you can choose."

THIS SUMMER, TWO of my daughters join me in the Catskills. Their husbands and Chaim will drive up on Fridays and stay until Monday. My daughter, Shira, has a child Tanya's age, and the two girls are almost inseparable. In the afternoon, we'll all go down to the pool. Tanya's much more confident in the water than she was. I feel like she's almost there. All she needs is the confidence to let go of me or the float, and she'll be swimming alone.

"How I wish you all lived nearer," I lament to Shira while we're sipping lemonade on the porch one morning.

"I know, Mommy. We wish we did too."

Shira knows the script already. I repeat it almost every time I talk to her.

"At least you have Tanya, though," Shira says, nodding in the girl's direction. "How's she doing?"

"Great… as you can see."

"What's with the adoption?" Shira asks.

"The procedure has started now. Things began to move quicker once there was official confirmation that her father's not alive."

"How much does she understand?" Shira keeps her eyes on the girls.

"Pretty much everything. We've always been very open."

Shira turns to face me. "You've been incredible… the way you've dedicated your life to her."

"Thank you," I say, blushing a little.

My other daughter Devora suddenly comes out to the porch and hands me my cell phone. "You've got a call," she says.

At first I don't recognize Mrs. Cooperman's voice on the end of the line. Maybe that's because her usually calm demeanor is now peppered with panic.

"There's been a new development," she says. "You need to come home."

CHAIM AND I are frozen in shock. "When did this happen?" Chaim says.

Mrs. Cooperman sighs. "Well, apparently her condition's been slowly improving, but now she's much better and has decided to move back to New York to be closer to Tanya."

I don't know what to say, to think, to feel. An enormous boulder is rolling over me, pinning me to the ground.

"H… how often?" Chaim stammers.

"Once a week to start with… just for an hour. We have to see how it goes. After all, Tanya doesn't know her mother."

"W… what do we tell her?" I suddenly find a voice, not mine but someone else's, outside of my own body.

"The same as I just told you. That her mother's getting better and wants to see her." Mrs. Cooperman studies our distraught faces and a look of sadness passes over hers. "Obviously, we'll have to put the adoption proceedings on hold for now. I'm sorry."

THE FIRST MEETING is arranged in a blur of feverish anxiety. Chaim and I sit Tanya down the night before to prepare her. We remind her that it's not that her mother didn't want her, only that she wasn't well enough to take care of her, but now she's feeling better so she's come back. I say it all with a golf ball in my mouth and the feeling of rodents gnawing the lining of my stomach.

Even though I'm expecting it, when the doorbell rings, I jump. "Mrs. Cooperman's here," I tell Tanya gently.

She screams. Full blown curdling screams that would make one think she's, *chas v'shalom*, being murdered. She clings to me desperately, her arms around my neck just like they are in our swimming lessons. Unlike then, though, I don't want her to let go. I want her to hold on and stay curled around me forever.

"You have to go," I whisper, gently prying her fingers open. "It's only for a short while, and then you'll come back home and we'll go meet Daddy and buy bagels and chocolate milk."

"Nooooooo… I don't want to go," she cries, tears gushing down her cheeks. "I won't stay there. I'll run away."

"You mustn't do that, *zeeskeit*." I hug her tightly even though I know I have to let go of her. "Come now," I say eventually. "Mrs. Cooperman is waiting."

Tanya screams and kicks all the way to the social worker's car, and I'm almost envious that she can do that because it's exactly what I'd like to do myself.

A short while later Tanya comes home, marches up the stairs and hunkers down in her room, the promise of meeting Daddy and the bagels and chocolate milk forgotten. As I try to coax her out I am mad… spitting hot oil, angry at a woman who feels she can just walk back into her child's life and turn it upside down.

Before Tanya leaves for the second visit, she punctuates the air with her shouts and cries, and I begin to wonder if the old Tanya is coming back, the little girl whose rage smoldered inside her, waiting to be ignited. My heart is smashing against the rocks of my pain, each jagged edge making another rip in my soul. After she leaves I am spent, utterly lifeless, the blood sucked out of me.

But gradually the visits become part of our routine. Tanya no longer throws a tantrum before leaving, and sometimes even returns with a smile on her face. The hour stretches out to a full afternoon and eventually into a Shabbos. We negotiate the Shabbos in exchange for Sunday and, *baruch Hashem*, succeed, winning a small but significant victory.

On Sunday evening she skips through the doorway, arms bundled with parcels from their shopping spree. She takes me upstairs to show me her new purchases: the short-sleeved tops and cut-off jeans she knows I won't allow her to wear. And when she tells me she wants to go back again next Sunday, I am not just pained and angry, but down-right frightened.

"I WILL FIGHT it!" I say angrily. "We'll hire the best lawyers and go to court to get custody. Clearly, Tanya should be with us. Her mother's unstable, hasn't been in touch with her for *five* years, and now she thinks she can just waltz back in here and claim the last dance. Well, I won't let it happen."

Chaim sits quietly, letting me rant until I've no juice left and need to stop for a refill.

"Mindy, I feel just the same as you," he says in a calm voice that makes me want to scream. "I'm just not sure that you'll win, though. Legally, Tanya's mother has custody rights, unless she can be proved unfit to parent, which no longer seems to be the case. I'd hate to see you put your energy into a fight you'll probably lose."

"What about the religious aspect?" I shoot back. "We've raised her to be *shomer Shabbos*, *shomer mitzvos*. Her mother isn't *frum*. Surely that's an important point?"

Chaim sighs. "Of course it is, but it's not going to make any differ-ence in court. Tanya's mother can take her back. We always knew that was a possibility." I drop my head into my hands. He's right, of course, we've always known that Tanya's mother could reclaim her like a lost baggage item; we just didn't think it would actually happen.

I look up at my husband through watery eyes. "There must be something we can do. We can't just... we can't just let her go."

Chaim gives a sympathetic nod. "I didn't say not to try. Just don't get your hopes up. The law's on her side."

Now that makes me boil. "Who says?" I blast. "What about the five years of emotional and physical neglect that Tanya suffered? What about the fact that she's religious now, and the responsibility we have to a Jewish child? What about the upheaval and confusion this is causing Tanya?"

"Actually..." Chaim bites his lip. "Tanya seems to be adjusting much better now."

"Whose side are you on?" I shout, almost jumping out of my seat. I know it sounds immature, but at this moment I am feeling like an abandoned child myself, an insignificant slip of a thing who has been discarded on the street.

Chaim tilts his head in that sympathetic expression that I know so well. "Yours, of course," he says. "*Ours.*"

I stare down at the floor and then back at Chaim and for the first time I notice the anguish in his eyes. Because the one thing I've left off the "what-about list" is the most painful thing of all. And that's, "what about" the fact we've simply grown to love her?

MY DAYS ARE filled with lawyers' meetings and appointments with social workers and child advocates. My nights are spent tossing and turning, waking between bad dreams that are consumed with strategies and plans to keep Tanya with us. The lawyer says we may have a good chance of winning based on the early years of neglect and the fact that Tanya's mother has not been in the picture for five years. I wonder if he just says that so we'll keep paying his fees, because according to the research that Chaim's done, the rights of the biological parent usually prevail. And yet, knowing this, I fight on.

I think of nothing else. Nothing else is important except for the overseas phone calls from the children, shopping and preparing for Shabbos and keeping up with the house. One thing I do still do, though, is take Tanya for her swimming lessons. There's a certain comfort in diving into the pool headfirst and swimming to the other end underwater until I'm forced to come up for air. I need that, to stay down there protected by the water, because once I surface all I have to face is emptiness, the silence echoing along the hallways that reminds me that Tanya isn't here but away on another visit with her mother.

THE LAWYER CALLS. He says that the judge will want to speak to Tanya alone… ask her what *she* wants. Suddenly my blood turns to ice. I say okay and close the phone.

"What happened?" Chaim asks, looking up from a new *sefer* he's recently bought.

I tell him.

"Oh," he says. "So you're frightened."

Am I? Is that why my hands are trembling, my pulse throbbing wildly in my neck? Why does the thought of Tanya talking to the judge fill me with fear? Because I know! Yes, I know what she will say. I've watched the tentative steps of the baby duckling toward its mother until it was able to shelter beneath her wings. And I've seen her waddle back to us, torn in two, pulled from side to side.

"My goodness… *what* am I doing?" I say in horror. "How can I put her through this?"

Chaim says nothing, only sits and stares.

"How could I be so selfish?" The revelation is as dramatic and shocking as a comet landing at my feet and showing me that there is life in outer space. I clasp my head in my hands and shake it from side to side. "Who am I to say we'd be better parents than Tanya's own mother?"

Chaim's eyes are glistening. "Don't be so hard on yourself, Mindy. You only wanted what's best for her."

"Did I? Or did I want what's best for me?"

Chaim closes his *sefer*. "Both, I guess."

"All I'm doing is making her feel guilty," I say. "Like I make the kids feel just because they live in other parts of the world."

"You miss them," Chaim says. "What's wrong with that?"

"Because I'm living through my children… can't you see? Once the house became empty, we got Tanya. She filled my spaces for me instead of me filling them myself."

"And you also grew to love her," Chaim murmurs.

I nod. "Yes, I do. But if I truly loved her I'd give her back to her mother. I'd let her go."

TANYA WRAPS HER arms around my neck as usual. I'm standing waist deep in the water.

"You're not mad, Mommy?"

"No, *zeeskeit*, I'm not mad."

"I want to have both of you… two mommies."

"And you will. You'll live with your real mother and you'll come to visit us too, especially on Shabbos… how's that?"

I wade out a little deeper. "Today you're going to swim," I say. "A leaving present."

There's a brief flicker of fear in Tanya's eyes.

"Don't be scared," I say. "I'll be right next to you."

I feel the water lapping around my waist. With one hand I scoop some up and pour it over our heads. I'm in awe of this mysterious clear liquid that can keep us alive. Tanya giggles.

"Ready?" I say.

She nods her head, her strong chin jutting out determinedly.

"Okay. So you need to take your hands from around my neck. You know the strokes. All you have to do is let go."

I gently pry her fingers apart until her arms slither down my chest.

I give her a gentle push to start her off. She looks back at me briefly, the familiar pleading expression on her face, but I shake my head. Suddenly she's swimming. Small, urgent strokes, pawing at the water like a dog. She throws her head back and squeals as she gains confidence in the water.

Slowly, I stretch out my empty arms in front of me, unused to the lightness of my hands. A smile unfurls across my face. I have let go!

This is a beautiful story, if I may say so myself! It still moved me even now when I read it again, and that's surprising because it's a recent piece so I'd expect to be fed up of looking at it already. (Usually, by the time my work goes to print, I can't stand the sight of it anymore.)

I wrote this story at spring time, the edge of summer when beaches beckon and trips to the swimming pool are a pivotal part of my family's life. My girls and I literally live in the water during the summer. I think we must have been mermaids in a past gilgul.

So it was in this atmosphere that I wrote "Swimming Lessons." But it was also in another headspace as well. One of my daughters had been going through a difficult time, and during therapy with her it had emerged that she and I were too closely enmeshed. We had always had a close relationship, but this was the first time I was hearing that there was such a thing as being too close. I had always tried to protect her when she was growing up, fight her battles for her, even. I had been too quick to jump to the rescue instead of letting her figure things out by herself. My daughter needed to unravel herself from me and stand alone. I needed to separate.

Initially, her pulling back was painful. I'll admit that I took it personally. I, who had been there for her through thick and thin, was insulted. But gradually, I learned to accept, to understand and to realize that this process was necessary for the sake of our relationship, so it could blossom even more. I had a lot of processing of my own. One stark reality was the realization that my children will grow up and do their own thing. I pray that means they'll stay near us, but there are no guarantees of that. And that means that one day, when our nest is empty, we mother and father birds need to know how to fly without our chicks. Of course, we will welcome them into our nest whenever they want, but we must not pressure them to come just because we are lonely. That means having our own lives, creating our own fulfillment both separately and together.

It is hard for parents to let go even once their children are married. Seeing our kids as unique individuals with their own thoughts and ideas can be a lifelong challenge. Even if the words are unspoken, the silent pressure to make Mommy and Tatty happy can be suffocating.

That summer at the pool, I observed the many mothers in the shallow end, teaching their children to swim. It struck me how healthy it is to have your child cling to you, desperate for your protection, and then to teach him to let go of you, to swim alone. And once your child is out there swimming, you know that he's safe; he doesn't need you anymore. If he falls in the water he doesn't need you to help him get out. Isn't that the ultimate we strive for? The analogy was striking.

So that's what I learned while I watched those swimming lessons. That teaching your child to swim is a lesson for life!

Chains

"WHAT DO YOU expect me to do with this?" Zev Michlin flinched as Mr. Caldwell slapped the file down on his desk.

"It… it's the end-of-the-year report," Zev stammered.

"I know *that*. Again… what do you expect me to do with it?"

Zev looked blankly up at his boss. Was he imagining it or was there actually fire coming out of his boss's mouth? Most likely it was smoke from the Cuban cigar in his hand that was not nearly as fat and pompous as he was.

"Well?"

"Y-you're supposed to read it."

"I did that and there is nothing in this pile of drivel that is vaguely useful!" Zev's boss picked up the file, leaned forward and waved it in front of Zev's face.

"Oh," Zev said. "I'm sorry."

"You're sorry? That's pathetic! I'm running a major corporation here and all you can say is you're sorry? Get out of my office and have a new report on my desk first thing in the morning."

"Yes, yes… will do." Zev grabbed the file and hurried out of the room.

Several of his coworkers flashed sympathetic looks as he stumbled past them. A minute later he was seated at his own desk, staring at a blank computer screen, hands trembling as he reached for the keyboard. He started to log on, then stopped. Suddenly, his mind was as vacant as his desktop, passive and unresponsive unless he activated it.

He dropped his head into his hands. What exactly was he doing, scurrying around like a little dog after its master? Slowly, Zev raised his head and clenched his fists. He could almost feel the handcuffs closing around his wrists, the heavy chains banging on the hard table. For a moment anger bubbled up inside him until he was like a bottle of Pepsi about to explode. In his mind he could see the handcuffs popping off, pieces flying in the air and his disbelieving stare at his hands as they shook free. Suddenly, his office door flew open.

"What're you doin' Michlin? Not sitting there wasting time, I hope!" Mr. Caldwell leaned against the wooden door frame, puffing on his cigar.

"No, sir, not at all." Zev sat up straight in his chair. "I'll have the report ready by morning."

After his boss left it seemed as if the very air was quivering. Zev slowly brought his hands to his face. *Just who was he kidding?* he thought wryly, trying to steady the tremor in his fingers. Those handcuffs were still there, locked tight, and he didn't have the key to open them.

ZEV MICHLIN WAS not really a wimp. Nope, he was no pushover. At least he never used to be. In the old days, when life was bursting with blue skies and golden promises, he'd been filled with dreams. Ah, those were the good times, when the blessing of youth meant that almost nothing intimidated him and he felt like he owned the world.

Later that evening, after he'd finished drafting a new report, he climbed wearily into his car. Resting his hands on the steering wheel, Zev examined them again, turning and twisting them this way and that. The skin was already thinning and small brown liver spots fanned out like freckles towards his knuckles. Who would have thought he'd have signs of aging at fifty-one? Nobody had warned him about *that*. Not that he had any control over it — any more than over most things in his life. Zev turned the key in the ignition. *Just who was driving whom?* he wondered as he pulled out of the parking lot and headed home.

Zev unlocked his front door and, after wiping his feet carefully on the mat, proceeded down the hallway. A spicy tomato smell tickled his nostrils as soon as he entered the kitchen. His wife turned around from the stove and smiled at him.

"Soup?" Zev queried, walking over to her and lifting the lid off a pot.

Miriam nodded. "And spaghetti and meatballs."

"Hmm… just what the doctor ordered," Zev said, tossing his briefcase onto a chair and sitting down at the table.

"Hard day again?" Miriam asked as she ladled the steaming liquid into a bowl.

"The usual," Zev grunted. "Caldwell's giving me a hard time, as always."

Miriam sighed. "He seems to delight in picking on you. I've always said it's because you're Jewish."

Zev shrugged. "Whatever."

"You should get out of that place, find a job where you'll be given the respect you deserve."

Zev held his spoon in midair. "We've been through this a million times. You know it's not simple. American companies are firing, not hiring, these days."

"Still worth a try," Miriam said. "That boss of yours treats you worse than a slave. You must be able to break free somehow."

Zev sighed and stared into his soup bowl. It wasn't as if he hadn't tried to find other employment; it was just that at his age most companies weren't interested. They wanted young stock; the older ones were being put out to pasture.

"I can't just leave unless I have another job that pays me the same salary," Zev mumbled. "Don't forget about Yakky's medical and therapy bills. We can't pay for those with Monopoly money."

"That's a shame… it would be so much easier," Miriam laughed, trying to lighten the load that was weighing down the room. Her tone grew serious again. "I'm sorry that you have to endure this day after day, but…" she trailed off.

"But what?"

She let out a big sigh. "I just wish you'd get out of there, that's all. You're so… stuck."

"Yes, I know… you tell me that at least once a month," Zev said. He reached for a napkin and wiped his mouth. "Anyway, how were the kids today? How did Yakky's occupational therapy go?"

"Fine. Naava says he's making progress with fine motor skills and his handwriting's improving. Oh, and by the way," Miriam paused. "Eli's upstairs. He'll be coming down soon on his way out."

Zev groaned. "Where's he going?"

"Friends… you know." Miriam raised her arms in a helpless gesture.

Zev's face darkened. "*Those* friends. Well, I'll have none of that." He rose from his chair, scraping it backward on the tiled floor and headed for the door.

"Zev, *please*… leave him," Miriam begged. "It won't help and you two will only get into another fight."

Zev stopped in the doorway and turned back to his wife, his face a mixture of anger and despair. "I may be helpless at work," he said stonily, "but I will not be helpless in my home!"

CHAINS! ZEV FELT the weight of them on the way to *minyan* the next morning; the shackles clamped around his ankles and pinched his flesh, clanked on the cold floor as he dragged his feet. Last night's fight was just as Miriam had predicted: him shouting and threatening all kinds of punishments, Eli staring defiantly, then picking up his duffle bag and storming out of the house. Just when did his sixteen-year-old son become such an angry teenager?

Zev shuffled into shul and made his way to his seat. Strapping on his *tefillin* gently, he took his *tallis* and pulled it over his head, hoping he could hide as if he were inside a tent. As he *davened*, his mind meandered like a stream making its way down a mountain. Once, his *tefillah* had been passionate, heartfelt, his connection to his Creator palpable, an intimate conversation. Now, he mouthed the crusty words that formed on his lips while his thoughts flitted in and out. The *brachos*, the *amens*, the *Shema* sailed right over him. His thoughts returned to a later conversation he'd had with Miriam the night before — yet another discussion about his biggest and most unfulfilled dream of all.

"Yes, I know we said we'd make *aliyah* after we got married," Miriam had said, sighing heavily. "But how can I leave Mommy and Tatty? Who will take care of them?"

Who, indeed? And who had been expected to be there for them these last twenty-five years? Oh, the victory of emotional blackmail. Too bad he hadn't tried using some himself. Perhaps then he'd have held onto his dreams instead of watching them slip through his fingers.

"HELLO!" ZEV ENTERED the house and closed the front door behind him.

"I'm on the patio," Miriam called out. "Come and join me. The weather's beautiful."

Zev stepped onto the patio where he found his wife soaking up the Brooklyn sun.

"How did your learning go?" she asked as he sat down.

"Pretty good… actually… I enjoyed it." Zev tilted his face up. It was a beautiful Sunday, the sky a perfect expanse of blue, birds twittering amongst the trees that bordered their small garden, a rare moment of peace in his stressful life.

"Nice, isn't it?" Miriam said, closing her eyes.

"Mmm," Zev murmured, sinking down into a chair. "Where are the kids?"

"Yakky's playing next door by Shraga, Eli's out, Devora's upstairs with Zissy, and Tova and Naftali are coming over with the baby soon."

Zev smiled. "That's nice." He closed his eyes, too, allowing himself the luxury of dozing off. His mind was drifting, his head growing as heavy as a sandbag.

Suddenly, Devora burst through the patio doors. "Did you hear what happened?" she shouted, her face flushed. Miriam bolted upright while Zev turned his head and rubbed his eyes.

"There's been an earthquake in Israel... a big one!"

"Whaaaat?" Zev was fully awake now. "When, where... how serious is it? How do you know?"

"Zissy's brother just called to tell her," Devora said. "He's learning at the Mir in Yerushalayim, remember?"

Zev nodded, although he really didn't have any recollection of where his daughter's friend's brother was learning.

"It hit Tzfas the hardest," Devora continued. "It's really bad up there... lots of people injured."

"Tzfas?" Miriam interrupted. "Didn't Yossi go there with his yeshivah for Shabbos?"

Zev felt his stomach lurch. Yes, he did recall something about his nephew and a *Shabbaton* up north. "I'm sure he's back in Yerushalayim by now," he said, trying to stay calm. He stood up quickly and made a dash for the phone, but Miriam was there before him. He stood, scrutinizing his wife's face while she spoke to Shuly, his sister. As he listened to the one-sided conversation and watched her eyes darken in fear, he knew. Miriam laid the phone down gently, tears glistening in her eyes.

"He's there," she said. "The yeshivah was supposed to travel back Sunday afternoon. Yossi and some other boys are missing."

NEWS GUSHED IN and raced through Jewish channels like a river in flood. The stories overflowed, until no one could be sure what was fiction and what was fact. One thing was certain: Yossi and his two friends were missing, probably buried under piles of rubble, unaccounted for amid the chaos. Pictures punctuated the front pages of the newspapers. Photographs showed overwhelming devastation: concrete ripped apart; sidewalks shredded; apartment buildings imploded in piles like collapsed Lego blocks; fortunate, disheveled survivors being treated for shock. Zev devoured the newspapers, searching hungrily for news of his nephew, hoping that maybe, just maybe, he'd find his face in one of the pictures of the survivors.

Zev roared into action. Desperate to help, he organized twenty-four hour learning *sedarim* at his shul. Miriam held *Tehillim* groups in their house and Zev even took time off work to attend *tefillah* rallies, much to the wrath of his boss.

"Sorry, it's an emergency," Zev said, leaving his office early the next day. And when he walked out on a seething Caldwell, who was waving his beloved cigar at him, Zev felt a moment of triumph. Let his boss threaten and fume all he wanted; he simply didn't care. He felt the familiar chains loosening a little, allowing him a drop more freedom, and it felt good.

"It's a pity that it takes a tragedy to motivate us," he said to Miriam later, before he left to study with his *chavrusa* for their study session. "But my *davening* is back to the way it used to be. I just wish it wasn't because of this."

His wife gave a sad smile. "Never mind the reason," she said. "Just keep on with what you're doing. May it be in Yossi's merit."

"*Amen*," Zev said before disappearing out the door. With newfound energy, he hurried down the garden path and jumped into his car. For the first time in recent years, Zev Michlin had a reason to get up in the morning.

DAYS PASSED. ONE day... two days... then three. Hope was fading, dwindling with the buried boys' diminished oxygen supply. Some of the missing persons had been found, but Yossi and his friends were not among them. Around the Jewish world people prayed and learned, women took challah in the boys' merit, committed themselves to not speaking *lashon hara* during two hours every day. And they waited. Jews across the globe held their collective breath.

By day five the rescue teams were ready to give up. It was reported that, sadly and with heavy hearts, they had begun to leave the scene. "Noooo!" Zev cried aloud when he heard the news. "You can't stop searching! There's still hope, even if it's only a slight one."

But, of course, no one out there heard him. A desperate silence had descended on the city of Tzfas. Yet the boys were there... someplace... but where? It seemed as if the land had opened its mouth and swallowed them.

On day six some rescue workers returned to comb the disaster area one more time, but they reported that there was no movement amid the wreckage. Zev felt his spirits sinking, his newfound energy gurgled out of him, leaving him flat and deflated.

"Come on, Zev, get out of bed," Miriam coaxed the next morning. "You can't give up hope."

Zev swung his legs over the side and sighed. "Let's not fool ourselves. The chances are almost zero."

"There have been stories," Miriam said, "miraculous stories of people getting out alive after days, even a week buried in wreckage."

"Miracles," Zev muttered. "Like a modern *Yetzias Mitzrayim*, I suppose."

A look of sadness flickered across Miriam's face. She stared at him pitifully and left the room. Zev glanced at the clock. He was too late for *minyan* now; he'd *daven* at home. He dressed, and with leaden feet shuffled over to the shelf to get his *tallis* bag. It felt heavy today as if filled with stones. Through the curtains, Zev caught a glimpse of an overcast sky and its grayness matched his mood. The chains were wound tighter than ever, weighing his arms down when he pulled his *tallis* over his head… and just when he'd thought he would soon be free of them.

ZEV WAS AT a staff meeting, slumped in a chair and trying not to nod off, when the call came. The shrill ring of his phone blasted its way through the vice president's monotonous speech.

"Sorry," Zev apologized, fumbling in his jacket pocket for his cell phone. He had barely pressed the answer button when his wife's voice surged out.

"Shuly just called. They've found them! They're alive!"

"W-what?" Zev stared at his phone.

"They're *alive*! It's a miracle, a miracle… *hodu laShem*!"

Zev shook his head. "I can't believe it. *Baruch Hashem*! How? What…?"

"I'll tell you everything… just come home."

Zev closed his phone and leaped out of his seat, sending his chair tumbling over backward. "They're alive!" he shouted, punching the air.

Twenty-two sets of eyes stared at him blankly. Caldwell stood at the head of the conference table, his mouth hanging open.

"My nephew!" he cried. "They found them and he's alive!"

The air quivered with anticipation but nobody spoke.

"Oh," Zev said, looking around and suddenly realizing where he was. "I'm awfully sorry, but this is an emergency and I need to go home."

"That's okay. Go ahead," the company's vice president said quickly, heading off Caldwell, whose lips began to twitch.

"Thanks!" Zev said and scooped his briefcase off the table, tucked it under his arm and headed for the door.

402 Ready to Fly

"Michlin!" Caldwell boomed, his face black as thunder.

But Zev was gone, clattering down the staircase, too impatient to wait for the elevator, and out into the bright light that momentarily blinded him. He shaded his eyes with the back of his hand until he could see properly. And what he saw was a sun that was smiling, soft fluffy clouds hugging each other in the sky, a street that glistened when he stepped onto it, a warm world filled with people who glowed. He paused for a moment outside his office building and looked around, marveling how everything had suddenly changed, and he simultaneously realized that he wasn't feeling any chains at all.

As he threaded his way through the traffic, his thoughts raced. Was Yossi injured? How had he and his friends survived? Who found them? Where were they now? So many questions — he couldn't wait to get home and hear the answers.

Forty minutes later, Zev burst through the door. Sounds of laughter and animated voices reached out to him. The children were in the living room jumping up and down, neighbors chattered excitedly, a small group of women sat in the corner saying *Tehillim*. Miriam quickly finished her phone call when she saw him. Her face was a cocktail of tears and joy.

"What happened?" Zev asked breathlessly. "How were they found?"

"I'll tell you… come outside onto the patio," Miriam beckoned.

"Where is he now?" Zev asked.

"He's in the hospital. They all are. They're severely dehydrated. Yossi has a broken arm and his friends both have leg fractures… one has a broken collar bone. All in all, they've been very, very lucky."

"How," Yossi said, shaking his head in amazement, "did they manage to survive?"

"They were in an air pocket," Miriam explained. "And they had some food and water in their backpacks… they'd just returned from a hike when the earthquake hit. Apparently, they stayed inside the air pocket for a few days hoping they'd be found, but when that seemed unlikely, Yossi began to dig his way out."

"With a broken arm?"

"Yes," Miriam nodded. "With a broken arm."

Zev listened in awe to his wife's retelling of the boys' dramatic escape. He sat without interrupting as Miriam related the details, how they'd recited *Tehillim* and *davened* together, imagining they were in the *beis medrash*, and all the while they'd been in excruciating pain. She described the terror they'd felt, the fear that no one would find them, that they'd die there underneath the debris. He heard how it was Yossi's idea to leave the safety of the air pocket and try to get out; that he'd offered to go because the other two couldn't walk but he could; that he'd put his life at risk for them.

Over the next few days more details emerged. Shuly's husband, who had stayed behind in Brooklyn while she had flown out on the first available plane to Israel, was the source of the news. The boys were unquestionably heroes. They had done everything they could to hold on, to believe that Hashem would save them. They'd been brave and resourceful, and Yossi… Yossi had been selfless and gallant!

With the boys recuperating in the hospital, as his initial euphoria wore off, Zev found himself wandering about in a daze, almost as if it was he who had emerged from the wreckage. He returned to work and received the expected dressing down from Mr. Caldwell about his recent behavior, but it flew right over his head. Somehow, it was getting harder and harder to concentrate. The chains had tightened again, squeezing hard enough at times to cut off his circulation. Perhaps that was the reason why his head was so fuzzy, why he groped around in a fog. Soon, he reflected, Caldwell would actually have good reason to fire him. Maybe, deep down, that's what he wanted.

"HAVING TROUBLE SLEEPING again?" Miriam asked, rubbing her eyes as she shuffled into the living room.

Zev nodded.

"Want some company or should I leave you alone?"

Zev looked up and smiled. "Always glad to have you here."

Miriam sank into the navy-blue leather sofa and settled herself comfortably against the cushions. "Do you want to tell me about it?" she said.

Zev stared ahead of him, his eyes wide and searching. He waited a moment before answering.

"I am ashamed," he said at last.

"Ashamed? Whatever for?"

"Look at me! I've been pathetic. All I've done is complain about my situation over the years but done nothing to change it."

Miriam bit her lip. "Well, like you've always said, it's not so simple."

Zev turned to his wife sharply. "No more excuses! I'm finished with that. It's time to act."

Miriam looked down and said nothing. A gentle rain was knocking on the window, begging for recognition. Through the curtain they could see the sky beginning to brighten in the predawn light.

"It's Yossi, right?" Miriam said finally. "He's what's caused this."

Zev inhaled deeply and drummed his fingers on the armrest. "I'm trying to sort it all out in my mind, but one thing I do know is that Yossi and his friends put me to shame. Look what they did! And look at me! What have I done?"

"You've done a lot," Miriam said softly. "You've made sacrifices for the sake of your family, put up with situations that have sometimes been intolerable."

"And done nothing to change them... just resigned myself to things never being different... I just gave up, shackled myself with imaginary chains."

Miriam's cheeks glistened in the glimmer of the dawn. "I am

sorry," she said, "because maybe I've added to your unhappiness too."

Zev regarded Miriam carefully. "Do you think we will make *aliyah* one day, that you could ever leave your parents?"

"Possibly," Miriam murmured, lowering her gaze. "I don't know. We could try… go back to the Rav… see what he says."

Zev's expression grew disappointed. "It will never happen, I know that. Not until they won't need you anymore and then it will be too late."

Miriam looked up, her eyes flashing in the semi-darkness. "I have my chains too, you know… we all do. They are there whether we like it or not. But they don't have to shackle us."

"What do you mean?"

"I mean that sometimes we can release our chains just by accepting that we have them. I'm going to try to do that. I'm not saying I'll succeed all the time, but… I'll try," she said.

Zev fell silent, shrouded in thought. "Maybe," he began hesitantly, "maybe acceptance is also a form of change. Perhaps if I learn to accept that we can't leave just yet, I won't be so bitter?"

Miriam nodded slowly. "There's something to that… freeing oneself from negative thoughts."

"It's funny, because you've tried to tell me this before but I never listened until now."

Miriam gave a weak smile.

"But there's something else that's bothering me," Zev said, his mood pensive. "It's about courage… being brave enough to change the things I can change. I never had it… that courage."

"You have to find it inside yourself… no one can give it to you. It comes with *emunah*."

"And *davening* for it too," Zev said. He sat quietly, thinking about courage and faith and the comforting thought that he wasn't alone in his struggle, that he had a family and Hashem to help him.

"Those boys are an inspiration," he said suddenly. "The way

they didn't give up, the way they fought to stay alive." He gave a small laugh. "They really *were* trapped, unlike me who just thought I was."

Miriam said nothing because there was no need for words. Together they watched the blackness papered across the sky peeling back, preparing it for a new day. Zev was going over things in his head: the therapy he wanted to arrange for Eli, to which he would accompany him; the new *shiur* he wanted to start at shul. He gazed out the window, seeing the sky, mostly milky now, just a little bit black.

"I'm going to leave my job," he said more to himself than to Miriam. "I'm going to look for something else."

Miriam smiled. "Good for you."

"There are others. Hashem will help me find something."

"*Amen*," Miriam said softly. "*Amen*."

Orange and yellow streaks slid across the sky as the sun rose. It was a new day.

After successfully writing my first story from the point of view of a male protagonist ("Taking the Leap"), I decided to dabble again with this genre. I always thought it virtually impossible to write from a perspective I couldn't relate to, but I guess writing as a cloud in first person ("When it Rains") changed that for me. Also, I had a male family member who was "stuck" in a certain rut at the time (although nothing like Zev) and that gave me the impetus for this story. As with all my stories, they can start with a tiny spark of an idea that jumpstarts into major electrical activity.

My family member's "rut" situation got me thinking. I began reflecting about the times we feel stuck in the mud, unable to climb out, whether it's in a professional area of our life, our attitude towards child-raising or in our personal growth. Often, the fear of changing causes us to stay there, bogged down. Sometimes, a challenge of some sort can catapult us out of our complacency, which is what happened in "Chains." Unfortunately, that surge of energy didn't last because the stimulus for it remained external and when Zev didn't get the outcome he wanted, he slipped back down again.

In this story I wanted to show how we need to "want" to change from a deep internal place and not to be frightened by it. And when we decide to do that, we can free ourselves of the chains that drag us down, imaginary or otherwise.

Getting Even

"TAKE YOUR DIRTY fingers away from there," I say to my daughter, gently pushing her away.

"Aw, Ima, just one." Tzippi's hand is poised above the miniature pizzas on the baking tray. She looks at me with her puppy dog eyes.

"Go wash your hands first," I say, laughing, as I steer her towards the bathroom. "Then you can sit down at the table and eat like a *mentch*."

Tzippi runs off and she's back in seconds.

"Wow, you're hungry," I say, watching her pile four pizzas onto her plate.

"I didn't eat my sandwiches," Tzippi says. "My water spilled over them so they were all soggy."

I sigh. "That's the second time this week, Tzippi. You must make sure to close your bottle properly."

"Um." Tzippi attempts to smile with her full mouth.

Suddenly, I realize somebody's missing. "Where's Mina?" I ask, looking over my daughter's shoulder. "Isn't she supposed to come for lunch?"

"No," Tzippi says between bites. "Change of plan or something. She went home with Shaindy Rothstein instead."

"Really?" I raise my eyebrows. "Since when has Mina been friends with Shaindy Rothstein?"

Tzippi wipes her mouth. "Dunno. I think the mothers are becoming friends or something."

A little alarm bell rings in my head; not a shrill pitch, but a low drone that nevertheless makes me sit up and take notice. "That's interesting," I say, reaching for the pitcher of apple juice. "But Mina's coming tomorrow, right?"

"Maybe." Tzippi shrugs her shoulders as if trying to be indifferent. "She said her mother might want her to go to Shaindy again."

I watch my daughter as she wipes her face with her napkin and I know she's trying to pretend she doesn't care. But she does, and so do I. And why shouldn't I? Mina has been coming home with Tzippi for lunch every day for the last four months, so why the sudden change? Maybe the menu's better in the Rothstein house, though I doubt it. But clearly there is something Mina's mother likes better there, if it's not the food.

MINA DOESN'T COME the next day, nor the day after. Tzippi wanders into the kitchen and slouches at the table, looking lost and lonely without her best friend. The fourth graders have been virtually inseparable since kindergarten, stuck together like glue. Until now, there was no tear in the relationship.

Mina's mother, Tova, is my neighbor and friend; we live across the courtyard from one another and often talk to each other from our balconies while watching the girls play. Although Tova and I are very different, we gel well. My relaxed, easygoing nature complements her more serious, nervous one. Tova loves rules; at times I find myself taking some of hers to use in my own life.

I guess you could say we're like earth and air. I would float away on butterfly wings if someone wasn't there to pull me down and ground me. Of course, my husband, Levi, does a good job at that, but it never hurts to have a little extra weight on the line.

I remember when Tova asked me if I could host Mina every day at lunchtime.

"Esti, are you sure you don't mind?" she asked, her forehead scrunched with worry. "I suppose she could always stay in school for lunch."

"Don't be silly," I said. "I'm making lunch for Tzippi anyway, and Mina's like my daughter."

Tova smiled gratefully. "You can't imagine how relieved I am that she has a place to go where she feels comfortable. After all, she's used to me being home all the time."

"I'm only too happy to do it," I said. "And Tzippi will be thrilled."

So that was that. I didn't think twice. Tova was free to attend her psychology course five days a week, knowing that her daughter was taken care of, and all I had to do was chop up a few more vegetables, or make some extra pieces of French toast. And that's the way I expected things to continue for the rest of the year.

TOVA SEEMS TO be avoiding me. Granted, she's very busy with her studies, but even in the evening, when I try to catch her to talk about the lunch arrangement, she manages to wriggle away like a slippery fish.

"I wonder what I've done," I say to Levi while we're lingering at the table after supper.

"Why do you think *you've* done something?" he asks. "It seems to me like the issue is with her."

I ponder this for a minute or two. Come to think of it, Tova is changing. For a start, she rarely wears *sheitels* anymore, but covers her hair in those colorful *tichels* and scarves. And I remember her telling me that her husband was planning to learn full time from the next *zman* and they were going to start keeping Rabbeinu Tam.

"You know what?" I say. "I think Tova's becoming more *frum*."

Levi looks at me over his glasses, which are halfway down his nose. "So?"

"So maybe now I'm not *frum* enough!"

Levi grimaces. "Oh, come on. And what's that got to do with Tzippi and Mina?"

"I don't know. It's the only thing I can think of."

Levi sips the coffee I made him, a little bit of caffeine to wake him up for his evening *shiur*. "I don't think you should worry too much about it," he says. "I'm sure it will pass."

He's right, I decide, soaping up the dirty dishes and staring into the bubbles I make. I wash the dishes. But then Tzippi walks in.

"What's wrong?" I ask, taking one look at her face.

Tzippi isn't a crier and she rarely complains, but I can see that she's fighting back tears. "Mina isn't going to study with me for the big *Chumash* test. She's learning with Shaindy instead."

I bite my lip, feeling her pain, and I'm not sure what to say. I stand up to go hug her, but she shies away and goes to the living room.

I follow and sit down beside her on the couch. "That must be very hurtful," I say.

"Whatever." Tzippi shrugs.

I put my arm around her shoulder and we sit quietly for a few minutes. I rack my brains to come up with an explanation for why my daughter's best friend is snubbing her. "Have you and Mina had a fight or something?" I ask eventually.

Tzippi shakes her head. "No."

"So why do you think Mina's going off with Shaindy? Are you sure nothing happened?"

Tzippi turns to look at me, her pale brown eyes swimming in pain. "Mina doesn't want to do it, Ima. It's her mother. She's making her."

I feel as if an arrow has just speared my heart. For a moment I grapple with unfamiliar emotions, which frighten me. Because all I want to do is send that spear back across the courtyard, straight into Tova's heart.

"SINCE WHEN HAS their relationship been unhealthy?" I ask angrily, grasping the phone hard.

Tova stumbles over her words. "I… er… it's since they're togeth-er all the time. Mina doesn't know how to handle it. It's too intense."

"So teach her *how* to deal with it," I say, trying hard to keep control. "Isn't that better than breaking up a friendship they've had for years?"

"Um… well… Mina's getting too obsessed," Tova hedges. "It's really not good for her."

"Really? Since when?" I'm almost shouting now. I want to fight like a tiger for my daughter.

"Well… it was always a problem. It… it… er… just got worse when they started being together all the time."

"Oh… I see." I spit the words out, sarcasm dripping from my tongue. "It was after you sent Mina to my house every day that you suddenly realized they shouldn't be friends anymore."

Tova's voice hardens on the other end of the line. "A mother has to do what's right for her child, and I believe that Mina needs to make friends with other girls."

"Fine," I say through clenched teeth. "But just remember while you're so busy doing the right thing, all the pain you have caused to another ten-year-old child!"

THINGS HAVE CHANGED. Tova and I no longer shmooze with one another across the courtyard while our girls play down below. In fact, we don't shmooze at all. If we pass each other in the street we behave as if the other one doesn't exist, sometimes even crossing over to the other side.

Just like I suspected, Tova has become more religious, and the people she once considered friends no longer have a place in her life. Now it's people like the Rothsteins who have earned a posi-tion of honor, while Levi and I have been discarded. All of that unhealthy relationship stuff was just a cover story.

But that's not what stings so much. Hurtful as it is, I can live with the rejection. But I absolutely cannot accept the anguish that Tova has caused Tzippi. My normally happy, confident daughter follows me around like a shadow. This once popular, fun-loving girl is sometimes so quiet I forget that she's there. She simply can't fathom what was wrong with her that justified such rejection. And as much as I reassure her that it's not her fault, it doesn't matter, because the bottom line is — she has lost her best friend.

"SO WHAT DO you think about that new school?" I ask Levi before he rushes off to work.

He nods his head from side to side. "Sounds good. We need to find out more information, though…"

"I'll make some calls today," I offer, eager to grab hold of the hook that was recently thrown me. This school, which my friend Shulamis told me about, could be just what Tzippi needs. She could get three good years there before going on to high school.

"Fine," Levi says, gathering his coat and briefcase. "Let me know what you come up with."

What I "come up with" is a relatively new school, about two or three years old, small and cozy with a high level of education, the right *hashkafah* for our family, and a principal you could only dream of.

I bring up the topic with Tzippi casually at suppertime.

"Oh, yes, I've heard of it," she says, her eyes unusually bright. "A girl in my class is switching there next year. I've heard that it's a great place."

"That's nice," I say, trying to keep my voice even. "So what about you? Do you think you'd like to go?"

Tzippi's response is so enthusiastic, so eager, that my gut feeling about her unhappiness is immediately confirmed. She hasn't said much about school and the situation with Mina during these past months, but it's what she doesn't say that tells me everything. The main issue is her loneliness. By fifth grade, the girls have their groups already, and even though Tzippi is accepted in most of them, she still seems to find herself offstage, like an understudy.

"I think she needs a fresh start," I say to Levi later that night.

We talk to our Rav. The following week, we take Tzippi for an entrance exam and interview. She passes with flying colors, and she's in!

TZIPPI IS SOARING. It's beautiful to see how she's spread her wings and started to fly. In her new school she's popular again, the happy, easygoing child she once was. If I harbored any doubts as to whether we were doing the right thing, they have flown way up high, together with my daughter. I delight in her development, her personal growth, and the myriad of friends she is making.

Her best friend, Avital, is a regular visitor to our home, and my heart swells with happiness when I see them studying for tests together or going to shul on Shabbos. My Tzippi's back! I can almost forget about everything that happened.

Except that I can't. In the deepest of places inside of me lies a bitterness that gnaws at my bones. On the rare occasions when I see Tova on the street and she gives me a sickly sweet smile, like everything's okay between us, the resentment that's been simmering comes to a boil and I want to wipe that sickening smirk right off her face. I continue with my life as usual, but whenever I think of what she did to my child I'm consumed with an overwhelming urge to hurt her. At those times I am ashamed and unable to recognize myself, but try as I might, I just cannot let go.

"GUESS WHO'S IN my class?" Tzippi announces as she dumps her bag on the table. She looks so grown up all of a sudden in her brand-new high school uniform.

"I've no idea… who?"

"Mina Sternberg."

"*What?*" For a second I'm thrown. I haven't thought about Tova and her daughter in months, and now all of a sudden they're back on my radar again. "How do you feel about that?" I say, once I regain my composure.

Tzippi shrugs. "Fine. It doesn't bother me. I have my friends."

I look at her closely. Has she really moved past everything, or has she tucked her feelings inside an envelope an d sealed it closed?

"She's really changed, Ima," Tzippi says as she spreads chocolate spread on her bread.

"Oh," I say. "How so?" I desperately wish we weren't having this conversation. I wish that Mina Sternberg and her mother would stay firmly out of my life, behind the steel door where I've placed them. In general I manage to keep the door closed, but sometimes a gust of wind blows it open, reminding me that the bitterness and resentment inside of me remains and can come gushing out any minute.

Tzippi gets up to wash and comes back to the table. She makes the *brachah* and takes her first bite of bread. "She's just... different," she says. "I can't imagine us having something in common anymore. When you see her, you'll understand."

Come to think of it, I haven't see Mina in a year or so — since we moved to a different part of the neighborhood. That means I haven't seen her mother either, and that's exactly the way I like it.

That's why I get such a shock when, two weeks later, I meet Mina at the bus stop. Interestingly, she actually says hello to me. For a moment I'm not sure who this short-skirted, heavily made-up teenage girl is.

"It's Mina Sternberg," she says, obviously noticing my confusion.

"Oh," I say, hoping the surprise isn't plastered all over my face. "How are you?"

"Fine, thanks." And then she bounds up the steps of the bus and disappears. As I walk home, I reflect on Tzippi's words. "When you see her, you'll understand." Oh, yes... I definitely do.

BARUCH HASHEM, TZIPPI'S turning out to be a lovely young girl. Clever, talented, popular, easygoing and responsible, she's like one of those triathlon athletes who excel at more than one thing. She's forging ahead in high school, well-liked by both students and staff. Every day I count my blessings for being given this wonderful child.

Tzippi hasn't mentioned Mina much since the beginning of the year, but the little she has said tells me quite clearly that Mina is struggling. Her friends are the girls who are out of the box, the ones who test the boundaries beyond just sticking a toe in the water. I don't know exactly what has caused Mina's deterioration, but whenever I think about it I am overwhelmed by a disturbing feeling of satisfaction. Yes… ashamed as I am to admit it, there's a sense of triumph in my heart, like I've just knocked all the pins down in the bowling alley in a single shot. There is a mean, nasty part of me that wants to jeer in Tova's ear and say, "Ha… serves you right!"

But revenge is not so sweet. Despite the sugary satisfaction, I don't like the bitter herbs that are sprinkled over it. It's not a taste I want to keep in my mouth, yet no matter how many times I wash it out, it always returns. Sometimes I think I'm making progress, but whenever I remember what Tova did to my daughter, wham! There it is again, and despite how hard I try, I can't get rid of it. I wish there was a magic recipe that would get rid of it once and for all.

THE PHONE CALL catches me in the laundry room, knee-high in whites. I rummage through crumpled sheets and pillow-cases to find my cordless.

"Hello, Esti." It is a familiar voice, but one I haven't heard in years.

Flustered, I drop the shirt I'm folding. "Ye… es," I answer tentatively.

"Long time no speak. How are you?"

It's *her*. No… it couldn't be. But it is. I'd recognize that voice anywhere. "T… Tova?" I say.

"Yes," she says. "Right… first time."

I can feel my pulse pounding in my ears. What does she want?

As if she's read my mind, she answers me. "I know we haven't spoken in a while," she begins. "But I really need your help. I have an enormous favor to ask you."

"Oh," I say, waiting.

She plows on, no small talk or pleasant formalities as an introduction. She's thrown me right off, and I flop down onto the pile of laundry so I won't lose my balance.

"Mina is going through a bit of a hard time," Tova is saying. "To be honest, she's got in with a group of girls who aren't the greatest influence on her." She pauses, probably for a refill of whatever it is that's fueling her. "So... I was wondering whether you could ask Tzippi if she'd mind inviting Mina into her group. I hear that Tzippi's friends are really good girls."

Never in my life have I been unable to find words like I am now. I am simply speechless. "I... I..." I open and close my mouth, stuttering.

"Esti... are you there?" Tova's voice continues to come at me, like a guided missile.

"Y... yes."

"So what do you think?"

Think? What I *think* is that she's got the most tremendous chutzpah! To call up like this, no apologies, not even an acknowledgement of everything that's passed between us; just another example of ruthlessly doing what's best for Mina without a single regard for anyone else along the way!

But I don't say any of this, because I'm so angry that if I verbalize my fiery thoughts, I'm afraid they will consume me.

"Esti?"

"Yes." I wonder why I'm bothering to answer her at all. "I'll *think* about it," I say before hanging up.

I PUT THE phone down, pull myself shakily to my feet, and go find Levi.

"What happened?" he asks in alarm. "You look furious."

I sink down onto the couch and relate the phone call from Tova.

"Whew," he says after I finish. "That's heavy."

"How *dare* she?" I splutter. "Who does she think she is to use our daughter again for her own benefit?"

Levi raises his hands. "What can I tell you?" He looks thoughtful. "It seems like she honestly doesn't realize what she's doing. Sometimes when a person becomes completely focused on a cause, he becomes blind to everything else around him."

Angry tears sting my eyes and I ball my fists in frustration. "I'm not going to let her hurt Tzippi again," I say fiercely. "She can find someone else for a scapegoat."

"So the answer is no, then?"

I look at Levi, startled. "Well, of course… what did you expect?"

Levi shrugs. "Just asking."

"What?" I shake my head questioningly. "You think I should say yes?"

"*You* shouldn't, no."

I gape at my husband. Am I the only one still normal around here? "So, *who* then?"

"Well," Levi says tentatively, "maybe we should let Tzippi decide? She's older now, more mature. I think she could handle this by herself."

For the second time today, no sound comes out of my mouth. When I finally find some words, they tumble out, flipping over each other like somersaults. "No. Absolutely not. Been hurt once. Enough!"

"I'm serious," Levi presses. "Why don't you ask her? Even if she says no, I'm sure she'll be happy to have been told about it. Whatever decision she makes, she could finally put this all behind her."

As soon as his last sentence is in the air, I have a sudden realization. "Actually," I say, "I think she already has."

"So," Levi says knowingly, "maybe you'll find a way to get some closure too."

FOR DAYS I toss the idea around like lettuce in a salad. I want to throw away the rotten leaves and start over with newly-picked produce, to pour honey-mustard salad dressing over my acidic thoughts.

While I'm debating whether to pass the ball to Tzippi, an unsettling idea comes to me. What if Mina is struggling now because of me? What if all my years of bitter, negative feelings towards her mother have affected Mina on a spiritual level?

This notion has me reeling. One thing I'm beginning to realize is that Tova loves her daughter just as I love mine, and is only doing what she believes is best for her. If, G-d forbid, I might be responsible in any way for Mina's difficulties, I could never live with myself.

My Rav tells me that there is no way of knowing if this is the case, but that for my own sake it's better to let go. It's not the first time he's told me this, of course, yet I've simply been unable to break free; maybe because the hurt runs so deep that I cannot find what it takes to forgive. There *is* a way, though, I know. Maybe, if I truly want it, I just have to ask Hashem to help me find it.

When I finally sit down with Tzippi to tell her about Tova's request, she isn't surprised.

"I don't mind including her in my group, Ima, but I don't think she'll want to join," she says simply.

I stare at my daughter in amazement. Wow! She's willing to reach out, just like that!

"The thing is, she probably won't fit in." Tzippi shrugs her shoulders casually and goes back to her homework.

I watch her, head bent over, fully absorbed in geometry. Can it really be so simple? Why can't I forgive and forget like she has? What is it that has enabled her to let go? I have my own homework to do, plenty to learn. But for now maybe I'll take a lesson from my daughter. I rub Tzippi's shoulder gently and smile. My lips move slowly with a whispered prayer — that Hashem should help Mina find her way.

This story is unfortunately based on true events. It happened to a daughter of a friend of mine. She decided to tell me her story and have me write it up in the hope that it would allow her to release certain negative feelings she still held onto.

As parents we make mistakes. Sometimes we lose the ability to think for ourselves in our desire to fit in and sad consequences can occur as a result of decisions we make.

I am not going to get into the issues that plague our educational system today; we all know what they are. My friend switched her daughter to a different school because of the social difficulties she was having in the old one — her child was ostracized with old friends being forbidden to play with her because she wasn't "one of them" anymore. In the end, though, it was the best move my friend could have made. Her daughter thrived in a different environment and has grown up to become a remarkable young lady, bli ayin hara.

So, as much as we scrunch ourselves up into the most uncomfortable of positions to fit inside the various boxes, Hashem always knows where we need to be. And my friend knows that too... now!

Lessons

MY BEEPER GOES off somewhere between the sweet potatoes and the cauliflower.

"Sorry," I say to the lady pushing a cart next to me as I fumble to find the beeper in my jacket pocket and knock the bag of apples out of her hand. *Nice batch*, I observe while crouched on the floor trying to help her gather them up: red, succulent, shiny. An irrelevant observation, of course, but one I need to make anyway, something nice and normal before taking the call which will be anything but... otherwise I wouldn't be being paged.

"Dr. Reich," the ER nurse says into my earpiece. "I'm sorry to bother you."

"That's fine," I say, moving away from the vegetable section. "That's what specialists are for."

The nurse ignores my attempt at humor and I don't blame her. "We've got a serious traffic accident... head-on collision. One of the passengers is a young woman in serious condition and we're having difficulty stabilizing her. Dr. Cunnings is about to insert an ET tube now and he asked me to call you in."

"No problem," I say, quickly doing the mental calculation: *Forget the shopping... there's leftover stir-fry for Yehudah's supper.* "I'll be there in ten minutes."

"Oh, and Dr. Reich —"

"Yes?" I say.

"Just so you know… the patient's name is Ina Malwarski."

"Oh," I say ignorantly. "And she is…?"

"She's a famous pianist," the nurse says. "A prodigy."

"Oh," I say again. I watch a lone apple that escaped from the dropped bag roll slowly across the floor. It's still shiny, red and juicy… for now.

AS AN ORTHODOX Jewish doctor in a New York City hospital, I'm often unfamiliar with the famous personalities who enter our doors. I don't follow the news or the social media, and even if I did, it's not important to me because I believe in treating everyone the same.

But when I walk into the cubicle where Ina Malwarski is lying intubated, the first thing I notice is the young pianist's mangled right arm, twisted now at her side like a gnarled tree branch. I stare at her crushed fingers, imagining them once dancing across the keyboard.

"Dr. Reich." Alex Cunnings rushes over. "Glad you're here." He nods at the girl underneath all the tubing. "She's sustained a severe head injury… the CT shows severe intracranial bleeding. Her pressure's dropping, pupils responsive but dilated… we need to get her to the OR right away."

"What about her hand?" I say, still staring down at her arm. "How will she play?"

Dr. Cunnings looks at me oddly. "We'll get to the hand, Dr. Reich. But right now we need to save her *life*."

WHEN I FINALLY rip off my gloves and mask, throw them in the wastebasket and emerge from the operating room, I'm not sure how many hours have disappeared since I walked in there. We… all the team… counted six hours and twenty-three minutes, but that means nothing because time spent like that can't be measured.

We've done our best. The neurosurgeons, orthopedic and plastic surgeons, and of course, the trauma team. Only time will tell now. Ina is in serious but stable condition in the recovery room and as soon as she's able, she'll be transferred to the neurosurgical ICU. As for me, I've done my part, coordinating the crew, orchestrating the band of accomplished performers. Each member executed his piece magnificently. But the harmony is not quite complete. There's something missing — a pianist.

On the way to the on-call room, I phone Yehudah, who has waited up to talk to me despite the late hour.

"Go to sleep," I say. "It makes no sense for us both to be exhausted."

"Soon," he says, fobbing me off. "How did it go?"

"She's a pianist," I say, "the girl in the accident… Ina something-or-other… quite famous."

"I guess that's why I haven't heard of her," Yehudah laughs. His tone grows serious. "Will she be okay?"

I sigh. "The next forty-eight hours will tell. One thing I'm sure of, though… she'll never play again."

Yehudah sighs too, a deep, heavy, familiar expiration of breath that is coming from something other than sadness over a young woman's shattered dream.

"How's Meira?" I ask, immediately understanding.

"She called this evening. Aaron's being difficult about the *get* again. She didn't complain, but I could tell from the sound of her voice that she's trying to hold it together."

I arrive at the on-call room, unlock the door and flop down onto the bed. I have no strength to hear about my daughter's estranged husband and his efforts to shackle her in their failed marriage. I am tired… so tired that my eyelids are slipping like shutters over my eyes and I have to keep forcing them to stay up.

"What is it this time?" I ask, even though I don't really want to hear the answer.

"Something to do with the custody of the children. She didn't go into details."

"Whatever," I say, my thoughts wandering unexpectedly from Meira to Ina the pianist — two young women whose lives have not gone at all the way they'd expected.

I STOP BY to see Ina in the ICU before I leave. She is lying like a slab of white marble, tubes running into and out of her inert body. I check the charts at the end of her bed and make a quick note of the respirator settings and her vital signs that flash from the wall monitor.

"I see she's gone down on the oxygen," I remark to the nurse, Stacy, who is fluttering around the bed. I was once an ICU nurse, too, until my restlessness moved me on.

I remember the first conversation with Yehudah when I told him I no longer wanted to be a nurse. "It's not enough for me," I lamented. "I want to do more."

"I understand that," Yehudah said. "But medical school takes a long time and it's tough, not to mention expensive."

"I can get a grant," I said unconvincingly. "And my father said he'd help out."

"I don't know." Yehudah shook his head. "A *frum* woman. It's one thing being a nurse… but a *doctor*? Do you realize how hard that will be? And the on-calls you'll have to do. You'll never be home."

That was admittedly a problem. I really didn't look forward to those all-night shifts that ran seamlessly into the next day, but after six years Yehudah and I had still been alone, so at least I didn't have any guilt feelings about neglecting young children. Even so, it wasn't a simple decision.

It was my dear husband who decided for me. "Look," he said, "I know you need to do this, and if you don't do it…"

"Yes?" I held my breath.

"... you'll be frustrated, unhappy, held back from reaching your potential. If the Rav gives his blessing then I think you should do it."

I wanted to sing and dance on the roof of our apartment building after we came back from the Rav's house.

"Once medical school is over it will get easier," I told my *tzaddik* of a husband. "Then I'll leave the hospital and go into private practice."

Indeed, I did leave the hospital — to take care of baby Meira when she finally made her debut. But as she grew and I had less to do at home, I felt the need to do more, to give more, to be part of the cutting edge — literally. So I went back to the hospital, but this time to the operating room, where I learned to remove leech-like lesions wrapped around people's brain stems or to sew up burst aneurysms with the precision of a seamstress, and give people another chance to live.

"There's been a slight improvement," Stacy says, showing me the results of the blood gases on a little piece of paper.

I nod. "Much better. But let's keep the ventilator settings the same because we want to get the brain swelling down. I'm off duty this Shabbos so Dr. Silas is on call. I'll be back Sunday."

"No problem, Dr. Reich. I'll pass the message on," Stacy says cheerfully and bounces off to the treatment room to prepare Ina's medications. I smile as I watch her go. After all these years the staff have gotten used to the novel Orthodox Jewish woman with her *Shabbosos*, holidays, that kosher food stuff and various other strange behaviors. Besides, I'm good to have around, because whenever someone is needed to work the non-Jewish holidays or Sundays, that's me with my hand in the air. Now that I'm senior surgeon, though, I'm only called in for a real emergency. Life is *supposed* to be more normal.

The room is painfully quiet, even with the sound of the ventilator pushing oxygen into Ina's lungs and the beep-beep of the heart monitor. I take a lingering look at the young girl, a human being with thoughts, feelings, memories and longings, who is in there somewhere, trapped amongst the machines, and I wonder who she is. On the way out, I pop into the doctors' offices and take a moment to read her file. And that's when I discover that Ina Malwarski, the famous young Russian pianist… is Jewish.

"WHAT ABOUT HER fingers? Will she play again?" Ina Malwarski's mother asks me, bringing her own older but intact hands before her face and clasping them together tightly.

"Well," I say, trying to buy time for my response. "The fact that she's regained consciousness is a good sign."

"But will she *play?*" A middle-aged woman who is standing beside Mrs. Malwarski moves forward.

"Um…" I look back and forth between the two women.

"This is Larissa, Ina's music coach," Mrs. Malwarski explains.

I nod.

"What about her hand, doctor? Can you save it?" Larissa asks, her eyes pleading like those of a prisoner begging for freedom.

I clear my throat. "It's too early to say at the moment. Ina's general condition is still very precarious… we're pleased with her progress so far."

Larissa twists her fingers together and brings them to her lips. "Such a talented girl," she says in her heavy Russian accent. "This is a tragedy."

I turn to look at Ina, who is now breathing on her own with an oxygen mask. Yesterday she opened her eyes and responded when spoken to. It's a good sign, but there's a mountain still to climb.

"We're doing everything we can," I tell Larissa and Mrs. Malwarski. "We want Ina well again as much as you do, but you must understand that she sustained a very serious head injury…"

"Just save her hand, doctor," Larissa cuts me off. "Millions of people are depending on it."

SHE'S A FEISTY one, Ina. If only she would use her will and determination to get well. Now that she's over in rehab I don't see her as much as before, but even so I stop in regularly. Her progress was good until it depended on her to continue it and that's when her resistance set in. When I arrive today I find her in a wheelchair by the side of her bed.

"Hi, Ina, it's good to see you up," I say cheerfully. I nod toward the chair. "Does this mean you've been outside a little?"

"I want to go back to bed," she says without looking up.

"What's the rush?" I ask. "I can take you for a walk if you want."

"I want to go back to bed," Ina repeats sulkily, leaning over the chair on her good arm while the bad one lies limply across her stomach.

"Are you sure?" I say. "Not even for five minutes to get some fresh air?"

Ina raises her head and scowls and I know it's no use pursuing it. The only kind of "fresh" thing I'm likely to get is a new argument. I wander down the corridor looking for a nurse. I honestly don't know why I keep coming to see Ina. Most of the time all I get is a cauldron of anger thrown in my face; red-hot accusations of "you don't understand"; frothing declarations of "my life is over."

"It almost was," I tell her. "But, thank G-d, it was saved. That means you must have a lot more left to do in this world."

Ina hates it when I say that and I don't blame her, but something makes me keep saying it anyway — probably the same thing that pulls me in like a strong undertow to her bedside each day. Yehudah says it's because Ina's around Meira's age that her situation touches me so deeply. I guess it could be, although she's nothing like Meira either in looks or personality. All they have in common is their shattered lives.

"Meira needs to fight harder," I tell Yehudah constantly. "She's letting that man run circles around her... he'll never give her a *get* at this rate."

Yehudah usually shrugs. "She's trying. You know Meira, she was never the pushy type."

Of course I know. The girl who always shared her sweets until she had none left for herself; the child who let everyone go ahead of her in line, that's my Meira. I get a twinge of guilt when I remember those things. If only I'd been around more to help her develop confidence, give her tools, maybe she'd have been better prepared for marriage.

The nurse accompanies me back to Ina's bed and I shake myself out of the past. As I watch Ina struggle and argue with the nurse I wonder if that's what draws me to her. Maybe because she has so much strength she isn't using? If only I could take just a little of it and give it to my daughter.

"Better now?" I ask Ina after she's reinstalled in bed.

Ina scowls, her creamy porcelain face shadowed by a dark cloud.

"I guess that means yes, then."

Ina slowly turns her head toward me. "Why do you keep coming here?" she asks.

"I keep asking myself the same question," I joke.

"Then you should save yourself the trouble," Ina says. "Save your energy for more important things."

I pat Ina gently on her arm and smile. "I think that's my call to make, not yours. Anyway…" I try changing the subject. "How's the walking coming along?"

"Don't know." Ina shrugs her shoulders. "And don't care."

"Really?" I raise my eyebrows. "You don't care whether you walk or not? What do you plan to do… get around in this wheelchair forever?"

Ina tilts her chin. "What does it matter whether I walk or not?" she says, her dark eyes flashing. "I have nothing to live for anyway." She gestures to her useless arm. "I'll never be able to play."

I pull up a chair and lean in close. "Listen," I say, "you're not just a pianist, you know. You're also a person."

Ina turns away.

"I know you think I don't understand. And you're right… I don't. I cannot imagine how devastating this is for you. But I do know one thing. There have been many people who've lost arms and legs, paraplegics with only half the use of their body… but they haven't given up. They've had to redefine themselves, yes, but that didn't stop them from carrying on."

Ina keeps her head turned aside, away from me, but I can see the two sad tears rolling down her cheeks. "It's all I know," she says at last. "Since I was five years old… it's what I was groomed for."

A sudden thought pops into my head. "Do you like it?"

Ina looks at me, puzzled. "Like what?"

"Playing the piano. Do you enjoy it or is it just what's expected of you?"

"What a dumb question. Of course I *like* it," Ina responds, her face flushed.

I regard her carefully, saying nothing.

"*What?*" Ina challenges me, then looks away. She grows quiet for a moment, her eyebrows knitted together in thought. "Well, I think I like it," she says hesitantly. "As I said, I don't know anything else."

A nurse arrives with Ina's medication. "So you were saying," I continue after Ina swallows her pills and the nurse leaves.

Ina leans back against the starched white pillows and suddenly she looks so vulnerable that I want to take her in my arms and hug her. "I never really thought about it," she says tiredly. "It's who I am, who I've always been."

I reach out tentatively to stroke her arm. "Well," I say, "maybe it's time to find out who you really are."

INA'S PROGRESS IS impressive. She barrels along like a steam locomotive speeding down the tracks. She is taking small steps now without the walker and last week the feeding tube was removed from her stomach. The hand, of course, is a sore subject, painful like an open wound. But it *is* healing… slowly. A few more skin grafts on those two crushed fingers and there is hope that she may have limited use of them. Will they ripple across the keyboard like they once did? Doubtful… but I have to remember that Hashem's in charge, not me, and there are always miracles.

I'd like to think that it's because of our blossoming relationship that Ina finally decided to cooperate with her treatment, but perhaps that's somewhat arrogant of me. And yet I cannot help but notice that since that day when Ina began questioning her identity, the wall between us came down. I look forward to our visits, enjoy the stimulating discussions, and I even tentatively introduce concepts she's never heard of before in a life devoid of anything Jewish. I talk to her about the idea of believing that everything that happens is for the best and trusting that things will turn out well. When I speak, it's for Meira too.

This evening I stop by on the way to the on-call room. Ina looks up when she sees me and there's a light in her previously dull eyes that warms me.

"What's with the linens?" she asks, gesturing towards the sheets and blankets under my arm.

"On duty," I say. "I agreed to switch with a colleague who's going out of town."

Ina grimaces. "That's a drag."

I shrug. "It doesn't happen often." I look at her closely. "You seem to be in a good mood."

"Oh, I am," Ina enthuses. "Today I talked to my parents about going to university to get a teaching degree and for the first time they reacted positively… none of the 'but our daughter was a famous pianist' stuff."

"That's great," I say enthusiastically. "Real progress for all of you." I sit down on the edge of her bed. "I'm proud of you," I say. "You've learned to accept what's happened to you and begun to make changes. That's what we Jews do."

Ina rolls her eyes. "Don't give me that Jewish business," she says.

"You've got a Jewish soul, Ina, there's no escaping it." I punch her playfully on her arm.

"If you say so… whatever that is."

"I *know* so." And I also know that the months of encouraging her, teaching her about *emunah* in a roundabout way, have paid off.

My cell phone rings suddenly. "It's my daughter," I say, looking at the number on the screen. "I'll call her back soon."

"How's she doing?" Ina asks, and for a second I'm surprised because even though I've told her about Meira, she's usually too self-absorbed to ask after her.

"She's much better. Tomorrow she should be finally receiving her *get*… you know, the Jewish divorce I told you about. It's been a rough ride, but hopefully after that she'll be able to remarry and rebuild her life again."

Ina grows thoughtful and frowns. "I'd like to go for a walk, get some air. It's stuffy in here." She sits up, pulls her legs over the side of the bed and reaches for her walker. "I don't understand this *get* thing," she says. "It sounds like she's trapped."

"I guess it does sound like that." I slowly escort Ina down the corridor. "It's not an easy concept to explain if you're not familiar with it." I pause to pick up the hem of Ina's nightgown that's trailing on the floor. "But there are many different ways to feel trapped."

We're just about to exit through the double glass doors of the day room and enter the garden when my phone rings again. This time it's Yehudah.

"Can you manage to go out by yourself?" I ask Ina. "I need to take this call, so just find a bench and sit and wait for me. I'll be there soon."

I retrace my steps, go back to the ward and slip into an empty office where I can talk privately with my husband.

"Hi… everything okay?" I say, detecting an anxious tone to his voice.

"It's Meira," he says. "Aaron's not going to give her the *get*."

"*What?*" I sink into a chair in disbelief.

"He's found another excuse… something else to do with the children… he wants to fight for custody now."

For a moment I don't move, stunned into a stony silence. And then I start to feel anger bubbling up inside me, boiling blood coursing through my veins. The rage is fierce and massive and before I realize it a volcano of pain and frustration is spewing out. I cannot contain the words which fly like missiles out of my mouth, ready to strike anyone in their path.

"This man is *evil*," I scream into the phone. "He's destroying Meira's life! I hate him!"

Yehudah is silent on the other end of the line.

"How is she going to continue like this?" I rant. "He'll never give her a *get*. Her life is ruined!"

Tears fizz effervescently down my cheeks as I continue to shout and cry and repeat the mantra, "Her life is over!"

"Dr. Reich." There's a loud knock on the office door. I've no idea how long the nurse has been standing there witnessing my breakdown. "Dr. Reich…" She peers tentatively around the door. "I'm sorry to intrude, but you didn't answer when I knocked. Is everything all right?"

I stare at the nurse uncomprehendingly and I blink. She has broken the spell. And as she opens the door a little wider I look past her and down the corridor where the figure of a slender young woman pushing a walker is disappearing from sight.

"Ina!" I call out breathlessly as I run to catch up with her.

"Don't touch me," she says, brushing my hand off her arm.

I back off, surprised and offended. "What's the matter? Are you upset because I didn't come to join you outside?"

Ina doesn't respond, just pushes hard on the walker until she reaches her room.

"Come, let me help you back to bed," I say, moving her chair and nightstand out of the way.

"I don't need your help," Ina says stonily. "I can manage."

I stand back, my heart aching as I watch her shuffle to the side of the bed and struggle to heave herself up with her good arm. "Please, Ina… at least let me call the nurse."

"No," she says. "Just go away."

Yehudah always says I have a stubborn streak, which comes out now as I remain, not budging until I see she's safely back in bed.

"Look, Ina," I say, "I'm sorry if I let you down. I just had to take an important phone call."

Ina looks at me pitifully. "You don't get it, do you?" Her lips begin to quiver. "Yes," she says, "you have let me down. It shouldn't take much to figure out why."

I speak to the nurse who knocked on the office door and I am able to put the pieces together and figure out that Ina overheard my conversation with Yehudah. She heard my cries, my outpouring of ire, the final explosion and I am ashamed. Ina's right to be angry at me; that was hardly the role model behavior of a doctor. In addition to all my roiling emotions centered on my daughter, I want to slither home in embarrassment.

It's only after my apologies to Ina fall on deaf ears that I realize it's more than that. I've let her down in a deeper way. All of my encouragement means nothing to her now. In her eyes I'm a fraud, not matching my deeds with my words, and in her raw, self-preoccupied state she cannot see beyond herself to understand that.

WHENEVER I GO to see Ina now, she sends me away with an angry shake of her head. I can live with that, but what I can't tolerate is seeing her deterioration, her gradual regression like a fetus curling back inside the womb. The staff in the unit tells me she doesn't cooperate anymore with physical and occupational therapy and she no longer takes even the tiniest of steps.

Friday, before I leave work, I gather my things and go downstairs to visit her. She waves me away as usual.

"No," I say as I pull up a chair. "I'm not going."

Ina shrugs and turns her face away, her hair spread out fanlike on the pillow.

"You don't have to look at me," I say, "but you're going to listen." I place my bag on top of the cupboard while I choose my words. "First of all, I understand how you feel," I begin. "And I'm truly sorry for the way I behaved that night… it wasn't right of me. But," I pause, "what I did is no excuse for this." I sweep my arm out and over the bedcovers. "You're using that one incident as an excuse not to get better and I think I know why. You're afraid of failing. You're frightened that you won't succeed in anything else except playing piano!"

Ina turns toward me, her green eyes flashing, jaw tight. "You still don't get it, do you?"

I look at her, startled. "What?"

"I don't *believe* you anymore. All of these months of convincing me that I still have a life even if I can't play… all of this faith and acceptance business… you can't even do it yourself for your own daughter!"

I feel as if I've been punched in the stomach and instinctively, I bend forward, winded. Maybe my head's also taken a blow… I'm not sure, because my thoughts are reeling, bouncing around like ping-pong balls inside my head.

"Meira's life is over! That's what you said!" Ina hurtles on. "What about mine? *She* has two good arms and legs… she's healthy, right? So if *her* life is over, what about mine? Why should I listen to anything you say?"

I raise my head up slowly, the pain spreading from my stomach to my heart. I look at this young woman whose life has been shattered, who is almost child-like in her dependence and vulnerability. I see the confusion and bewilderment in her eyes as she searches for something to hold onto, a reassurance that one day she will be well. And that's when I really understand.

"You are so right," I say softly, my voice quivering. "I let you down and I'm sorry."

Ina stares at me and says nothing.

"It's easy to say the words, to think your faith is strong, until you're called upon to test it... and I blew it."

Ina's bottom lip trembles as she fights back tears.

"This was a lesson," I say. "A hands-on opportunity to learn. And seeing that I'm only human, I'll have to keep trying and failing and trying again."

Ina closes her eyes, small rivulets of water seeping from the edges and she nods slowly to herself. "Like me."

This time it's my turn to be silent.

After a few minutes Ina opens her eyes and looks at me. "You're a doctor," she says with a tremulous smile. "I expected you to be perfect."

"Well, I'm not. And I'm not meant to be." I tuck a stray strand of hair behind her ear. "Remember what I once said... 'It's not what you are but who you are.'"

Ina nods her head. "Like I'm not just a pianist..."

My eyes glisten and a lump forms in my throat. I reach out to Ina and clasp both her hands tightly. "There are no promises, Ina... nothing's engraved in stone... but you still have your whole life ahead of you."

GENTLY, I PUSH open the door to the music room, slip inside and slide along the back wall behind the rows of chairs. Parents eagerly await their daughters' performances, and they chatter amongst themselves while waiting for the recital to begin. I slip into a seat and blend in with the audience. I don't know much about music, but Ina's students sound pretty good to me. When I watch the girls' hands fluttering along the keys of the piano, I imagine Ina once playing like that, her fingers brushing the notes lightly like butterflies wings and my stomach sinks a little, grieving for her loss. But Ina looks happy in her new role. She is passing her birthright, her love of music, on to her students and it emerges naturally. I smile as I watch her, the mother hen surrounded by her chicks.

We've come a long way, Ina and I. Once a week we meet in my home and study together from a *sefer* on *emunah* and *bitachon*. Even though Ina says "this Jewish stuff is stiff and outdated," she grudgingly admits that the material we learn helps her get on with her life, especially in the tough times. Often Meira joins us as well. She definitely needs a lifesaver to hold onto while waiting for her personal salvation. Without it, without the knowledge that Hashem is running her life every single second she would drown.

As for me, I'm still learning my lessons — always will be. The challenge is to take the theoretical knowledge and bring it inside so that the words that leave my mouth pour out of an inner font of spiritual wisdom. Of course, I don't always manage to do it, but I'm trying.

The last of Ina's students finishes her recital and all the girls bow to resounding applause. I stand, clapping with the proud mothers and feeling like I'm one of them. Ina looks searchingly into the audience and catches my eye. She grins, raises her bad hand with its two deformed fingers, and waves.

As a writer, I am constantly aware that my talent comes from Hashem. It is not a middah I have worked on; it doesn't make me a better person. It is purely a gift from Hashem and therefore I have a responsibility to use it in ways He would be proud of. At the same time, I also know that Hashem can take that gift away from me whenever He likes for whatever reason. I could just wake up one morning and poof — it's gone!

So what would I do if I couldn't use my talent anymore or anything else, for that matter? One does not have to be a famous athlete to mourn the loss of a limb.

My story, "Lessons," began as a way to explore this issue and the emotions involved — anger, loss of identity, a sense of hopelessness. But then it went further. What about the reactions of others who are trying to help the victim cope? Do their words comfort the victim or does he silently think, "What do they know? They're not in my situation."

The issues raised here are too complex to be fully explored in one short story. In the end, I decided to focus on authenticity; that Ina should find her authentic self and figure out how to express it with her physical limitation; that Dr. Reich should understand the power of her words and actions on a vulnerable young woman and be able to live in her heart what she knows in her head.

This is a lifelong avodah, of course. Recently, I began attending Rebbetzin Tzipporah Heller's webinars. I frequently hear the question to the Rebbetzin, "How can we take what you say and put it into our hearts?" Of course, I don't remember her answer... sigh. But what I do remember is that it's possible, and if I ask Hashem to help me internalize His messages, He will.